For my parents.

Both of them, because I couldn't choose.

The boy was watching them. Donovan had seen him before: number 53 by his jersey, ginger-haired, stocky. On Thursday afternoons, the boy ran drills up and down one end of the field in Scotts Bluff Center alongside his teammates in the youth football clinic. Afterward, he waited at the bus stop for his older sister to pick him up. He was waiting there now, wiping his brow with the sleeve of his shirt, and watching them. He was maybe ten years old, still too young to be marked. That made Donovan wary. Terrorists weren't above recruiting kids.

"Security log checks out. Infrared scan is clean, electronic scan is clean. Dull as toast out here. I'd say we're about done." Jet tapped the comm unit in his hand, marking off the last stop on their usual patrol route.

Donovan stifled a yawn as he let his gaze wander back up and down the street. Usually, Jet was the one who was wide awake in the mornings and fighting fatigue by the evening, right around when Donovan got his second wind, but after twelve hours on duty, at the end of their last patrol before a two-day break, they were both tired. Next week, they'd rotate onto night patrol.

As if reading his mind, Jet said, "Next week is going to suck."

"I'd take nights over waking up at oh six hundred any day."

Jet shrugged. "I can't sleep much past oh six hundred anyway."

"You're some sort of freak," Donovan told his partner, lifting a hand to shield his eyes against the evening sunlight as it sank to the horizon. It stabbed through the arched, soaring, woven metal struts of the stadium behind them. Named after the nearby steep hills that had been an ancient historical landmark, Scotts Bluff Center was the newest, grandest human-made structure in sight, a testament to the growth of the Ring Belt. One month from today, forty thousand people would descend to fill its stands for the centennial Peace Day celebration. Security would be a nightmare.

On Peace Day, the President of West America would stand up onstage to commemorate a century of peace and cooperation between humankind and the zhree. He would speak about the lessons learned from the War Era and the importance of continued human self-government. When the President sat down, Donovan's father would take the podium. Donovan pictured his father walking across the stage, in his stiff gait and dark suit. His father would tug on his lapels and clear his throat softly before speaking. Everyone watching—in the stadium, or at home—would shift forward and pay attention to what the Prime Liaison had to say, because even though the President was still nominally the head of state when it came to human affairs, was there anything of real importance that was purely a human affair anymore?

"Don't look now," Jet said, "but that kid is coming over here."

The boy was crossing the street, walking toward them with short, half-jogging strides. His shoulders were curled forward, and he glanced left and right nervously. Jet paced away, acting casual, scanning the street for any sign of danger. Donovan watched the boy's approach. The kid slowed and stopped a few feet away, as if uncertain whether to come nearer.

Donovan took a step toward him. "Hi there," he said.

"Uh, hi," said the boy, eyes on the ground.

"What's your name?"

"Horatio."

Donovan pointed to the boy's football cleats. "You must be really good at football. You're here practicing a lot."

"I suppose." The boy relaxed a little. His shoulders came down and he looked up at Donovan's face. "Do you play?"

"Sure, a little. My buddy Jet over there is better than I am. We can't play when we're on duty, though."

Donovan tended to be the one to talk to the public when talking needed to be done. Jet didn't have the patience for it, and his good-natured but aggressive energy, like that of a caffeinated lion cub looking for stuff to wreck, could be a bit intimidating to civilians. Donovan knew that even with the uniform and markings, he didn't look much like a soldier in comparison, just an earnest, clean-cut teenager. True, he had his father's jawline and eyes, but his hair, despite being trimmed short, always insisted on being unruly, and the smattering of tiny freckles across the bridge of his nose, which he hated to no end, did at least help with the whole youthful and friendly look.

The exocel, however . . . there was no getting around it. Anyone with an exocel could expect to draw a few frightened or hostile glares out here in the Ring Belt. Armored soldiers-in-erze could expect worse.

Horatio didn't seem scared or hateful. He shuffled his feet. "Can I see your gun?"

"Sorry, buddy. I can't take it out for show."

The boy looked disappointed. He kicked the ground with his toe.

"I'll show you something else, though," Donovan said. "Come here."

Horatio took a few steps closer. Donovan held up his hand, watching the child's reaction. The broken stripes across the backs of his hands mirrored the zhree body patterning of his master erze. Soldier's markings. They unnerved some people, which was often useful, but he didn't want to scare the kid. "You know how to play rock, paper, scissors?"

"Yeah." The boy held up his own hand, skeptical.

"Okay, ready? One, two . . . three!" Donovan stuck out his first two fingers and snapped them into sharp blades. "Scissors beats paper."

"No fair," said Horatio. "You saw what I was going to do." But his eyes were wide.

"Oh, all right." Donovan armored his fist, encasing it. "Paper beats rock. You win."

The boy grinned, impressed. Donovan quirked his lips up in a smile but glanced to either side quickly, glad he could count on his partner to be vigilant. You had to be careful with kids. You had to keep them at arm's length and not drop your guard, but at the same time, you had to be friendly and approachable. You wanted them to see past the biotechnology, to understand that you were one of the good guys—as human as them, and trustworthy.

Horatio's grin faded. He shifted his weight from foot to foot, then reached into his pocket and withdrew a folded, wrinkled pamphlet. "I . . . uh, I found this." He held on to it tight, frozen with indecision for a second. Then he handed it over quickly.

The paper was thin and gray, cheaply printed, and tri-folded. Donovan had seen something like it before and only needed to read the first few lines.

A CALL TO ARMS!

There can be no doubt we are in a struggle for the survival of our species. The Accord of Peace and Governance is a fiction, the greatest lie ever told to humanity. We are being lulled like sheep to a slow slaughter by our oppressors and only if you open your eyes will you see it all around you. Ask yourself now: Are you prepared to FIGHT, to KILL, and to DIE for what you believe in??!!

Donovan refolded the paper. "Where did you find this?" He kept his voice curious, unconcerned.

The boy chewed the inside of his cheek. His eyes flicked to the bus stop, as if considering whether to run back to it.

Donovan slowed his words. "Horatio, you're doing the right thing."

"My uncle's place."

"Just the one copy?" This was important. Possession was a misdemeanor; distribution was a felony.

"No, a whole big stack of them. And . . . other stuff. Like equipment or something." In a rush, "I was just looking for a screwdriver, I didn't mean to go snooping around, honest."

"What's your uncle's name?"

"Sean. Sean Corrigan." The name spilled from the boy's lips like a large mouthful of water held too long. "My mom says it's none of our business. We barely know him; he stays away from the rest of the family. I don't want him to get in trouble or any-thing . . . but I don't want him to hurt anyone, either."

"You think he might do that?"

"I . . . I don't know. Nothing bad will happen to him, will it?"

"Not if he hasn't done anything wrong yet."

Horatio nodded, a fearful look creeping into his eyes. "I don't want him to find out I told you."

"He won't," Donovan promised.

"I better go. I'm supposed to get picked up." The boy backed away, stuffing his hands into his pockets as he turned to dart back across the street.

"Horatio." Donovan caught the boy's backward glance. "Don't worry, okay? You did the right thing."

Donovan watched the boy hurry back to the bus stop. Then he returned to where Jet was waiting by the skimmercar. Jet turned over the pamphlet Donovan handed him. "More scribblings from our writer friend Max, huh?"

"Must be the latest issue. At least this one doesn't urge killing us 'soulless exo dogs.'"

"He probably got in trouble from his readers for insulting dogs." Jet opened the door to the skimmercar and punched open a line to Central Command. They were supposed to radio in any civilian tips they received while on patrol. A pamphlet handed to him by a kid wasn't urgent, not like a bomb threat or anything, but Donovan spoke into his transmitter.

"PT 202. We have an unsolicited civilian lead. Over."

The voice of Liz, one of the dispatchers, came back over the line. "Patrol Team 202, go ahead."

"What have you got on Sean Corrigan? A boy claiming to be his nephew says he found a stack of Sapience propaganda in the guy's house. Some of the recent stuff from Max." Donovan took the pamphlet back from Jet and rubbed the thin paper between his fingers. "Max" was the name printed on the bottom of all of these. A code name for the terrorists' most prolific writer, or writers. Who knew if Max was one person or several.

Jet nodded across the street to where the boy's sister had just pulled up in a blue sedan. "His sister's marked."

Donovan squinted, trying to catch a glimpse of the teenager's hands on the steering wheel. "You're sure?"

"Scientist erze. I saw it."

A point in favor of the boy's credibility, then, if the rest of his family was marked. Liz's voice came back over the radio. "We have a red file on Sean Corrigan, going back five years. The civilian police put him away for ten months, for theft and arson, but didn't find any direct links to Sapience at the time. Picked up again at a checkpoint three months ago on suspicion of weapons smuggling, later released. Unmarried, lives alone. One brother: Andrew Corrigan, a scientist-in-erze. A niece, Olivia, also Scientist erze marked, and a nephew, Horatio."

So the boy's story checked out. Donovan leaned back against the hull of the skimmercar, still warm from the afternoon sunshine, though the orange glow of the September evening would be gone in half an hour. They were near the end of their shift, and his father, whom he sometimes saw on the news more often than in real life, would be expecting him home tonight.

Jet crossed his arms. "This *is* the first interesting recon we've had all day," he said slowly.

"I'm sure Cass and Leon would appreciate a fresh lead."

Jet shrugged, smiled. They'd known each other for too long to need to throw down a dare out loud.

Donovan sighed. "You have an address for Corrigan?" he asked Command.

"Sending it over."

Jet slapped Donovan on the shoulder and climbed into the skimmercar. He dropped into the driver's seat and programmed in the address. Donovan got back on the comm. "PT 202. We're following a civilian lead out of sector. Over."

Vic's voice piped up a second later. She and her partner, Thad, would be their nearest backup. "202, aren't you almost off shift? Don't you two have lives outside of work?"

"That depends," Jet replied, guiding the skimmercar into motion. He lowered his voice in an attempt to sound suave. "What are *you* up to this evening, Officer Kohl?"

A pause. "Oh, the usual. Putting *bad boys* in their place."

Jet whistled. "What's your location? A couple of bad boys here would really like to know."

Donovan shook his head in mock exasperation. "Ignore my partner, I'm not responsible for anything he says. Especially if it's being monitored." He leaned over to punch the line closed, then rested back in his own seat. He looked over at his friend. "Stop that. You look like a moron."

"Stop what?"

"Thinking about Vic with your mouth hanging open and drool running out."

"I can't help it, man. I'm in love with her. She's the hottest girl in the Round."

"Which is why you have to play it cool. Pique her interest. You're being too obvious."

"Girls dig obvious. Anyway, I don't *drool*. Much."

Buildings and trees blurred as the vehicle reached cruising speed. The body of the patrol skimmercar was a sleek zhree design, optimized for agile, multi-directional movement, but the inside, thankfully, had seats and controls proportioned for humans. Jet let the automatic navigation take over, then stretched his arms above his head and yawned. "I'm so glad we're off tomorrow. Commander Tate has been working everyone like mules all month. At first I thought it was a good thing to have graduated early, but whatever happened to downtime? Hey, why don't you get your old man to pull some strings and set us up with something easy for a while? Like guarding the shipyards or the algae farm."

Donovan snorted. "Come on, you know my dad." His father would never use his position to do anything that might smack of favoritism. He also did not approve of shirking hardship or duty. Besides, Donovan knew Jet wasn't serious about wanting a dull post. The guy might make a show of complaining, but when push came to shove, you would probably have to knock him unconscious to keep him away from his job. Like right now: chasing this end-of-shift lead when they could leave it to someone else. Despite his restless, devil-may-care attitude, Jet was as dependable a partner, and as competent a soldier-in-erze, as anyone could ask for.

The skimmercar banked slightly as the freeway curved. Donovan oriented himself automatically by looking for the Round. There it was, to his right: the circular city. From this distance, the only thing that stood out were the Towers, jutting up into the sky, metallic yet organic-looking, appearing like a cluster of stalagmites, perhaps, or termite hills, but too symmetrical, too obviously the work of intelligent designers. The tips of the Towers glowed faintly pink as the last of the evening light slid into the skimmercar's windows and tinted the immense expanse of sky that stretched over the wide prairie landscape.

Donovan had seen an old photograph in a museum once that showed this area from a time before the War Era, before the Landing, even: just miles and miles of waving grass and grazing cattle with only the occasional small human town to break it up. It was hard to imagine such a time, when all around them sprawled evidence of activity and growth: construction equipment, busy roads running every which way, new neighborhoods filled with houses and shops and people hoping for erze status and work. The fluid curves of modern zhree-style architecture mingled with blocky, traditional human buildings. Skimmercars buzzed past ground cars, electricycles, and pedestrians. Donovan had seen another photograph in the same museum, of the Ring Belt some eighty years ago, in the early days of peace, when it had been part trading post and part refugee camp, burgeoning with displaced humans hoping for some livelihood or profit from working with the new governors. Now the urban sprawl encircled Round Three (for it was the third out of eighteen Rounds all over the world) in a messy, vibrant swath of humanity, like algae glommed around a pond rock.

The Ring Belt had its bad parts, though. The skimmercar slowed, began making tight turns to navigate the narrow streets of an old, crumbly neighborhood of small, square brick houses and weed-choked front lawns.

"This has got to be War Era housing," Jet remarked. "Crazy that this stuff is still standing."

Donovan checked the navigation screen and pointed down the row of near-identical dwellings. "Third one on the left," he said. "Park over there, out of sight. I don't think anyone out here in the place time forgot is going to be friendly to stripes."

Jet took manual control of the skimmercar and guided it to a strip of gravel alley at the end of the block before lowering it to a stop. He checked his handgun, pocketed extra ammunition. "Let's go hunt us down some sapes."

Donovan drew his own sidearm—a standard 9mm electripulse pistol, modeled after a classic human weapon but built with off-world metal composite and outfitted with zhree battery technology. He made sure the magazine was full, then holstered it and stepped out of the car after Jet.

They spaced apart defensively as they approached the house. Donovan watched for movement in the tiny windows of the neighboring homes. Evening had turned the world a shadowy blue, and the temperature was plummeting fast. The banter between them was gone, as was their earlier sense of fatigue; there was nothing like the possibility of danger to clear the mind. This place made them tense, focused. All the buildings on the street had flat, walled roofs and radiation-shielded basements. They had been built for a time of war, and the people who lived here—poor, unmarked Sapience sympathizers—probably felt like they were still in one. Donovan's exocel crawled up, responding to cold, and nerves.

They circled Corrigan's house. "Someone's home," Jet said through his transmitter, his voice low in Donovan's earbud.

Donovan scanned the front door and the street. There was a car parked at the curb and a pickup truck in the side driveway. Sudden, silhouetted movement in the windows. Two, maybe three people. Donovan's pulse quickened. *Corrigan's supposed to live alone, isn't he?* The guy had a criminal history, stacks of seditious material, and visitors at night? Donovan toggled his transmitter. "PT 202 to Command, we have a suspected terrorist safe house here. Request permission to search."

Liz's voice came back a second later. "202, you are unsupported outside of your coverage sector. Flag it and come back in."

"Scorch that," Jet's voice interjected. "We chased a live lead and we're standing in front of the house now. If we don't engage, this guy is going to spook and the place will be empty when we come back."

Donovan ground his teeth. He thought of the boy, Horatio. If they didn't nab Corrigan, the man would be free to find out his nephew had turned him in. "Command, this is a reliable civilian lead on a prior record. We're going in."

"This is Command One." Commander Tate's voice broke through on the line. "202, we have teams tied up dealing with a bomb threat on the other side of the Belt. Your backup is fifteen minutes away. You are on your own right now."

"Understood."

"PSO," Tate snapped.

Probability of Successful Outcome. Donovan pictured the Commander's interrogative glare; no doubt she had pulled off her glasses and was leaning over Liz, rapidly tapping one arm of the thin wire frames on the dispatch monitor. She wanted his soldier-in-erze judgment: How reliable was the lead, how real and urgent was the threat, how likely was it that they could apprehend the suspect without endangering innocent civilians or making the Global Security and Pacification Forces look trigger-happy or incompetent?

Soldiers-in-erze on patrol said that what PSO really stood for was Please Screw Off. As in, "Command, please screw off and let us do our jobs." Donovan looked at the house. One building, no more than a few people inside, empty street. "PSO is high."

"Keep your line open."

"Jet." Donovan jerked his head, and his partner advanced swiftly up the short walk to the front door. Donovan followed. He pressed his back against the brick wall beside the doorframe and drew his electripulse. He went to full armor, his exocel rippling from node to node, the living machine cells knitting their microscopic lattice structures across his skin.

Jet pounded on the door. "This is SecPac! Open up!"

2

They waited several heartbeats, then exchanged a nod. Jet drew his pistol. He stepped back, ready to kick the door in when it opened.

Jet pushed into the house without hesitation. Donovan followed on his partner's heels, scanning the room, his weapon pointed down, finger off the trigger but his thumb hovering next to the coil charger. Three people in the room—two men, one woman—all of them tense, staring in silent, undisguised hostility.

"Sean Corrigan?" Jet asked the man who'd opened the door.

A stiff nod. Sean Corrigan was a thick-necked man with a short beard. He glared at the invaders from beneath heavy eyebrows, his jaw working back and forth as if he were chewing something nasty he wanted to spit at them. Donovan could feel the hatred emanating from him like heat off of sun-baked black tar.

"Face the wall, over there, all of you," Jet commanded. "Hands on top of your heads."

Slowly, the man obeyed. "This is my house," he said, voice thick with stifled rage.

"Come on, move," Donovan ordered the other two. He lined them up next to Corrigan. Not so close that they could talk. Then he swept the lower floor, fast, his gun up, moving entranceway to entranceway in a few seconds. The house was small and the other rooms were empty. He cleared the basement to make sure there wasn't anyone else hiding down there, then returned to the living room. Jet had the three suspects kneeling with hands laced behind their heads. He held up a powder-based handgun. "Found this on Corrigan," he said.

Corrigan's face was flushed, apt to combust. The olive-skinned man next to him was sweating, the whites of his eyes encircling wide pupils. The woman—Donovan startled a little. She was a teenage girl, about their age, maybe younger. Her hair was tucked up into a black wool cap. She stared up at him, quiet and unflinching, her chin lifted.

Donovan holstered his gun, turned on all the lights, and got to work. He and Jet had conducted enough searches that he knew all the usual places to look, and covered them in minutes. He emptied out drawers, went through cabinets, knocked around for loose floorboards and false walls. He slit open the mattress and the sofa cushions. Dust and fluff swirled in the air.

Jet kept a watchful guard over the suspects. "Find anything?" he called.

"Not yet." Donovan paused, surveying the wreckage uneasily. With a solid lead, they usually found something—sometimes small things like unregistered weapons, sometimes big things like explosives-making labs. Occasionally, though, they found nothing. Two weeks ago, they'd searched the house of a married couple, Jim and Mila Guerra; intelligence had linked the Guerras to several local Sapience operatives, but the search had come up empty. The woman had answered all their questions with hostile monosyllables while her husband stood behind her, arms crossed, the eagle tattoo on his bicep glaring at them as balefully as he did. Those two were sapes, he and Jet were sure, they just couldn't prove it. This evening was looking like it would end the same way.

Leaving a house after an unsuccessful search was the worst feeling. It meant they'd either made a mistake or been duped. It meant they'd just made SecPac look cruel and impotent, made people who hated exos hate them even more.

Commander Tate's voice crackled to life impatiently in his earbud. "Command to 202, what is your situation?"

Donovan exchanged a frustrated look with Jet. "Command One, we have three suspects under guard. We're still searching. Stand by. Over." Had Corrigan removed all the evidence? Had Horatio been lying? Donovan saw Corrigan's mouth twitch; he was stifling a smile. *He thinks he's won. He thinks he's going to get off scot-free.* Donovan's jaw clenched. They weren't making a mistake here. He tried to remember what Horatio had said. The boy had seen pamphlets and equipment. He'd been searching for a screwdriver . . .

"Toolshed," Donovan said under his breath. There had to be a toolshed.

He rushed to the rear of the house. Through a yellow linoleum-tiled laundry room, he found the back door leading out into the yard. In the dark, he didn't see the shed at first; a screen of thick shrubs shielded it from view. Donovan pulled the penlight from his uniform breast pocket and flicked it on, playing it over the weathered, gray cedar siding. He put the light between his teeth and tugged on the shiny new padlock. When it didn't give, he bladed his hand and thrust it into the door slit. Splinters frayed and snapped as he shoved his arm in almost up to the elbow. After a bit more wood wrecking, he tore the padlock off. Donovan swung the door open.

"Erze almighty."

Stacked against one side of the shed were crates of rifles: two dozen M4 clones and three (*three!*) SecPac-grade, laser-sighted E201s. A filing cabinet against the back held pamphlets bundled with rubber bands and thousands of rounds of ammunition in boxes. Donovan lifted the wooden lid covering a metal tub and stared at what must have been at least three hundred pounds of C4 plastic explosive. There were two rocket-propelled grenades, their tubes in a corner. There was even a stolen fission engine starter coil.

He ran back inside the house. Jet smacked Donovan's hand in a high five. "Sean Corrigan." Donovan made his voice stern and official, though he was flying high with relief. "By authority of the Global Security and Pacification Forces, I charge you with possession of weapons, distribution of seditious material, and involvement in an illegal organization with the intent to commit acts of terror. You will be taken into custody to answer for these crimes before a court of law."

Jet prodded Corrigan between the shoulder blades with the muzzle of his gun. "You hear that, you terrorist scumbag? It's the atomizer or penal camp for you."

Corrigan's back went rigid, his whole frame quivering with helpless fury. The man beside him sagged like a deflating balloon, but the girl turned her head to stare at the two exos with a curious mixture of resentment and fascination. "Aren't you awful young to be soldiers for the shrooms?"

Donovan looked at her askance. "Aren't you awfully pretty to be a terrorist?" He turned away and called in the triumphant news to Command.

Tate took his report silently. Another moment passed

before she said, "Bring them in. I'm sending a cleanup crew your way." She sounded as no-nonsense as ever, but Donovan could hear the satisfaction in her pause. "Fine work tonight. Reyes—your father will be pleased to hear of it."

"I'll bring the skimmercar around." Jet headed for the door. "Not too shabby a way to end the day, eh, Lesser D?"

"Not too shabby," Donovan agreed. Six months on the job; he and Jet might be the youngest team in SecPac, but they were holding their own.

A few years ago, after his father's reappointment banquet, Donovan had griped to Jet, "You know, no matter what I do, I'll always just be the kid of a famous dad. I'm always going to be Reyes Junior."

"McReyes," Jet intoned. "Son of Dom."

"Reyes the Second."

"D. Reyes the Lesser." That was a good one. Jet had turned it into Donovan's permanent nickname.

The skimmercar settled in front of the house. Jet came back in, nudging an overturned drawer out of the way. "Okay, let's take them out one at a time. I'll take Corrigan first if you stay with the other two squishies."

"Civilians," Donovan mock-chided him. They weren't supposed to call non-Hardened people squishies, even the criminals. Just last week, Tate had given all the exo soldiers-in-erze a lecture about it.

"All right, *squishy*, get up." Jet nudged Corrigan to his feet. He handcuffed the man behind his back and shoved him out the front door. A few minutes later he returned and escorted the other man out. It was important to be extra careful about suspects trying to escape; in these parts, anyone might be a sympathizer and it would be easy for someone to disappear into a friendly house if they got away.

With a SecPac patrol vehicle parked out front, Donovan wondered how many hostile neighbors were watching from the nearby houses. Unease seeped into his skin, tingling up and down his exocel nodes. "Jet," he said into his transmitter, "let's hurry it up." He kept one eye trained on the girl still kneeling on the floor and stepped back so he could see his erze mate coming back up the walk. A dog barked outside.

And the night erupted in gunfire.

3

Donovan saw his best friend knocked forward off his feet by a spray of bullets.

He threw himself across the room, falling to a crouch inside the doorway. *Where are they? Where are the sapes?!* He scanned the street wildly. Another burst of gunfire peppered the skimmercar like hail and ricocheted off the street around it. There: powder-weapon muzzle flashes from the roof of the house next door, lighting up the darkness like sparklers. Donovan tabbed the coil charger on his gun as he swung it up and unloaded shots. The pistol kicked in his hand; he surged armor over his wrists, steadied his aim, and fired until he heard the snap of electric coils on an empty chamber.

He ejected his magazine and fumbled for a new one from his uniform pocket. "Jet!" he shouted.

Jet groaned and climbed painfully to his feet. "Man, that hurts bad. I am going to be *sore*."

It could be worse, Donovan thought. At least Jet hadn't seen it coming; it was actually better not to be too tense when you took a bullet. As it was, Jet being laid up for the better part of a week would be the best outcome they could hope for. There was only so much lead an exocel could take, and his erze mate was still a sitting duck.

Jet started to half run, half stagger back toward the relative safety of the skimmercar. Another burst of gunfire tore up the ground around him. Donovan slammed in a fresh magazine and leapt out onto the front walkway, opening himself up as a target as he poured fire back at their ambushers. The roar of blood in his ears drowned out even the gunshots. The only thing on his mind was laying down a barrage to cover Jet's run.

A bullet whined past him. Another grazed his shoulder, making him stagger. Donovan had just enough time to process, *There's gunfire coming from the other direction!* before a round slammed into his thigh. The impact shuddered through his armor in a radiating wave up his leg and into his pelvis. He dropped to one knee, teeth gritted, and let off two more shots before rolling back into the cover of the doorway.

The gunfire fell silent. Commander Tate was going ballistic in his ear. "202! SITREP!"

"We're taking fire," he gasped. As if that wasn't obvious. "Gunmen on the roof of the house on the right, and . . . *somewhere* on the left . . ." Sweat wicked up through his armor; he wiped his palms down his pants and rubbed his throbbing thigh. His exocel knit frantically over the impact site. The crushed bullet worked free and fell down into his pant leg.

"Hold your ground!" Tate ordered. "Don't let them take back the house, or Corrigan and his accomplices. Backup will be there in three minutes."

Donovan kept his gun raised and edged his head and shoulders through the doorway to see what was going on. He let out a breath of relief. Jet was bent over and grimacing, but he'd made it back to the skimmercar. Then, a flurry of movement: Corrigan and his friend jumped from the open skimmercar door and started running.

Corrigan didn't make it far; despite his injuries, Jet launched himself after the man and tackled him to the ground. With his hands still cuffed behind his back, Corrigan's face smacked into the pavement and he let out a muffled howl. His companion kept going, running a wild zigzag across the neighboring lawn.

"Stop RIGHT NOW, you—" Jet started after him, but bullets began raining down again from the determined rebels covering their comrade's escape. Donovan braced himself in the doorway and opened fire. Jet dragged Corrigan back to the skimmercar with one arm and let off rounds after the fleeing man with the other. Answering shots sparked all around them. Bullets gouged the doorframe around Donovan and chipped the brick walls. The man jerked and went down. Donovan couldn't tell if he was dead or alive, and he had no idea who'd hit him.

The hum of a speeding skimmercar preceded the distinctive pulse of SecPac patrol lights sweeping the street, barreling closer and brighter. The shooters broke off. The night fell suddenly, incongruously silent.

"D, you okay?" Jet's voice.

"Yeah. You?"

"Yeah." A pause. "I think those bastards cracked some ribs."

Donovan slid down against the doorframe. He leaned his head back and closed his eyes, exhaustion flooding in as adrenaline flooded out. Thank heaven and erze. That had been rough. He'd been under live fire countless times in training, and a couple of months ago they'd had to arrest someone who'd fired on the skimmercar, but this had been so much more real, and so . . . *disturbing*. The terrorists were just squishies. But they were so fanatical about their agenda they were willing to risk their lives just for a chance to take his and Jet's.

The night had not ended smoothly, but at least they were both okay, and still had—

He opened his eyes. The girl was gone.

He bolted to his feet. She'd been in here during the firefight. Where had she gone?

There was a faint click from the laundry room. The back door closing.

Donovan raced across the main level and threw the door wide. A slim, dark shape was hurtling past the shed, through the shrubbery, into the next row of houses.

He sprinted after her. *Tricky little*—Donovan cursed himself for not keeping a closer eye on her, but in all that madness back there . . . "Stop!" he shouted. She put on more speed.

Donovan pushed himself. His right thigh was still numb and he rebalanced his armor to compensate, letting his exocel stabilize his gait. She was fast, for a squishy, but she couldn't outrun an exo. He'd almost caught up with her when he realized she wasn't just running *away* from him, but toward something. Toward a parking lot. At the far end of the lot, the red engine lights of a van turned on. It growled to life with a dirty, petroleum-burning cough.

The girl dodged a bush and hurdled over a low retaining wall. She made it a short distance across the lot before Donovan grabbed her. His hand came down on her shoulder and pulled her back. She spun to face him. Her black wool cap tumbled off her head. For a second, her face was close to his—auburn hair falling around her ears, fine pixie nose and small mouth bared in a cry of anger—before she thrust a short black object at his torso.

It was far too small to be a gun. He assumed it was a knife—a desperate, foolish act on her part—and didn't even bother to defend himself. Only it wasn't a knife. Electrodes sprang out, pouring fifty thousand volts into him.

His entire body cramped violently. Pain and shock flooded in. His exocel spasmed uncontrollably, trying to defend against something that wasn't there. Donovan lost his grip on the girl and fell. He couldn't put his arms out to break the fall, and there was a sharp white flash across his vision when his temple hit the pavement. He heard the girl running again, and the sudden, very nearby skittering crunch of tires. A slamming car door, followed by urgent footsteps, and then a man's harsh voice. "Don't shoot it, you idiot. The zebrahands are crawling all over the place—they'll hear. Hand me that iron."

The realization that he had made a terrible, fatal mistake coursed through Donovan's mind. He willed himself to *move*, to scream a warning through his transmitter. Still half paralyzed and twitching, he managed to push up weakly on his hands and open his mouth, and then a blinding pain connected with the base of his skull.

4

"Is he still alive?" The girl's voice.

"Of course it's alive. You know what it takes to kill one of these things?"

Donovan kept his eyes closed and his body still. His head seemed to be unreasonably heavy, and there was a steady, throbbing pulse behind his eyes. He realized he was in a sitting position, and his chin was slumped forward on his chest.

The man who had just spoken was nearby, but his voice was moving around. It was a hard, unrelenting voice—a voice that steamrolled over other voices. "Honest to God, I'm surprised the stripes didn't nab Corrigan earlier. Didn't I always say he was careless?"

"You did, Kevin." Another man's voice, younger and less assured.

"Carelessness will get you shot or atomized, sure as hell. Gareth, though, poor bastard."

From the way the voices echoed, they must be in a large, empty room.

The younger man said, "You're some kind of crazy lucky to have gotten away like that, Anya."

"Nerves of steel and a good head on your shoulders, more like," was Kevin's reply. "The expression on this one's face, man, that was sure worth something, wasn't it?"

The girl said, quietly, "I think I saw him move just now. Do you think he's awake?"

A long pause. Some shuffling sounds.

A wave of cold water slammed Donovan in the face. He jerked back, gasping, eyes flying open. His exocel rippled reflexively, straining against the steel wire that bound his wrists and ankles to the metal chair. The man standing in front of him tossed the empty tin pail aside. "Now it's awake."

Donovan coughed, sputtering. He was indeed in a large, windowless room, lit by a strip of fluorescent lighting that gave the gray walls and bare concrete floor a sickly yellowish-green hue. The three people in the room stared at him as if they were expecting him to do something—shout, swear, struggle. He blinked dripping water from his eyes and tried hard to gather his muddy, panicked thoughts. He dug his chin into his uniform collar, feeling for—

"Looking for this?" The man who'd doused him, Kevin, held up the crushed remains of his transmitter and earbud. He tossed the bits of scrap in the direction of the water bucket. "You're alone, zebrahands. Your pals aren't coming for you."

"Yes they are." Donovan tried to make his voice come out confident and unafraid. It sounded rough and too fast. He steadied his gaze on Kevin. "You're making a really big mistake. Let me go now, and you *might* live when they get here."

Kevin walked forward slowly. The man was as wiry as a coyote and had the feral look of one. His jawline was as hard as his voice, and dark with stubble. Curly black hair stuck out from underneath the brim of a denim ball cap. "Look around you," he said. "You're not in a position to make threats. That uniform, those stripes on your hands, that alien armor in your body, it doesn't mean jack in here."

Despite himself, Donovan felt fear slime his throat. The man was right.

"Brett," said Kevin, "set up the camera."

The younger man leapt to obey. He unlatched a big carrying case on the floor and started pulling out pieces of equipment. Though he worked with practiced speed, Brett moved with the twitchy servility of someone who'd been beaten up as a kid one too many times and was always waiting to be jumped. Dark patches of sweat showed in the armpits of his frayed gray T-shirt. In a few minutes, he had a tripod set up. He fiddled with the recording device, then sat back on his haunches and scratched his nose nervously. "Um, it's out of batteries."

"Out of batteries?" Kevin burst out. "Chrissakes, why do I keep you around?"

"Don't worry, don't worry, I'm sure I have some more in the van," Brett said quickly. He gave the other man an apologetic, kicked-dog look and hurried from the room. The door clicked closed behind him.

Donovan's fear congealed from amorphous dread into solid terror.

Sapience distributed a series of videos among its members as propaganda, and to SecPac and the government as intimidation. They called it Alien Dissection, though most of the victims weren't zhree but exos. The extremists didn't differentiate; anyone with an exocel was a fair target in their minds. The message in any case was the same: *Armor can be beaten. We can kill them. They die just fine.*

Donovan pulled against the loops of wire binding him to the chair. He surged and furrowed his exocel along his wrists, trying to break or cut the steel, but his armor scraped across the flexible metal cables uselessly.

Kevin made an impatient noise and turned his attention to Anya. He put an arm around her shoulders and squeezed, a little too tight and a little too long, considering that the girl held on to her elbows, not resisting but not returning his embrace. "You're in now, for sure." His lips moved near her ear. "I'm going to vouch for you, and when I vouch for someone, they're in. But you've got to want in. Things got scary for you tonight. You still want this?"

The girl looked up at him. Her fine features were resolute. "Yeah. I do."

"You've got the nerves for it, that's for sure, but you've got to have the stomach too. You think you have that?" When she nodded, Kevin gave her a pleased shake. "Now, that's a girl."

Brett reappeared, holding up the video recorder in triumph. He attached it to the top of the tripod and swiveled it to point at Donovan. He gave Kevin a thumbs-up. "Showtime," he said.

Kevin unzipped his jacket and tossed it aside. The vest he wore underneath had a gruesome pale sheen. It was woven through with panotin—the stuff exocels were made of. Donovan's guts lurched. The only way to get panotin was off the corpse of a zhree or an exo. The rebels had no qualms about harvesting the technology they despised from the bodies of their enemies and using it for themselves.

Donovan shuddered. He was going to die, and it was going to take a long time and hurt a lot. Afterward, the terrorists would salvage what panotin they could from his remains and leave the rest for Jet to find. They would send the video of his death to Commander Tate, who would have to break the tragic news to his father.

His father. His father would be so . . . *disappointed*.

Donovan's breath rasped in his throat. Where were his fellow officers, his erze mates? When would they rescue him?

Kevin drew his pistol, ejected the magazine, and slid in a fresh one. "You're lucky, you know," he said. He drew back the slide. It released with an ominous click. "You get to redeem yourself to your species. Not every shroom pet gets that chance." He nodded toward Brett, who pushed a button on the video camera. A red light blinked on.

"Do you have anything you would like to volunteer?" Kevin asked. He sounded genuinely interested now. Concerned. Acting like a talk show interviewer for the camera. "Any confessions you would like to make? This can be easy. You were born human. You can still prove yourself to *be* human in the end by helping the cause."

Donovan looked at the red light focused on him like a laser sight. He thought about what he wanted to say to anyone who might be forced to watch this—something defiant and dignified— but he didn't trust his voice not to shake. Instead, he turned an imploring gaze on Brett and Anya. They didn't seem as pitiless as Kevin. Couldn't they see this was wrong?

Brett didn't look at him. He stood behind the camera, hands stuffed into the pockets of torn jeans, elbows sticking out. He hung on to Kevin's words with an eager, worshipful attentiveness, nodding whenever the man paused. Anya, though, stared at Donovan steadily, as if he were a strange animal in a cage. She was now sitting on top of the closed video equipment case, her arms resting on her knees. Her lips moved very slightly, as if encouraging him to speak.

"Nothing to say? Not even your name? All right." Kevin's voice shifted from query to demand. "Who led you to Sean Corrigan?"

That was an easy one to refuse; like hell he was going to give up an innocent little boy. In training, he'd been taught one line to repeat over and over again if he was ever captured. At the time, the possibility of needing it had seemed so remote; it was the sort of thing you figured was there just in case, but you would never have to use, like fire escape exit maps and weight limits for skimmercars. The line came back to him now: *I'm under orders to provide no information under enemy interrogation.* Even an officer's identity could be used by terrorists to target his family and fellow cooperationists.

"I asked you a question." Kevin took a step forward. "Who led you to Corrigan?"

Donovan said, "You know I'm not going to answer that."

Kevin shot him in the chest.

The impact crushed the breath from his body and detonated a shuddering wave of agony as it rocked through his exocel. His head whiplashed back; for a second everything went blurry.

Kevin gave him a minute to recover. "Who is your source? We know SecPac has informers. Did one of them give you Corrigan?"

Donovan panted in time with his throbbing torso.."Go to *hell*," he wheezed.

Through watering eyes, he saw Anya cover her ears. Kevin shot him again, in the stomach. The gunshot reverberated in the closed room, like pain. Donovan barely heard it; the world had gone strangely muted beyond the gong ringing inside his skull. Kevin's persistent voice sounded as if it were traveling underwater. "What is the code word you use with your informers?"

Donovan's mind tried to search for the answer in a treasonous bid for self-preservation. The code changed every two months and was given to patrol teams on a need-to-know basis. Wallaby? *Wapiti.* He swallowed. There was no moisture in his mouth. His words came out in a groan. "I'm under orders to provide no information under enemy interrogation."

The next bullet struck him in the ribs, and he howled. For the first time in his life, Donovan wished he was not an exo. Exos could stay alive long past what a normal human could endure. The remarkable biotechnology that made the zhree so invulnerable was now guaranteeing him a very slow death. The fourth shot slammed into his shoulder. Donovan's head jerked back. The harsh strip of overhead light danced in his vision. He fought wildly against the restraints, dignity forgotten, cursing Kevin in a string of half-sobbing, inarticulate profanities.

Kevin came and squatted down next to Donovan's chair. "The shrooms made your kind so damn hard to kill. I used to hate it. Now I kind of like it." He draped his long arms over his knees and dangled the gun from his fingertips. "Tell me, what's the fastest way to kill an exo?" When Donovan didn't answer, he called across the room. "What do you think, Brett? Anya? What's the fastest way to kill an exo?"

"Put a gun in its mouth and pull the trigger," Brett suggested.

Kevin stood and pressed the barrel of the pistol to the side of Donovan's mouth. "What do you think, zebrahands? You want to

31

suck on this and take the easy way out?" He moved the gun upward and fitted it against Donovan's left eye. "Bullet through the eye works too, doesn't it?" Donovan squirmed as the metal ground against the socket.

Kevin moved the gun away. "Well, that's not how it's going to go." He walked over to where a rifle was propped against the wall. He returned with it and crouched back down to Donovan's level, resting the firearm on its stock and giving it an affectionate pat. "This baby is a real War Era relic. Fires five-point-seven by twenty-eight millimeter, armor-piercing rounds. It'll punch through just about anything, even panotin. It's probably been a long time since you've seen yourself bleed, hasn't it? Humans *bleed* when they're shot. You curious about what that's like?"

Donovan chewed hard on the inside of his cheek. He wondered if he could *force* himself to drop his armor so the bullets would kill him. He doubted it. It would be like trying to keep his hand unarmored while pressing it to a hot burner. His body would rebel, try to save itself, like it was doing now. His exocel was working frantically, pushing out the flattened bullets, knitting and rebuilding at the site of impact . . . but slower each time.

Kevin slung the rifle over his shoulder. He backed up again, moving the pistol in a lazy, indecisive motion, as if considering which part of Donovan to aim for next. "Start saying something useful."

I'm under orders to provide no information . . . He said it silently to himself this time. Exos were nothing if not loyal to their oaths. His armor rippled, trying to anticipate where the next blow would land. He closed his eyes.

"Stop it."

Donovan opened his eyes. Anya was on her feet, her sharp chin jutted forward. As he watched in dim amazement, she stalked in front of Kevin. "Stop shooting him."

Kevin's mouth warped. "What do you think you're doing?"

"It's not working." She perched slightly forward on the balls of her feet, her small hands balled into fists. "And it's cruel. Plain cruel. He's just a boy."

In spite of everything, Donovan blinked in wonder. *He* was just a boy? She was just a girl, a *squishy* girl, standing in the path of a loaded gun. A bullet would kill her—punch right through bones and tissues and organs. Even though she was the reason he was in here, Donovan felt like shouting at her to get out of the way. Kevin was a psychopath, a killer.

"A boy?" Kevin's face reddened. "Is that what you think he is? 'Cause he looks like one? Like someone who might smile at you and ask you to the school dance?" He shoved Anya aside and strode over to Donovan, his expression empty of compassion. "He's nothing of the sort. The shrooms change them when they're little kids. They start training them as soldiers as soon as they turn twelve. Isn't that right?"

"That's the age that all erze born are marked," Donovan blurted. "You're just making it sound—"

"*Is that right or isn't it?*" He dug the gun muzzle into Donovan's temple. Donovan nodded.

Anya pushed Kevin's gun arm down, glaring up at him. "If you're going to kill him, then kill him. But don't keep hurting him. We're supposed to be the good guys here. We're fighting for humanity, not losing it."

"Stop recording this, dammit!" Kevin shouted in Brett's

direction. He grabbed Anya by the arm and dragged her aside. "I'm changing my mind about vouching for you. You said you had the stomach for this, but I should have known better. You think there's room for nicety in war? You've got to be willing to do anything for the cause. *Anything.*"

"Not this," the girl said. She looked birdlike in the shadow of Kevin's wrath. "Give me the gun. I'll kill him, if you ask me to. But I don't want to be a part of *this*." She pointed to the video camera.

A long moment of stalemate stretched between them. Donovan stared, transfixed, knowing he was dead either way but unable to help feeling a stir of conflicted admiration. The girl was fearless, the way she stood staunchly in front of the terrorist sergeant, her small frame tense with determination.

Kevin flipped the pistol around and offered her the grip. "Do it, then."

Anya paled. She pressed her lips together and took the gun.

Kevin pulled an extra magazine from his back pocket and slapped it into her other hand. "You might need more rounds." The left side of his mouth tugged up in dark humor.

A strange fog was descending over Donovan. He felt inexplicably disconnected from what was going on, as if it didn't concern him anymore. He wondered if he was going into some kind of shock—a combination of adrenaline overload, and his body channeling all physical and mental reserves into his exocel in an ultimately futile bid to keep him alive.

He watched Anya approach. She really was a fragile-looking thing. Underneath a baggy jacket, she wore a thin, wide-collared black shirt that slipped off one shoulder and exposed her sharp collarbone. The waist of her pants sat low on bony hips beneath a hollowed stomach and small chest. Donovan looked into her eyes; he wanted her to know what she was doing. Strangely, the fact that he was going to die seemed a secondary tragedy.

Once she pulled the trigger, there would be no turning back. As an exo-killer, there would be no life for her besides a criminal one; no path but Sapience. SecPac took a terrorist off the streets, and another, like Anya, took his place, and so it went on. Donovan managed to work just enough saliva into his mouth to form words. "Don't do this, please. You're not like him. Not yet. You don't have to choose this."

She looked down at the gun in her hand. He saw hesitation and nervousness, but also a deep, resolute rage.

"My name is Donovan." His voice was a dry whisper. "I'm seventeen."

She lifted the gun with both hands and walked forward until the black hole of the muzzle filled his vision, like a telescope lens into oblivion. It was all he could see. There was nothing else but the gun—the gun, and the drenching fear. *Let her hands be steady*, he prayed. *Let it be over quickly.*

A second passed. An eternity. *What is she waiting for?*

"Guys!" said Brett. "Hold up, you might want to see this."

"Not now," Kevin warned.

"Seriously, Kevin, look at this." Brett's voice rose. "That's him, right? Anya, come and look—you know who he *is*?"

Anya lowered the gun. For a moment, she and Donovan stared into each other's eyes as if they had passed together through some invisible threshold, and the strange face before them was the first sight on the other side. A shadow passed across Anya's features: relief, or regret.

Brett was gesturing at the screen he'd just handed to Kevin. "It's on the news. While you two were arguing, I figured I'd check the news, and what do you know? The stripes are saying he's missing—presumed dead or captured—and the news is making a big deal out of it." He pushed aside the dirty-blond hair that kept falling across his eyes and stared at Donovan with a heightened sense of interest. "They're saying he's Donovan Reyes. *Reyes*, as in—"

"Prime Liaison Reyes," Anya finished. Her voice fell to a hush. "He's the son of the Prime Liaison?"

Kevin's eyes jumped between the screen and Donovan. "Is this some kind of trick?" he demanded in a murmur, speaking mostly to himself. "Is SecPac screwing with us?"

"He said his name's Donovan," Anya said. "I heard him say it."

Donovan felt the air shifting in the room. The three terrorists seemed to sway in a crosswind, as if they had been sailing in one direction, only to have been suddenly buffeted in another. Brett and Anya looked at each other, and then at Kevin, expectantly. "He's got to be one of the most valuable stripes in the country," Brett said. "This is good news, right?"

"Is it?" said Kevin.

Yes, is it? Donovan's heart had begun beating again, optimistic he might continue living. But he felt sick and confused. He'd been prepared to do his erze duty, to die without giving these criminals any scrap of information they might use. Now that they knew his father was the most powerful man in the country, what would they *do*? They would want to use him—or his death—in a more dramatic and calculated way.

"Kevin, what are we going to do?" Brett exclaimed, more animated than he'd been all night. "This is really big! Maybe we shouldn't kill him right away. Maybe we can bargain for him, use him to go after SecPac, even the head dog Reyes."

"You're supposed to make bombs, not give opinions! Shut up and let me think." A weird parade of emotions was shuffling across Kevin's face: excitement, disappointment, suspicion, sober deliberation. He took off his ball cap. Underneath, his mess of dark curls was permanently imprinted by the hat's rim. He ran a hand through his hair and jammed the cap back on, tugging the bill back and forth with nervous jerks. "We take him. And we get the hell out of the Ring Belt."

5

They fled in a different car, a silver petroleum-burning SUV with tinted windows. The sort of inexpensive, common human vehicle that wouldn't attract attention, it rolled along the ground at an erratic, rumbling pace and had to be manually controlled at all times. They put Donovan in the middle seat, his hands cuffed behind him. Steel wire was fastened around his ankles, then looped around the metal base of the car seat for good measure. Brett drove. Kevin and Anya sat in the backseat behind Donovan, weapons in hand.

Donovan was in pain. The bullets he'd taken had bruised him terribly. "It won't work, you know," he said. His voice sounded hoarse. "You won't get any concessions or ransom. My father won't negotiate with terrorists."

"That would be a real shame," Kevin said from behind him, "for you."

Donovan closed his eyes briefly. "You don't know my father." Prime Liaison Reyes was the lead diplomat between the human government and zhree oversight in West America. He was responsible for the entire erze approval system upon which cooperation between the species rested. He couldn't afford to put his personal feelings first, and he surely wouldn't be cowed by Sapience, not for anything. He knew the risks inherent in Donovan being a soldier-in-erze; on SecPac's trainee graduation day, he'd looked Donovan up and down in his crisp new uniform and said somberly,

"Be careful, son." He still said it whenever he sa

on patrol, as he had yesterday morning. Because

worst, Dominick Reyes would not treat his sor

any other soldier—ultimately expendable. Mayl

was under the impression that Donovan had some worth as a

hostage, but the more Donovan thought about it, the more cer-

tain he became that torture and death had merely been delayed,

not averted.

He dropped his exocel way down, to save energy. Fatigue and

injury were sapping him fast. He could not tell where they were in

the Ring Belt. He'd gotten only a two-second glimpse outside

before he'd been shoved into the SUV, and all he saw through the

windows now were streetlights casting orange light on unfamiliar

roads. Even if he managed to escape, he wouldn't make it far.

Kevin and Anya fished bagels from a brown paper bag. Kevin

tossed the bag up front to Brett, who pulled out a bagel and chewed

it as he drove. Donovan's stomach hurt as he watched them. He

could ignore hunger, but thirst was a different matter. He licked

his dry lips. "Can I have some water?" he asked.

No one answered him. After a few minutes, he heard Anya

unscrewing the top off a water bottle. She held it up to his face,

and he tilted his head back so she could tip the water into his

mouth. He drank greedily, trying not to let any of it spill. It tasted

stale and a little funny, as if the bottle had sat in the sun for too long

and absorbed the flavor of plastic, but it was the best water he'd

ever had. When she took the bottle away, too soon, he said, "Thank

you," then wiped his chin on his shoulder and leaned his head back

against the headrest. His head felt too heavy, as did his eyelids.

They drove on in silence.

ould tell now they were traveling north. The sky to his
had lightened. The buildings were thinning, the country-
de broadening into a sea of windswept grass rolling over low
hills. They were coming to the outer edge of the Ring Belt. Once
they left the Belt, it would be harder for SecPac to locate him. They
would not give up, though. Jet would never give up. Donovan had
to stay alive long enough to be rescued.

The vehicle slowed. From the driver's seat, Brett said, "Oh,
scorching *hell*."

The road was blocked. In the gray half-light of early morning,
a crew of workers was directing heavy machinery—diggers, earth-
movers, assemblers. Two workers were setting up signs indicating
the road closure and detour. The three cars ahead of the SUV were
slowly turning around, heading back the way they had come.

Brett edged the vehicle forward. "Kevin?" he asked anxiously,
"What do we do?"

Anya pressed a hand to the glass, peering out the window.
"The detour will take us back into the Belt."

"We aren't going back into the Belt," Kevin said. "SecPac will
be crawling all over it by now."

"Drive right through the barricade?" Brett's foot came a hair
off the brake.

"Like that won't set alarm bells off," Anya said. "They'll call
SecPac in five seconds flat."

Indecision clouded the inside of the car. One of the construction workers began walking toward them, pointing meaningfully
at the detour sign. Kevin leaned forward over the seat back. His
voice grew low and urgent, all business. "What do you see, Brett?
Are those people clean, or are they marked?"

"They're marked," said Brett.

"How many of them?"

"Three. And one shroom."

"Any of them exos?"

"I can't tell for sure . . . I don't think so."

Kevin ducked down and brought his rifle up. "All right. When I say go, gun the engine. Drive right through those signs and stop next to that digger. We throw the doors open and take them out, all of them." He braced the stock against his shoulder. "I'll go for the shroom, you two handle its pets. You think you can manage that?"

Brett reached for the glove compartment. He took out a handgun and held it in his lap with his right hand, tightening his grip on the steering wheel with his left. His twitchy eyes skipped between the road and the rearview mirror. "Got it, Kevin."

Anya took Kevin's pistol in her hands. He nudged her with his shoulder. "No chickening out this time, Anya. This is for *real*. Trial by fire. You've got what it takes, or you don't." She set her jaw and nodded.

"Don't do this!" Donovan swiveled his body around, twisting his injured shoulder painfully. These sapes were crazy. Kevin was crazy. Those were innocent people they were planning to massacre.

Kevin jabbed Donovan with his rifle. "On the floor. Facedown."

"No."

"Do it, or I'll make you *stay* down."

The worker walking toward them slowed, puzzled that the SUV hadn't moved yet. Donovan's hands clenched behind his back helplessly. He couldn't just let four people die. He would have to start yelling and struggling, and hope the commotion warned them before he was silenced with enough lead.

Kevin jerked his head from Anya to Donovan. "Fry him again. That'll keep him out of it. Brett, you ready?"

"I can get us through!" Donovan blurted.

Kevin flashed a sharp scowl. "What do you mean?"

Donovan pinned the man with a wild, imploring glare. "I'm an exo and a soldier-in-erze. I can talk to them, I can get us through. No one has to die. Take these handcuffs off and let me go out there."

"Scorch that."

"Listen, you asswipe." He was talking as fast as he could now. "Even if none of the humans are Hardened, you have maybe even odds of killing the zhree. Soldiers will arrive in minutes and they'll know you were here. I can get us through without leaving a bloody trail."

The man hesitated. Anya said quietly, "Let him try, Kevin."

"He'll run out there and warn them, then turn on us."

"I won't," Donovan said. "I don't want anyone getting killed. One of you can come with me. You'll hear everything I say. If I make a wrong move, you go back to shooting everyone. Just decide, fast."

"What do I do, Kevin?" Brett called. "Should I run this guy over or what?"

Two heartbeats of silence and tension so thick it felt like fog, trapped inside the vehicle. Kevin cursed. He leaned down with a pair of wire cutters and snipped the metal binding Donovan's ankles, then reached around the seat and unlocked Donovan's handcuffs. "This better work, zebrahands," he hissed. "You better not be messing with me."

Donovan opened the door and stepped out of the SUV. For a second, he wobbled and put a hand out to steady himself against the side of the car. Then, with effort, he brought his armor up to half strength, an on-duty level, and walked forward as authoritatively and confidently as he could manage, trying not to limp or wince.

The man he approached had a ruddy, sun-roughened face and broad shoulders. The blocky patterning on the backs of his thick hands marked him as a builder-in-erze. "Morning," Donovan said, making his voice bored and a little weary. "I can see you're setting up a work site, but I'm afraid we're going to have to get through here."

The man raised his brow, then furrowed it back down. Donovan watched the squinting eyes take in his exocel, his youth, his erze markings, and his damp uniform, streaked with dirt and torn with bullet holes. Gruffly, "You look like you've seen some trouble, Officer."

"You could say that." Donovan forced a grim smile and looked down at himself. "We flushed out a terrorist hideout last night. It got pretty ugly. Haven't had much sleep." All true. Donovan motioned toward the roadblock. "I'm heading north on urgent SecPac business. I can't afford to lose time to this detour."

The builder-in-erze looked past him. Donovan glanced over his shoulder. Anya had come up just behind him and was listening warily. He turned back to the man in front of him. "I've got three civilians with me. No one else behind us. Once we're through, you can close it off."

Would the man recognize him? Had he seen the early morning news already, with Donovan's face plastered on the screen? No, he obviously hadn't. He blew out an annoyed breath. "You'll have to talk to the boss."

The Builder was in discussion with the other two members of his crew, a man and a woman. As Donovan drew near, he saw that the man was an exo. He was lightly armored, and his dark skin made his exocel nodes less visible, so it wasn't surprising that from a distance, Brett had not seen what he was.

Another exo! Donovan's mind sprinted over the possibilities. Two exos and one zhree were more than a match for three squishy insurgents. Could he communicate his dire situation to this man somehow? Ask for his help?

The exo and the Builder were having a disagreement, the man's patterned hands gesturing around the perimeter being marked out by landscape survey drones. The zhree was replying with equal vehemence, limbs waving, his voice hitting high excited notes. The mobile translation machine between them trilled and jabbered madly, trying to keep up with the rapid conversation. Finally, the Builder said something in the staccato rhythm of command, fins gesturing sharply to indicate the end of the discussion.

The exo's shoulders tensed with internal struggle. He looked ready to keep arguing, but it was hard to defy a direct order from one's erze master. The man grumbled something, scowling, but dropped his armor in acknowledgment. As he turned away, he looked up briefly in Donovan's direction.

Donovan hesitated. What should he do? He had seconds to decide. Anya's eyes were drilling into his back.

Kevin and Brett were crouched in the vehicle with high-powered firearms. The Builder and his exo foreman were unarmed and trained to use their exocels for construction work, not combat. What if they froze or cowered? The two non-Hardened human workers wouldn't stand a chance.

Only the foolish aspire to die fighting. That's what his father would say. *Planning for survival—that is difficult.*

Donovan stepped up to the Builder and dropped his armor respectfully. Panotin retreated across his skin. "Excuse me, zun," he said. "I realize your crew just finished blocking this road, but my vehicle needs to pass through on urgent SecPac business."

The translation machine began relaying his words in strumming musical notes and chirps, but the Builder didn't wait for it to finish. Clearly, he understood English well enough not to need the machine's help. "Soldier Werth did not inform me that any of his humans-in-erze would be interrupting this project. The construction of the auxiliary communication tower is extremely high priority."

Everything was high priority these days, it seemed. Coincidentally, the centennial Peace Day wasn't the only major event coming up; the Mur Erzen Commonwealth had a new leader, a new High Speaker, from the distant zhree homeworld of Kreet, who'd never been to the outer colonies. In a couple of weeks he was scheduled to visit Earth for the first time. It was a great honor that the High Speaker would begin his planetary tour at Round Three, and according to Donovan's father, the momentous occasion had zhree of every erze—and, by extension, a great many humans—scrambling in preparation.

"I understand, zun," Donovan said, not waiting for the translation either. "This came up unexpectedly."

From slightly behind him, Donovan could feel Anya staring so hard her eyes were surely drying out. Was this the first time she'd been close to a zhree? It was hard for Donovan, who'd grown up in the Round, to remember there were still millions of humans who went about their daily lives only rarely, if ever, interacting with members of Earth's governing species. He wondered fleetingly if the experience was living up to Anya's expectations. Was she surprised? Repulsed? Disappointed?

The Builder was taller than average. Most zhree stood around four feet, but this one came up to Donovan's chin. His domed, exocel-clad body bore the blocky pattern Donovan had seen scaled down on the hands of the workers. Each of the limbs arrayed circularly under the zhree torso could be used as an arm or leg; right now the Builder was standing on four of them and holding a computing disc with the other two. The "head" was not separate; it bulged up from the center of the torso. Six solid yellow eyes, like opaque glass lenses, were spaced equally around it. With a large heaping of imagination, Donovan could see where the derogatory term "shrooms" came from. Enormous, armored, six-legged mushrooms—that's what War Era humans thought the zhree resembled.

"What is this urgent business?" The Builder spoke by drawing his tiny seventh limb across the hollow, ridged speech organ on the underside of his torso, like a violin bow across strings. The light and dark fins on top of the rounded body flashed in concert with the musical speech, like semaphore flags.

"I'm afraid I can't say, zun. Erze orders." That should end further questioning.

The Builder focused on Donovan by closing three of his eyes and regarding him intently with the others. "Why are you in that old human vehicle? Where is the rest of your squad, and who is this unmarked human you have with you?"

Crap. He was getting far too curious. Donovan fought to keep calm. If he began to armor reflexively, out of stress, it would only raise more suspicion. It didn't help that the translation machine relayed the message a second later in a stern male voice that reminded Donovan of his father on his most humorless days. The Builder was not really male—the zhree were hermaphrodites—and the high, lilting musical tones sounded almost feminine, especially since he could see this Builder's swollen egg sac. But Donovan thought of all zhree as male, because of their translated voices. The aliens had learned long ago that humans obeyed a low male voice more automatically.

"Every SecPac skimmercar is being used to patrol the Ring Belt, zun," he said. "Only the undercover vehicles could be spared." Donovan grasped for a plausible story as if hurriedly collecting spilled toothpicks. "I'm escorting three unmarked civilian witnesses to a detention center up north, to help identify terrorist suspects. That's all I can disclose."

"You are an adolescent," the Builder observed. A curious pause. "But you do not look too healthy."

Donovan swallowed. *No kidding.* Was it the flushed face? The sweat on his brow? The hitch in his movements? Facial expressions were totally foreign to most zhree, but those that worked closely with humans were more perceptive. Donovan turned his open hands palm up—a gesture the Builder would understand—and tried to give off a sense of weary good humor. "It's been a tough week. With the High Speaker's visit and Peace Day coming up, everyone in SecPac is being worked to the ground."

The Builder flicked his fins in a gesture Donovan would have translated as a snort or tsk. "Soldier Werth ought to take care not to wear out his exos." He closed two eyes and opened a different two in sequence, shifting his gaze to look in the direction of his own exo foreman. In a rhythm of grudging affection, "Sometimes it is easy to expect too much and forget that you are only human." He lifted a third limb off the ground and waved to the man by the road whom Donovan had spoken to earlier. "Danielson! Let this soldier-in-erze through, then send out a Belt-wide detour alert and move the signs farther down the road." To Donovan, "Go in erze."

"Thank you, zun." Donovan walked back to the SUV as casually as he could muster. Anya trotted close behind him, casting backward glances the whole way. Donovan went to the passenger's side and opened the door, climbing into the front. As soon as both he and Anya were inside, he said to Brett, "Okay, you can go."

"Drive," came Kevin's voice, low and dangerous, from behind. "Slow and normal-like."

Donovan opened his window and waved thanks as they rolled past. A minute later, the SUV was speeding down the freeway, the Builder and his crew gone from sight. Brett let out a loud breath. He swiped his brow with the sleeve of his shirt. "Man, oh *man*. That was close."

"Stop the car," Kevin ordered.

Brett cast a darting glance at Donovan, then slowed the vehicle and pulled it to the side of the road. As he did so, Donovan felt the barrel of Kevin's handgun come to rest against the base of his neck.

"What are we doing?" Anya asked.

"Waiting," said Kevin. "To see if we're being followed."

Brett put the car into park but left the engine running. He rolled down the window and leaned out on his arm, fingers jiggling, watching the side mirrors. Silent minutes passed. In the distance, a pair of turkey vultures drifted over the old wreck of a wooden windmill. The rising sun reddened the long clouds streaking the sky. Donovan felt hot and woozy. He'd used what little energy he had left in the charade back at the construction site, and now he felt as if the inside of the car had become a strange, moving echo chamber throbbing in time to the pulse behind his eyes.

Kevin said to Anya, "What did he say to them? Anything that might have tipped them off?"

Anya thought about it. "I don't think so."

Kevin grunted. "You can't ever be too careful. Don't forget that. You never know how the shrooms are going to try to get you." In a half whisper to Donovan, "That was a nifty stunt you pulled, Reyes Junior. Playing your cards real clever, just like your daddy. Now, move over to the middle seat, *slow*, and lie down with your hands behind your back."

Donovan envisioned whipping around and closing armored fingers over the man's throat. Instead, he did as he was told, because lying down had never seemed like such a good idea. He crawled between the two front seats and lowered himself across the middle row. He could feel how weak his exocel was when the handcuffs went back around his wrists. Everything was hurting again, worse than before, and when the SUV started moving, he couldn't tell if it was traveling forward, or up and down, or spinning in place. His eyelids dragged shut and consciousness drained from him.

6

Donovan's father had a lecture he used on any occasion he thought his son was not living up to expectations in some way, which by Donovan's estimation was often. "The future depends on people like you—those who can straddle the divide between the species," he would say, as preamble to why Donovan's skills rating ought to be higher, or his academic evaluations better, or his comprehension of the zhree language more fluent. Sure. No pressure or anything. The last time Donovan had stewed silently under the barrage of heavy-handed Dominick Reyes rhetoric, he'd wanted to snap back, "*You're* the Prime Liaison! Shaping the future between the species is *your* job, not mine!"

The first incarnation of the lecture had been given right before his Hardening. His mother had been gone less than a month. It had happened suddenly, without warning. She had dropped him off at school one morning, and partway during the day, his father had picked him up—something he had never done before. Donovan's mother had gone on a trip, his father explained. One that might last a very long time. No, there was no telling when she would return. Sadly, she would not be there for his Hardening, but not to worry, his father was going to do something else he'd never done before—take a day off from his new, Very Important Job, to spend time with Donovan beforehand. They would go to the park and the ice-cream shop.

The reality of his mother's abandonment came gradually. At first, Donovan kept expecting her to be there when he got out of school, or at least for her to show up in time to tuck him into bed at night. If she wasn't there today, then surely the next day. It took weeks for him to realize that she would *not* be there the next day, or the day after that, or the day after that. Her belongings disappeared from the house; his father put out boxes of her clothes and shoes, her personal items, her little notebooks of scribbled poetry—and men came and took them away. That was distressing enough, but the thing that convinced Donovan that his mother was truly gone was the silence in the evenings. The raised voices, the arguments he had gotten used to overhearing before he fell asleep—they had been replaced by silence. Even his crying was silent.

His Hardening Day arrived.

His father had woken him early. Donovan was starving. He hadn't been allowed to eat for eighteen hours beforehand, but he was too anxious to complain. They had driven to the center of the Round, to the Towers. Donovan had only visited the national seat of zhree government once before (so the place would not be too frightening for him on Hardening Day) and it was not yet familiar to him, the way it would be later. That morning, he was awed by the alien magnificence of the buildings, the way the curved walls and rounded entryways appeared to be knit together from unearthly metal fiber. He stared nervously at the battle-armored Soldiers guarding the entrances, their unblinking eyes watching in all directions.

They went into a special building that his father explained was used just for making exos. It was separate from the Hatchery, where the Nurses cared for zhree broods and oversaw the Hardening of their own kind. The Hardening of a human was different. The zhree had residual natural exoskeletons, an evolutionary trait left over from thousands of years past, before they'd developed the exocels that would enable them to become a space-faring, multi-planet civilization. For the zhree, living machine cells fused with organic structure in a seamless rite of passage that had been going on for innumerable generations. Not so for humans. Exos were still a tiny minority. Hardening was painful and dangerous.

Donovan stood in a semicircle with the other boys and girls. They ranged from four to six years old. That was the window of time that worked for humans; any younger and the child might not be strong enough to handle the procedure, any older and the body would reject the integration of panotin-assembling cells. Donovan's father stood behind him, hands on his shoulders, as did the other parents behind their children.

Donovan looked around the circle of faces. There were thirty-eight kids, from all around the country. He recognized three of them from school. Jet looked anxious, his face screwed up a little, as if he might start crying. Vic and her twin brother, Skye, were standing side by side, giggling and poking each other in the ribs, while their mother admonished them to stay still and pay attention. Donovan dropped his eyes to the ground, his face heating with fear. Sometimes people died from Hardening. A lot of these kids didn't know that because their parents didn't want to scare them. Donovan knew.

"Jet said that it hurts," he'd blurted to his father days ago.

"You will be unconscious," said his father. "Afterward, there will be pain, but it will be manageable."

"Is it true that some kids *die*?"

His father nodded. "One in twenty times, the process does not succeed. Either the child dies, or survives but must live with an exocel that is deformed or nonfunctional."

Donovan's face trembled. "Will *I* die?"

"You will not die," said his father firmly.

"But what if I do?"

"You will not," his father repeated.

"How do you *know*?" Donovan demanded, tears flooding his eyes.

Suddenly, his father's voice took on an edge of anger. "Because you're my son. I've sacrificed too much for you to die. Now, stop crying. The Hardening process is much safer than it used to be. You have nothing to fear."

Donovan learned later that there were two casualties out of his batch: a four-year-old named Susannah Morrows, and Vic's twin brother, Skye. He also learned, much later, that sixty years ago, the mortality rate had been 30 percent. Who knew how many people had died at the very beginning, almost a century ago, when the zhree had first attempted to Harden the legions of human war orphans who had fallen under their care.

A Nurse was making his way around the semicircle, walking on three legs in a rotating motion. With the other three limbs he was marking children off a list on a computing disc and scanning them for signs of illness or infection. He stood slightly taller than the children themselves, and when he reached Donovan he bent his supporting limbs so two of his solid yellow eyes were level with Donovan's face. He seemed kind, and he moved his fins in a gesture of calming as he checked Donovan's pulse and temperature. "Don't be scared, hatchling," he strummed, too quietly for the translation machine, but Donovan murmured, "Yes, zun," politely, as he'd been taught.

As each child was checked off, the two nurses-in-erze, a plump, friendly young woman named Evangeline and an older grandmotherly woman named Theodosia, led the kids away from their parents and through an arched door. There were hugs and tearful partings. Some of the younger children cried and had to be carried out. Some of the grown-ups cried too; the others smiled with false bravery. Donovan looked up at his father. His father looked serious but unconcerned, as if they were standing in line in a store. Donovan relaxed a little. Everything would be okay. He just wished his mom was here.

"Do you remember what it means to be an exo?" His father held him at arm's length.

Donovan nodded.

"When you wake up, you'll be better and stronger than you are now. You'll have erze status for life, and when you grow up, there's nothing you won't be able to do. Maybe one day you could even fly in a spaceship to other planets if you want to."

Donovan nodded. His bedroom at home was cluttered with small toy spaceships, and he was jealous that one of his classmates, whose parents were engineers-in-erze, had visited the zhree orbital stations *and* the Moon.

"You will have enormous advantages and responsibility. Do you understand?"

He didn't. He was only five years old. But he said, "Yes, Father," and then Evangeline led him away. He looked over his shoulder. His father was standing silently, watching him go. He didn't know it at the time, but everyone else, zhree and human, had been watching Dominick Reyes as well. They observed the new Prime Liaison's public display of loyalty, his calm confidence as he sent his only child to be Hardened.

Evangeline led Donovan into a clean white room with a stool, strange-looking machines with long arms and tools, and a Hardening tank. He'd never seen one before. It looked like a large oval fishbowl, three-quarters of the way full with a slightly pink, viscous liquid. "Okay, can you take your clothes and shoes off for me?" she asked. He did so, folding his clothes neatly and setting them on the stool. He put his shoes on top of his clothes. "My underwear too?" Yes, his underwear. When he stood naked, shivering slightly, Evangeline said, "I'm going to give you a little shot now, okay? My, you are a brave little boy."

To distract himself from the shot, he studied the gentle, swirling erze markings on Evangeline's hands. "How did you become a nurse-in-erze?" he asked.

"Well, sweetheart, I had to apply. The shr—I mean, the zhree only need a certain number of human workers, so the Liaison Office has an application process to decide who's qualified to be in erze. Unless you're an exo, of course. Then you'll be in erze automatically when you turn twelve and get your markings." She smiled at him.

"My father works for the Liaison Office," Donovan said proudly. He kept on talking, much faster now, because he was starting to feel nervous again, and he wanted his mom. "Do you know what 'in erze' means? It means a member of the erze, like a member of the family. The zhree don't really have families, though. My father says it's more like a . . . um, a tribe. And everyone in the tribe works together, as Nurses or Builders, or whatever. So that's why 'in erze' also means, 'correct' or 'good.' 'Cause that's what you have to be, to be in the erze, right?"

"You sure are smart," said Evangeline. "Why don't you get into that big bowl of pink jelly and see what it feels like? I bet it would be super fun to swim in." She helped him up the two steps and into the tank.

"It feels wet and squishy," he said.

"Can you put this little mask over your head? That's it. See how it's connected to a tube with air in it? You can even put your head underwater and still breathe. Now, just lie down and relax . . ."

— — —

His father had been wrong. When Donovan woke up, he didn't feel better and stronger. He felt like he was dying. He sweated, and thrashed, and sobbed for his mother. His heart raced so fast he thought it would burn up in his chest, then throbbed so slowly he was sure each beat would be its last. A Nurse came by his bed regularly to check on him, trilling and humming instructions to a fat nurse-in-erze, not Evangeline, someone whose name he didn't know. They gave him fluids, and medication for the pain, but not too much, so the drugs would not interfere with the Hardening.

The Hardening was like having a million fire ants crawling under his skin and inside his bones and in his brain. He wept and begged for it to stop. His frail human body was being conquered and remade. For four days he burned with fever, shook with chills, and passed in and out of consciousness and delirium. He halluci-nated that his mom was there, soothing him and kissing him with cool lips. His father was not there during the day, but twice

Donovan awoke at night to see him sitting by his bed, watching him with hands folded in his lap, a motionless shape in the darkness. He hated his father.

On the fifth day, the Nurse declared he would survive. The fat nurse-in-erze duct-taped fleece mittens to his hands so he couldn't scratch and pick at the erupting exocel nodes, which burned and itched. They broke out in the usual pattern: up the length of his spine to the crown of his head, across his collarbones and down the front of his torso, along the outside of both arms and legs. His hair fell out, in patchwork clumps. By the eighth day, he could get out of bed, and by the tenth, he and the other surviving, half-bald, newborn exos had started playing games of tag in the curved hallways of the infirmary.

Jet was the first to do it. He wasn't watching where he was going and accidentally bowled over a bad-tempered boy named Tennyson, who took a retaliatory swing at him. Jet flinched back and armored, just like that, but lost it an instant later and got punched in the ear. Still, everyone was so excited, even Tennyson, that Jet spent the rest of the day begging people to hit him so he could figure out how to do it again. Donovan was jealous. He could *feel* his exocel but couldn't do anything with it, not yet. When the time came, after fourteen days, for the parents to take their children home, Donovan could only armor up by concentrating so hard for thirty seconds that beads of sweat popped from his forehead. Jet was already showing off by hitting himself with sharp rocks, which the nurses-in-erze immediately ordered him to stop doing.

It was exciting, discovering their new bodies. The only one who wasn't giddy was Vic. She didn't care. She sat curled in the corner, crying for her brother.

In a rare show of indulgence, Donovan's father let him spend his first few days back at home doing whatever he wanted: staying up late, watching cartoons, eating cake in the morning. His father was busier than ever. He arranged for a fifteen-year-old exo named Jamieson to watch over Donovan and help him begin to control his exocel.

Jamieson set Donovan's toy tool bench on the floor between them. "Look," he said. He extended his armor out to a flat point on the tip of his index finger and used it as a screwdriver on one of the plastic screws. He made a fist, encased it in armor, and hammered down one of the nails. He formed the outside flat of his hand into a sharp blade, set it against a block of wood, and tapped it with his other hand, making a small pile of shavings.

Donovan was impressed. "I can't do that," he said morosely.

"You'll learn, little guy. You're going to love it."

"Do *you* love being an exo?"

Jamieson hesitated. "There are people who don't like us," he said. "People outside the Round, people who aren't in erze. But so long as you stick with your own kind, it's great. If you get chosen and marked by a good erze, you've got it made. You'll always have a good job, a nice house"—he gestured to Donovan's home—"and you'll live twice as long as those poor suckers who are just made out of meat. Maybe you'll even have your dad's job someday."

Donovan made a face. "I hope not." His father's job sounded terribly dull and complicated. Jamieson laughed.

— — —

Donovan went back to school, into an exo class. Much of their time at first was spent learning to build control and coordination. For the first few months, their exocels were erratic and flickering. Sometimes Donovan's would start insulating him when he was already too warm, or go to full armor for stupid reasons, like someone sneezing nearby. But it got better quickly. Control came to him slowly, but when it came, it was fine and consistent.

One day, the teacher led the group of exo children, their heads fuzzy with new hair, into a grassy, fenced play yard where a Scholar stood waiting, surrounded by a cluster of older zhree hatchlings. Ms. Reynolds said, "Class, we're going to be sharing our outside playtime once a week with our friends from Scholar Elni's brood cell. Remember what we talked about: Always drop your armor before you ask a question, and pause so everyone who's listening can hear the translation. We're going to have a contest afterward to see who can remember all the erze markings."

Donovan wasn't paying attention to his teacher; he was fascinated by the concentric ripples of the Scholar's markings, which he had not seen before. Earth, his father had explained, was primarily a military and trade outpost, whatever that meant; there were plenty of Administrators, Soldiers, and Builders, a fair number of Merchants, Engineers, and Nurses, and colonists of other erze, like Scientists, Scholars, and Artists in fewer number.

The two groups, humans and zhree, regarded each other silently from across a wary distance.

"I don't like humans," one of the adolescent zhree said at last, shifting his weight squeamishly. The translation machine was indiscreet enough to repeat him. "They look strange."

"You cannot judge a species by its appearance," said Scholar Elni, addressing his pupils. "Humans are not so savage and unpredictable as some of those War Era elders would have you believe. No matter your erze, it is important that you understand how to interact with the natives. They were the apex species on this planet long before we arrived."

"Do they play?" asked a small Builder.

"What kind of question is that?" the Scholar said. "Of course they play. All sentient creatures play."

Both groups eyed the balls and toys scattered strategically around the yard. Jet dashed out, grabbed an inflated red ball, and raced back to the human side. Emboldened, a few of the other kids made similar runs. The zhree milled toward and around them cautiously. "Don't squeeze them," one of the Soldier hatchlings warned his fellows. "They break."

"These ones are Hardened," Scholar Elni said. "When they are a little older, they will be erze marked. So you see, they are not all that different from us. Treat them respectfully and humans will reward an erze with hard work and loyalty."

Donovan managed to claim a bucket and shovel. He had barely half filled his container with rocks when he looked up to see Jet standing in front of him, red ball still held with both hands. Donovan thought Jet looked like the kind of kid who might be here to steal his bucket. Very deliberately, he picked up another rock and put it in.

"Is your dad really the Prime Liaison?" Jet asked.

"Yeah."

"Do you get to fly on his plane?"

Donovan stuck out his lower lip. "No."

"You don't look that special," Jet challenged. "I'll bet you can't even catch me before I get to that tree." He ran away.

Donovan dropped the bucket and chased him but did not catch him. Jet was really fast.

"Do you know how to sneak up on a zhree?" Donovan asked, trying to think of something to impress the other boy.

"You can't. They have six eyes. They can see all around."

Donovan pointed to a zhree standing awkwardly off to the side by himself. "Run in front of that one and do something really silly. I dare you."

Jet hurled his ball away without a word and ran in front of the young Nurse, whose name, they would later learn, was Therrid. Suddenly, Jet tripped and fell, hard, on his face. He lay still, unmoving.

The Nurse's fins shot up in surprise, then froze. After a long hesitation, he approached Jet slowly. Donovan imagined the zhree was wondering if he would be blamed for whatever inexplicable harm had befallen the human child. He nudged Jet with one of his limbs. He strummed some nervous words. He bent over, four of his eyes sliding shut, focusing his multi-directional gaze on the prone boy.

Donovan padded up behind him, trembling with his own daring, and yanked hard on the zhree fins.

The Nurse let out a startled, high-pitched trill. Jet leapt to his feet with a shout of laughter. He and Donovan ran away as fast as they could, hearts pounding in their ears. Therrid would get them back later, though, by stealing their shoes and hanging them out of reach from a tree.

At regular intervals each year, an Administrator would come to observe and evaluate the children in the class. Donovan always did well in the evaluations. He knew it wasn't because he was particularly gifted, but because he had an educational advantage. Dominick Reyes had business in the Towers at least once a week; now he brought Donovan along. The rules were simple: If Donovan followed along behind his father, silent and observant, he stayed. If not, he would be confined at home under the eye of one of his father's humorless staffers, chosen especially for the task based on lack of empathy toward children. It was a no-brainer. When Donovan was not at school, he was trailing after his father, absorbing the zhree language and picking up the mundane details of his father's work.

Nothing about this seemed special or unusual to Donovan. Boring, yes, pointless even, when he would prefer to be running around enjoying himself, the way his mother used to let him. It wasn't until he was a teenager, marked, in training to be a soldier-in-erze, that he seriously contemplated the idea that there were millions of humans out there, growing up so very differently from him and his friends. People in the Ring Belt and beyond, with no erze to belong to and no exocel to protect them. Squishies.

7

A hand touched Donovan's shoulder. For an embarrassed instant, he thought he'd fallen asleep in the skimmercar on the way home from patrol. He began to mumble an apology; then everything came crashing back so fast he jerked fully awake, armoring, wrists tugging against handcuffs.

Anya pulled her hand away quickly. She gathered the collar of her jacket to her throat, warding off the wind blowing through the open SUV door, and stared at him over the top of pale knuckles. She held out a yellow blueberry muffin sealed in plastic and a stick of beef jerky. "You want something to eat?"

Donovan looked at her blearily, then down at the food in her hand. His stomach was a tight knot of ache. If Kevin or Brett had been offering, he would have refused. They would only have pulled it away from him, maybe eaten it themselves in front of him. Anya wasn't like that, though. He struggled up to a sitting position, then armored down and nodded.

She popped the plastic on the muffin and climbed in beside him. Her thin fingers tore off a piece of the crumbly pastry and held it to his mouth. He leaned forward and ate it. It was as tasteless as baking powder, and he wondered pessimistically how old it was, but when she held out another piece, he took it eagerly. He chewed and swallowed, eyes averted. It was strange to be eating from her hand like this, his lips unavoidably touching the cold tips of her fingers. She smelled faintly sweaty—not locker-room sweat but girl sweat.

When he'd finished the muffin, she took out her water bottle, opened it, and let him drink. She offered him the beef jerky and he tugged on it with his teeth to take off a piece. She watched him the entire time, her gaze as inscrutable as it had been when she'd placed the muzzle of the gun against his eye, her finger on the trigger. He felt helpless and humiliated. Also grateful and uncomfortably intimate.

He turned his face away and looked around as he worked over the tough, dried meat. It was midday. The sun was shining down, clear and white, through the tall black stilts of scaly tree trunks. They had left behind the flat, open prairie and climbed into craggy hills, densely forested. The breeze coming in through the still-open door stung Donovan's nostrils with the crisp scent of ponderosa pine. He knew where he was: the Black Hills. SecPac referred to it as RA3-1. The Risk Area of nearest proximity to Round Three, rated as having high levels of terrorist installations and activity.

Donovan bit off another piece of the beef jerky and looked up at the empty blue sky. Scanner planes flew over the hills frequently, but there were a lot of places here for terrorists to hide. How much longer before SecPac found him? Would Soldier Werth send in zhree Soldiers for one missing human? It was unlikely but possible.

They were parked on a narrow gravel road, in front of a steel sentry gate. Brett was pacing about fifty meters from the vehicle. Every few minutes, he would lift the rifle he carried to his shoulder and sight into the woods at nothing in particular. Kevin was nowhere to be seen.

Donovan turned back to Anya. She fed him the last bit of jerky, and this time he met her unwavering gaze. Neither of them looked away, neither spoke. Donovan still felt weak, but the few hours of sleep, and the food, had taken the edge off the pain. He could think clearly again as he studied Anya's face. Why would this girl want to be a terrorist? Kevin was a zealot, and Brett was a follower, but Anya didn't seem like either. She was young and pretty, she had a conscience. She'd stood up to Kevin, twice. Would she go further? Would she help him if he could find the right thing to say, now, while the man wasn't here?

Before he could think of what that might be, she spoke. "You understand their language."

Donovan swallowed the remaining stringy mouthful of jerky. He nodded slowly. "Most of it."

"It sounds like music." Her head tilted slightly. "What do they call you? Do you have a name?"

"Yes," he said. He looked at the water bottle in her hand. "Can I have some more water?"

She poured a little into his mouth.

"So what is it?" she asked him.

"What's what?"

"Your name."

Donovan cleared his throat. He whistled the three notes that made up his name in Mur, the predominant zhree language of the Commonwealth. The first long vibrating note, the same as his father's, but the second and third notes tripping down the scale, while his father's rose briskly.

"That's nice." She didn't smile as she said it.

"It sounds different when they say it." A human voice couldn't make the strumming, vibrating sounds of a zhree speech organ.

"And there's a visual pattern that goes with it, otherwise the same three notes might mean something else." He shifted slightly forward. "Long names translate better, but Anya might be—" He whistled two short notes. "Or maybe—" A slightly different variation.

Her expression turned cold and sharp. "Why would I want a shroom name?"

The crunch of boot steps, and Kevin's voice approached. Anya hastily capped her water bottle and stuffed the empty plastic wrap in her pocket. "Wait," Donovan said quickly as she scooted away from him and climbed into the other seat. "Where are you taking me?"

Anya grabbed Kevin's gun off the seat and slouched back with her legs drawn up. She rested her forearms on her knees, gun aimed casually in his direction, as if she'd been sitting that way all along. "To the Warren," she said.

Donovan craned his neck to see out the windshield. Kevin had paused at the sentry gate. He was talking to a tall man in camouflage fatigues and an M4 slung over his shoulder. The two of them shook hands, then embraced warmly. The tall man gave a signal to some unseen eyes in the forest, and slowly, the sentry gate swung open.

Kevin gestured Brett back to the SUV, then returned to it himself. When he saw Donovan sitting up, his eyes traveled suspiciously from him to Anya. "He say or do anything?"

"No," she said. "He just woke up."

Kevin fished a granola bar from his pocket and unwrapped it. He held it out to Anya, but when she shook her head, he took a big bite of it and took his time eating it looking at Donovan the way a hunter might study an animal in a trap. Donovan felt a fresh wave of hatred for the man and another small ripple of gratitude toward the girl.

Brett came up, and Kevin jerked his chin toward Donovan. "Doesn't make sense, does it? For the Prime Liaison to risk his own kid as a SecPac officer."

Brett said, "What're you saying, Kevin?"

"I'm saying"—Kevin squinted at Donovan—"how can we be sure he really *is* Donovan Reyes? SecPac might be feeding us a false identity to keep him alive. They could be playing us. Pretty convenient how he got us through that little hiccup back there, wasn't it?"

Donovan stared at the man in disdainful wonder. "Does life as a terrorist get tiring?" he asked. "Being paranoid all the time, knowing we're going to get you eventually?"

Kevin's face darkened. He leaned forward, his voice a hard whisper. "Let me tell you something, you worthless shroom pet. If you get me, there'll be more patriots who come after. There will always be more, and you better believe we'll keep fighting."

"Well, Kevin," said Brett, "you're the boss; if you think it's safer to kill him, we should do it. But I don't know . . ." Brett shifted his weight from one foot to the other. "I think it's him. I mean, look at him. He friggin' *looks* like Reyes, man. What are the odds of that?"

Kevin scowled. Finally, he grunted. "Once in a blue moon, Brett, you do have a good point." He walked around the front of the car and got into the driver's seat. Brett climbed in beside Anya and pulled the door shut. The SUV grumbled to life and rolled through the sentry gate. For ten minutes, it navigated packed gravel roads that wound through forest and hugged steep rock walls, before Kevin eased it off the path, onto a flat spot well concealed by trees, and cut the engine. "Let's go."

The three of them gathered gear and weapons from the vehicle, then nudged Donovan out at rifle-point and made him walk ahead down the path. The crunch of gravel gave way to the thud of dirt. The dust from the end of a long, dry summer rose up around the toes of Donovan's boots. Birds warbled, flitting from tree to tree. The trail all but disappeared; overgrown shrubs dragged across their legs as the SUV fell out of sight.

Just as Donovan began to wonder if they weren't leading him deep into the forest to kill him after all, part of a building emerged: a short concrete structure thrusting out of the hillside, shaded by rock overhangs and tree cover. It would be almost impossible to notice unless a person was approaching on foot and searching for it.

Kevin said to Brett and Anya, "They'll question you both, separately, to check you out, make sure you are who you say you are. But it's nothing to worry about. They'll know you're with me." From the corner of his eye, Donovan saw Kevin put his arm around Anya's waist and pull her close for a minute as they walked. "You're not nervous, are you?"

"No," she said. "I'm not nervous."

Donovan could not say the same for himself. The little food in his stomach balled into a hard knot as he watched the steel doors begin to slide open like the maw of the hill itself. People weren't taken to secret Sapience camps and returned alive. Once he went through those doors, the odds of SecPac finding this hideout that had eluded them thus far and storming in to save him were despairingly slim. He was walking into his own tomb.

For a brief instant, he considered sprinting away into the forest.

It would be a hopeless ploy. He might survive being shot, but he'd be injured and handcuffed with no way out of the wilderness.

And now it was too late; his steps carried him through the entrance. Kevin walked close behind, his rifle never wavering. Two armed men, wearing helmets and panotin vests, shut the doors behind them with a metallic clang.

They were in a cave. A crowd of about thirty people had gathered for their arrival, but at the sight of Donovan, they fell back as if jolted by an electrical barrier. A murmur of shock rose up and echoed against the rock walls and low ceiling. Donovan felt the muzzle of Kevin's rifle jab into the small of his back. He walked forward, his heart pounding in his throat. Everywhere, he saw hostile stares, rough clothes and faces, unmarked hands—all of it stark under the intermittent glare of LED lights running down the tunnel walls, leading him deeper into the hillside. "Home, sweet home!" Kevin shouted. "Someone find Saul, will you? I've been out hunting and bagged a big one!"

Donovan bit down. *You had nothing to do with it.* It was Anya who'd caught him in an unguarded moment of stupidity. He wasn't sure why it mattered at all, but the thought of Kevin taking credit for his capture infuriated him. A rock flew out from the crowd and struck Donovan in the chest. "SecPac filth!"

Donovan flinched. His armor responded, layering instantly in response to attack. The sight set the crowd off.

"Shroom pet!"

"Traitor! Collaborator!"

"Exo scum!"

Another stone came hurtling at him, then another. One hit him in the collarbone, the other glanced off the side of his head. They stung, but they were only small rocks. They couldn't hurt him, not badly. These people, though—Donovan staggered from the force of their hatred. Their faces were twisted, their voices raised. Donovan's hands felt hot and swollen in their cuffs. He fought against the instinct to battle-armor; it would only stir the crowd's bloodlust. When these people realized rocks wouldn't work, they would lynch him in some other way. His step faltered.

"He's a prisoner!" Anya's shout was drowned out. "You're not supposed to hurt prisoners!"

Donovan half turned, worried for some insensible reason that by calling attention to herself, the girl might get hit by one of the flying stones. Before he could spot her behind him, the steeply descending tunnel ended. He took one more step and found himself stumbling into an enormous chamber—and into the center of a rebel camp. Behind the growing mob, Donovan glimpsed racks of weapons, ammunition cans, and pallets of supplies. The sound of machines being repaired clattered in the background; the cool, damp air was thick with the smell of engine grease and cooking food. Donovan raised his eyes. The cave arched like the nave of a cathedral, a few thin beams of sunlight stabbing through metal grates high overhead. More people stood on the catwalks that ran along rock walls encrusted with white crystal formations that looked as if they bubbled, webbed, and dripped throughout the cave. Men and women, even a few children, pressed close to the railings, staring down at the scene below.

"What in the name of creation is going on here?"

The rumbling voice preceded a man with a wide face and shaved head, striding toward them with a glower. The crowd pushed forward, bold and excited now. Someone shoved Donovan hard, and he fell to his knees on the stone. The approaching man bellowed, "That's enough! We're soldiers here, not a mob!"

The spectators grumbled and swayed resentfully, but hushed and waited.

The man looked down at Donovan, stunned. He turned to Kevin. "Warde, have you lost your mind?"

Kevin stepped forward. "Nice to see you too, Saul. There are three tubs of supplies sitting in the back of the SUV. Blankets, antibiotics, ammunition, whatever I could get my hands on this time around. Toilet paper too, y'all!" At this the crowd laughed and a few people clapped. Kevin smiled as wide as a pleased hyena and motioned Brett and Anya forward with deliberate casualness. "I brought a couple of good recruits. This is Brett. He's been operating with me in the Ring Belt for nearly two years. Knows his way around anything you can blow up or light on fire. Anya here—don't be fooled by her pretty face. She's going to be a crackerjack operative. I vouch for both of them."

Saul's eyes shifted over. He inclined his head toward Brett and Anya. "Patriots of humanity," he said, lifting his arms to the expansive cavern, "welcome to the cause."

"To the cause!" The underground chamber thundered with the unanimous reply.

A slow grin of relief crawled across Brett's bland face—the first strong expression Donovan had ever seen on the man. Anya raised her eyes, overwhelmed, a small smile of disbelief curling the edges of her mouth, as if she were a child surprised to find herself suddenly in a club with adults. Donovan turned his eyes away, a sick feeling unwinding in his stomach.

"We'll get you both sorted soon enough," Saul said. He turned back to Kevin, his frown returning. "Now, you want to explain what possessed you to bring an exo soldier *here* of all places?"

"It was a moment of opportunity." Kevin squared himself to the other man but spoke so everyone could hear him. "The kind of opportunity you don't pass up, because a higher power is placing it in front of you and telling you to *take it*."

Saul dropped his voice. "You know how I feel about those videos. But at least they're brief. Holding a prisoner is different— it's too risky."

"This is worth it," Kevin said. "It's a game changer, Saul. A blow to the heart of the beast."

Saul could not have been old, but his face was lined, his stubbled head deeply furrowed. He looked like a hard man, as solid as the limestone, the kind of man accustomed to giving orders and seeing people die because of them. He regarded Donovan with deep-set eyes. "What's your name?"

Donovan lifted his chin. "Donovan Reyes."

For a second, the silence was such that Donovan could hear only the low background hum of electric generators. Then murmuring disbelief cascaded through the gathered rebels and rose up the cave walls. "Donovan Reyes!" Kevin repeated loudly, throwing up his arms. "The son of the Prime Liaison. Think about the information he has. Think about what the government would be willing to do to keep him in one piece."

Donovan climbed slowly to his feet. The terror of dying had lost some of its power in the last twenty-four hours. Now the idea of being killed seemed less awful than the likely alternative—being *used*. "They'll do something, all right," he said, forcing a confidence he didn't feel. "They'll find this place, and they'll tear it apart." He spoke to Saul, praying the man would see more sense than Kevin. "If you force my father's hand, you're asking for SecPac, maybe even *Soldiers*, to show up here. All these people will die. You can still offer to return me now, before that happens."

"You're a good talker, zebrahands. Like father, like son," Kevin sneered. He turned back to Saul. "We keep moving him, cell to cell, camp to camp. I can set up the relay. Keep SecPac guessing as to where he is. Feed them false leads along with our demands. They won't find him."

Saul looked unmoved. "We need Max in on this decision." He called, "Someone get Max down here."

Max? The same Max responsible for the Sapience propaganda that had led Donovan and his patrol team to Sean Corrigan's house last night? Kevin looked displeased but kept talking. "Things are happening, Saul. I'm on the ground in the Ring Belt more than almost anyone else; I can feel it. This is going to give all the cells the jolt in the arm that they need, 'cause if we can get that one"—he pointed to Donovan—"we can get *anyone*. We declare an ultimatum. All shrooms and SecPac presence out of major urban areas, starting with Denver, Phoenix, and Seattle—make them free human cities."

Despite his situation, Donovan choked on a laugh of derision. "There are hundreds of thousands of marked people in those cities! You really think we'd just pull out and leave them defenseless?" If *that* was what Sapience was envisioning for starters—millions of unmarked humans in a state of anarchy, taking out their pent-up hostility on those who were in erze, all the best scientists, engineers, and civil servants—they might as well put the end of a rifle in his mouth and shoot him now. His father would never, ever in a million years consider such madness. "What world are you living in?"

"We would offer amnesty to those who renounced alien allegiance. An act that your kind is incapable of." Saul motioned forward three of the biggest, meanest-looking armed men. "Lock this shroom pet up. Two guards on him at all times."

Donovan glared at the men who stepped forward. "Don't touch me," he warned. He was an exo at the humiliating mercy of squishies and rapidly realizing what his duty compelled him to do. Despite what he'd said to Saul, he couldn't count on being rescued. This underground terrorist bunker was bigger, better equipped, and held more people than he suspected SecPac knew about. Maybe he couldn't escape, but if he could find a way to get free of his restraints, he would do as much damage to this place as he could. He'd get his hands on a weapon, start a fire, set an explosion—he didn't know what yet, but one Hardened, trained, and armed soldier-in-erze could cripple a Sapience nerve center. He let his fatal resolve steel him, then took two steps forward on his own— before coming to an abrupt standstill.

A woman was hurrying desperately through the crowd. People moved out of her way, letting her pass. When she reached the front, her eyes fell on Donovan, and she reeled as if she'd slammed into a wall. She let out a high gasp. The blood drained from her cheeks, as if he were some appalling apparition. "My God," she whispered.

Donovan stared at the woman. A sliding sensation began to tilt the solid rock beneath his feet.

He must be mistaken. It couldn't be.

"Max," Saul said, looking between them, "you know who this is?"

"Yes." The woman's lips moved almost inaudibly. "He's Donovan Reyes. He's my son."

"Your *son*?" Saul said the word as if it were foreign.

Fresh murmurs rose from the few people near enough to hear and cascaded back through the crowd.

"When I told you I used to be married, I didn't tell you to whom." The woman calling herself Max did not take her eyes off Donovan. "Before he was Prime Liaison, Dominick Reyes was my husband. We had a son. I left him behind when he was only . . . a small boy." Her voice broke, strangling the words. She came toward Donovan with short, hesitant steps, her raised hands turned upward and reaching slightly forward, as if she were cupping some delicate object in her palms and offering it to him. "Donovan . . . do you remember me?"

"Yeah." Donovan heard his voice come out expressionless from shock. He knew it was her—after three thudding heartbeats of disbelief, he knew for certain—but he didn't really recognize her, not in the way one recognizes familiar things. It was as if he'd seen the same photograph in profile over and over again, memorizing half a face and now seeing the other half for the first time. The same, but not the same. His feet clenched inside his boots, gripping the ground. His mind scratched feebly for understanding. "*You're* Max?"

"You've got to be kidding me." Kevin's eyes jumped disbelievingly from person to person. "Saul, you going to *do* something?" he demanded.

The woman Donovan knew but did not recognize as his mother drew close. She was shorter than him. She had storm-colored eyes and thin skin that showed even the finest lines. He remembered, abruptly, that the constellation of freckles speckling her nose and cheeks used to scrunch up when she smiled at him. She did not smile. She laid the flat of her hand against his cheek and he felt her long fingers tremble. A fist closed in Donovan's chest.

"I've wanted and feared this day for twelve years," she whispered.

"Get away from him, Max," Saul said.

She did not move. "Max, *now*," Saul said sternly, but she did not seem to hear him. He motioned to the three burly men; two of them clamped their hands on Donovan's shoulders and pulled him backward, while the third stretched out an arm to keep the woman back. She turned then, wildly. "Don't hurt him, Saul! He's my son! *My son*." In the profound silence that had gripped all the assembled onlookers, her voice climbed high and urgent. Her eyes raced around the circle of watching faces, finding stunned sympathy but no help. With a choked sound, she tried to reach Donovan again, to push past the man who stood in her way. He took hold of her arm, holding her in place.

Something tore inside Donovan. The sight of her reaching for him as he was pulled away—it stabbed deep. He fought against the arms dragging him back. "Get your hands off me," he snarled. "Let me *go*!" He tensed like a bent wire, throwing the surface of his exocel into a landscape of edges, sharp as cut glass.

The two men on either side released him at once. "My hands!" one of them howled, staring at his lacerated palms. "He *cut* us!" The crowd broke into shouting, and cursing, and movement. Rocks began flying at Donovan again, and the other man unslung his M4 and swung it like a heavy metal club across Donovan's back.

He bit his tongue as he fell. It hurt so badly, a sharper and more concentrated pain than the blow to his body, that he yelped and tears pricked his eyes. He tasted blood in his mouth as he plowed into the ground with his knees and the side of his head. Above the tumult, he heard his mother cry out, as if in pain, something between a curse and a plea, and he heard Saul also, bellowing for order.

Donovan raised his head and saw Anya. She hadn't moved. Everyone else was moving and shouting, but she was standing still in the maelstrom. "Get up," she urged him. He couldn't hear her, but that was what she said. He tried to push up; two men took hold of his handcuffs behind his back and forced his bound arms upward painfully, so he swore loudly and scrambled to stand before his shoulders came free from their sockets. He tried to turn his head, to look for his mother, but she was gone, swallowed up or borne away by the crowd. The rebels did not touch him again; they drove him through the cavern at the points of their rifles.

— — —

They locked him in a small, dark cell at the end of a long tunnel. The cell had a single cot with a thin mildewed mattress. The frame of the bed was bolted to the stone floor. There was a drain in the corner to piss into. The cell was not designed to hold someone who was armored; a resourceful, determined exo might be able to find and exploit some weakness in the bars, so two guards armed with collapsed stock submachine guns stood some distance away, sharing a smoke and keeping a watch over him.

Donovan was grateful they had taken off the handcuffs. His wrists had been bound together behind his back for so long that his shoulders and arms had lost all feeling beyond dull heaviness. An hour later, it was still hard to move them. He lay on the bed, groggy from constant hurt and the emotional fallout of the world dropping out from under him. He wondered when his mother— when *Max*, the Sapience terrorist and propaganda writer—would come to see him. He wanted to see her again. In the dim quiet of the cell, it was hard to believe any of what had happened. He needed to see her again, for confirmation, even though the thought filled him with sickly confusion.

He shivered in the cold of the cave. Shivering was a bad sign. It meant his exocel was too weak to insulate him properly. He eyed the ugly gray prisoner's jumpsuit that had been deposited through the bars onto the floor of his cell. His SecPac uniform was destroyed; filthy, damp, punched through by bullets and torn by his own battle armor. He drew it tighter around himself and turned his head away.

For years, he used to secretly speculate about where his mother might be living, what she might be doing, whether she had another family now, one she loved more. His imaginings, based on how he remembered her—lively and spontaneous if a bit preoccupied and distant—were glazed with nostalgia and bitterness, but often fanciful. She was a vagabond in Asia. She was remarried with four kids. She was dead. It didn't really matter. His father had never offered anything in the way of information, no matter how insistently Donovan questioned him.

"But *why*? Why did she go away? Where did she go?" he'd asked, up until he was in his teens and stopped caring.

His father's face would darken. "She wasn't happy."

"What wasn't she happy with?" Donovan asked, with a child's terror that the answer was: you.

"With this life. With me. With all of it." His father always looked at him then, in a way that made Donovan suspect he was holding back. "She wasn't from the Round. She didn't really know what she wanted when she moved here." Regret and anger traced the furrows of his face. "She shouldn't have been marked. That was my fault."

Donovan was bewildered by this. Plenty of people aspired to what they had: erze status, a good home, a life in the Round—that was why his father had such an important and busy job. Why would his mother want to leave, to leave *him* for anything else? "But why doesn't she ever call or visit? Don't you know where she *is*?"

Dominick Reyes had no patience for this descent into petulance and resentment. "No, I do not. And if I did, it wouldn't matter. We all make our own choices, Donovan, and she chose badly. She chose to leave us."

Only she didn't just leave. She left to join Sapience, to fight an unending war of terror against the zhree-supported government. Against his father, and against SecPac, and by extension, against him too. A nauseating grief filled Donovan's aching stomach and seeped into his throat. He curled onto his side. Reality was becoming too strange and painful to handle.

— — —

Time passed. He had little sense of how much. Three shifts of guards came and went. They didn't speak to him. Donovan got colder, and thirstier, and hungrier. "Hey," he called to the guards. "Aren't you at least supposed to give me some food and water?" They didn't answer him. They weren't the hateful and impulsive rebels who'd been yelling and throwing rocks. These men had the look of hardened revolutionaries. When Donovan cursed them—"Hey, I'm talking to you, you squishy bastards!"—they went on smoking and watching him impassively, as if he were an angry dog flinging itself against its leash, well out of range. Donovan licked his chilled lips. They didn't treat him as human because to them, he wasn't.

He took the gray jumpsuit into a corner and changed into it. It was made of heavy fabric, dry and intact. It made him feel warmer right away. He folded his ruined uniform properly and placed it on the end of the mattress. Doing so made him feel less ashamed about this small initial surrender. He was a prisoner of war now and facing a battle of will against his captors. His two current guards wore thick coats, and as he watched, they pulled on gloves to keep their hands warm. When they breathed, he saw the faint mist hanging in front of their faces. Donovan had heard the hum of generators in the main cavern; there was heat and light in this bunker, but they were depriving him of it.

He slept in exhaustion-induced fits and spurts that made it even more difficult to judge the passage of time. Each time he awoke, it was in a near panic. It was terrifying to feel his armor deteriorating, to feel the cold reaching his skin and chilling his flesh. Even so, his exocel would pull everything from his body before it failed; he would fall into an anemic coma before hypothermia set in.

They're screwing with me. Making me feel as weak as a squishy.

He was surprised when the slight figure appeared in front of his cell. "Anya?" Relief bubbled up inside him. He went up to the bars and reached his hands through. She was holding a plastic cup of water and an open silver pouch, both of which she placed into his eager grasp. He could smell that the pouch was filled with food, and his insides contracted with need. He had been in here at least a day, though he was only guessing, and the last thing he'd eaten had been the muffin and beef jerky Anya had snuck him the day before that.

He downed the water, then tipped the pouch to his mouth. It was an MRE in a self-heating package, the sort of thing he'd had to eat during field training. Apparently, Sapience camps stocked them as well. It was lukewarm and stewlike; chicken and beans or something like that. Donovan didn't care, and he barely tasted it. Anya hadn't given him a utensil, so he had to squeeze most of it into his mouth. It was gone so fast he wished he had slowed down. He was still ravenously hungry as he looked at the empty pouch, wanting to take it apart and lick the inside of the foil but not wanting to stoop to that level under Anya's watchful gaze. She would probably report everything about his condition and behavior to her superiors.

She held out her hands and he reluctantly handed the cup and pouch back to her. "I didn't think I'd see you again," he said. "I thought you'd be getting the Sapience orientation for new recruits, not feeding prisoners."

Anya shrugged. "They figured you wouldn't try to hurt me," she said. "And Max didn't want anyone to hurt *you*."

The thought of his mother trying to protect him made Donovan angry. "Why didn't she come herself, then?"

"They won't let her."

"You mean Saul and Kevin." Donovan gripped the bars. The metal was as cold as ice. "So do you like it so far? Joining up with terrorists, hiding in a cave—this is what you wanted, right?"

"I have to go," she said. She turned and began to walk away.

"Wait," he said, immediately regretting he'd said anything to make her leave. She was the only one who would speak to him, the only one to bring him food and water, and right now, she was his only connection to the world beyond these bars. "What are they going to do to me?" he called after her, but she was already turning a corner in the tunnel.

—— —— ——

In the damp cold, he began to cough. He had to hold his sides from the pain of it. He coughed up blood; it speckled the sleeve of the mottled gray jumpsuit and the piss-yellow fabric on the cot. He felt light-headed and wheezy. Kevin's bullets had done a number on him, and frozen and weak as he was, he wasn't going to get better.

He thought about his closest erze mates and wondered if he would see any of them again. Jet, of course, whom he'd been Hardened with, marked with, trained with, and loved like a brother. Tamaravick Kohl, with the face of a model and the work ethic of a draft horse, was a bit too serious and grown-up but had a sensitive, considerate side that came out for those she cared about. Leonidas Hsu, sleepy-eyed and soft-spoken, handled combat with ice water in his veins and at all other times carried a sketchbook and drew elaborate pictures of fantasy creatures. Cassidy Spencer, always the first into any room, was sharp-tongued and quick-witted, five foot three but able to deal with anyone—from calming senior citizens to talking down a roomful of men with machine guns. And Thaddeus Lowell, their class captain, an assigned mentor a few years older than they were, was already a lieutenant at the age of twenty-one, a natural leader, bighearted, unflappable, and able to drink anyone under the table and hit a quarter-sized target with an E201 at three hundred meters.

Jet, Vic, Leon, Cass, Thad—they were his fellow soldiers, his erze mates, and erze was closer than kin. If any of them needed his help, Donovan would stop at nothing to give it. They would come for him; he still believed that.

Whether they found him alive or dead was a different question.

— — —

He waited anxiously for what he could only estimate was at least another full day before Anya returned. Again, she brought him a cup of water and an identical pouch of preserved food. "I can't live on only this, you know," he said after he'd devoured the small meal. He was even more ravenous than yesterday. *Screw it.* He tore the pouch and licked every last drop of gooey stew from the crevices. "Do they know that? Exos need certain things . . ." He shook his head. He felt slow and stupid now, worn down by cold and malnutrition. Of course they knew. They were giving him enough to stay alive, for a *squishy* to stay alive. If his panotin-assembling cells starved, leaving his exocel crippled, no one here would care.

"What's going on?" he asked her. "Have they tried to make demands?" He needed to learn something, *anything*.

Anya's face was a shadowy oval. She was wearing different clothes and they did not fit her very well. There probably weren't many Sapience operatives in the Warren from whom she could borrow clothes in her size. The bottoms of her pants were rolled up and the shapeless sweater she had on under her own jacket hid the sharp slope of her chest and made her breasts all but invisible. "I don't know." She shifted her gaze from his. "Even if I did know, I couldn't tell you."

She reached to collect the cup. Donovan shot a hand out and grabbed her wrist through the bars. She gave a small gasp. "Anya," he pleaded in a whisper, hoping the guards had not seen or heard. "I need your help. I really do, or I'll die in here." He knew the desperation was plain on his face. "Please. You're a good person, I know you are."

She looked down at his hand. The stripes across the back of it stood out even darker than usual against his paling skin. Slowly, she raised her face. "What do you need?"

— — —

The next day, Anya didn't come. Instead, one of the guards gruffly ordered him to put his hands through the bars. Donovan was surprised to hear the man talk. He'd started to think of him and the other sentries as gargoyles, impassive and immovable. "We've been real nice to you, zebrahands." The man had a droopy lower lip and the words LIVE FREE tattooed across his knuckles. "Saul told us not to touch you, not to talk to you, not to so much as breathe on you, and what Saul says around here goes. But if you try to slice or gut me with your armor, I will shoot you dead and see to it the good parts of you are sewn into my new panotin vest. We clear?"

Donovan nodded. He put his hands together through the bars and the man handcuffed him. The cuffs ratcheted tight against his wrists and were the thickest manacles he'd ever seen; even an exo couldn't hope to break or work free of them. The guards opened the cell and escorted him down the tunnel.

9

The room the guards took him to was warm and brightly lit. Donovan couldn't adjust to the difference and kept blinking because of how sharp and yellow everything looked. The rectangular space was plain and institutional; it did not look like it was part of the inside of a cave. There was a steel table in the middle of the room and two steel chairs, one on either side of the table. Donovan sat in one of the chairs, his hands—handcuffed in front of his body this time, thank erze—resting in his lap. The wonderful warm air blowing in from the ceiling vent made him irresistibly sleepy. He knew he needed to be alert and focused, but his skull felt like lead and his eyes hurt.

The door across from him opened. Saul strode in. He was carrying a brown paper bag, which he dropped on the table before sitting down across from Donovan. The overhead light cast a sheen on the smooth center of his shaved head but didn't seem to penetrate the deep crevices of his face. The man pulled a packet of smokes from his back pocket. He clamped a cigarette in his mouth and lit it, then tossed the packet on the table and leaned back in his chair. For a minute, they studied each other. Saul turned his head and blew twin streams of smoke through his nostrils in a long, thoughtful exhalation. Donovan glanced around the room. The two of them were alone. There were no obvious cameras, no big burly men ready to hit him or throw him against the wall, no suspiciously painful-looking equipment.

"I brought you something," Saul said at last. He opened the brown paper bag and upended the contents onto the table: a half-full bottle of water, a dinner roll, and a small disposable plastic cup with a lid—the sort of container in which takeout restaurants packaged sauces or salad dressing.

Donovan reached across the table with his bound hands and picked up the cup. He popped off the lid. There was a thick, clear liquid inside. All-purpose machine oil, he guessed. Neutral-tasting, at any rate. He sniffed it. His fingers were shaky as he tore off a piece of the dinner roll, dipped it into the cup, and brought it to his mouth.

He'd told Anya, "Mineral oil, or machine oil, or gun oil, it doesn't matter. As long as it's clean."

"You eat oil?"

He didn't like the incredulous, revolted tone of her voice. "No, usually I just take the supplement that all exos get. But without it, I need some hydrocarbons in my diet. My body breaks it down to make panotin. If I've been, oh, say, *shot a bunch of times*, I need more of it to heal."

"So if you don't get it, you can't armor?"

He dropped his forehead to the bars. How could he make these squishies understand? "You can't affect my armor without affecting me. If I can't armor, it means I'm pretty close to being *dead*."

Donovan wiped the last bit of bread around the inside of the cup. He struggled to unscrew the water bottle, then drank eagerly, clasping the bottle in both his cuffed hands like a squirrel holding a nut. Saul watched him, expressionless. "Better?" he rumbled, when Donovan was done.

Donovan leaned back in his chair. Now that he was finally warm and no longer painfully hungry, he wanted nothing more than to close his eyes and lie his head down on the table. He blinked hard and focused on the outline of the closed door behind Saul's chair. "Where is she?"

Saul crossed his thick forearms. "Your mother? Or the girl?"

Donovan hesitated. "Max. She's the same Max who writes those pamphlets, isn't she?"

"She's a wreck. In shock. Crying and asking to see you."

He tried to process how he felt about this. Was it even true? "You haven't let her come."

"No. You're too dangerous."

He was dangerous? He was trained to keep the peace, to be judicious but effective when it came to using violence. *They* were the ones who'd been flinging rocks, baying for his blood. Donovan bristled. "You think I'd hurt my own mom?"

"So you still think of her as your mother."

"I . . ." He didn't know how to answer that. "I suppose that's what she is. Even if she is a terrorist."

Saul's straight chin tilted down. "And I suppose she still thinks of you as her son. Even if you are an exo. A biotechnological abomination designed to support an alien race in the oppression of your own species."

Donovan opened his mouth to spit an angry retort, then clamped it shut. He wasn't going to let himself be baited into a ridiculous ideological argument with a fanatic. "I want to see her."

The man leaned forward, elbows on the table. "Do you think that's a good idea? She'll be ashamed. Disgusted. It might be better for both of you to pretend the other person—the one you remember—is long dead. That's what I've been telling her."

The same thoughts had occurred to Donovan during his long

hours of isolation, but hearing them voiced aloud in such a matter-of-fact manner by this Sapience commander seemed to transform them from worry into truth. Donovan's hands closed into fists. "You're probably right. But I still want to see her."

"What you want doesn't matter here. You're a prisoner. A bargaining chip." Saul lifted his eyebrows. "Whether you go home or not depends on what your government decides to do."

Donovan's eyes narrowed. "Give me a break. We both know you're not going to send me home."

"You sound pretty sure of that."

"I'm not stupid."

"No, you're not." Saul leaned back, impassive. "The Prime Liaison's office has issued a statement: 'Under no circumstances will we negotiate with terrorists.' There've been no attempts to make contact or to bargain for your release."

Donovan had expected as much, but that didn't mean his throat didn't burn with the sour taste of abandonment. He swallowed it down. *Nothing cracks you, does it, Father?* "I told Kevin before, I wouldn't get any special treatment. I'll bet he's disappointed I'm not as useful as he thought I'd be."

"Oh, he still thinks you could be very useful. You're a trove of information about SecPac and the government."

Donovan sat still. "He's already tried to get it out of me."

"He didn't have much time the first go around. He figures you'll be more cooperative now."

Donovan's pulse began beating against the handcuffs. "If you hand me over to him, it'll be for his sick entertainment and nothing else. You won't get anything."

The man rubbed his jaw. "I suspect you're right. You exos are as bound to your erze as shrooms. Something they do to your brains when they Harden you. It would take a truly heinous amount of torture to break your compulsion to observe an erze oath, wouldn't it?"

Donovan remained silent. Saul made the loyalty and discipline of exos sound unnatural, something to be disparaged, as if humans hadn't always valued those traits as well.

"So what are the choices now?" Saul asked. "We execute you as a political statement or keep you locked in that cold cell. Killing you risks heavy reprisals and might stir up a backlash from moderates within Sapience. But holding an armored prisoner is too risky, we're not equipped for it. Sooner or later, we'll slip up and you'll make us pay for it. Simpler to get it over with. Wouldn't you agree?"

Dealing with Saul was different from enduring Kevin. The man said everything straight up, no malice involved. Just discussing the situation as it now stood. Donovan found himself starting to nod, even though it was his *execution* they were talking about. Saul balanced risk against gain; he was deliberate and calculating. Between people like him and unpredictable mad dogs like Kevin, it was no wonder Sapience was so hard to beat.

"Here's the problem, though." The map of deep lines on Saul's face shifted and his voice softened into something quite unlike what it had been before. "I'd hate to lose Max. She's a special lady, your mother—been with the cause a long time, like me. To think, after everything we've been through together, all the things we've survived, I'm going to lose her over this . . ." He let out a sigh of deep resignation. "She'll never forgive me if I order your death. I'll do it—God knows I will—but I'd lose her forever." He took a slow drag on the last part of his cigarette. The tip of it glowed red. "This life, zebrahands. It turns you to stone inside, it has to. But we're not all what you think: unfeeling killers. Even killers are not all unfeeling."

Donovan almost smiled. He couldn't help it. This whole situation was some kind of dark comedy. "Sounds like you've got a real dilemma."

The crevices in Saul's brow deepened and his contemplative air vanished, replaced once more with straightforward authority. "I'll let you see her," he said. "I'll move you out of that cell. You can have food and a warm shower. I'll even let you out of those handcuffs."

Donovan stifled the urge to lean forward and give away how good that sounded. "What's the catch?"

"You swear an oath to me, like what you have with the shrooms."

A noise of disbelief escaped him. "You're not of my erze! You're not even marked. I'm not going to swear anything to you. Even if I'm trapped here, do you really think I'd turn around and start helping Sapience?"

Saul stubbed out his cigarette on the surface of the metal table. "No. You wouldn't be able to. You lack the free will that pure humans have."

Slow rage boiled behind Donovan's eyes. There it was again, the insinuation that because he was an exo, he was a tool, unable to think for himself. Extremist lies that Sapience spread to make uneducated squishies fear and hate exos. It shouldn't have the power to affect him, but it did. He was worn down, hurt, and confused, and it was one more smack across the face. "You don't know what you're talking about," he said.

"Prove it, then. Can you honor an oath to me, a human being, the way you do with your alien masters?"

"Your reverse psychology crap isn't going to work on me."

Saul nodded. He pushed his chair back and stood; his head nearly touched the overhead lamp hanging from the low ceiling. "I'll let her know your decision." He crossed the room and turned the doorknob.

"Wait." The thought of going back to that dark cell, to debilitating hunger and cold, isolation and despair . . . Donovan's heart began knocking against his ribs. If—no, not if, *when*, he told himself firmly—when his fellow soldiers-in-erze arrived, they would need him to be ready and waiting, not locked away in the deepest part of the cave, helpless, crippled, half dead. He had to get out of that cell. He had to see the only person who might help him. "What . . . what kind of oath?"

Saul paused, his hand on the doorknob. Slowly, he turned around. "An oath of neutrality." He stalked back to Donovan. "You won't harm anyone or anything in the Warren. You won't try to escape or to contact anyone outside." Saul leaned his hands on the table. The broad set of his shoulders blocked the lamp light filtering through the smoke-fogged air. "You'll act like a guest here, not an officer of SecPac. Swear to this, and I'll let you see your mother."

Donovan turned the words over in his head. What choice did he really have? Saul seemed to be sincere, and what he was proposing was infinitely preferable to all the other alternatives: torture, execution, long imprisonment. He wasn't going to *help* the terrorists, just not give them any reason to kill him, cripple his armor, or keep him frozen and starved.

"Okay," he said finally.

"Say it, then," Saul said.

"I won't act against you or any of your people while I'm here. I won't try to escape or contact others. While I'm in your custody, I won't behave as a SecPac officer." Saying it out loud was harder than he'd expected. He found himself speeding up, trying to get it over with. He touched his lips to the backs of his bound hands. "I pledge this on the Accord of Peace and Governance, which I protect, on the markings of my armor, and on the erze that defines me, from now until the coming of the Highest State."

There, it was done. Donovan felt relief, and a squirmy sense of guilt and discomfort. He'd only recited formal vows twice in his life: at twelve, when he'd been marked as a soldier-in-erze, and earlier this year, when he'd graduated from training to become a full-fledged SecPac officer. What he'd just done was surely blasphemy of some serious variety. He'd sworn an oath to a terrorist leader. He'd invoked the Accord, and his erze, and even the religion he didn't really follow, in front of a man devoted to destroying all of those things. And in some bizarre twist of logic, Saul was accepting it. Donovan averted his eyes. "Satisfied?"

The man straightened up, looking down at Donovan with unreadable, heavy-lidded eyes. "Yes. And here's my promise in return. If I think for even one second you're not keeping your word, I'll do what Kevin should have done to begin with: I'll break Max's heart and end your sorry life."

10

Saul left without another word. When the door opened again several minutes later, Anya came in. At the sight of her, something loosened inside of Donovan's chest. He smiled at her, and for a second, she smiled back, her small mouth rising before she caught it and made her face serious again. It had been there, though, for a moment—a real smile.

Anya held a key. She unlocked his heavy handcuffs and he rubbed his wrists, gingerly layering his armor from his elbows out to his fingertips, trying to return feeling to his hands. The girl took a step back at the sight of his sluggish exocel crawling across his skin. "Don't worry," he said. "I won't do anything. I promised."

"I know."

She led him out of the room. The two guards outside the door followed several paces behind, tense and suspicious, cradling their rifles. Donovan caught them exchanging disbelieving glances. *Can you believe this? Saul is letting an armored stripe walk around.* He kept his hands visible, and his movements steady and deliberate. If he spooked them, he wouldn't be surprised if they sent a volley of bullets ricocheting through the tunnel, hitting Anya and each other in the process.

They took several sharp turns through corridors marked with symbols—upside-down triangles, hash marks, random letters—

their meanings known only to Sapience operatives. This place must be huge and well designed to be defended. Donovan ran a hand along the concrete-reinforced wall nearest to him. His fingers came away damp. The ceiling was bare cave rock with curious mineral formations that looked like popcorn and others that looked like frost. "This place has been here a long time."

"Since the late War Era, is what they told me," Anya said. "The army back then dug out and fortified miles of caverns."

Donovan looked around, impressed. Did those War Era generals know that more than a hundred years later their underground fortress would still be in use as a terrorist bunker? Maybe they saw the end of the war coming and built this place to last for centuries so their descendants could hole up and keep fighting long after they were gone.

They reached a wing of the Warren dug out into small individual rooms, one after the other, like a subterranean dormitory. None of them had doors, just heavy canvas draped across the openings, like tent flaps. Donovan tilted his head to peer around the edges of some of the draping. "They're empty," he said.

"I think it's overflow space for when a lot of recruits or refugees show up," Anya said. "But Kevin said that with winter coming, anyone who isn't on SecPac's target list would rather take their chances living in the Ring Belt, or up in Rapid City, where there's reliable work, and food, and heat." She pushed aside the flap concealing the room at the end of the row.

It was a simple, bare bedroom. Compared to the dungeon he'd been in for the last several days, it was a luxury suite. The bed had clean, if worn, sheets and a pillow. The dresser had a heat lamp next to it, and through a narrow doorframe in the grayish plaster wall he could see a tiny bathroom with a toilet, a sink, and a showerhead over a stone floor and circular drain. "There's a timer on the faucets; you get five minutes of water twice a day," Anya said.

Donovan turned to face her. "Thank you for what you did."

She gave a small shrug. "They told me to bring you food so that's what I did. I told them what you said you needed." Her hair hung loose around her shoulders. The damp underground made it frizzier than he remembered. She was wearing a better-fitting shirt today, though her pants were still too long.

"I know, but . . . no one ever asked you to be decent to me, and you have been. So, thanks."

Anya bit her bottom lip. Her small white teeth were slightly crooked. "It's not your fault, what you are. We don't all have a choice in our lives, you know? So it's not fair to judge people for stuff they don't control." She spoke with such righteous indignation that it reminded Donovan immediately of how fearlessly she'd stepped in front of Kevin's gun. He shuddered at the memory, and all of sudden, he wanted to hug Anya.

He missed his friends terribly. Exos did not do so well separated from the erze for long periods of time.

An awkward moment of silence passed. "I . . . would really like to take a shower," he said.

The girl seemed relieved to be pulled from the brink of what might have been further conversation. "There are towels in the drawers. At least there were in my room. And soap. I'll try to find you some clothes." She turned and pushed through the canvas draping.

Donovan followed a few paces and stood holding up the flap as he watched her walk away. The two guards were still in the corridor. They'd taken up position several meters from his room, where the tunnel widened. Oath or no oath, he was still a prisoner. Saul wasn't stupid enough to leave him unguarded, or give him access to the rest of the Warren. Then he remembered the crowd of squishies who would've been eager to continue the stoning they'd been giving him, and it occurred to him that the protection of Saul's guards went both ways.

He went to the drawer and found two slightly threadbare folded towels and a bar of clear soap. He couldn't get out of the rough jumpsuit fast enough. He was tempted to shred it in his hands but settled for kicking it into a corner. His boots stank from days of constant wear; he shoved them under the bed. In the closet-sized bathroom, he cranked the timed faucet to the very end of its range. A stream of just-barely-warm-enough water spat from the shower-head. Donovan closed his eyes in the spray and rested his forehead against the wall. The water ran off his head, down his shoulders and back. It was heavenly. He scrubbed and scrubbed, taking off a week's worth of grime and flakes of dried and damaged panotin. The water ran out before he'd had enough of it.

He dried himself, then wrapped a towel around his waist and went back into the bedroom. There were no clothes in the room and he didn't want to put the prisoner's jumpsuit on again, so he sat down on the bed and turned on the lamp. He probed the places where he'd been shot: his sternum, stomach, shoulder, thigh, and ribs. The deep-tissue bruises were tender to the touch and hurt when he moved too quickly or took a deep breath. For the first time in days, he tried to armor himself fully. His nodes felt weirdly sensitive, which could not be a good thing, and his exocel faltered over the wound sites, as if it were hitting speed bumps all along its normally flawless run. He hoped Jet, who'd taken several bullets as well that night, had been treated in the Towers and was doing a lot better than he was.

Donovan lay down on the bed, which sagged slightly under his weight. It felt so good to be out of that cell. He felt guilty for luxuriating in it. Some soldier he was, swearing on his erze in front of a terrorist leader in exchange for a nice room and a meeting with his mother. Jet, warrior that he was, would probably have gone down fighting before ever reaching the Warren.

What was he going to do now?

Accomplish one thing at a time. Donovan grimaced at his father's voice in his head. It was right, though. He was alive and no longer behind bars. Yes, he'd given his word to Saul, but immediate duty to erze superseded all other allegiance; if his fellow stripes burst into the Warren right now, there would be no contest: He would fight with them. He needed to be ready. He needed to recover and regain his strength. And he was going to talk to Max. The thought filled him with a sick, eager anxiety.

His head hurt. He was too tired to think anymore. He closed his eyes.

— — —

He opened them again when he smelled food. Something hearty and sweet, mixed with the sharp smell of fresh coffee. He sat up slowly, confused at first. He must have fallen asleep. For the first time in nearly a week, he'd awoken to something pleasant.

Anya stood at the foot of the bed, holding a tray. Her eyes traveled immodestly over his body, and for a second, he felt a jolt of embarrassed excitement to be caught wearing nothing but a towel wrapped around his waist. Then he realized her gaze was following the line of exocel nodes—each one dark and slightly raised, the size of a pinky fingernail—running up his torso, branching across his collarbones, and marching, closely and equally spaced like soldiers, down his arms. He tensed, then swung his legs over the side of the bed.

Anya turned away and placed the tray on top of the dresser. "I brought you some clothes." She pointed to a stack of badly folded garments at the end of the mattress. Donovan picked them up without looking at her. He shook out a pair of pants and two pullover shirts. "They even look like the right size," he said, impressed. "Where'd you get them?"

"From Kevin's closet."

Donovan nearly dropped the clothes. He felt the urge to wipe his hands on the towel.

"They're clean," she said.

Wearing something that had touched Kevin's body was preferable to the dirty, ugly prison jumpsuit by only the narrowest of margins. Donovan grimaced. He took the clothes into the tiny bathroom, faced the wall, and put on the pants and one of the shirts. They *did* fit him, although the waist on the pants was too loose, made more so by the weight he'd lost. He envisioned how pissed Kevin would be to see where his clothes had gone. It was really too bad, he thought, that the promise he'd made to Saul meant he couldn't go find Kevin and pay him back for the four 9mm rounds to the body. A beating with a cement block would probably be a fair trade, for a squishy.

The cafeteria tray Anya had brought had a bowl of oatmeal

topped with bits of dried fruit, chopped nuts, and two slices of cling peaches from a jar. Next to it was another disposable plastic cup of oil and a mug of coffee, hot and black. Donovan pulled the tray into his lap, poured the oil into the oatmeal, and tried not to eat so fast that he scalded his mouth.

"That's about as good as food gets around here." Anya sat down on the edge of the bed, leaving a space between them. "Most of it is canned, or dried, or frozen. And MREs. Lots of MREs."

Donovan slowed long enough to sip a mouthful of coffee. He glanced at her. "The life of a criminal militant not living up to its glamorous reputation?"

Anya's face stilled. "I never expected it to be glamorous." She stood back up and he was surprised to see her fierce anger suddenly directed down at him. "I don't have to take mockery from your kind." She pivoted to leave.

He caught hold of her by the arm, tipping the tray precariously and splashing scalding coffee over his hand and into the rest of the oatmeal. He righted the tray just in time, his fingers still gripping her elbow. "You're right. I'm sorry."

She stared down at his hand on her arm, then back up at him coolly.

Donovan let go. "I didn't mean to mock you. And I shouldn't have assumed anything about your reasons for being here. It's just that, for a lot of people who join up, it doesn't end well. I would know. You seem like a good person, so I guess I was hoping you'd change your mind once you got here. That's all."

The fire faded from her eyes. Donovan pulled a napkin off the tray and sopped up the spilled coffee. Without saying a word, she took the second napkin and helped him. He dried his coffee-drenched hand. Without warning, Anya placed her hand over his. Her fingers brushed lightly across the armor that had sprung up to shield him from burn. He held still until she lifted her hand away, and then he wished he'd done something, or said something, before she had.

"I was curious about what it felt like," she admitted. "Your armor."

Slowly, to hide his confusion, he ate the remaining three spoonfuls of coffee-flavored oatmeal. "And . . . ?"

"It's warmer than I expected. It doesn't feel like skin, but it's not *unlike* skin either." An odd concern touched her voice. "Does it hurt? When they Harden you?"

Donovan set the tray back on top of the dresser. The girl mystified him. She was so proud and vulnerable at the same time. She was resolute about being a rebel, but she seemed so naive and curious about the enemy. "Yes," Donovan said. "It hurts."

"A lot?"

"A lot."

She nodded as if she understood. "But if you get through it, if you choose the hurt and survive, you come out strong. So strong that almost nothing can hurt you. And afterward, they make you a soldier, part of a family as strong as you are, that'll never let you down." She fixed him with a burning, interrogative gaze. "Isn't that worth it?"

Donovan looked at her, not knowing what to say. He wished he could say yes, but he could see where she was going with this, at least in her own mind, and it didn't make sense to him. How could she compare taking up with Sapience to being Hardened, or suggest a band of terrorists was anything like an erze, or draw parallels between his experience and hers? Yet her weird logic seemed real when she said it the way she did.

Donovan lifted the bottom of his shirt and dropped his armor to nothing, as if he were paying respect to an erze master. Underneath the panotin, his torso was a mess of giant blotchy purple and green bruises. "You still get hurt," he said. He let the shirt fall back down. "People still let you down." He thought of his mother. And his father. "And sometimes, you're not even sure if what you're doing is right, or if it's worth it." He thought of the hatred he'd seen in the eyes of the people in the Warren, the same rage he'd seen on Sean Corrigan's face and on the faces of other people whose family members he'd arrested, whose doors he'd kicked in, whose houses he'd searched, not always successfully.

Donovan reached for Anya's hand. "Exos don't get to choose. We're too little at the time; our parents make the decision for us." He squeezed Anya's small, breakable hand. "*You* can decide for yourself."

The canvas hanging rustled. Donovan looked up. Max stood in the entrance of the room.

11

Donovan dropped Anya's hand. The girl looked between Donovan and Max, then picked up the tray with its empty dishes and walked past them out of the room.

"Anya. That's your name, isn't it?" Max's voice came out scratchy and pitched slightly above a whisper. The woman cleared her throat uncomfortably. "Thank you for what you did. If it wasn't for you . . ."

Anya looked over her shoulder, meeting Max's gaze for just a moment. "Don't thank me," she said. "Thank Brett."

Her words gave Donovan sudden pause. It was true; if Brett hadn't been watching the news at that moment, Anya might have done as Kevin had asked. Pulled the trigger. Put a bullet through his eye and into his brain. How had he managed to almost forget that? He had begun to think of her as the only person in this place he could almost trust.

Max, his mother—he still found it hard to think of her as either one—turned to face him. They were alone. She was very pale, though her cheeks were slightly flushed and her eyes were rimmed with pink. She looked as if she had been crying. There was a certain forced staunchness about her; her lips were firmed and her back straight. Her throat moved as she swallowed. The way her eyes alternated between staring at him and jumping away—Donovan imagined it was the way a recovered alcoholic would act if locked in a wine cellar. Like her greatest dream and worst nightmare were coming true.

His throat had gone as dry as sand.

"Hello, Donovan." A long pause. A dimple formed in the space between her eyebrows. "God. You do look like him. The way he was when he was young."

Donovan felt as though he really needed to sit down. He leaned heavily against the dresser. She didn't look as old as he'd expected, not as old as his father. Still, there were hard, pitiless lines around her mouth and eyes that he didn't remember her having. "What should I call you?" he said at last. "Max isn't your real name."

"It's my middle name. Maxine. I've gone by it ever since I left the Round."

He had not remembered his mother's middle name. His father would have, though. "Does he know?" Donovan asked, growing realization turning his voice wooden. "My father . . . does he know you're a member of Sapience?"

"Does he know?" She let out a short, bitter laugh. "He forced me to choose: leave you behind or be arrested for treason. He threatened to come down hard on my family, my friends, anyone I knew who might be connected to Sapience, unless I fled like a dog and never came back."

Donovan's fingers curled around the edge of the dresser. "He never told me."

"Of course he didn't." She took a halting step forward. "I always meant to take you with me, Donovan, to save us both. If I'd had a choice, I would never have left you. I would never have let him do what he's done to you."

"What he's done to me?"

"Turned you into one of *them*. Something more shroom than human."

A moment of shock before anger flared in Donovan's skull. "Exos are as human as anyone else." He pushed off the dresser, onto his feet. "Using zhree biotechnology doesn't turn us into zhree! We have just as much right to the benefits of an exocellular system as—" He stopped, hopelessly bewildered. This wasn't going anything like he'd imagined or hoped. Even though he knew he was right, he sounded like his father—the man he'd just found out had been hiding things from him for years. He drew a breath through his clenched jaw. From the bleak look on Max's face, he saw she was having as hard a time as he was.

"I've messed it up," she said quickly. "I started this all wrong— blaming him instead of talking to you." She turned her face aside, composing herself, before looking back at him. "Can we start again? Please?"

Donovan swallowed. He nodded mutely.

His mother sat down slowly on the edge of the bed. "Okay, then. How . . . how are you doing?"

A grimace of derision began to twist the muscles of his face before he forced it under control. "Considering I've been knocked out, tortured, and imprisoned without food or heat, I'd say I'm doing all right. Better than yesterday."

Max closed her eyes for a second. "I'm sorry."

"Why didn't you come earlier?"

"I couldn't. Saul wouldn't let anyone—"

"Bull. I'll bet you didn't even try."

She looked stunned by his accusation, as stunned as he was at himself. "Maybe . . . maybe I wasn't ready, Donovan." To his horror and satisfaction, her eyes filmed with sudden tears. "How could I explain? How could I face you? You don't understand . . . leaving you was the worst thing I've ever done. I've given everything for the cause: family, friends, erze status, a career, a marriage, a comfortable life . . . None of it mattered, except when it came to you. That was too much. Losing my son was too much."

Donovan found he couldn't look her in the face, not when tears began sliding down her cheeks. He stared instead at her hands, curled into fists at her sides, the knuckles white, the backs crinkled with circular scar tissue where the interlocking rings of the Administrator erze markings had once been before they'd been stripped away. Nasty pale shapes in the same pattern as the bold, curved lines on his father's hands. She lifted them to wipe her eyes and he turned his gaze away.

"It started as just a few articles," she said. "I wanted to be a writer when I was young, did you know that? I used to write essays and poetry for my college newspaper."

Donovan said nothing, though it was perhaps one of the few things he actually did know about her; as a child he'd managed to steal away one of her notebooks from his father's purge—it was still hidden, half forgotten, in the bottom of a desk drawer in his room.

Max said, "When I moved to the Round, some of the realizations I began to have, the things I wanted to say . . . I couldn't say to anyone I knew, certainly not your father. Then I met some people who felt the same way I did, and I wrote more articles, and I started going to meetings, and it just kept growing . . . I felt closer and closer to the cause even though I was leading this double life as someone who was marked and respectable. Until the day arrived when I knew we had to leave for good."

"Why?" The word came out short and strained.

She raised her eyes to him. They were dry now, slightly puffy. "He volunteered you to be Hardened. I told him it was evil, I would never agree to it. There was such a great wedge between us already; this snapped us apart. Neither of us would give in. I made plans to escape, to take you away from there, but I didn't act fast enough. It's something I'll regret until the day I die. Things could have turned out so, so differently . . ."

She let out an unsteady breath. "One morning I took you to school and was on my way to work when two SecPac officers and one of your father's staffers stopped me. They brought me into a room in SecPac Central Command. Your father was there. He had had me under surveillance for months. They showed me all the evidence they'd gathered: the articles I'd written, the money I'd given, the meetings I'd gone to . . . it was enough to send me to prison for life, if not to the atomizer, and to implicate many of my friends in the cause. I panicked, Donovan. He gave me an out: If I was gone in an hour and never came back, he would seal the file and pretend it had never existed. I did it. I left you behind. It was the worst decision I ever made. He forced me into it, and I will never forgive him. Just as I'll never forgive myself."

She rose and came toward him. Donovan fought conflicting urges to step closer to her and to shrink away. "You never sent any messages," he said. "You never tried to come back."

"I did send messages. You never replied, so I knew he never gave them to you, or had taught you to hate me. He told me that if

I ever tried to take you back or contact you again, he would reopen my file. He would elevate me to a Priority One Target and use his power as Prime Liaison against everyone I knew. He promised to hunt me down. He would do it too, I knew he would. He's a ruthless man, more ruthless than you can imagine.

"After that, Sapience sent me abroad, to where no one knew me. I trained with cells in Mexico and ran missions in the East. For more than a year, I didn't even know if you'd survived the Hardening. It took several risky connections for me to finally find out. I knew I'd lost you . . . but it was enough for me to know you were alive." She reached for his hand, tentatively, and when he let her take it, she folded it into both of hers. He could feel her hands shaking slightly, and his own, as still and clammy as meat. His mother's voice grew small. "I stopped trusting in God a long time ago," she said. "But in the last few days, I've come to believe this must be a sign. When I found out years ago that you'd been given Soldier's markings, I fell into a dark place for a long time. *This*—the fact that we're standing here, talking to each other . . . it's a miracle, Donovan. God *is* on our side, and He gave you back to me, to the cause, so we could finally be together again."

Max's words were like a vortex spinning in Donovan's head. He felt them disrupting everything in his ordered view of the world, flinging things around pell-mell, sucking at him, dragging him along as he tried to keep up with them. He was finding it hard to get past a few simple facts. His mother hadn't wanted to leave. His father had found out she was part of a terrorist network and forced her out of his life, then kept the truth from him for all these years. And now . . . now what? She thought they could be reunited for good, mother and son again. Part of Sapience.

He pulled his hand away, not too quickly, but firmly. "I'm an exo," he said. "A soldier-in-erze. As long as you're in Sapience, we'll be on opposing sides. You can't just *undo* twelve years."

"I know." Her shoulders sagged. "Saul told me not to bother trying to reach out to you. He said I was better off thinking of you as dead already. But I can't—I *won't* accept that. I pleaded with him, to let you out of that cell, to give us a chance." She rocked back slightly, holding her own elbows. "He told me you swore to be neutral here. You agreed not to pose any threat to us. You said you'd stop thinking of yourself as one of them."

"I didn't have much of a choice," he said. "But yeah, I did."

"That's a start," she said. "Something we can build on so we can begin to get to know each other again. That's all I want—the *only* thing I want now. We had so many years stolen from us, Donovan, I want to take back at least a little of what we lost. Do you?" She searched his face, imploring. Donovan wondered what she saw: the little boy she'd left behind, an enemy soldier, a copy of the man she hated, or just a very confused teenager.

He realized he was nodding slowly, because he didn't know what else to do. He had to admit he did wish he'd had a mom around while growing up. He'd always wished that, deep down. As awful as this whole situation was, he couldn't regret meeting her now. He supposed . . . he *did* want to talk to her more, to understand her a little, even. Maybe.

"What about the others?" he said. "I'm an enemy hostage. A bargaining chip. Saul said so himself."

Max shook her head. "*He*—your father—has refused to bargain for you. The Prime Liaison won't negotiate, not even to save his own child." Her mouth twisted in an ugly way, as if she'd swallowed an insect. Despite everything he now knew, it surprised Donovan to see her face so full of righteous fury. "He kept you from me all these years, but now he won't compromise to get you back. It's not you he cares about but his own pride, his grip on power."

Donovan stared at the ground, his thoughts burning. How could that be true?

She had come into the room so anxious, but now Max seemed to be straightening, growing taller in her conviction as she spoke. "All the better for us that he's shown his true colors. You don't have to go back to him, not anymore."

It was Donovan's turn to shake his head. "The people in this place want me dead. If it were up to that psycho Kevin . . ."

"It's not," she said at once. "Kevin may be volatile, but he won't go against Saul. And Saul and I go way back, trust me on that. I won't let anyone hurt you or take you away from me again."

A weird shiver went through Donovan's stomach. He wasn't sure if he felt touched or insulted by Max's newfound protectiveness. Did she really think she could play at being a real mom now, when he was practically an adult, an exo, a soldier? But he keep his thoughts to himself. He was in enemy territory, after all. She had engineered his freedom from that cell. He needed her on his side.

Max moved to put her arms around him. She didn't hug him tight, the way Donovan vaguely remembered being hugged when he was a boy. She placed her arms around him just enough so it didn't feel right to tense or draw away, or to squeeze her back either. Slowly, he put an arm around her and she stood, welcoming his loose embrace for a long minute, until he dropped his arm and stepped back to open a small space between them.

She nodded, as if to say again: *It's a start.*

"Everything will be okay," she promised.

That sounded like the sort of thing adults said to kids to reassure them. Something his father would never say. But he wanted in that moment to give her another hug, a better one, and to believe her. "Okay," he said.

12

Days passed. Donovan couldn't be sure how many. He spent most of the time sleeping. He was still in terrible pain, still coughing up blood, but by the third or fourth day, both the pain and the blood lessened. If he'd been in the Round, being treated by a Nurse in the Towers, he would have healed quickly. That wasn't the case, but at least now he had a real bed with blankets, and the room was warm, and Anya or his mother came by three times a day with his meals.

"Do you need a doctor?" Anya asked when she saw him wincing as he rolled his shoulder experimentally.

Donovan shook his head. What could a squishy Sapience medic do for him? What he needed was to get his exocel back up to full strength, so it would properly stabilize anything broken and speed recovery. He'd asked for iron supplements as well as hydrocarbons, and Anya had brought him a bottle of ferrous sulfate pills. He tapped half a dozen into the palm of his hand and swallowed them with water.

Anya watched him. She watched him a lot. Sometimes he woke up to discover she'd come in with his food and left it there while he was sleeping, but twice now he'd woken to find her sitting just as she was now—perched on the dresser, legs dangling, staring at him. She stared in the unselfconsciousness way a toddler might stare—not looking away even when caught. It was very disconcerting. He was pretty sure she'd never known an exo, maybe she'd never even seen one except from a hateful distance. Her long-lashed eyes were large relative to the rest of her face, and that made her expression seem even more childlike when she stared.

He didn't call her out on it. He didn't want to risk her ire, to drive her away like he almost had before. He needed what little information she could give him, and if he was honest with himself, he needed her company, because the alternative was crushing loneliness, and he was more comfortable with this strange girl than with his own mother.

"What's going on out there?" he asked her.

She swung her heels against the dresser. The bridge of her nose furrowed. "SecPac is shaking down the Ring Belt. Door-to-door searches in the sympathizer neighborhoods, hundreds of unmarked people brought in for questioning. That's what I heard from Kevin. He says we're sure to get a wave of people coming over to us soon after this."

"Maybe I'll get some neighbors down here, then," Donovan said wryly. Kevin was probably secretly pleased by SecPac crackdowns. It was the same old story: The terrorists provoked the government to react with harsh measures, which inspired more bitter people to join their cause. Convenient.

"It's serious." Anya crossed her thin arms and glared at him accusingly. "People's homes are being invaded. Armored stripes are taking them away from their families in the middle of the night."

He set the cup of water down with a hard bang. "I know that. I've done it before and it's not fun. And it wouldn't be happening if you sapes hadn't kidnapped me. So whose fault is that?" They matched scowls across a short distance that felt like an impassable gulf.

Anya dropped her eyes first. A little uncertainly this time, she asked, "You think they're still looking for you?"

Donovan hesitated. Every passing day made him less sure of the answer to that question. "Let's just say that if it was one of my friends that was taken? I'd smash down every door in the Ring Belt if I had to."

"Even if you had to hurt a hundred people for one of yours?"

"Yes."

"So you're saying your lives are worth more than ours." She didn't raise her voice this time, but the bitterness was plain. "That's how your kind always think."

"It's not a calculation like that." Donovan felt his own temper rising. Did she *like* to goad him? "*My* kind, as you call us—soldiers-in-erze—we're family, and you'd do anything for family. Wouldn't *you*?" When she didn't answer, he said, "I know you would. You stood up for me, just because you thought it was the right thing to do, and I'm an enemy soldier who doesn't mean anything to you. So you'd do a lot more for someone you cared about. If you'd been born in the Round, you'd have made a good stripe. You'd have been screened for those kinds of traits and marked, just like me. So don't paint me as an evil villain and act like we're so different."

Anya picked at her fingernails. She wasn't looking at him now. "I'm not . . . saying you're an evil villain." She seemed as if she had something else to add, but then she simply bit her lower lip and said nothing else.

Anya was a maddening puzzle. Donovan sighed and said in a softer voice, "Have there been any other statements? Has my father said anything?"

She shook her head. "Not that I've heard of."

Anya wasn't really the right person to ask; she was just a new recruit. He ought to be asking Max, but discussing the conflict between SecPac and Sapience with his stranger of a mother was uncomfortable territory. He wasn't sure he would get the straight truth from her in any case. She seemed intent only on making him feel safe and comfortable.

Every day she came to spend time with him. Mostly to talk. She asked whether he was feeling better, and if he needed anything else. She wanted to know about his life, his friends, what he liked to do. She told him about living in Mexico and East America, and some of the places she'd seen and the people she'd met. They skirted around anything that highlighted the fact that she was a terrorist lieutenant and he was an exo soldier-in-erze. After a few days, the conversations had started to feel less horribly awkward, but she still did most of the talking.

Two or three times now, she'd mentioned how she'd missed him all these years, how she regretted not being there for his childhood, and how grateful she was now. "I hope you'll feel able to ask me anything," she said. "If not now, then someday soon." Donovan listened and nodded. She wanted to be friendly. Fine. He had questions for her, all right, but he hadn't worked himself up to asking, *"What turned you into an extremist?"* and *"Do you really believe exos aren't human?"* and *"Have you killed anyone?"*

After a while, when she stood to go, she looked at him with a patient but tense smile, as if he were a locked chest she was resolutely trying to open with different keys.

— — —

"I'm going stir-crazy in here," he told Anya, after he started to feel recovered enough to be bored. Although the room was far better than the cell, it was still small, dull, and underground. How did these insurgent fighters live like this, like mole rats, with so little in the way of modern amenities, and without fresh air and sunlight? At least they had the run of the Warren and were able to come and go. When Donovan paced out of the room, whichever two guards were on duty at the time casually hefted their submachine guns and shifted to block off the end of the hall. They eyed him suspiciously but didn't look too worried. If he tried anything, they would see him coming, and even his promise to Saul and Max notwithstanding, there was no way he'd plow through a burst of automatic gunfire.

The next day Anya said, "Max says I can take you to the library. If we're escorted."

Donovan was willing to go anywhere, so long as it was out of the room. Now that he wasn't in constant pain, he'd been thinking: He was oath-bound not to do any damage, or escape, or contact anyone outside the Warren . . . but that didn't mean he couldn't try to learn about this place. Gather intelligence that might be later useful. He followed Anya down the hall. Brett happened to be one of the guards today, along with the man Donovan remembered from earlier, the one with the tattooed knuckles who'd threatened to turn him into a panotin vest.

"Hey," said Brett. "Where're you taking him?"

"Library," said Anya. "Max said I could."

The second guard ran his eyes over Anya. "You're getting a little friendly with that thing, aren't you?" His droopy lower lip curled inward. "Just 'cause Kevin brought you in, don't think people won't talk. You want to last around here? Wouldn't be good for you to start being called a pet lover."

Anya's shoulders went rigid. "Scorch off."

"Cool it, both of you," said Brett. "Anya's one of us. She's no pet lover; she nearly put a bullet through this one's eye, cold as a dead man's balls." He turned a strong look on the other man. Donovan was surprised. Brett was Kevin's accessory—he didn't seem like the type of person to stand up for anyone, or anything, but now he said, "Anyway, I wouldn't be throwing stones if I were you, Tom. I hear your brother's restaurant business is real popular with the Hardened crowd."

Tom's demeanor changed. His hands clenched; LIVE FREE lined up on his knuckles. "Don't you talk about that, you hear? Maybe he's a coward, but he's got a family to feed, man. I don't want anyone labeling him a cooperationist, going after his business or his kids. Got it?" He shoved his face closer to Brett's. "Got it, new guy?"

"Sure thing, Tom." Brett nodded quickly, looking earnest, if not as sycophantic as he was with Kevin. "No reason to go accusing people of being cooperationists just for making ends meet."

"Right," Tom said, clearly uncertain as to whether Brett was being sincere or goading him.

"So, the library?" Brett motioned Anya ahead. Donovan followed, catching a glimpse of Brett eying him as he and a chastised Tom fell into step close behind.

The library turned out to be more like a storage space. It was slightly larger than the room Donovan was staying in. Metal shelving units with rusty hinges were crammed up against each other along the walls. They held dozens of musty-smelling cardboard boxes, some turned onto their sides so that the spines of the old books inside were visible. There were two matching metal-frame chairs in the corner, but not enough light to read comfortably by. A piece of paper in a plastic sleeve, labeled *Sign-Out Sheet*, was stuck to the inside of the door.

"So this is the library," Donovan muttered. The library in the Prime Liaison's house was an expansive room with cherrywood floors and huge windows below a high vaulted ceiling. His father paced its length when deep in thought, worked at his desk late into the night, and used the room to meet with his staff, fellow members of Cabinet, and other important officials. Long glass shelves held historic copies of books from throughout human history, as well as memory discs containing translated versions of the seminal works of literature from the Mur Erzen Commonwealth. There was a cluster of comfortable armchairs in a patch of afternoon sun that Donovan had grown accustomed to falling asleep in.

A jolt of homesickness speared him.

Brett and Tom waited outside, even less impressed than Donovan was. Donovan ran his finger along the spines of a row of books in a sideways cardboard box. There were classics from the War Era, bleak works like *Cliff of Stars* and *The Last Salute*, mixed in with even older works like *The Great Gatsby* and *The Hobbit*. It was strange to see paper copies unceremoniously packed together in a Sapience storeroom; he would have thought such historic documents would all be in government or private collections, or museums. It made sense, though. The people who built the Warren, and the insurgents who now occupied it, would want to hang on to their own copies of classic human literature for safekeeping, until the day they prevailed in taking control of the planet.

Donovan stooped to lift the lid off a closed box on the bottom shelf. It was filled with folded pamphlets, just like the stacks he'd discovered bound with rubber bands in Sean Corrigan's toolshed. Insurgent propaganda written by Max. He held on to the lid, thinking he ought to set it back onto the box. This was his mother's heinous work. His hand moved against his will to extract one of the papers. Small, dense text filled the single page.

> **Humans are not only justified but obligated to kill zhree. By coming to our planet, they are asking to be killed. What's the proper thing to do if a garden is attacked by an invasive species? Merciless extermination of the weeds—by burning, cutting, poison, or whatever means necessary—so that the rightful native species can flourish again! For the same reason, exos must also be killed. They are unnatural creatures, tools of the oppressor, and it's not murder but mercy to put to permanent rest the souls of the humans they used to be.**

There was more, but Donovan couldn't read any further. With a shiver of revulsion, he dropped the pamphlet into the box and shoved the lid back on top. As a SecPac officer, he'd always felt tainted even reading that garbage. Now that he knew who the author was, the feeling was a hundred times worse. How could his own mother believe this crap, much less write it? After he'd hidden away her little writing notebook in his drawer at home, it had taken ten more years for him to realize how bad her poems were, but at least they were only benignly overwrought (*snow crusted on the ground cracking underfoot like the inexorable burning frost of solitude on the soul,* etc.) but these pamphlets . . . they incited people to violence. These past several days, his mother had been caring toward him, seeking some connection or reconciliation. How was he supposed to match her kind, hopeful face to these hateful words?

He turned to look for Anya so they could leave. She was standing next to an old screen, its surface coated with a scummy layer of dust. Her back was to him, and when he came up behind her, he saw she was shuffling through a stack of memory discs she'd pulled from a box. She paused on one labeled *Archive Compilation— Landing / War Era.* Before Donovan could suggest he'd had enough of this place, she slipped the disc into the screen's read slot.

Nothing happened. Perhaps the screen was so old it didn't work anymore. But then it flickered and came to life. Donovan wasn't sure what he was looking at; it appeared to be grainy old news footage. The newscaster's voice sounded crackly and distant, as if she were shouting into a microphone during a windstorm. *"Russia, China, and the United States have now all denied any involvement in the shocking events unfolding across the world. The consensus appears to be developing that the vessels are indeed extraterrestrial in origin . . ."*

Donovan blinked, and suddenly the image made sense. It was a nighttime aerial shot of Round Three! Only there was no Round at all; the surrounding landscape looked vaguely familiar but shockingly empty. The camera was focusing in on the area that would later grow into the Round: a circle of devastation that must have been twenty miles wide, just bare earth, flattened and charred trees, and white smoke rising from the scorched ground. The reporter was saying that four hundred and twenty-three people from the affected farmland near the border between Wyoming and Nebraska were missing and presumed dead. It was the first day of the Landing.

The footage cut away to other locations. The sound and image quality on the disc wasn't great; the newscasters' excited voices were interrupted with static as the view jumped all over the world. There were twenty landing sites in total, established in sparsely populated locations across Earth. In the center of each blackened demolition area was a zhree ship. Donovan leaned closer to see that they were expedition-class planterships—huge cousins to the construction and transport paverships he'd seen refueled in the shipyards. On-screen, though, they looked small, and they *were* small, compared to the Towers that would replace them.

Donovan glanced over at Anya. She was paying rapt attention to the old footage. He'd seen the next clip before: a somber-looking man wearing a dark suit in the style of that era, seated at a desk in front of a striped flag. He assured viewers that military forces had been mobilized and steps were being taken to establish communication with the aliens. He urged all governments and citizens to remain calm.

The next scene on the disc showed a chaotic river of people filling the traffic-jammed streets, raiding stores for food and water, boarding up buildings, or swaying together and praying.

"Didn't you learn about all this in history class?" he asked Anya.

The girl shrugged. "The teachers gloss over a lot of the War Era." She paused. In a smaller voice, "I didn't go to class much."

Donovan turned back to the screen. The level of panic was almost comical. The zhree hadn't been hostile, not at first. For two weeks, they made no attempt to engage with humans. Watching scenes of zhree drones circling the perimeter of where the Towers would be, any knowledgeable person today would see that the first priority had been constructing surface bases, establishing communication and supply lines, and building a defensible position in the solar system.

Earth, it turned out, was a previously overlooked habitable planet occupying a strategic area of space contested by the two most powerful zhree civilizations: the Mur Erzen Commonwealth and the nomadic Rii Erzen. When the Mur Erzen occupied Earth first, dealing with the native species was a distant third consideration after building the Rounds and setting up a military cordon between Mars and Jupiter. The homeworld of Kreet had intended Earth to be not just a vigorous frontier colony but an important beachhead against Rii incursion into Mur territory.

Of course, the human leaders of the day hadn't known that. On-screen, many stern, uniformed people were insisting that the appearance of drones preceded an all-out assault on humankind.

Anya pulled over the two metal chairs so they could sit down. The glowing tails of launched missiles streaked across the greenish on-screen night sky. The War Era had begun. Hours earlier, the zhree had finally finished decoding the multitude of human languages and broadcast their first message simultaneously from all the landing sites.

RESIDENT SENTIENT SPECIES: THIS PLANET IS SECURE UNDER THE JURISDICTION AND PROTECTION OF THE MUR ERZEN. ANTICIPATE SUCCESSFUL INTEGRATION INTO THE COMMONWEALTH OF COLONIES. CEASE

HOSTILE OVERTURES AND STAND BY FOR FURTHER COMMUNICATION.

By then, it was too late. There was no standing by. Alien integration was not something humans wanted.

The footage from the War Era went on for a while. Some of it Donovan had seen before, but Sapience had gotten hold of clips that weren't usually shown, not even to soldiers-in-erze. Disturbing images: squads of Soldiers descending on human military encampments, unstoppable in their perfect coordination and bristling exocels, terrifying in their stripes and yellow eyes and many limbs. A particularly heinous clip of a captive Soldier being subjected to fire, electricity, gas, and all manner of torture in an attempt to discover how to overcome exocel technology. Mushroom clouds over two of the Rounds before the zhree disabled the rest of the nuclear weapons from orbit. Entire human cities obliterated in retaliation.

It was horrible stuff, three decades of death and destruction condensed into thirty minutes of footage. What a waste, Donovan thought, all because both sides had made epically bad assumptions. To humans, the Landing portended mass invasion, enslavement, extermination—the sort of thing human history and fiction stories told them to expect. And in their ill-prepared rush to beat their enemies in securing the valuable piece of galactic real estate that was planet Earth, the zhree had played into those fears.

"They underestimated us." Donovan leaned forward to wipe some of the dust off the screen with his sleeve. "They assumed that because we didn't have light-plus travel and were confined to a single planet we weren't advanced or intelligent. The War Era was a lot harder on them than we knew at the time, did you know that? We had home-planet advantage; they were dealing with higher gravity, lower oxygen, dwindling supplies . . . If Earth hadn't been so strategically important to the Mur Erzen, they might have decided it wasn't worth it."

Anya turned to stare. "How do you know that?"

"One of them told me." An old Soldier, at the trainee graduation ceremony last spring. There weren't many veterans of the War Era left; Soldier Wysse was one hundred and seventy-two years old. He was fond of talking to humans and could do so for hours; he'd cornered Donovan to expound on his immense admiration for General McDaniel's heroic last stand at the Battle of Pittsburgh. "Such a noble species," he'd said wistfully. "Such pluck."

On-screen, the War Era was finally coming to an end. One by one, the nations of Earth capitulated to zhree control. It wasn't a clean process. Some parts of the planet ceded quickly after the Landing and endured practically no War Era at all. Erze employment and interstellar trade had begun flourishing there even as other parts of the planet were being reduced almost to stone-age wastelands. Half of North America agreed to peace with Round Three before the other half did with Round Four. But watching the first Peace Day scenes of human leaders meeting with zhree Administrators, and of people celebrating in the streets, it seemed to Donovan that the emotion on everyone's faces was one of relief.

Anya made a skeptical noise in her throat. "They look so happy to be conquered."

Donovan shook his head. "They're happy to be *alive*." To no longer be at war. The zhree were reasonable governors. They brought technology, trade, military protection, and jobs. They would allow the natives to live in peace and manage their own affairs. Humans were no longer the dominant species on the planet, but they could adapt. Life could go on.

The disc ended. Anya ejected it from the screen and put it back into the box.

"Well, that was cheery," Donovan said.

She didn't seem to notice he'd spoken. She riffled through the other discs absently but didn't take any of them out. Her gaze was almost unseeing, sunken into herself. He thought she looked . . . . terribly sad.

Donovan had slouched down in his uncomfortable chair, arms crossed. Now he sat up and leaned his elbows onto his knees, tilting his head to try to catch her eye. "What are you thinking?"

"I'm thinking about how many more will have to die," she said. "Back in the War Era we had big armies, and nuclear weapons, and millions more people. We have a lot less now. How long will it take for us to finally win and drive the shrooms off of Earth? A lot longer than I'll be alive."

"Longer, as in never, you mean." Donovan stood up and stretched. "Face it. The war ended a hundred years ago. You can't roll an avalanche back uphill. The zhree are here to stay."

"That's accepting defeat."

"No, it's accepting reality." For the very first time, he thought he saw her hesitate and it made him want to press. "The only reason you're thinking in terms of victory or defeat is because Sapience *wants* you to think that way. It's not black and white like that; even if you kicked every zhree off the planet and established new human-only governments, what would you do then? Go back to living like we did centuries ago without modern technology like exocels or light-plus travel? Cut ourselves off from the Commonwealth and pretend we're the only species in the universe, when we know that Earth is valuable and we'll just be in danger again?"

Anya didn't reply. Donovan took a step closer to her. "The only thing Sapience will *ever* achieve is more of that—" He pointed to the now-dark screen. "More war. More people dead on both sides. Didn't seeing those video clips change your mind, even a little bit?"

She dropped her chin for a minute, her hair falling forward, concealing her expression. "No. We're still fighting for the same thing we were fighting for back then." She lifted her eyes back to his. "There's nothing more precious than freedom. Freedom is worth any cost."

"We're self-governing. We have freedom."

"The freedom to determine our own destiny—we don't have that."

He could think of a dozen counterarguments, but when he opened his mouth, every one of his retorts died on his tongue. Reason wasn't the right way to convince someone like Anya. He moved close and took hold of her arms. Lowering his voice so Brett and Tom out in the hallway couldn't overhear, he said, "I like you, Anya. I've seen a lot of people who throw their lives away to join the cause, and I'd hate to see you become one of them." He searched her eyes, wondering if his words were reaching her. "Even if I never get out of here, it would make me feel better if you did. It's not too late to change your mind. To go home."

She took a half step even closer and gazed straight at him, her lips slightly parted, and for a second, Donovan forgot what he'd been saying. He could feel her breath on his chin as she spoke.

"This is the only home I've got now. It's like you said. Sometimes you can't go back, only forward."

She rocked forward onto the balls of her feet and kissed him.

It wasn't a long kiss, but it wasn't a peck either. Her mouth pressed against his for two slow heartbeats, then tugged gently on his bottom lip as she pulled away. Donovan swayed back. "What was that for?" he croaked.

"For caring about whether I throw my life away."

Donovan ran his tongue over his lower lip, where her teeth had lingered lightly a moment earlier. His head buzzed. He badly wanted her to do it again. He also wanted her to listen to him. "I—"

A sudden resounding detonation rocked the room.

13

The dull explosion came from somewhere overhead, convulsing the layers of rock and soil above them. Donovan grabbed for Anya, steadying her as the ground and walls shuddered. Both of them looked up, half expecting to watch in horror as the ceiling split open and caved inward, burying them alive in the hillside. It held, though the single light flickered, and the metal shelves swayed and creaked.

"What was that?" Anya cried.

Another boom, much farther away, sent a second, faint tremor through the soles of Donovan's feet. "Air strike," he said.

They're here. His fellow soldiers-in-erze were in the sky right above him, dropping bombs.

Brett rushed into the room. "We have to go! Now!"

"Where are we going?" Anya shouted as they ran after him.

"To the holds," said Tom, taking up the rear. "This is your first air strike? Don't worry, they're not so bad. You just have to wait them out. We split up between four gathering holds; they're the most secure parts of the Warren. If any one of them goes, at least we don't lose everyone." He grunted as another muffled explosion shook the ground. "Wouldn't want to be caught outside right now, though."

People were rushing through the tunnels, quickly but without panic. Donovan followed, turning left, then right, then left again, until he was carried along into a wide, low-ceilinged room rapidly crowding with a couple dozen insurgents. There was no furniture in the room, but one corner was stacked to the ceiling with gym mats, and another held large plastic tubs, presumably filled with supplies in the event the stay grew long.

A hand fell on Donovan's arm. "Thank God." It was Max. Her taut face slackened with relief. "I couldn't find you in your room. I thought—" She didn't finish the sentence. Instead, she pulled him aside. "I'm glad you're safe."

Donovan was relieved she was safe too, but he only nodded distractedly, waiting and listening for the next bomb to fall. What was SecPac trying to accomplish? Had they scoured the Ring Belt and were now moving into the Black Hills, trying to flush out terrorists? Did they know or suspect he was down here? Or was this air strike in retaliation for some other Sapience activity unrelated to him?

The next boom sounded closer. The planes must have swung back around to do another pass on the area. The following explosion was directly on top of them. The entire room concussed with horrific force, and the air itself seemed to quake. A few people screamed, and almost everyone ducked, throwing their arms over their heads, though the instinct was comically pointless. Another equally massive impact a few minutes later made Donovan's teeth rattle in his skull. He caught sight of Anya's pale face, hunched between tense shoulders.

"It's okay," he whispered to her. "These air strikes aren't really targeted to kill anyone. They're mostly meant to destroy roads and communication towers so it'll be difficult for Sapience to use the area."

It was true, but with the next explosion, Donovan began to doubt his own words. If SecPac knew the Warren was here, maybe they were going after it in earnest now, trying to blow the hill to rubble. He imagined the tunnels buckling, collapsing, turning this room into an instant, silent tomb. A sweat broke out on his neck. He berated himself; he was a soldier, a Hardened soldier, for crying out loud. But right now, crouching in a bomb shelter with no erze mates and no uniform, he didn't feel much like one. He felt as vulnerable, as hunted, as the rebels. His mother grasped his hand, and without thinking, he squeezed it.

Another bomb struck the ground above them. The room went dark.

Gasps and profanities broke out. Flashlights came on. Beams of light swung around the enclosed space, crisscrossing one another and throwing moving shadows across the walls.

"Why isn't it over yet?" a man's frustrated voice demanded.

"They know where we are," someone else murmured. "They've got to know."

"Calm down." Max's voice rose over the small crowd. "They don't know. They're just trying to frighten us."

"Well, they're doing a bang-up job." A nervous grumble of widespread agreement.

"Aren't you all forgetting something?" The first man's voice cut through the others. "They know *exactly* where we are." A flashlight beam suddenly turned on Donovan's face, blinding him. "*It's* right here, telling them."

More beams of light swung around to congregate on him. Donovan shielded his eyes with his hand. "*What?*"

"You heard me." Behind the glare, Donovan couldn't see the man's face, only hear the certainty in his accusation. "The shrooms have a kind of psychic link with each other, like birds, or bees. He's leading them to us. That's been the plan all along. Maybe they're reading his mind right now."

"That is the *stupidest* thing I've ever—" Another shock wave cut off Donovan's reply and made all the beams of light shake.

Max let go of Donovan's hand and stepped in front of him. "Back off, Javid." Her voice was deceptively calm, and strong with authority. It made everyone pause, Donovan included. "This is my son you're talking about."

A silhouette of a tall woman moved next to the man who had spoken. "Max, you're one of us, you have been for a long time. We all feel terrible about the boy you lost, but the enemy is standing among us right now, and you refuse to see that." She looked around at the small group, gathering shadowy nods. "Like Kevin said, your judgment can't be trusted anymore."

Max swung her head over slowly. "And you believe him, Kathy?"

The people in the room shifted forward and back. The darkness, the continuing assault on the hillside around them—it made them scared and reckless. The explosions seemed to be coming even more frequently, one after the other, like a series of hellish thunderclaps. "What do we do?" another voice cried.

"No one does a damn thing," Tom said. "Saul says no one touches him, so no one touches him."

"I don't see Saul anywhere, do you?" said the first man, Javid, sweeping his flashlight. "Unless we handle this ourselves, we're all going to die down here. I'm telling you, that thing is a homing beacon."

This was getting out of hand. Donovan pushed past his mother and stepped forward with his arms held out. "No matter what you think, I'm not zhree. I don't have any mental link. I'm not giving away where we are. If this place caves in, I'm as dead as any one of you." His voice bounced in the tight quarters.

"Doesn't prove a thing," spat Javid. "It would be worth it for them to sacrifice one of their pets to get all of us."

Donovan kept his expression unchanged, though he envisioned grabbing Javid's flashlight and smashing it into the man's teeth. "I made a promise not to hurt anyone here, and I won't. Not unless it's in self-defense." He armored hard and fast. "In which case, all bets are off."

The lights wavered and bobbed as the rebels hesitated. Donovan enjoyed a moment's grim satisfaction. He was no longer weak, handcuffed, and alone. They were afraid of him, as they should be.

The shape of a weapon rose with Javid's arm. Donovan heard the click of a safety being released right next to him before Max spoke. "Put it away, Javid," she said a low, even voice. "Or I swear I'll shoot you myself."

"Listen!" Anya shouted. "It's stopping."

Everyone fell silent. A low boom thundered in the distance, then faded. Nothing followed.

Endless seconds passed in the darkness. No one breathed. Would the planes come back around? Would the next explosion be on top of them again? More silence. Suddenly, there was an electric crackle and the lights came back on, along with the low hum of generators.

A collective sigh of relief spilled from the group. Donovan squinted against the overhead lights, piercingly bright after the long minutes of blackness. Javid didn't move, didn't relax along with everyone else. He had a soft face, brown-skinned with startlingly light eyes, and the muzzle of a short carbine trained on Donovan's chest.

"They're gone," Anya said. She raised her voice, insistent. "It's over."

Donovan stood in place, watching Javid's gaze flicker suspiciously. "I had nothing to do with it," he said.

Kathy put a hand on Javid's arm and pressed it down. The menace in the man's face didn't recede, but he let his firearm drop to his side. Donovan waited until he heard Max, Brett, and Tom relax their own weapons, then armored down. The air in the room sagged from the broken tension.

The door of the hold slammed open. Kevin's unmistakable, brutal voice demanded, "Is it in here?"

"Yeah, we got him," Brett called back.

Donovan turned. He hadn't seen Kevin since the day he'd come to the Warren. The man's denim ball cap was pushed up on his forehead, and the skin of his stubble-shadowed face reflected a faintly damp sheen. The sight of him made Donovan's gut clench in remembered terror, and his fists close in violent longing.

Kevin's pitiless eyes found Donovan at once. The corners of them twitched. "Are those *my clothes*?"

Saul strode in after him. "Excitement's over," he declared to the room. "Count your blessings—we're all in one piece, though it's not going to be pretty outside. Everyone out. Now." He pointed to Donovan. "Except you."

People hurried to leave. Donovan saw Javid pausing to exchange hushed words with Kevin.

"You too," Saul said, motioning Brett and Tom from the room. "Warde, you stay."

Anya hesitated, as if reluctant to go, until Kevin seized her by the arm and tugged her close. "I can't believe you gave it my clothes."

Anya lifted her shoulders, a gesture both defiant and helpless. "They fit."

Kevin stared at her, then laughed. "I'll see you later," he said, bringing his face close to her cheek, as if he were smelling her. "Don't you worry about anything."

Anya nodded and left the room.

Donovan's stomach churned with bile. He could see how some of the Sapience fighters weren't all bad. Some were sucked in because they didn't have better prospects. Some were driven by noble, if misguided reasons. Kevin, though, was vain, and cruel, and remorseless. And the way he looked at Anya, the way he handled her as if he had a right to her . . . *I'm going to put you away,* Donovan promised. *I'm going to see you in a penal camp or an atomizing chamber, you worthless piece of terrorist scum.*

When the last person had gone, Max said, "What's this about, Saul?"

Before Saul could answer, Kevin slapped a hand to his 9mm and swung it up to Donovan's temple. "Don't lie, you striped bastard. Did you tip them off? Are they tracking you somehow?"

Donovan turned a cold look on him. "Do you really think I would be here if that were the case?"

Saul casually tapped Kevin's handgun aside, shaking his head at Max before she could draw her own. "That air strike was closer and more sustained than it's been before. Doesn't seem like a coincidence."

"Javid thinks the shrooms have some way of finding it," Kevin said. "Like a transmitter in its brain."

"Javid wouldn't have any experience with a brain." Saul tapped his back pockets, pulled out a pack of cigarettes. "Can't take the risk, though. We're moving him."

Max stepped back as if he'd slapped her. "He hasn't been a threat at all. He's kept his word. You said that if—"

"I said I'd give you a chance. I did that, Max. You're the only reason this shroom pet isn't dead or in chains." He clamped a cigarette in his mouth and lit it. "The plan was to keep moving him, keep SecPac guessing and chasing. We've waited too long, letting them get close. We need to protect the Warren."

Donovan's mother spoke before he could. "Where are you sending him?"

Saul blew out a smoky breath. "Warde's set up the details. We're moving him north, up to Widget's crew. Sending false leads out in a few directions at the same time."

"Has Widget made assurances for his safety?"

"Not in so many words. I filled her in on the situation. You know her, she'll leave her options open. I'm not going to tell her how to run her cell." He slid a sober gaze over to Donovan, then back again. "No one is going to want to hang on to an armored prisoner for long, no matter how valuable. Widget will pass him like a hot potato, until we can get him out of the country."

"Out of the country?" Donovan cut in. "Why? You said the government wasn't bargaining for me."

"Just because they won't bargain doesn't mean SecPac isn't using you as an excuse to crack down hard wherever it can. We keep you out of their reach, and it won't be long before the people rise up against their tyranny." Saul took a hard drag, smoking his cigarette down fast before grinding it out. "Maybe then they'll reconsider their position."

"Or maybe they're not worried about him at all," Kevin said with a dark look of contempt, "since momma's keeping him safe."

Max ignored this. "When are you moving him?"

Saul looked to Kevin.

"As soon as I flip the switch and say go," said Kevin. "Tomorrow."

Max straightened. She turned to Saul, her expression pained but resolute. "I'm going too."

Saul nodded without meeting her gaze. "I thought as much."

"Who else is coming?" She spoke to Kevin reluctantly.

"To meet Widget's guys? The fewer the better. I'll take Brett as a second driver but that's it."

"I want the girl to come."

Anya? Donovan was confused, until he saw Kevin's smirk. "If it makes you feel better." Of course; his mother didn't trust Kevin, certainly not with Donovan's well-being once they were away from the Warren and Saul's authority. She wanted someone Kevin cared about within her own reach, as insurance. And Anya might even be an ally; she'd stood up to Kevin on Donovan's behalf already.

"We're going up through Rapid City?" Max asked.

"That's the plan."

"Then we can arrange a visit with the doctor."

Kevin paused, one eye squinting. "It's awful short notice."

"You can make it happen, though." Max turned back to Saul, her expression almost pleading. "This can't go on. Maybe there's a way . . . to solve everything."

Saul looked grave. "You can't hope for that."

"We can ask."

"Sure, why not," said Kevin suddenly, as if it were all the same to him. "I'd like to see what Nakada has been up to."

Donovan felt lost. He didn't know what they were discussing and apparently agreeing to, but it was all happening so fast. He wanted to interject, to demand explanations, but he seemed unable to, struck dumb by the sight of his mother in her element: a senior Sapience leader in counsel with her colleagues. All he understood right now was that they were leaving the Warren tomorrow, both of them.

"One other thing." Max squared herself to Kevin. She was several inches shorter than him, but she faced him the way a wolverine faces a bear. Her voice scraped nearly as hard as his. "Don't *ever* point a gun at my son again."

A wicked light flickered in Kevin's eyes. Donovan felt the sudden urge to reach out and pull his mother back; did she not know how crazy Kevin was? The man cocked his head slightly. His voice grew soft and cool, the way it had been just before he shot Donovan in the chest. "The cause isn't personal, Maxie. If it were my kid, showing up striped and armored? I'd kill him myself, no matter how many bullets it took."

Max stood her ground, unmoved. "You're not a parent."

"'Sacrifice everything for the cause, because then there will be nothing they can take from you,'" Kevin quoted. "A real patriot wrote that a few years ago. What happened to her?"

"Warde," Saul growled warningly. He put a hand on Max's arm and pulled her toward him slightly. "You're sure about this? We need everyone we can get, especially people with experience. We need you here. You know that." His voice fell, turned gravelly. "*I* need you here."

Donovan's mother gave a slow nod. "I know. I'm sorry, Saul."

She moved to hug him, but his large hand caught her by the chin and he kissed her, long and hard.

Donovan was flabbergasted. He had no memory of his parents ever kissing like that. Perhaps, in their better moods, there had been brief, dignified kisses on the lips or cheeks. Nothing sad and passionate, the way Saul and Max were kissing. As if there were no one else in the room. Donovan jerked his gaze aside, his face warming. Even Kevin seemed to squirm.

"Take care of yourself," Saul said roughly when they broke apart. Max started to say something, but he laid a thick finger over her lips. "Remember, these hills are sacred. You'll always be welcome here."

"Saul . . ." Max started again, emotion twisting her voice.

"Not another word, Max. You say anything to make me think you're not coming back someday, and I won't take it well." Saul's face was a landscape of tight edges. He jerked his head at Kevin. The two men left.

Max's shoulders sagged as if all the air had gone out of her. "I'll take you back to the room," she said to Donovan quietly.

Donovan followed her through the Warren's corridors. Neither of them spoke. Some sections of the halls were lit, others were still without power. The people they passed stepped away from them, their gazes cold with suspicion.

When they reached the room that had been his for almost a week, Donovan let out a breath of desolate relief. This small space felt safe, the only place where he hadn't been hurt or in danger lately. Now things had been shaken up again. Was the air strike a sign that SecPac was still searching for him? He couldn't let Sapience spirit him out of the country, but what could he do? How could he escape without betraying, maybe arresting, his own mother—this strange, unyielding woman who was leaving her comrades, and the man she loved, for him?

"Try to get some sleep." She spoke gently to his back as he stood in the room.

He turned. "I've read the things you've written, you know."

She was silent for a second. "This isn't the right time to talk about it."

"The things you said about exos, about how we're not human, how we ought to be killed—you believe them." It was a question, but he heard his voice flatten it into an accusation.

"I do. I did." She rubbed a hand over her eyes. "In a war, you wield every weapon you have, including words. Especially words. If what I write convinces one more person to take up arms for the cause, then I've succeeded. We can't win unless we rouse the people to fight. Once a fire catches, it will spread. The people, the masses of unmarked people—they're like dry kindling. Sapience is the spark." She hesitated, and he thought he saw a different war being waged openly across her face, laying bare for a moment a bleak vulnerability. "Donovan . . . exos are a terrible thing, made more terrible by the fact that people willingly allow—no, *want*— their children to be Hardened. I'm sorry to hurt you by saying it. It's not your fault at all, not something you had any control over. No matter what, you're my son. I hate exos, but I love you. I always will. Do you understand?"

His chin moved indecisively as he tried to shake his head and nod at the same time. He didn't understand her motives, not at all, or how she could condone *murder*. But he thought he understood caring about someone while hating what the person was. His voice fell. "What's going to happen to us? What are we going to do?"

"We're going to take things one step at a time," she said. "I don't know how yet, but we'll find a way out of this. We'll get away from SecPac. We'll leave Sapience if we have to, even. I would do that, Donovan. I'm not leaving you again."

Donovan didn't answer, but curls of relief and dread wound through each other in his chest.

"It'll be okay. Tomorrow . . . it'll be okay." It seemed to him that she had been saying that a lot lately. "Good night, Donovan." She pushed aside the canvas flap that separated his room from the corridor.

"Good night . . . Mom."

14

Donovan paced the small room, waiting for Anya to come. His stomach told him it was around dinnertime, but it was a different kind of hunger that made him anxious when she didn't appear. Thinking about the kiss in the library warmed his face, clouded his mind with anxious desire. But then the image of Kevin's arm around Anya's waist, his face near her cheek, would intrude and poison the feeling entirely. It troubled him, how much he'd grown to rely on Anya's visits to give meaning to the passage of time in this place. *Where is she?* There was only one guard out in the hallway right now; he could shove his way past in order to go look for her, but after the standoff with Javid, just about everyone in this place would probably welcome an excuse to shoot him.

Donovan sat down on the edge of the bed. The adrenaline of the air strike had snapped things back into focus for him. By tomorrow night he'd be out of the Warren—and away from the neutrality oath he'd sworn to Saul. From here on, the insurgents would try to keep shuffling him out of SecPac's grasp, holding him out like a lure attached to impossible demands his father would never accept, ratcheting up tension and violence on both sides. Max, for all her rekindled maternal tendencies, couldn't protect him indefinitely from her fellow rebels; she'd only be placing herself in danger from both SecPac and her own people by staying with him. That much had been made apparent tonight.

Clearly, he had to escape.

He would wait until they were near the border. Hopefully, that would give him time to convince his mother not just to help him but to go with him, to get out of Sapience for good. She was already leaving the Warren, leaving Saul; she'd said she would leave Sapience if she had to. That was an opening he could use; if he could persuade her to give up her criminal ways and flee the country, they'd be able to stay in contact somehow, without being a danger to each other.

It was the best possible outcome he could think of. He might not ever see her again, but she would be safe. She was a terrorist, he hadn't forgotten that, but she *was* still his mother. These last several days of being around her had made him remember small things he thought he'd forgotten: the dimple between her eyebrows, the fact that she was left-handed, the way she used to call him "sweedy-dee" and let him do things his father didn't approve of, like run around with no shoes and skip Mur language class. He didn't want to see her end up in an atomizing chamber.

Donovan sank down onto the pillow and closed his eyes. When the mattress shifted, rousing him, he lifted his head, confused about whether he'd actually fallen asleep or not. It must have been for only a few minutes. Anya was kneeling next to him on the bed, holding out a wrapped sandwich. "It's what I could find," she said. "I was trying to help clear the rubble from one of the entrances, and by the time I looked for food, this was all that was left. It's ham and cheese."

Donovan sat up and took the sandwich. It looked a little squashed, but he didn't care about that; he was glad to see Anya. "Have you eaten?" When she shook her head, he unwrapped the sandwich and handed half of it back to her. She kicked her shoes off and pulled her legs up onto the bed. They ate together in silence.

When he was done, Donovan crumpled the wrapping and said, "They're moving me tomorrow."

"Yeah. Kevin told me."

"They want to pass me from cell to cell until I'm out of the country."

She nodded.

Donovan leaned in, trying to read her expression. "Remember what I was saying in the library? This could be your chance too. You could leave with us. With Max and me. Leave this place. Go to a new city, make a new life for yourself."

She shook her head as she finished chewing. "You're sure stubborn, aren't you? Like I told you already, *this* is my new life. Besides, Kevin wouldn't let me go."

A red coal of anger flared in the pit of Donovan's belly. "Kevin doesn't control you. You don't have to put up with . . ." *With the way he looks at you. Touches you. Orders you around, manipulates you.* "With *him*."

Anya stiffened. "You don't understand. Kevin and I . . ." She sighed, exasperated. "I owe him for a lot of things. He's not really a bad person."

For a second, Donovan was speechless. Then he exploded. "Not a bad person!" He wanted to fling himself against the wall in disbelief. "He's a murderer. A torturer. A terrorist. The way he treats you, it's obvious *exactly* what he wants from you. And he's . . . what? Twenty-eight? Thirty?" His lips twisted. Anya folded her arms across her chest, her face reddening. Nasty ideas crowded into Donovan's mind. He was stunned to hear them escaping his mouth in a tone of revulsion. "Just what is he getting from you, for bringing you into Sapience?"

Anya's mouth opened in a small oval of shock. Then she slapped Donovan across the face. He couldn't help armoring in reflex, and even though he turned his head with the blow, she yelped in pain. Her palm smarted red as if she'd smacked it into a brick wall. Tears sprang to her eyes as she clutched her wrist. "Who do you think you are?" she sputtered. "That is *none of your business*, and what makes you think you can judge me or tell me what to do with my life? Just 'cause of those marks on your hands? They make you think you're so much *better* than the rest of us?"

"That's not what I think." Remorse ripped into him immediately. "You're right, I was way out of line. Way out. Look, I'm sorry. I just . . . blurted it without thinking. I didn't mean . . ." He reached out to check her hand. She pulled it away from him, turning it into a fist. Swiping at her eyes, she grabbed her shoes from the floor and shoved them on.

Donovan leaned back and thudded his head against the wall. He couldn't believe what he'd just done. He'd wanted to sway Anya into making a different decision but horribly offended her instead. He was usually careful with his words, able to talk people down—it was part of his job, after all. But when he thought about Anya and Kevin together, his hands all over her . . . he lost it. All he could taste was the venom in his mouth.

She stood up to leave. "Scorching hell, Anya," Donovan said. "Please, just hear me out. I know I've got no right to judge you. I barely even know you. But I know for damn sure you deserve someone better than *Kevin*. He's everything I've sworn to fight against, and *you*—you're the one decent thing that's happened to me during this whole nightmare. Not my mom—" He gave a dry laugh and ran a shaky hand through his hair. "No, she's definitely *part* of the nightmare—but you . . ."

"You think I'm a slut," Anya said ferociously.

"*No.*" Donovan sprang to his feet. "I think you got dealt a raw deal, one you felt like you had no choice but to take. If only SecPac could stop people like Kevin from getting to people like you, we'd put an end to Sapience. You're a good person on the wrong side, and even if I can't do anything to change your mind, I'm still glad to have met you, and I . . . I care about what happens to you, is all."

Anya's lips jammed together. Her shoulders were turned away, as if she was still going to storm out, but then slowly, she sank back down onto the bed. She didn't look at him, staring fixedly instead at her hands and picking at the dry cuticles, her anger still smoldering but rapidly cooling into frail resentment.

Donovan sat back down next to her, leaving a space between them. "I'm sorry," he said again.

"There were sixty of us," Anya said, still not looking at him. "Fifteen families that wouldn't take the relocation payout. My dad said we would stay no matter what, because it was our land, it had been in our family since before the War Era, and he didn't give a damn what the shrooms wanted to build on top of it. But no one cared what he said. The shrooms don't need ranchers. No one in my family had ever been in erze."

"You were . . . How old were you?"

She pulled her sleeves down over her hands and tucked them under her bony knees. "I was eleven."

"The algae farm standoff," Donovan muttered, half to himself. "You were part of that." Five years ago, the expansion of the

Round had necessitated the construction of a huge new algae farm. Donovan's father had worked day and night for weeks, scrambling to qualify enough new builders-in-erze. Located roughly a hundred miles southeast of the Ring Belt, near Lake McConaugh, on the North Platte River, the vast hydroponic complex was amazing. Donovan had seen it before; there was always a rotating SecPac detail guarding the facilities. It employed five hundred humans. It supplied 60 percent of the food for the zhree population in Round Three, and four of its satellite bases, greatly reducing dependence on supply vessels from other planets.

"The shrooms sent SecPac officers to evict us," Anya said. "If your dad fires on a stripe and gets thrown in jail, you know what your chances of erze status are after that? *Zero.* Not that I cared, but my sister might've gone to college. They moved us into the Ring Belt, to the Transitional Habitation grids. What were we supposed to do in a city?

"Do you know who helped us when my dad was in jail, when we had *nothing*?" Anya raised her chin and pinned him with a fierce look that defied him to answer. "Kevin did. He found us a place to stay. He got us an old car and medicines for my mom. When she passed away, he helped us with everything. Sapience kept us fed, found us work, took care of us. He can be a jerk sometimes, and I know he goes over the top. But Kevin cares about the people that no one else does, people the shrooms and the government throw away."

"It doesn't mean you owe him. Not like this," Donovan said.

"The rotten parts of a person are as much a part of them as the noble ones. People are never just what you expect." She glanced back up at him and her voice took an uncertain turn. "*You're* not what I expected, that's for sure. The stripes that came to kick us out of our house . . . they were like monsters. They had guns and masks and this second layer of skin that moved like it was alive. They were shouting at us, and my dad had the shotgun and he was yelling at them and my sister and my mom were crying."

Donovan didn't know what to say. He thought he ought to apologize, but he hadn't been there, and those stripes were his erze mates too; they'd only been doing their jobs. He placed a hand on Anya's back, between her shoulder blades. Anya shook her head as if bewildered; strands of crinkled auburn stuck to her chin. "I thought you'd be scary like them. Alien. People say exos aren't really human anymore, but under that armor you still seem pretty human to me."

"Glad someone here thinks so," he muttered. Was that what she was doing when she stared at him? Waiting for him to turn into one of the "monsters" from her childhood? Trying to puzzle out if he was human?

"She told me to try and make friends with you, you know." Anya turned her head to look at him abruptly. "Max. She thought if you had a friend here, you wouldn't feel like a prisoner. That you might even want to stay."

Donovan went still. *Now* it made sense.

"Kevin didn't like it, but Saul said there was no harm, might as well, since I'd be keeping a close eye on you and no one else would want the job."

"Right," Donovan said. He let his hand drop away from where it had been resting on Anya's back. Anya's time with him had been a Sapience *assignment*. Even more humiliating was the fact that he'd been so easily emotionally manipulated. It had *worked*. He *had* felt less like a prisoner, had begun to think of Anya as a real friend. "I get it," he said woodenly. "I know I've been a chore to you."

Anya frowned. "That's not what I was about to say . . ."

"Was kissing me part of the job too?"

"You stupid stripe, will you just shut up and let me finish!" Anya burst out. She closed her eyes tight in exasperation and opened them again. "When they asked me to try to be friends with you, they said it all apologetic-like, as if they were sending me to Siberia. Everyone here's got some reason to hate your kind; who wants to spend any time with one, pretending to be friendly? But it wasn't like that at all. Not at all. In the library . . ." Anya's gaze flickered away in uncharacteristic embarrassment; her tongue moved across her lower lip, as if still feeling that moment. Donovan's fingers twitched; he nearly brought them to his own lips, so strongly did the ghost of that touch tingle on his skin.

"They did *not* tell me to kiss you, I'll have you know," Anya said. "I just felt like doing it. I never thought I'd want . . ." She faltered, as if the words weren't coming together in the right way. "You're just different, okay? *You're* the one who's a good person on the wrong side. I wanted to think for a second that the sides don't matter, and . . . anyway, I'm . . . really glad I didn't shoot you."

Donovan moved next to her, their legs touching. He put a hand under her chin and tilted her face up to his, a droll smile creeping onto his face. "Me too," he said. "I wish the sides didn't matter. And I'm also really glad you didn't shoot me." Anya rolled her eyes and began to reply, but Donovan brought his mouth down over hers, cutting off whatever she'd been about to say.

The kiss was molten alloy spilling out of a furnace; it was jealousy and frustration, it was recklessness and fierce want. Anya's lips were moist and soft and a little cold. He kissed her harder, more determinedly than she'd kissed him; he put his hands on either side of her face, moving his tongue in her mouth. She gave; her body loosened and pressed against his. When they came apart for air, she followed his mouth with her own, reclaiming it, and they were kissing again, with even more frantic, desperate neediness, as if they would be forced apart at any second, as if there were mere minutes left until the end of the world.

"Donovan." Anya whispered his name. She'd never said his name before. The way she said it now, it sounded as if she believed she could only use it once, like a nonrefundable ticket, and had been waiting, holding it in her mouth until the right moment. Donovan made a low noise in his throat. Anya's hand reached up and touched his stubbled jaw. It cupped the back of his head; it ran down his neck, fingertips caressing the line of exocel nodes. A mingled jolt of alarm and tingling pleasure shot down Donovan's spine. He gasped and pulled back slightly, his brain pulsing with a vague if eager unease.

Anya said, with worry, "Doesn't that feel good?"

"No, it . . . it really does . . . It's just that . . ." *She's a sape.* *You're a soldier. This isn't good for either of you. What are you* *doing, kissing her, leading her on? She's with Kevin, of all people.* His body railed against all his protests. Wild desire blotted out nearly everything, obscured even the previous days of trauma and confusion. Anya's eyes were the color of a clear prairie sky and just as endless and unknowable. He could get lost in them, like a bird on the chinook wind. Reluctantly, he forced his gaze aside, trying to collect himself. "You know that after tomorrow, we'll probably never see each other again," he said.

She was silent for a moment, then her eyes turned sad and she laid her cheek against his shoulder, her breath warming the crook of his neck. "We're both soldiers. Who knows how long we have to live anyhow?"

"I don't want you to think of yourself that way." He wrapped his arms around her and she shifted so that they were curled together on the bed. "And I'm not going to stop hoping you'll listen to me and choose differently."

"See, this is just what I mean. Trying to change people proves you really are hopelessly human." They stayed cocooned together in a moment of uncertain silence until Anya said, "You do eat machine oil, though, which is plain gross."

Donovan blinked, then snorted incredulously into Anya's hair. "I don't eat it when I have a *choice*. You'd eat bugs for protein if you had to."

"No," said Anya firmly. "I'd never eat bugs."

"You would."

"I wouldn't."

"You'd squish them and lick them off your fingers." He pretended to flatten insects off the wall, then sucked the tips of his fingers with apparent relish. "Or worms. You'd eat worms."

"I'd sooner starve," she said, but he could see the side of her face and tell she was fighting a smile. It made Donovan keenly happy to think he'd made her smile. Her body was so soft and pliant; he felt as if his hands were digging through layers of bulky, shapeless clothing, jealously questing just to touch the smooth skin of her flat stomach. He spread his hands wide, his armor completely down, getting as much skin on skin as he could.

A heavy but strangely comfortable silence wrapped itself around and between them. After a while, Anya said, softly and a little sleepily, "I know I shouldn't wish for this, because it's going against the cause. But whether it's leaving with Max, or your own people finding you . . . I hope you get free."

He hoped so too, but at this instant he was content to be nowhere else. He kissed her again, very gently this time, and allowed himself to touch her a little more, and even though he didn't think he could *possibly* fall asleep with Anya so near, with the curve of her body fitted into his, remarkably, he did.

— — —

When Donovan awoke the next morning, the bed was warm where Anya had fallen asleep next to him, but he was alone. He guessed he'd slept well into the daytime, though it was impossible to tell inside the Warren. A tray with a meal of toast, canned baked beans, and coffee had been left outside the canvas flap door of his room.

Late that afternoon, Max came to collect him. She was dressed in a black turtleneck sweater and her hair was pulled back in a stern clasp. She had a canvas pack over her shoulders and was wearing a fitted vest that Donovan did not want to examine closely in case it was lined with dead panotin.

"It's time to go," she said.

15

Donovan followed his mother, retracing the path he'd taken on the first day here, navigating narrow passageways and passing through the vast cavern with its metal catwalks and rock crystal–encrusted walls. He had no idea what lay ahead, but he was not going to miss this claustrophobic bunker, that was for sure. Kevin, Brett, and Anya were waiting for them at the steel double-doored entrance. Donovan caught Anya's eye for a hesitant second and his chest clenched, before both of them shifted their gazes away.

Kevin jerked his chin at Donovan. "It's not handcuffed."

"There's no need for that," Max said.

"I'm not about to have my throat ripped out."

"We need you to get us out of here," said Donovan. "I'm not going to kill you." *Yet. Even though you'd deserve it and I'd die happy.*

The man curled his lip. "Unlike some people, I'm not cracked in the head enough to trust a stripe."

"I won't have him treated like an enemy prisoner," Max insisted.

"That's what he is."

"Mom, it's okay." Donovan stepped forward and extended his hands. "Fine. Do it."

Kevin nodded at Brett, who came forward with a pair of handcuffs and clapped them around Donovan's wrists.

"It's 'Mom' now, is it?" Kevin snorted. "You are walking one hell of a tightrope, Max—with me, with Widget, with everyone. If he tries anything at all, Brett and I aren't going to blink twice. Just so we're clear."

"We're clear."

Kevin nodded to the sentries, who killed the entryway lights and opened the doors.

Donovan lifted his face to the remaining light fading over the hilltops and took a deep breath of crisp forest air. He swayed in relief; after so many days underground, staring at blank rock walls and dim lighting, stepping outside was like plunging from a desert cliff into a cool lake. The breeze on his skin, the sharp scent of pine, and the sight of the open wilderness lit his senses. He lifted his eyes, searching for scanner planes. There were none, only pinprick stars winking into existence in the east as darkness unfurled across the sky.

They walked the narrow, hidden path down to the gravel road where a nondescript black van with off-road tires was parked under the cover of trees. It was amazing how many cheap petroleum-burners Kevin seemed able to get his hands on. The man banged once on the hood and swung himself into the driver's seat. He cranked the engine and the creaky old contraption rumbled to life. The windshield wipers squicked back and forth, twice, smearing dead insects.

Donovan felt his mom's hand fall gently on his back. "Let's go."

He climbed in and scooted to the end of the middle seat. Brett got in the back, and Max followed. She pulled the door closed and sat next to Donovan. Anya jumped into the front passenger seat.

Kevin jerked the van into gear, and the tires began to shudder forward over uneven dirt and gravel.

It took over three hours to drive into Rapid City. The evening quickly turned into full dark, and twice they had to backtrack to detour around areas made impassable by fallen trees and rocks, very likely the result of yesterday's air strikes. The roads were narrow and winding, and Kevin drove with the headlights dimmed, so the going was slow. They didn't want to attract any attention from the sky, he explained, nor meet a deer through the windshield. The man was a jackal, but he was careful. You didn't live long as a Sapience operative if you weren't careful. Every once in a while, he looked back at them in the rearview mirror. From the way he was sitting, he must be packing in a shoulder holster. Donovan glimpsed the shape of another, larger firearm on the floor under Anya's feet.

"You awake back there, Brett?"

"Sure am, Kevin."

"Keep it that way."

Max was gazing out the window as the forest crawled past. The inside of the van was so silent the hum of the road was like a distant surf, carrying them slowly through waves of dark and rocky landscape. Donovan shifted, surreptitiously testing the handcuffs and wondering, now that he was feeling better, if he could get free of them if he had to. Earlier in the day, he'd run his exocel through its paces. It was still worrisomely weak in spots, but his control was fast and flawless. If anything went wrong on this trip, at least he wouldn't be helpless. Brett breathed loudly behind him, his pistol resting on his knee.

They made much faster progress once the hills were behind

them; the van was trundling down flat roads. Max put a hand on his arm. "Can you see it?"

Donovan followed her gaze. "See what?" he asked. They had reached the outskirts of Rapid City. It looked far older than the Ring Belt; many of the shadowy buildings that filed past with increasing regularity were old concrete-and-steel structures, though some were modern, rounded, and shimmering with imported metal weave. Streetlights pulsed by. There were many other vehicles on the road now, cheap petroleum ground cars chugging along in the right lane as expensive skimmercars shot past them. The green lights of a transport ship blinked across the night sky, perhaps carrying seeds or wood to distant planets.

"Everywhere you look, we're becoming like them," Max said. "Buildings, cars, even human bodies . . . it's all becoming more alien. After the War Era, we fell off our own path, we stopped being inventive and started striving only for what they dangled in front of us." Her whitish reflection in the window glass was somber and ghostly. "Do you want to know what first brought me over to Sapience?"

He did, but he didn't say anything. He let her continue. She said, "It was a little girl. She was about a year old, the same age you were at the time, waiting by one of the entrances to the Round with her unmarked young mother. The mother had brought the girl to be adopted by a couple inside the Round. Whatever the woman's reasons for giving up her child, she must have thought her daughter would have a better life being erze marked, maybe even being changed into an exo. That toddler didn't understand, she just cried and cried as her mother walked away." She closed her eyes for a moment, as if the memory were from yesterday instead of sixteen years ago. "Tell me, Donovan . . . do you know how the Liaison Office—your father's people—how they approve applicants for erze status?"

Did he know? He could probably recite the criteria in his sleep. "There are a lot of factors," he said. "Mental and physical health, intelligence, obedience to the law, learned skills, psychological profile . . ."

"The zhree choose the healthiest, brightest, most obedient humans as their aides," his mother said. "They offer more comfortable, peaceful, prosperous lives, working for the good of the Commonwealth. They harness our work for their own purposes, and they Harden our children. The luckiest of us are second-class citizens on our own planet, but we feel grateful and entitled, because we enjoy it at the expense of those who are lower. We are being remade into a servant species, and your father's co-operationist government is helping to make it happen. That night I wrote an angry letter about that little girl, and I published it under a fake name, and that's how it began."

Donovan shifted in his seat. This was the side of his mother he'd never seen. This was Max, the ideologue, who made all of society sound like an evil conspiracy. Of course there was disparity. Yes, there were cities that badly needed modernizing, and the erze system was far from perfect, but there were good things too: enduring peace between nations and species, exocels, cheap and clean energy, interstellar trade, longer and healthier lives . . . "Haven't you read history?" he said. "We humans weren't exactly doing such a great job for ourselves before the Landing. There were all sorts of awful things going on. You can't say everything's worse now because of the zhree."

"Sure you can," Kevin cut in. "Whatever problems we had before, they were *our* problems. Now there's only one problem. They're it." He turned the wheel and drove into a near-empty parking lot. He stopped the van but left the engine running. On the other side of the lot, a pickup truck was parked by itself. It flashed its headlights: once, twice.

"Okay." Kevin nodded to Anya. "You know what to do."

The girl opened the passenger-side door and hopped out. She zipped up her jacket, closed the door, and began walking across the asphalt, toward the pickup truck.

"What's she doing?" Donovan felt a throb of anxiety, watching her stride away by herself.

Kevin peered through the windshield, forearms leaned over the steering wheel. One hand moved to his vest, feeling for the weapon concealed underneath. "Meeting our contacts. The guys in Rapid City know me, but they're still real careful. SecPac spies got to their cell last year; they lost a bunch of good people." He slid Donovan an accusing glare from the corner of his eye, as if he'd had something to do with it.

The door of the pickup truck opened. The figure of a large man in a leather jacket stepped out. Donovan's anxiety sharpened. The man met Anya partway across the parking lot. Donovan could see them speaking to each other. Were they exchanging secret codes? Asking questions only the other person was supposed to know the answer to? Donovan pressed a hand to the glass. Anya looked like a child next to the hulking figure. "Why is she the one who goes?"

Kevin scowled. "The most junior operative always goes."

"She knows what she's doing," Max said. "She has to earn her way up in Sapience. We all did."

Anya turned and came back to the van. Donovan released a silent breath of relief.

"We're good," she said, climbing back into the passenger seat. "They'll take us to the doctor now."

Kevin grunted in satisfaction and pulled the van forward. The pickup truck's lights came on. It drove out of the parking lot, and Kevin followed. A hint of tense anticipation pervaded the inside of the vehicle. Kevin had his eyes fixed on the pickup's taillights, both his hands on the wheel. The illuminated bumper stickers included the old United States flag, a stylized bald eagle, *Give War a Chance*, and *Proud to Be an Extremist*.

"Who is this doctor?" Donovan asked. "Why are you going to see him?"

"Dr. Nakada is a scientist who does research for us," Max said.

"A Sapience scientist?" It was bizarre to think of cave-dwelling insurgents having scientists.

"He's a patriot," Max said. "I think he might be able to help us. To help you."

"What do you mean?"

The pickup truck turned and slowed to a stop behind a square, gray brick building. Kevin parked the van behind the other vehicle and turned off the engine. He waited a second, then opened the door. The rest of them followed, stepping out to meet the two men who'd emerged from the cab of the truck. The big man who'd met Anya introduced himself as Dixon and his shorter companion as Reed. Donovan doubted those were their real names, but he filed them carefully in his memory, along with the men's appearances. Dixon was soft-spoken, had a trim black beard, and a scar over his left eyebrow. Reed would be easy to remember: He had round glasses, red hair, and a gap between his front teeth.

"Warde, you're still alive and kicking?" Reed exclaimed. The two men shook hands, then embraced. "You've got more lives than the devil's cat. Planning to quit while you're ahead?"

"Never." Kevin grinned. "Saul sends his best."

"Which one of you is Max?" Dixon asked.

"I am." Donovan's mother stepped forward. "Thank you for meeting us on short notice. How's Widget?"

"Still got all her atoms," Reed said cheerily. A ripple of chuckles. Sapience humor, apparently.

Reed's eyes fell on Donovan, then traveled down to his bound, striped hands. "Jesus." He took an involuntary step backward. "You weren't kidding. An armored stripe. *Jesus.*" He looked at them and shook his head. "You've got stones, I'll give you that."

"He's not a threat to us," Max said. "He hasn't hurt anyone."

"Why's he in handcuffs, then?" said Dixon. "The only exo you can trust is a dead one."

"This is a special case," Max insisted. "The doctor is always asking to see a live exo. Well, we brought him one."

Donovan frowned, an alarm bell pinging in his mind. What was *that* supposed to mean?

Dixon and Reed exchanged a doubtful glance. "True enough," Reed said. "Widget must trust you something fierce to agree to this, but all right. I sure hope you know what you're doing. Let's go see the doctor." He fished a key from his pocket and unlocked the back door. It opened onto a concrete stairwell stretching up to the unlit floors above and down to a single closed basement door.

"Knock at the bottom. He knows you're coming. We'll stay up here and call down if there's any sign of trouble."

"You stay up here too," Kevin said to Brett and Anya.

"Hey, come on now, Kevin, can't we see what's going on down there?" Brett said.

"No." Kevin wound a hand behind Anya's neck and gave it an overly long squeeze. "We won't be long."

Max led the way down to the unmarked basement door. Donovan followed her, Kevin behind him. As he descended, apprehension wormed up Donovan's throat. He had a bad feeling about what was going on here. Max knocked and waited. A shadow fell across the sliver of light emanating from beneath the closed door—someone examining the visitors through the peephole. Bolts were drawn back, and the door opened.

"Quickly," said the man on the other side. The three of them filed through. Dr. Nakada closed and locked the door behind them.

They were inside a cluttered, half-lit laboratory. Donovan ran his eyes over labeled drawers, an examining table, rows of microscopes on counters, and shelves of jars filled with things he didn't want to examine too closely. Were they ... sweet erze ... body parts? With panotin still on them? And was that a ... miniature Hardening tank? The color of the viscous liquid inside was wrong, almost orange, but the attached tubes and instruments made him stare in queasy recollection.

This was definitely not right.

"Kevin," said the doctor, by way of greeting. "Max."

"Good to see you, Eugene," Max said. She put a hand lightly on the small of Donovan's back. "This is Donovan. He's ... my son."

Eugene Nakada was probably not old, just prematurely aged. His hair was jet black, but it receded in a dramatic widow's peak. The smooth skin of his curious face appeared pallid under the fluorescent lights illuminating one side of the basement. The doctor focused on Donovan with unsettling interest and shuffled forward with his hands in his pockets. "A living exo! I take it your exocel is undamaged and healthy? What year were you Hardened?" When Donovan told him, he nodded enthusiastically. "Eighth-generation technology. Fantastic." He added, "You must excuse my exuberance. I don't usually meet exos who can answer my questions."

A scrabbling sound erupted from the corner. Two rhesus monkeys were scrambling back and forth in a large cage. Donovan did a double take; there was something strange about the monkeys. They were *armored*. Except their armor was wrong—insofar as monkey exos could be right at all. Their exocels were incomplete, deformed. They couldn't possibly be functional. They covered some parts of their bodies and not others, thicker in places, creating a grotesque patchwork of panotin and fur. The effect was revolting, like looking at an animal with human skin partially grafted over it.

Donovan's stomach lurched, and he took a hasty step back. His eyes jerked away from the sight of the monkeys and landed back on the jars of body parts. The sickening realization hit him. "This is where you bring them. The exos that you kill." He stared at Kevin in horror. "You give them to this mad scientist to dissect and study so he can perform crazy experiments."

"Donovan." Max's voice was sharp. "Just listen first."

"They're not crazy experiments," said Dr. Nakada with a defensive sniff. "And I wasn't always a 'mad' scientist." He took his hands from his pockets and turned them over. At Donovan's stunned expression, he smiled wryly. "Yes, I still have them. They're faded, I know—haven't been renewed in years. But SecPac hasn't caught me yet, so they were never stripped off. Truth be told, I don't care to part with my Scientist markings. I worked hard enough for them, back in the day."

"You were a scientist-in-erze," said Donovan. "And now you work for Sapience?"

"The research I do now is the most important and fascinating work I've ever done. There are hundreds of thousands of exos around the world, yet we humans still know so little about how Hardening actually *works*." A shadow descended over his face. "And why it sometimes doesn't."

It took Donovan a second to understand. "Who was it?" he asked.

"My daughter." Dr. Nakada's unblinking stare made Donovan wonder if the man was hating him at that moment—hating him for being one of the survivors. "She was a beautiful little girl. I knew the odds, but my wife was an exo; I assumed our daughter would be fine. That the risks would be less for us. Not a very scientific assumption to make." He turned away and began rummaging distractedly in a nearby counter drawer. "After we lost her, I couldn't stop thinking about how ignorant I was. How ignorant we all are. The zhree have humans-in-erze working all over the world, in dozens of capacities, but exocel technology is still their secret."

"I know my own exocel," Donovan said.

"How to use it," the doctor agreed. "The more interesting question is: How to defeat it?" He took a small item from the

162

drawer and held it up. Donovan had one second to notice it was a small bottle with a spray nozzle before the doctor thrust it toward him and sprayed a fine mist into his face.

"The *hell*—" Donovan jerked his head back, armoring instantly out of reflex. Then, in one terrible moment, his exocel dropped. One instant it was there, in another, it was gone, his conscious connection severed as abruptly as if a limb had been chopped off.

Donovan's heart seemed to stop. One second passed. Two. Three.

Oh my God.

His armor sprang alive again. It poured violently across his skin, like water bursting through a dam. Donovan reeled with relief and fury, straining the short length of chain between his handcuffs. "What did you do to me?" he nearly screamed. For a few awful seconds, he'd been reduced to the helplessness of a five-year-old, unable to control his newly Hardened body. All the doctor had done was spray something in his face. How could his armor be disabled by something so mundane?

Kevin whooped. "Did you just do what I think you did?" he demanded. "Did you just *turn off* his armor?"

Max snatched the small bottle from Dr. Nakada, studying it covetously. "Can you make it last longer?"

Donovan choked back burning nausea. How could she be happy to see him defenseless and humiliated? Losing control of one's exocel was like losing control of one's bowels. Something that happened to the very young and the very old, the diseased and the disabled, and occasionally, to the very, very inebriated. He considered grabbing the bottle and crushing it in his hand, though no doubt it wasn't the only sample. Instead, he lunged for Nakada and closed his bound hands over the front of the man's shirt, yanking him forward. "You are an erze traitor," he said through clenched teeth.

Kevin had the barrel of his gun up against Donovan's ribs in a second. "Watch it."

Max grabbed Donovan's tense, armored forearm. "Let him go, Donovan. He didn't hurt you."

"I'm giving you two seconds, zebrahands," Kevin hissed.

Donovan let go slowly, his shoulders still trembling with rage. "What is that stuff?"

Dr. Nakada smoothed the front of his rumpled shirt with a faint air of satisfaction. "Have you ever needed surgery?"

Donovan shook his head. "A friend of mine once did." Jet had had his appendix taken out when he was fourteen.

"How does a surgeon operate on an exo?"

"Exos don't go to the hospital. There are zhree Nurses in the Towers who treat us." He remembered visiting Jet after his surgery and asking him how they did it. "They put you so far under even your exocel conks out."

"Not precisely," said Nakada. "They do anesthetize you, but they also use a drug that blocks the neurotransmitters controlling exocel activation. I synthesized the compound in soluble form but haven't had a chance to test it until now." He tapped his chin. "Unfortunately, as you can see, inhaling the dilute solution produces only a temporary effect."

"Would it work on a shroom?" Kevin asked.

"No," said Donovan. "The zhree don't breathe the way we do."

"He is correct," Nakada said. "They filter and take in oxygen through the surface of their bodies. Sprayed particles would be too large to affect them. Furthermore, I am not even certain the neurotransmitter blockers used on human exos would work on a different species." He spread his hands. "As I said, we simply don't know how zhree Scientists developed human exocels, and how different they are from what the zhree themselves have."

Kevin grimaced, disappointed. "Well, it's a start. A good start. Taking out exos is the next best thing to taking out shrooms." He squinted at the jars with idle, nose-wrinkled curiosity, then wandered over and tilted his head toward the monkey cage. "It's good work you're doing here, Doc." He nudged the bottom of the cage with the toe of his boot, sending the horrible monkeys scampering. "If you need more money, more equipment or samples, we'll try to get them for you. You're getting close, aren't you? Getting close to something we can use."

The doctor smiled uneasily. He seemed to consider how best to frame his answer to balance reality with what Kevin wanted to hear. "We're still a long way from producing an effective weapon, but yes . . . perhaps we're getting closer."

A weapon. Of course Sapience would want a weapon that could disable exocels, but this was the first evidence Donovan had ever seen that they were actively developing it. This scientist-in-erze turned traitor might actually come up with something. Donovan's thoughts spun in escalating alarm. SecPac needed to know this.

Max's hand was still on Donovan's arm. She took a deep breath, then pressed her lips into a tight line, as if she were bracing herself to jump into ice water. She turned to Nakada. "What about a permanent solution? Could you remove an exocel entirely?"

Donovan froze. He could not have heard correctly. *"What?"*

The doctor shifted his sober gaze from Max to Donovan, then back again. "Ah," he said.

Donovan jerked away from his mother in a spasm of visceral horror. "You want to turn me into a *squishy*?" The word came out unnaturally high and squeaky.

She reached for him, stunned by the strength of his reaction. "To take the alien machine cells out of you. To turn you back into a normal human being."

A normal human being. So this was why she'd wanted to bring him here. This was what she'd meant by "helping him." Remove his exocel? He backed away, shaking his head. It was *insane*. Hideous to even contemplate. Like imagining the removal of one's spine, or being skinned alive. "You can't . . . it's not possible . . ."

"It wouldn't just be the biggest breakthrough in the war. It would save us, Donovan. Without your exocel, you're not useful to the shrooms, and you're not a threat to Sapience. You could be free. *We* could be free." She turned back to Nakada, eyes swimming with hope. "Is it possible?"

The doctor pursed his lips to one side, considering. "Long-term suppression *might* be possible. The effect would keep wearing off, though, and he would still be an exo—merely a weak and drug-addled one." Nakada was stalling. He rubbed the backs of his hands nervously and cleared his throat. "Complete removal of an exocel, however . . . I would have to say the chances of such a procedure succeeding are exceedingly slim."

"How slim?" Max asked.

Donovan felt sick. An exocel was as much a part of a person's body as blood and bones. You couldn't just . . . God, what would you be left with? A gory lump of flesh?

Nakada glanced at Donovan before speaking to Max again. "You must understand, the exocel is not an implant. It's a system-wide augmentation and rewiring. Imagine the body as a computer. An implant would be adding a piece of hardware; Hardening is changing the operating system. Even if I had a team of the best surgeons, it's extremely unlikely the exocel could be removed without killing its owner. Or at the very least, inflicting permanent brain damage."

The doctor's answer was so utterly obvious Donovan felt like screaming. He could have told Max the same thing if she'd bothered to ask instead of bringing him here with her impossible, mad idea.

Max's face slackened under the weight of disappointment. "Thank you, Doctor." Her voice was flat. She opened the door. Without another look back, she began to ascend the stairwell, one heavy step at a time.

"Don't mind her," Kevin said, clapping a hand to the doctor's shoulder. "You just keep me posted on how you're doing with that spray stuff."

Donovan caught the door with his shoulder before it could close. He took the steps two at a time, chasing his mother as she left the building. He shouted after her. "Even if that traitor scientist *could* remove my exocel, did you really think I would ever agree?" Roiling fury made it hard to get words out. "I'm not a little kid anymore. You can't stand what I am, but did it occur to you that I can't stand what you are either? You didn't want me to be an exo? Well, I sure as hell didn't want you to *leave* to become a scorching *sape!*"

He flung the words at the back of her head, but she didn't stop walking. Brett and Anya were talking with Dixon and Reed next to the pickup truck, shifting impatiently and stamping their feet against the chill. All four of them looked over at Max expectantly as she paused, halfway to the truck. She turned back toward Donovan, who shook with anger behind her. He saw her face; it had the saddest, most resigned expression he'd ever seen. It made her seem suddenly old. She said quietly, "I just want you back."

A sudden blast of gale-force wind hit the ground. Donovan staggered. A wall of air buffeted the others against the truck and slammed through the open door of the building, nearly pushing Kevin back down the stairs. Above the wind came the distinctive thrum that Donovan recognized at once as the sharp vertical descent of a micro-fission engine T15 stealthcopter. Blinding white light slammed down over them like an overturned cup. Donovan threw his arms up over his eyes. His heart skittered into his throat.

"This is SecPac! We have the building surrounded. Hands in the air—don't move and we won't shoot!"

The amplified voice echoed down, full of command and dead serious. It was Jet.

16

Gunshots rang out. It took Donovan a second to realize they were coming not from above him but from behind. Kevin, teeth bared, unloading at the open bay doors of the hovering T15. His bulging eyes, the irises ringed with white, blazed like those of a cornered animal. "It's a setup!" he bellowed. "We were set up!"

Everyone burst into frantic motion. Dixon and Reed scrambled for the pickup truck, yanking doors open and grabbing for weapons. Anya began to run for the van, but Max caught her by the jacket. "No. Back in the building. There's an underground escape in the basement, in the doctor's lab." She drew a pistol of her own and gave Brett a shove. "Grab Nakada and get him away from here. Go!"

Dixon and Reed emerged from the cover of the pickup's open doors, assault weapons barking to life in a burst of astounding noise. "Come and get me, you shroom-loving pricks!" Reed screamed up at the harsh light.

"Come on!" Brett shouted, grabbing Anya. He readied himself to make the short run across open asphalt to the building's entrance, thirty meters away. Gunfire erupted from the stealth-copter, pelting the ground like hailstones. Brett cursed and leapt back, flattening himself against the pickup's tires. Donovan yanked Anya violently into the shadow of his own body, pinning her against the truck, his bound hands stretched over both their heads. He braced himself, waited to feel the rocking, punching pain of bullets striking his tense body, but remarkably, nothing hit him in the volley.

"Donovan, go with them!" Max shouted into his ear.

"What about you?"

"I'll be right behind you," she promised. "Just go! Go!"

Adrenaline poured into Donovan's veins, not from fear but from an agony of indecision. Jet was up there. They had come: his erze mates, his fellow soldiers. Every bit of Donovan's training and conditioning told him to run toward them. His hands shook. *Get Anya out of here first.* "Stay right next to me," he told her. She drew a short breath and grabbed his arm. They ran.

Donovan matched his strides to hers, running nearly on her heels, ready to throw himself forward over her. A short burst of gunfire followed them. "Hold fire!" Jet shouted from far away. "Everyone hold fire, dammit!"

Anya reached the building's doorway and flung herself through it, Donovan with her. Brett plowed in right after them. Kevin was planted in the opening, his face twitching, red with rage. He barely seemed to register their arrival, pausing only to let loose a string of curses, adjust his aim, and fire at the blur of movement behind and above them.

Donovan snapped his head around. Ropes dangled from the black shape of the T15. Jet was descending in a straight fall, one armored hand whistling with friction as it slid down the cable like a carabiner on a line. Kevin's shot missed him, he was falling too fast; he let go and plummeted the remaining ten feet, his exocel shuddering visibly in the harsh spotlight glare as it absorbed the shock of his crouched landing.

Kevin aimed again; Donovan swung his bound hands like a club, knocking the man's arm aside before he could fire. With a snarl, Kevin whipped the pistol back around toward Donovan's chest. He pulled the trigger. His gun made an empty clicking noise. "Dammit!"

Brett barreled up to Kevin. "The doctor!" he gasped. "Max says to save him!"

Even in Kevin's fury, the message registered. The doctor and his work were more important to Sapience than anything else right now. More important than shooting stripes. Kevin hurled a final murderous glare at Donovan. Then he leapt for the stairs. "Move it, Anya!"

Anya had her pistol up, steadied with both hands, aiming out the doorway. She fired in Jet's direction. The recoil kicked the weapon in her grip—once, twice—before Donovan twisted his hands hard in the cuffs and clamped one of them over the top of the frame, jamming the slide.

"Let go!" She yanked angrily.

"Run. Go with Kevin." He dropped his hand and shoved her, hard. "*Run*, Anya."

Something in his voice or his face—both of them twisted with urgency—made her listen. She stared up at him. Tendrils of hair clung to the sides of her face, framing an expression unutterably bleak. For a moment, Donovan could not breathe; a firestorm of silent regret raged between them. Then Anya turned and raced down the stairs.

More figures dropped from the stealthcopter's dangling lines. Dixon and Reed greeted them with a wall of firepower. The noise was terrific. Donovan stared, mute with horrified astonishment, at the sight of his mother behind Dixon's shoulder, reaching into the bed of the truck. She came up with an M4 carbine and brought it up, smooth and practiced. Two SecPac officers went down in a combined hail of lead. One of them, an exo, screamed in pain, rolling on the ground. The other wasn't Hardened. The gunfire riddled his synthetic armor and a bullet passed through his neck. He went down without a sound.

The other officers opened fire at the truck. Shrill, high-pitched blasts filled the air as E201 pulse rifles perforated the vehicle's hood and siding. The windshield collapsed in a spray of glass. Dixon, half in and half out of the driver's seat, let out a roar and stumbled from the wheel. He took two steps before Jet and Vic, standing side by side, each put a round into his chest. The huge man staggered like a tipping boulder but didn't fall. His blood-flecked vest gleamed gruesomely in the harsh, burn-laced air. The next four shots tore through the dead panotin. Dixon went down with a jerky gurgle.

Reed popped up, emptying his magazine in a burst of guttural rage and sending officers ducking and scrambling for cover. The stealthcopter banked alarmingly, trailing ropes like tentacles, filling the air with a static whining.

Donovan uttered a hoarse noise, unintelligible to himself. His erze mates were out there taking fire—instinct screamed at him to go to them, to help them. But his mother was still behind the truck, a squishy crouched in a cone of flying bullets. He had to get to her before they did. He had to stop this. Run out there, scream, wave his arms, make them all *stop*.

Donovan strained against the metal binding his hands together. He poured armor over his wrists, thickening them until the panotin bulged against the restraints, widening them a millimeter. He strained his exocel until it felt as if the veins in his head and neck would burst. Then he dropped his armor all at once and pulled again. The handcuffs slipped up to the thickest point of his knuckles and stopped. Donovan gave a choked cry of frustration.

"Wait." Brett appeared beside him. Donovan hadn't realized he was still there; hadn't he followed Kevin and Anya? Brett reached over and unlocked the handcuffs. They fell away from Donovan's wrists.

Donovan turned his freed hands in confusion. *Why—?*

A momentary pause in gunfire; Donovan heard the voice of Thaddeus Lowell, his SecPac class captain, hollering, "This is your last chance! Drop your weapons and surrender!"

"You're not going to take me, you striped bastards!" Reed let off another burst of fire. He shook his weapon over his head. "Do you hear me? You're not going to—"

Bullets ripped through the man's arm, nearly severing it. Reed ran toward the officers in a wild, suicidal dash. His right leg exploded above the kneecap and he went down, spurting blood over the asphalt and still screaming defiance. SecPac officers advanced in a rush. From behind the hulk of the destroyed truck, Max looked across the smoke-obscured distance to Donovan. Her clothes and face were smeared with dust, and Reed's blood flecked her face and clothes. Never had Donovan imagined his mother could look like she did now—grim and scared and murderous.

He ran toward her. He might be caught in a shower of gunfire, but he ran anyway, his heartbeat one long indistinguishable throb in his ears. He was almost there. Max mouthed his name and shook her head. Then she wheeled out from behind the cover of the vehicle and fired a long burst.

Vic spun and went down.

The next part seemed to happen in slow motion. Jet swung his E201 around and squeezed the trigger.

No! The bullet punched into the truck, inches from Max's head. Donovan changed course in mid-step and tackled Jet before he could fire again. Jet's eyes flew open in surprise as he and Donovan tumbled to the pavement together. Donovan grabbed the scalding barrel of the rifle and yanked upward, hard, wrenching it from Jet's fingers. He hurled the weapon aside. Everything felt strange, horribly wrong. He was moving as if in a twisted simulation, none of it real, none of it sensible. "Call it off!" he shouted. Without knowing what he was doing, he clamped his hands over his friend's throat and shook. "Make them call it off!"

Jet's exocel surged under Donovan's steel vise fingers. He slammed his forearms down over Donovan's. Their exocels sheared against each other, layers of panotin vibrating down both their limbs. Donovan's grip buckled; Jet rolled him over and hit him in the face. "Donovan! *D!* It's me!" Donovan struggled mindlessly and Jet hit him again. The impact knocked the back of his head against the concrete. "Snap out of it!" Jet was yelling at him. "What the hell is wrong with you?"

There was a storm of movement and running. Donovan's arms were grabbed and pinned by several hands. He was pushed onto his stomach. Jet flattened him with the weight of a knee between his shoulder blades. "Vic!" Jet shouted, worry cracking his voice. "Someone check on Vic!"

"I'm okay," Vic called.

The muddy logic of the fight drained out of Donovan. He raised his face a few inches from the ground. The gunfire had stopped. Dixon and the non-Hardened officer lay sprawled, padded black lumps in slowly expanding pools of dark liquid. Someone was helping the wounded exo—Atticus—to sit up. Reed, horribly, was still alive, thrashing what remained of his leg and spitting at the officer who tried to get to him. The remaining SecPac officers—Tennyson, Ariadne, Katerina, Lucius—were running toward the building, weapons up, fast and focused, wary of any additional insurgents inside.

He couldn't see his mother. Had she gotten away? Was she dead? "Where is she?" he wheezed, too quietly for anyone to hear him over the sound and wind of the landing stealthcopter. Bits of churned gravel and grit pelted his face.

Brett stepped forward suddenly from the shadow of the building's doorway. The barrel of every SecPac rifle zeroed in on him at once. Donovan expected to see him go down in another explosion of gunfire, but Brett fell to his knees with his empty hands raised high over his head. "Wapiti!" he shouted. "*Wapiti*, for God's sake! Don't shoot!"

Tennyson kept his E201 steady but moved his hand from the trigger. "You're the agent?"

Brett nodded. His face was slightly turned, and his raised hands trembled, as if he were afraid the officers wouldn't believe him. "The basement," he said quickly. "Two sapes and the scientist who's working for them—they were headed for an escape route." The officers parted around Brett, running into the building.

Donovan's memory telescoped to a vivid moment: the muzzle of Kevin's handgun and the man's voice, demanding, "*What is the* code word you use with your informers?" He twitched under Jet's weight.

Brett? Brett is a SecPac agent?

Jet bent his head over Donovan's. "I'm going to let you up," he said. "Can you handle it?"

Donovan nodded, though he wasn't sure it was the honest answer. The pressure came off his back. Donovan rolled over and sat up. He felt light-headed, abuzz with a surreal, delayed panic that was just now hitting him full force. He rocked back and dropped his forehead into trembling hands. It was suddenly hard to breathe; his chest felt shrunken, as if a vacuum hose inserted down his esophagus had sucked the air from his lungs. It wasn't just the adrenaline crash from the firefight. Turning on your own erze was wrong, abhorrent to any normal exo. He'd *attacked* Jet. It didn't seem possible that he'd done it.

Jet knelt in front of him and grabbed him by the upper arms. They stared at each other uncertainly, paralyzed with relief, waiting to see what the other would do. Jet shook Donovan roughly, then crushed him in a fierce hug. "Heaven and erze, what was that all about? Do you have *any* idea—" He pulled back, holding on to either side of Donovan's head. "I thought I'd find you in bloody pieces. Command wouldn't green-light a rescue until tonight. Intel told us this place was some kind of torture lab . . ." Jet faltered. He searched Donovan's eyes closely, his own burning with furious confusion and worry. "What did they do to you? Did they hurt you? Brainwash you or something?"

Donovan tried to shake his head. "That sape . . ." He squeezed his eyes shut for a second. "She's my mom."

There was an uncomprehending silence before Jet dropped his hands. "What?"

"Prime Liaison arriving on site!" Thaddeus shouted. "Officers at atten*tion*!"

A second stealthcopter churned the air with a deep vibrating thrum as it touched down next to the first one. A figure stepped out. Dominick Reyes's unmistakable voice carried across the torn street: "Where is he?"

Every officer on the scene straightened, the Hardened ones dropping armor respectfully. For a second, Donovan felt frozen in renewed shock. Then he scrambled to his feet. The floodlights from the stealthcopter were gone; only blurry orange streetlights illuminated the shape of his father in his dark suit, bearing down on him with long strides. Donovan didn't see his father's face until a second before the man stopped directly in front of him. The hum of the T15's engine faded out. In the background, Reed was still moaning, and distant crashing noises floated up from inside the building behind them, but silence stretched between the two of them like a balloon. Donovan swallowed. He was wearing Kevin's clothes and had conducted himself nothing like a soldier-in-erze. "Father," he said.

His father brought his hands up and gripped Donovan's shoulders. His fingers were remarkably strong considering he had no exocel; Donovan could feel them digging against bone. His usually inscrutable face contorted with emotion. It was a baffling and awkward sight, as if the muscles were unused to such demands and ill-practiced for it. His voice was quiet, and rough like broken rock. "Are you hurt?"

"N-no. No, sir," Donovan stammered.

A small nod, nearly imperceptible. The sight of it punched something inside Donovan. He felt an abrupt urge to laugh. He was pretty sure if he began laughing, he wouldn't be able to stop, and then he would start crying or shouting. He'd already put on an incomprehensible display of madness in front of his fellow officers; now he was going to melt down and start sobbing in front of the Prime Liaison. Donovan clenched the ground with his feet, made his spine straight. *Keep it together. Keep it together. You're a stripe.* He kept it together.

His father held on to his shoulders for so long it seemed as if the world had stopped spinning. Slowly, his father's hands unclenched. They fell to his sides. He passed his gaze once more over Donovan's face, as if double-checking that it was really him. The skin around his eyes loosened a tiny bit. Then he turned to Thaddeus. He was himself again, stern and in control. "Report."

"We've secured the building, sir. There was a Sapience lab in the basement, like we suspected. The scientist and at least two other terrorists escaped through a hidden tunnel in the back of a closet. We're in pursuit; I've sent out an area-wide alert and given the order to have the landlord and all the other tenants brought in for questioning, pending charges of sympathizer activity. We'll catch them, Mr. Prime Liaison." Thad possessed the same laid-back poise regardless of whether he was enjoying a beer by a pool or reporting to the Prime Liaison after a firefight. He exuded *I got this* from every pore, and it endeared him to superiors and subordinates alike. Now, though, when he glanced at Donovan, his face sagged visibly in relief before he turned back to Donovan's father. "Thank erze he's safe, sir."

"Casualties?"

"One suspect dead, one in critical condition. One exo officer with non-life-threatening injuries." Thaddeus paused, somber. "We lost a non-Hardened officer. Marcelo Dawes. He shouldn't have been out here in the first place, but we're badly stretched tonight and using any stripe with combat training—Hardened or not."

Two other officers approached, pulling a stumbling, hand-cuffed figure between them. They forced her to her knees on the ground in front of the Prime Liaison.

Donovan felt faint. Relief and anguish swept over him.

"This is the other Sapience operative we captured, sir," Thad said. "She resisted at first but then surrendered."

Max raised her face. It was streaked with dirt and blood, but cold and calm and eerily hateful. "Hello, Dominick."

A backward shift of weight was the only sign of surprise the Prime Liaison made. He stared down at the bound Sapience rebel without betraying any triumph or malice. "Hannah," he said. "Or should I call you Max?"

Donovan's mother rose to her feet with slow dignity. "You've had SecPac after me for quite a while now, haven't you? If you'd known I would cause you this much trouble, you would never have let me leave the Round."

"No, I would not have. I did it to spare Donovan."

"To spare him." A dark curtain unfurled across her face. She looked as if she might lunge across the short space and attack the Prime Liaison with her bare hands. The officers on either side took a firm grip of her arms. She ignored them; she ignored everyone, even Donovan. Her eyes were fixed on Dominick Reyes. "To *spare* him?" she repeated, her voice knotting into something ugly. "You *stole* him. You turned him into a monster. You used him to get to me, and at the bidding of your alien masters, you are using him still, in your own selfish agenda against humanity."

Everyone was staring. Donovan felt cemented to the ground. His heart hammered against his ribs. The enmity foaming the air between his parents was like a solid mass, an expanding, impermeable shell. Perhaps he jerked forward anyway, without knowing it, because suddenly Jet had a firm grip on his elbow.

"It's over, Hannah." Dominick Reyes's voice was stony, but Donovan could see the anger squeezing down the corners of his father's eyes. The Prime Liaison raised his voice so that everyone nearby could hear. "Ten minutes ago, I was notified that tonight's Risk Area operation was a success. As we speak, SecPac forces are tearing apart Sapience's underground bunker in the Black Hills." He paused to let the news sink in, his eyes not moving from the woman who'd once been his wife. "The terrorists there have been killed or captured. The ones who fled into the wilderness are being hunted down and brought to justice. The war you think you're fighting is over; we will not let you extremists drag the country into another."

Cheers and applause erupted from the officers nearby. Thad shouted to get their attention back. "Two teams—171 and 190— you're staying here. Find those missing sapes! The rest of you, we're heading back to the RA—they're going to need our help over there." People scrambled back into motion.

Donovan was still staring at his mother. She looked as pale as chalk. He could see her mind trying to process the devastating news, wondering: Had any of her friends survived or escaped? Was Saul dead?

"You are traitors," she whispered. Her eyes were bottomless pits. "All of you."

"Take her away," the Prime Liaison said.

"Father, wait—" Donovan found his voice again, but the plea choked in his throat.

"*Donovan.*" His father's voice was quiet in the midst of the renewed noise, but it landed hard as an anvil.

His mother was being ushered roughly across the street to one of the waiting stealthcopters. "Wait," Donovan blurted again. "Don't—" He tried to move to follow, but Jet's grip on his elbow tightened. His mother looked over her shoulder. For a second, her gaze touched him. Then she disappeared into the aircraft. The T15 lifted off with a low bass hum, taking his mother, Dixon's body, and the sedated and mangled Reed. It hovered for a moment, then passed overhead, silent as an owl.

That's it, he thought. *It's over.*

His knees weakened. He looked for a place to sit down, that wasn't the middle of the asphalt, but the sight of Thad escorting Brett before the Prime Liaison shocked Donovan upright.

Dominick Reyes said, "Were it not for you, for the enormous risks you took, and the sacrifices you made, we would not have discovered the location or the layout of the Sapience camp. This country owes you its thanks, even if your courage is never publicly recognized." Donovan's father paused meaningfully and extended his hand. "After all you've done, you deserve to finally come home. And for helping to recover my son, you have my deepest personal gratitude."

"Thank you, sir." Brett was sickly pale, nearly as destroyed by the night's events as Donovan. He still looked like Brett—a twentysomething, bland-faced, working-class squishy insurgent. The sight of him shaking hands with the Prime Liaison nearly bowled Donovan over. Kevin's obsequious lackey—the man who'd stood by, recording his torture—was being praised as a hero? As Thaddeus led Brett away, Donovan exploded. "That can't be right! That man is a *sape*!"

"That officer," his father corrected, "has been embedded undercover in Sapience for nearly two years, at enormous and constant risk to his own life."

"You're telling me he was communicating with SecPac the whole time?" An odd, numb anger was descending over Donovan. He shook his head. It was all, unbelievably, starting to make sense. "You knew where I was all along. You didn't come for me because you wanted to get Brett inside the Warren. The Warren was the real prize." It was a good strategy. Tactically brilliant. His hands clenched into fists. "Then you stalled. You kept him in there, learning as much about the place as he could before the SecPac strike. You let them think—you let *me* think—that I was a lost cause."

"We're *stripes*," Jet cut in, sounding angry himself. "How could you think that?"

"You knew the whole time!" Donovan wished he could make his father react, that he could get that implacable face to move again, to twist like it had, just for a few seconds, earlier. "You knew about Mom being in Sapience!"

His father regarded him. Concern touched the outer edges of his stern expression. "You have been through an ordeal, son. I will ignore your disrespectful tone." He turned to Jet. "Vercingetorix, please see to it your erze mate is examined by a Nurse and debriefed by Commander Tate. Make sure he gets home safely afterward."

"Of course, sir," said Jet.

Donovan watched his father striding away, brow drawn in concentration in the midst of the continued swarm of activity, speaking to an aide that had magically materialized by his side. Wary crowds of curious onlookers had gathered across the street beyond the bright green SecPac warning tape cordoning off the building. Another stealthcopter was landing. Thad was yelling for everyone to get a move on *now now now what are you waiting for.*

The world wobbled alarmingly—Donovan squeezed his eyes shut hard, opened them, and it righted itself.

"Come on, Lesser D," Jet said. "Let's get you back where you belong."

17

The T15 climbed in a stomach-dropping straight ascent, then sped southwest. The lights of Rapid City shrank to pinpricks, then fell behind. In the cabin, there was only the background hum of the nearly silent engines. Donovan felt encased in some sort of mute bubble. His erze mates—Jet, Vic, and Thad—stared at him in undisguised concern.

"We'll drop you off at the Towers," Thad said. "Get you checked out."

Donovan shook his head. "I'm fine. We should join up with everyone else and help."

His friends exchanged skeptical glances; they'd seen his near meltdown back there, how he'd jumped his best friend and had to be wrestled to the ground. They were wondering if the time spent in enemy captivity hadn't knocked his screws completely loose. Was he still fit for duty? Still one of them, still in erze? "I'm not squishy-brained," Donovan insisted. An exo who lost control, of his mind, or his armor, was squishy-brained. "I've seen the Warren, I can help. I'm not leaving."

His immovability seemed to mollify them. His soldierly instincts were still intact. He seemed lucid enough. An exo belonged with his erze; he was compelled by its needs more than his own. The best thing his friends could do for him was to get him back among his fellow stripes.

Thaddeus looked down at the floor of the stealthcopter. When he raised his eyes, he said quietly, "It's good to have you back, Donovan."

Jet's face lost its composure. He turned to climb into the cockpit. Donovan heard him giving directions to the pilot.

Vic looked in Jet's direction, then back at Donovan. "He took it really hard," she said, her voice lowered. "When Thad and I got there that night . . . he was . . . well, I've never seen anyone wrecked like that. We went searching for you, kicking in doors. He could barely move after taking all those bullets, but he wouldn't give up. He broke every single one of that squishy's fingers trying to find out where they'd taken you. Soldier Werth himself finally had to get on the line to order us back in."

Donovan hadn't spared a lot of thought to how Jet would have suffered. If their positions had been reversed, if Jet had been the one captured by sapes . . . Donovan's chest contracted violently. Soldiers-in-erze could be stoic about being injured or killed, but being taken alive, or *worse*, having one's best friend taken alive . . . that was a different matter.

"How's your head?" he asked Vic, wanting to change the subject.

She touched her temple. Vic had heavy-lashed hazel eyes, a full mouth a guy couldn't help staring at, and short hair so colorless that the line of her exocel nodes showed through. Her armor bulged in a goose egg lump on one side of her forehead. "The bullet grazed me," she said. "A few inches over, and . . ." She made a face. Exos survived shots to the head half of the time, but the results were not pretty.

The slow drive from the hidden bunker in the Black Hills to Rapid City had taken hours in Kevin's van; it took less than thirty minutes for a T15 to reverse the journey. In the dark, the thickly forested hillsides rolled beneath them. Donovan gripped one of the metal handholds as the stealthcopter banked and circled. He peered down, barely able to make out anything more than the craggy landscape, until the T15's landing lights came on, illuminating a hole in the hillside: the entrance to the Warren. It must have been the same one Donovan had come out of earlier in the evening, but it was unrecognizable. The steel doors were blown off; smoke issued in occasional thin clouds from the tunnels within. Boulders and broken trees lay scattered nearby. Around the gaping black breach, the perimeter of a large space was guarded by SecPac assault scramblers. The stealthcopter maneuvered in for a tight landing in a demolished clearing next to two other T15s.

Thad and Vic jumped out; Jet and Donovan followed. As soon as they did, someone yelled, "REYES!"

"WHICH ONE?" someone else yelled.

"Which do you think?!"

People came running. The floodlights from several of the scramblers turned on, bathing the torn hillside in greenish light. Donovan stopped, stunned speechless by the sudden appearance of so many familiar faces. This was the most SecPac officers he'd seen in one place since graduation. At the sight of him, they broke into cheering and applause. Soldiers were an expressive lot; they swarmed Donovan with hugs, clapped him on the back, shook both his hands. Jet was mobbed too; he raised his arms triumphantly over his head. "I told you we'd get him back! Stripes never give up on their own!"

More cheering. "REYES!" The chant was picked up. "REY-ES! REY-ES!" Donovan grinned weakly. The joyful welcome of his erze mates blotted out the lingering sense of being tainted by everything crazy that had happened to him. It felt desperately good to be back with his own people, among those who cared about him. There was an essential rightness to being in erze. Still, the sound of his name being chanted over and over made him feel a little strange. It didn't seem like it should be for him; he hadn't done anything. It sounded like a spontaneous cooperationist rally for his father.

The noisy crowd parted for Commander Tate. "Cut the damn lights!" she shouted. "There are sapes crawling these woods like lice." Tate stopped in front of Donovan. She was the tallest woman Donovan knew, dark-skinned and ridiculously energetic, with the hypertoned build of a fanatical mountain climber and a voice strong enough to carry over a crowd of men. "Officer Reyes." She extended her hand. "It is awfully good to see you."

"Thank you, ma'am," Donovan said, shaking it.

A sudden blast of machine gun fire erupted from somewhere to the east. People scrambled for cover, grabbing weapons and returning fire. Tate stood unmoved. "Highest Erze almighty, I *said* cut those lights!" The lights went out, plunging the forest back into darkness. Tate said to Donovan, over the tumult, "Check in with Nurse Therrid in the medical tent. Then report inside. We could use your help. Lowell, Mathews—you as well." Tate stalked back toward the hole in the hillside. "And, Reyes—find a uniform! Those sape clothes look terrible on you."

Unsure of where the medical tent was, Donovan started walking, but at the boom of a nearby exploding grenade, he and Jet ducked behind the lowered body of one of the scramblers, next to Thad and Vic and a small group of other stripes.

"Leon," Donovan exclaimed.

"What's going on here, Hsu?" Thad asked.

Leon dropped back down from his perch on one of the scrambler's six legs, lowering his nighttime field glasses. "A bunch of sapes up on that ridge just won't give up. They have at least a couple machine gun nests and some stolen pulse cannons that will tear your armor *up*." To prove his point, he showed off his left bicep, bulging with damaged armor. The distinctive smell of burned panotin made Donovan wince.

"Squishy sons of bitches." Thaddeus studied the ridge like a wolf scanning a herd of sheep. "Let's get some bees in the air."

"On it." Vic climbed into the scrambler's control pod and swiveled it around.

Leon reached for his ever-present sketchbook. "I have something for you." He lovingly extracted a page he had removed from the book and placed inside a protective plastic sleeve. He handed it to Donovan, then thoughtfully turned on a penlight and shone it over Donovan's shoulder so he could see. It was a drawing of a nude she-demon cupping her breasts. "Leon," Donovan said, feeling oddly touched, "this is your best drawing yet. I don't know what to say."

"I worked on it the whole time you were missing," Leon said somberly. "When I finished it this morning I knew we'd get you back, 'cause you were meant to have it."

"Here we go," shouted Vic. Twin streams of heat-seeking micro-drones spat from the scrambler's undercarriage and swarmed across the terrain like a plague of red-lighted insects. Leon jumped back up with his field glasses and called out coordinates as the red lights coalesced on the ridge in a row of clear targets. Pulse rifles whined and field artillery barked to life. The eastern ridge lit up in a series of impressive explosions.

A brief cheer went up. Jet lowered his E201, wiped the night scope free of dust, and glared up at the ridge with a satisfied look of deeply personal vindictiveness. "That's what you sapes get for taking one of ours."

A strange sense of unreality was coming over Donovan. An hour ago, he'd been trying to save rebels from his own erze mates. Now he was standing on the other side, warm with camaraderie, his heart jumping in triumph as the enemy was blasted to smithereens. The soldier in him twitched with the compulsion to get his hands on the nearest weapon and help his friends; some other, confused part wanted to escape, to get away from all of it.

He found the medical tent easily enough; it was right by the Warren entrance and had Nurse erze markings on its quick-assemble frame. Inside, five injured exos were sitting or lying on small folding beds. The nurse-in-erze, a calm, older man named Sanjay, took a quick look at Donovan, decided he wasn't in critical condition, and instructed him to wait. Jet waited with him, shifting impatiently but apparently unwilling to leave him on his own.

"How's your back?" Donovan asked him. "After, you know."

"I had three cracked ribs and a ruptured spleen. It wasn't so bad, but I was stuck lying in a therapy tank in the Towers for a couple of days." Jet's voice fell. "Just about went out of my mind."

Donovan started to grin; he couldn't imagine Jet would be any good at lying still.

Jet wasn't smiling, though. He was uncharacteristically quiet, his arms stiff by his sides. "I had no idea if you were alive. Or what they were doing to you. I'd seen those videos . . ."

"Jet," Donovan said quickly. "I'm okay."

Slowly, Jet nodded. "Yeah." Then he looked at Donovan and his mouth curved in a smile that was more like himself. "You are so screwed, man. That is the last time I ever leave you alone with a girl."

Donovan laughed uncomfortably.

"You think I'm joking," Jet said. "Vic came to visit me, *three times*, while I was out of commission, and I was so worried I couldn't even enjoy it. What good is being shot up if you can't enjoy female sympathy?"

"Three times, eh?" Donovan said.

"D? Jet? That you?" The voice calling them was familiar.

"Cass?" Donovan made his way over to the cot at the other end of the tent. Cassidy reached out a hand and Donovan squeezed it between his own. Jet came up on the other side and took her other hand.

"Are you two ever a handsome sight for painkiller-addled eyes," Cass said, a wide, slightly loopy smile lighting up her face. "You made it back to us. I knew you would."

"Oath and erze, Cass," was all Donovan could say. "Your shoulder."

"Does it look bad?" she asked, nose scrunching with worry.

Donovan hesitated. Cassidy's exocel was ripped to ribbons down to the muscle under the skin. The panotin looked dark, slick with blood and bits of hanging flesh. It crawled in a creepy way, feebly trying to knit the flayed sections back together. "It could be worse," he said, trying to sound upbeat.

Cassidy turned her head to Jet instead.

"It looks like you went through a meat grinder," he told her.

190

Cass sighed in resignation. "TGINS."

"TGINS," Jet agreed. Thank Goodness I'm Not Squishy.

"Grenade explosion," Cass explained. "I'm being evacked. I'll be in a tank for weeks." She looked crushed. "It was insane what we found in there. Miles of War Era tunnels, filled with supplies and weapons and erze knows what else. We killed dozens of squishies. Captured dozens more. Fighting room to room the whole way." They paused at the sound of more machine gun fire and a distant mortar explosion outside.

Donovan swallowed a lump of shame. He was the one they'd all been worried about, but what he'd suffered suddenly seemed to pale next to the injured soldiers who'd been fighting for hours. "Why didn't they just blow the place up?"

"Command wanted all the data we could get our hands on—computers, files, prisoners." Her grip on his hand tightened. "And they couldn't blast the cave without knowing for sure you were out of it."

"Donovan!" A loud trilling exclamation preceded Nurse Therrid, who came up to them, trailing his translation machine and his nurse-in-erze. While Sanjay broke open packs of panotin replenishment gel for Cassidy's wounds, Therrid drew Donovan aside to another bed. His fins fanned wide in exuberant greeting, then folded in concern. "Thank erze you're safe. It makes me ill to think of losing exos I've known since they were Hardened." The translation machine started to repeat him in the voice of a young man, but Therrid smacked it off so they could converse without it.

Years had passed since those childhood zhree-human school encounters; Donovan saw Therrid far less often now. They'd grown apart, of course, separated inevitably by the status of their species and the work of different erze, but he still liked Therrid a lot. All the early exposure to humans must have had a formative effect on the Nurse; he now specialized in treating exo soldiers-in-erze. A third-generation colonist, Therrid understood several human languages fluently and garnered fin-flicking disapproval from some of the older zhree for his overly familiar manner toward natives.

"I'm all right, zun Therrid," Donovan reassured him.

"Let me be the judge of that, hatchling." Therrid would probably continue to call him a hatchling until he was fifty, Donovan suspected. He had Donovan undress, then took his temperature, looked in his eyes and mouth, examined his cerebrospinal nodes, and had him armor up and down several times. He made Donovan lie down and maneuvered a portable scanning array over him. "You have a bruised lung, and two of your ribs are fractured, though stabilized and healing. You're showing symptoms of panotin depletion, elevated stress, tissue trauma, and malnutrition." Therrid strummed a sighing low note. "It sounds bad, but it's nothing that enough rest and proper nutrition won't fix. You're lucky you're young and have an eighth-generation exocel. I'm clearing you for reduced duty but scheduling you for three therapy tank treatments, five days apart."

Therrid tapped out instructions on a computing disc and passed it to Sanjay. The Nurse's opaque yellow eyes closed and opened sequentially, shifting his focus back as Donovan sat up. "Donovan, listen carefully. You may suffer effects from your ordeal that aren't apparent yet. The stress of being separated from one's erze affects exos just as it does zhree. You were only gone for twelve days, but if you notice odd behavior or strong feelings of anxiety or depression, you must let me and your superiors know. Distrust, hostility, or a sense of isolation from one's erze could be signs of mental trauma."

Of going squishy-brained. Donovan stifled a grimace. "Yes, zun."

Jet had left during the exam and returned with a slightly-too-large spare uniform jacket. The Nurse cocked a fin in his direction. "I would think, though, that having Vercingetorix here as an erze mate would be traumatizing enough as it is."

Jet gave a slow shake of his head, the corner of his mouth hooking up. "Don't try being funny around humans, zun Therrid. The translator doesn't accurately capture your sarcasm."

"Thank the Highest State you've recovered, Vercingetorix. You're an insufferable patient even by human standards." The Nurse turned back and clasped his pincers tightly to Donovan's hand. "Go in erze."

Donovan took the uniform jacket from Jet and shrugged it on as they exited the tent. Outside, the sky had barely begun to lighten over the smoking eastern ridge. A team of scouts, Vic and Leon included, had begun to climb toward it on foot. Other officers were guarding the perimeter, but most were busy taking the Warren apart. Soldiers-in-erze emerged from the wrecked entryway carrying crates, weapons, boxes of storage discs, computers . . . and bodies, many bodies, wrapped in black bags. Everything was being loaded into T15s, which were now arriving and departing with regularity. A couple of Soldiers stood out among the humans, one of them walking the perimeter, the other speaking into a comm unit to coordinate scanner plane sweeps of the area. The sounds of battle had fallen mostly silent; any

Sapience rebels still alive and at large had by now probably fled deep into the wilderness.

Donovan faced the open tunnel into the hillside. The first time he'd entered it, he'd believed he wouldn't come out. Less than twelve hours ago, he'd walked out, eager never to see it again. He didn't really want to go back inside. Surely Commander Tate and his fellow officers would understand if he didn't want to revisit the scene.

"Hey," Jet said. "You all right?"

"Yeah." Donovan steeled himself; he wasn't going to beg out, not now, not in front of everyone. He straightened his borrowed uniform. *You're a stripe, dammit.* He went back into the Warren.

18

The Warren was a scene of carnage. Bullet holes, burn marks, and blood splatters marred the walls. Stone and metal rubble littered the floors and entryways. The clogged air smelled of dust, gunpowder, and burnt explosives. Donovan and Jet stepped over the debris, following the tunnel into the wide cavern Donovan had walked through yesterday and where days before he'd been pelted with rocks and forced to his knees in front of Saul.

Donovan's eyes drifted to the long line of bagged bodies against the wall. He wondered if Saul was among them. It was easy to imagine him stoically wading through battle, bellowing orders until the end. Most of the other rebels—paranoid Javid, white-haired Kathy, and Tom with his LIVE FREE knuckles—they were probably all dead too. All these tunnels, all those heavily armed insurgents . . . Like Cass had said, the firefight that had raged in here had been terrible: bullets spraying against limestone and metal catwalks, bodies sprawling across passageways, all the noise of enclosed gunfire and screaming.

Jet stopped someone and asked where the Commander was. They found her in a room just off the main cavern, one that had not been among the few Donovan had seen during his captivity. She was sitting with her elbows on a small table, chin propped on one set of knuckles, listening with a faint, attentive frown as Thaddeus give her the account of the rescue operation in Rapid

City. Under the harsh yellow light of a portable lamp, Tate looked different. Donovan had never been able to tell how old the Commander was; exos aged slowly, but the job had no doubt eaten away at some of that advantage. The tight black curls of the Commander's hair had gone a touch gray, and sometimes her hands trembled from a neurological disorder common to exos with fifth- and sixth-generation exocels.

"Reyes. Mathews." She noticed them standing, armor down, in the doorway and motioned them in. "The Nurse cleared you for duty?" she asked Donovan.

"Yes, ma'am."

"Good. We need everyone we can get. We've got the Risk Area more or less secure now, but it means there's barely a skeleton crew back in the Ring Belt patrolling the sympathizer-heavy neighborhoods. We're already down to calling in non-Hardened reservists." She pulled a screen toward her and dug thin wire-framed reading glasses from her pocket. "Things could get worse. We're already getting reports of hot spots in Rounds Four, Eight, and Eleven. There was a bombing in Rio just an hour ago."

That was to be expected; a SecPac crackdown in one part of the world usually incited terrorist cells in other parts of the world to retaliate with attacks and bombings. "Close the door," the Commander said. When it was shut, and they were seated on over-turned crates around the table, she said, "You may have noticed a few Soldiers roaming about. They're here to observe and provide logistical support, primarily. Don't fool yourselves, though; with the new High Speaker due to land tomorrow, you can be sure everything is under zhree scrutiny. There are some discussions I'd rather keep among exos." She turned to Donovan. "I know you've been through a rough time. But tell us everything that happened, in as much detail as you can."

Donovan swallowed, then nodded. He started with the firefight at Corrigan's house. "I was careless," he admitted. He told them about chasing Anya out the back door, Kevin and Brett knocking him out, taking him captive, torturing him. "They set up a recorder. One of the sapes, he makes those videos . . ."

Jet's expression turned dark. "Sick animals," he said under his breath.

"Kevin Warde." Commander Tate said it like a curse. She turned to Thaddeus. "Any word on the manhunt?"

"Every patrol team in Rapid City is searching for him, but like before, he's slipped underground like a rat," Thaddeus said. "His SecPac file is a mile long, but his list of sympathizer friends is even longer."

Donovan shifted uneasily. Kevin deserved to be hunted down and atomized, but the fact that he was so good at eluding death and capture meant Anya had a better chance of escaping, and for that, Donovan was weirdly grateful.

Tate scowled and turned back to Donovan. "Go on, Reyes."

Donovan continued recounting what he had been through. As he did, the questions became more specific, more interrogative. He grew nervous. Would they think he'd done something wrong? Been negligent in some way?

"Did 'Max' provide proof she was your biological mother?" Tate asked.

"Um, no . . ."

"When was the last time you saw her prior to these events?"

"When I was five. Before I was Hardened."

"But you still recognized her?"

"Yes."

Tate raised her eyes from her screen. Her gaze was not unsympathetic, but it bored into Donovan a little too long for comfort, as if she were trying to solve an equation and he was part of the answer. "It must have been very strange to meet her in a Sapience camp."

He squirmed a little under his commander's scrutiny. "It was. I was shocked. Confused." A little quietly, "I still am."

"Did you get the impression she still felt attached to you? Did she speak to you at length?"

A tightness was gathering in Donovan's chest. His mother was in a SecPac detention center by now. "Yes."

"Reyes, this is important." Tate leaned forward. "We met with fierce resistance when we attacked the Warren. The insurgents had enough time to destroy some of their files, in fact, many stayed to wipe out as much as they could. We think Sapience has plans for a major attack of some sort, on or around Peace Day, but we haven't found any concrete evidence, and the lower-level operatives we've interrogated are all in the dark." She pulled off her glasses and tapped them on the table; she did this when she expected answers. "Did 'Max' tell you anything you think might be important? Did she ever reveal anything, intentionally or unintentionally, or ever hint at what Sapience might be planning to do?"

Donovan tried to think back on the conversations he'd had with his mother. He could recall them in general, especially how he felt during them—awkward mostly—but had she ever said anything important, strategically? He didn't think so. If she had, he'd missed it; he'd been too weirded out by the whole situation, deliberately avoiding any topics involving Sapience instead of trying to glean useful military intelligence. "I'm sorry, ma'am," he said. "She didn't tell me anything about their plans."

After a moment, Tate nodded as if she hadn't expected any different but was disappointed nonetheless.

"Do you remember the other terrorists you met in the bunker?" Thad asked, shifting to other, more straightforward questions. "Kathy and Javid—what were their last names?" The queries continued. What types of weapons had Donovan observed the insurgents using, and how many did they have? Did he know anything more about Widget and the location of the cell they were planning to transport him to? Had Kevin mentioned the identities of any other exos he'd tortured and killed? Donovan's palms were sweating now. He wanted to help, to be as thorough as possible, but after the last question, he already felt as if he'd failed in some way. There were some things he plain didn't remember, and some he didn't know. And he didn't want to reveal too much about Anya. If he told them about her family being part of the algae farm standoff, SecPac might be able to locate her through her relatives.

Thad slid a screen in front of Donovan. "These are photos of the insurgents who were killed in the strike last night. Can you identify any of them as Saul Strong Winter?"

Donovan scrolled through the images. The faces of dozens of corpses flicked by, bluish-white and clinical. Some of them you could pretend were just sleeping, but others appeared to be frozen in the moment of anguish before they died, eyes and mouths still open. The photos had been taken on site with a bright flash so the morbid images looked washed out, unpleasantly stark. A lot of the faces had blood on them, some had head wounds, and a few were particularly gruesome—half a jaw blown off or a chunk of the skull exposed. Donovan found Tom, then two other men he recognized but whose names he did not know, their faces intact but so obviously dead. He did not find Saul.

"How about these prisoners?" Thad said, pulling up another set of photographs. "Recognize any of them?"

Donovan pointed out Kathy, looking haggard and hopeless, handcuffed and standing against a blank wall, just one of several defeated terrorists bound for detention centers, trial, and then prison or execution. An odd mixture of disappointment and surprisingly strong relief washed over him as he reached the last photograph. "I don't see Saul," Donovan said. Tate sat back, nostrils flaring in a frustrated sigh. Clearly, she'd been hoping that the senior Sapience commander would be among the dead or captured. Part of Donovan wanted to flip through the photographs a second time, to make sure he hadn't missed anything. The other part was inordinately glad he hadn't come across Saul's face, staring out at him with lifeless eyes, a cigarette still clamped between blue lips.

"We're still collecting bodies and searching the forest," Thad said. "We might find him yet."

Commander Tate got up and paced to the back of the small room. Donovan hadn't realized it at first, but now he suspected this room must have been Saul's. Hanging on the wall was a frayed blanket embroidered with an eagle inside a star-shaped design. Donovan studied the red-and-black design for a minute, trying to figure out why it seemed familiar, before he remembered that he'd seen it as a bumper sticker on Reed and Dixon's truck.

"The eagle is a symbol of freedom," Tate said. She cast a critical eye around the small room as if it might give her some clue as to the whereabouts of its former occupant. Besides the blanket, the space was spartan, a fugitive's hole revealing little of the man. Tate crossed her arms as she turned back to the wall. She snorted softly. "The insurgents are fooling themselves. No zhree has ever enslaved or oppressed humans the way humans have enslaved and oppressed one another. Can you imagine a world with Sapience in charge? It would be a return to tyranny, not an overthrow of it."

Thaddeus offered Donovan a half-full canteen of water, which he took gratefully.

"This Dr. Nakada," Tate said without turning around. "You said his goal is to develop a weapon for Sapience?"

Donovan brought his focus back again. "He didn't seem confident it would happen as soon as Kevin wanted, but yeah, that's what he's after." He described the lab, the monkeys, the spray bottle Nakada had thrust in his face. "The stuff he used on me only worked for a few seconds, but it dropped my exocel. There wasn't any warning. My armor just . . ." He trailed off. No one pushed him to continue; the other three exos understood. They were wincing in sympathy, as if he'd just admitted to pissing himself under torture.

"A weapon that can disable exocels," Tate mused. "In the hands of terrorists."

The room fell uncomfortably silent as everyone pondered the grim idea. Jet said, "There were whole governments trying to create something like that back in the War Era, and they didn't succeed. These are just guys in caves."

"Yeah, but there weren't exos back then," Thad said. "Maybe War Era people couldn't figure out zhree physiology, but if Sapience has scientists who can figure out a way to destroy exocels in humans, that would be—"

"Disastrous," Tate said with finality. "It wouldn't merely be a danger to the exo population but to all of humanity. It wouldn't matter if it worked on the zhree or not—the very possibility of hostile humans possessing the ability to disable exocels would be seen as a threat to the Commonwealth." In the pensive silence that followed, the worst-case scenario played out in everyone's mind, and Donovan realized why Tate hadn't wanted any Soldiers to hear their conversation. If such a threat was real, and the zhree knew about it, they might take things back into their own hands, descending en masse to eliminate it by whatever means necessary. A new War Era. She turned around. "We have to find Nakada."

"If only we could find Warde, we'd find Nakada," said Thad.

"What about the girl they're traveling with?" asked Tate. "This Anya—any leads on her?"

"We're not sure who she is. Probably a runaway. The name isn't matching anything in the system." He called up another file on his screen. "Donovan, these are all the unmarked teenage girls in the Ring Belt who were flagged in SecPac's database as having some possible connection to Sapience. Do you see her here?"

Donovan wiped his palms surreptitiously on his thighs and took the screen again. He studied each photograph for a few seconds before moving on to the next one. Anya was the sixth girl. She was staring into the camera with a sullen expression, her mouth slightly open in a disdainful pout, as if she were impatient from waiting to be photographed. She looked to be fourteen or fifteen in the photo. Her cheeks and shoulders didn't look quite as sharp as they did now, and her hair, he was startled to see, was dyed black instead of auburn. But it was her.

He flipped to the next photo without a word. There were five more girls. Donovan handed the screen back to Thad and shook his head. "Well, it was worth a shot," Thad said.

Donovan's heart started to pound. He felt an almost unbearable compulsion to take the screen back, to undo what he'd just done. *Let me take a look at that again, maybe I missed something.* He couldn't do that; how was he going to explain why he'd lied on the first pass? Because that's what he'd just done: lied to his superior officers, to fellow exos of his own erze. People who were in erze did not do that. For a moment, he felt immobilized by an inner war so fierce he was shocked it didn't spill onto his face. But Tate was checking the time, and Thad was reviewing his notes. By the time they turned back, Donovan had forced his expression into one of humble fatigue. "I'm sorry I couldn't do better. It's hard to remember everything."

"That's understandable. You were under a lot of stress." Tate stood up; they did as well. "Take it easy today. Go see your father. And for the love of all erze, keep a low profile and don't talk to the media." She stowed her glasses, then fixed Donovan with a long, steady gaze. "I need every stripe I have right now, but you have a troubling personal connection to this operation, Reyes. Will it compromise your ability to do your duty?"

Donovan stiffened. A rational part of him realized the question was justified—more than Tate even knew. *I let a dangerous scientist and a terrorist psychopath escape arrest. I attacked my partner. I just lied to protect a sape I kissed last night, and I want to know: How am I going to save my mom?* But the Commander's question felt like a slap. He was the son of the Prime Liaison and one of the highest-rated soldiers-in-erze from his graduating class; never had his fitness for duty ever been questioned.

He could feel Jet's eyes fixed on the side of his face like a laser beam. Donovan straightened to attention. "You can count on me, Commander."

Tate's face slackened very slightly in relief. "I'm glad to hear it. Go in erze, then."

Donovan followed Thad and Jet out of the room. "You wouldn't guess it, but after what we pulled off tonight? That's Tate in the best mood I've seen in a while," said Thad. He gestured around the cavern. The bagged bodies were gone, and though they could hear a lot of activity outside, the tunnels were now largely quiet and empty. "After we're done in here, we're going to collapse it all; the sapes won't be able to use it again."

They emerged from the Warren into hazy morning light. Donovan kept his eyes ahead, not returning any of the odd glances Jet kept sliding in his direction. Thad turned to Jet. "You know Vic likes you, right?"

Jet nearly tripped over a pile of rocks.

"The goofy flirting is cute, but you've got to make a real move."

"Is she . . . I mean, did she . . . what did she say?" Jet drew Thad aside urgently.

Donovan used their distraction to stop and lean against the nearest standing tree. He let out a shaky breath. What had he done? He'd told Commander Tate she could count on him to do his duty. If that were true, he ought to turn around and go back now, tell her everything that might help SecPac find Anya. Find Anya, and they'd find Kevin. Kill or capture Kevin, and take one of Sapience's most bloodthirsty terrorists off the streets. Save innocent lives.

He dropped his forehead to the tree trunk. He couldn't do that. Seeing Anya on the screen had only made him want to keep her safe, to prevent her from becoming another face in the other two sets of photos he'd seen. He didn't want to see the despairing mug shot of her in a prison uniform, and he certainly did not want to see her doll-like face bone-pale and splattered with gore. SecPac had killed and arrested so many Sapience members from the Warren, surely the escape of one girl—someone who wasn't an evil person, just a teenager with a sad history, a bad relationship, and a hankering to belong to something—wasn't a big deal. It wouldn't make a difference.

Donovan hurried to catch up with his erze mates.

19

Donovan was the first soldier-in-erze cleared to return to the Round after the injured exos had been evacuated and all the prisoners, captured evidence, and body bags were cleared out and transported from the Warren by stealthcopter. Even so, it was late afternoon by the time the T15 landed back at the airfield in Central Command, and early evening by the time he and Jet settled the skimmercar in front of Donovan's house. They'd both been without sleep for over thirty hours.

Donovan stared at the house, almost afraid to go in. Driving into his neighborhood, it seemed impossible to believe he'd ever been away, that everything that had happened to him had been real. The familiarity of the Round assaulted him: clean, curving boulevards, fluid metal architecture, zhree and humans passing one another casually on the streets. The sky was cloudless and the breeze mild today, as if even the weather were better here. His world—a world apart from the crowded, old human cities, and as different from the reality of Sapience as day was from night.

Now, though, staring out the skimmercar window, he felt as if he were looking at a house he didn't recognize. The Prime Liaison's state residence flew both the flag of West America and the icons of the Mur Erzen Commonwealth over a column-fronted entrance. It was a dignified, impressive building, but now it exuded a miserable aura that had been invisible to Donovan before. The hatred between his parents had grown out of this place. Like one of the cratered national military parks or preserved ghost cities that ensured the War Era was never forgotten, it seemed too awful and sad a place to enter.

There was no vehicle in the port. His father was not home.

Jet got out of the car and Donovan had no choice but to follow. He cleared them through the security system, led the way mechanically through the foyer into the living room, and collapsed onto the nearest sofa.

Jet went into the kitchen. He came back out with a bag of tortilla chips, a jar of salsa, and two bottles of "armor juice"—the ubiquitous orange-flavored, fizzy supplement drink that every Hardened person in the world ordered by the caseload. He set his findings on the coffee table. "There's never any food in your house."

"That's because no one actually lives here." His father was always working, eating his meals elsewhere, and Donovan hadn't been home much even before he'd been captured by terrorists. Donovan mustered himself off the sofa to raid his father's liquor cabinet. He poured two Hard-Ons—rum and armor juice on ice—and handed one to his friend.

"Cheers," Jet said. They clinked glasses. "Welcome home."

They sat in silence for a few minutes, passing the salsa jar back and forth, dipping chips straight into it, too exhausted from sleep deprivation and adrenaline fallout to turn thoughts into conversation. Finally, Donovan made himself speak. "About last night . . . I didn't mean to jump you. I just—"

"Forget it," said Jet. He drained the rest of his drink and sucked down two of the ice cubes, crunching them between his teeth. "I didn't know she was your mom." He shook his head. "That is really messed up."

Donovan nodded. "I'm not squishy-brained. I know I acted that way, but I'm not. I'm sorry."

"I said forget it. If I found out my mom had run off to become a terrorist, I'd probably go a little squishy-brained myself." Jet was no doubt trying to offer sympathy, but the comparison didn't really work. His mom was an exo like him, a high-ranking administrator-in-erze who oversaw low-orbit transport logistics and coached youth basketball in her spare time. She was about as likely to turn into a violent insurgent as Jet was.

Donovan was silent for a minute. "It blew my mind. I always hated my mom for leaving, you know? But secretly, I thought, maybe she had good reasons. My dad never told me what they were. He always knew, but he never told me."

Jet turned his glass in his hands. "You can't really blame him."

Donovan frowned. "What do you mean?"

"I'm not sure I'd want to know. I mean, I would, but I wouldn't. If someone so close to me was doing such awful things . . ." He looked at Donovan, then slumped back against the sofa and rubbed a hand tiredly over his face. "You were just a kid. I'm not saying what your dad did was right, I'm just saying you can see why he did it."

No, I can't. Donovan felt the muscles of his face tightening. It was the one thing that infuriated him about Jet sometimes—how his friend took his father's side. Best friends were supposed to agree with you that your parents were intolerable, but the Prime Liaison's halo of importance seemed to blind Jet to this one, obvious obligation. Maybe it was because Jet's own father was such an unassuming scholar-in-erze—a professor who taught Commonwealth history and ate the same type of breakfast cereal every day—that Jet sometimes said things like, "Your old man's got one of the hardest jobs in the world." Then, with a shrug, "He's probably doing his best."

Donovan didn't want to fight with Jet about this. Instead, he said quietly, "She's still my mom." When Jet didn't reply, he added, "I know what she is, I know she hates exos, but still." He leaned back and closed his eyes. "You know what's really screwy? She told me she'd meant to take me with her. I could've been an unmarked squishy. A hardcore sape, hiding out in those hills." He grimaced and opened his eyes, turning his head. "We could've been enemies."

"That *is* really screwy." Jet gave him a strange look. "Good thing it didn't happen."

The front door opened. Benjamin, one of the Prime Liaison's exo bodyguards, came in and took up a position to the side. Donovan's father walked in. His heavy steps rang off the polished hardwood floors as he crossed the foyer.

Jet got to his feet and stood to attention. Donovan shoved the bottle of rum behind a sofa cushion and followed suit. The Prime Liaison glanced at the two of them as he shrugged out of his heavy jacket and hung it up. "Vercingetorix," he said, "you will have to look more alert than that during the welcome ceremonies tomorrow. You ought to go home and get some rest."

Donovan blinked. He'd forgotten that the High Speaker of the Mur Erzen Commonwealth was scheduled to arrive tomorrow on his first visit to Earth.

"Yes, sir," Jet said, and headed for the door.

Donovan's father stopped Jet and clasped his hand in a long, firm grip. "Thank you for bringing him home."

"I always will, sir."

There were times, occasionally, when Donovan wondered if he and Jet had been switched at birth. Jet would have made an excellent Prime Liaison's son.

Damascus, his father's other bodyguard, showed Jet out, then he and Benjamin departed gracefully to check the grounds. Donovan's father came over to him, pulled the hidden rum bottle from behind the sofa cushions, and poured a splash for himself over Donovan's remaining ice cubes. He was still in the same suit he'd been in the night before, and two days' worth of stubble accentuated the grave hollows under his eyes. He said softly, "I told you to be careful."

A snort of disbelief escaped Donovan. He wanted to hug his father tight; he wanted to scream curses at him. "Is that all you have to say for yourself?"

His father's hand stilled in the act of raising the glass. The sudden arrested motion was like a held breath. Physically, there was nothing unusual about Dominick Reyes—he was of average height, average build, his face was careworn, and his voice was, if anything, softer than others. But he was the most intimidating man Donovan knew. A force of nature. As far as Donovan could tell, he rarely ever failed to get his way. He regarded his son with the expression of a lion about to turn on its cub. "Say what you mean, Soldier."

"You sent Mom away. You never told me why, you never told me she was a Sapience operative. You let me believe she abandoned us."

"She did abandon us. She chose to embrace extremism and violence." His father took a generous swallow from the glass, then set it down on the table with a bang. "I gave her several chances, before and after she left, to change her ways. I offered her immunity and the chance to be with you again if she renounced her ties to Sapience and co-operated with SecPac to apprehend terrorists. She refused. She chose the Sapience cause over us, again and again."

His father's words pushed against fresh splinters. Donovan quailed from them, then shook his head; the point wasn't that his mother had chosen the cause over him—he already knew that. "From the day I was marked, you knew I might meet her as an enemy."

"You wanted to be a soldier-in-erze. I had hoped you would go into the civil service, but you wished for something different." Every erze offered marks to the cohort of twelve-year-old exos at the same time, with one exception: the Soldier erze always had first pick. A chosen exo had to decide whether to be a stripe before any other erze could offer. Donovan's father said, "You were proud of your aptitude ratings and Soldier Werth's notice. You wanted to be in the same erze as your friend. I never influenced your decision."

"You didn't tell me I'd be fighting against my own mom!" Donovan's hands clenched the air. "Why didn't you just tell me?"

"Would you have given up a future in SecPac?" When Donovan failed to answer, his father said, "I thought it was better for you to believe your mother to be merely irresponsible rather than evil."

Donovan ground a fist helplessly into the back of the sofa. "She doesn't believe in cooperation, but she's not *evil* . . ."

"She plans bombings, assassinations, and sabotage. She publishes propaganda encouraging people to kill anyone who is marked. Her goal is war, against a powerful and benevolent race, a war that would likely result in the loss of countless lives and possibly the extinction of our species. Is that not evil?"

Donovan couldn't answer. He didn't know how.

"You've studied history in school," his father continued. "The War Era cost humanity over a *billion* lives. For what? Was life on Earth any better before the Landing than it is now? What right do a few extremists have to tear down everything humans have gained from a hundred years of peaceful coexistence?" He gestured expansively. "Your home, your markings, your erze mates, your exocel—everything you value is thanks to the Accord—which your mother and her fellow terrorists wish to destroy!"

"Why are you lecturing me?" Donovan shouted. "I'm a stripe! I swear on the Accord! But it's not that simple; not everyone in Sapience is the same. Maybe the group does bad things, but each individual—"

"Is personally responsible," his father finished. "You want to know the truth. Very well. 'Max' was questioned this afternoon. She confessed to being involved in last year's Denver bombings—the ones that killed thirty-two government workers, including two exos, and five innocent bystanders. She helped to plan the assassination of Dr. Stuckart, the leading scientist-in-erze studying light-plus transfer point stability—you might recall that his entire research team was murdered." His father held up the empty bottle of armor juice. "There was also the narrowly averted plot to poison half a dozen algae farms, along with factories producing dietary supplements for exos. Should I go on?"

"No," Donovan said miserably.

His father pinned him with a fearfully intense gaze. "She took you to a secret Sapience laboratory. Why?"

"She . . . she wanted to know if an exocel could be removed."

"And you were going to let her try?"

"No!" Donovan cringed. "Father, no. *God*. I'm not suicidal."

The Prime Liaison's face relaxed, very slightly. He placed the bottle back on the table. "She told me once that she would rather see you dead than armored. The entire time you were in Sapience hands, I was afraid she would find you and take advantage of your vulnerability to twist your thoughts, to convince you of things that aren't true."

Donovan sat down hard.

His father gave him a long look, then sighed. "Tell me," he said, "what do exos represent that Sapience fears so much?"

Donovan rolled his head back and groaned at the rhetorical questioning. "Everything they can't stand: cooperationism, zhree technology, the government—"

"*Progress*, Donovan." His father began to pace in front of the coffee table. "The zhree have advantages over us: They live longer, they cooperate better, they're hardier, more adaptable. The erze are more stable than human institutions, and exocels protect against radiation and harsh conditions on new planets. The zhree built a far-flung, space-faring empire. At the time of the Landing, we humans had never gone past the *Moon*." The Prime Liaison stopped pacing and dropped the entire weight of his gaze on his son. "Exos have the same advantages as the zhree. If we humans are to control our own destiny, it won't be through war with the zhree but by rising to their level. By reaching the stars ourselves. You are the future of humanity. That's what the reactionaries fear."

"Did you have me Hardened to get back at Mom? To prove you'd won so she'd never come back?"

A change came swiftly over his father's face. It was a subtle but menacing shift, like a storm cloud appearing in the sky. "I had you Hardened to give you a *future*." Ugly lines deepened between the Prime Liaison's nose and the corners of his mouth. His next words were spoken barely above a whisper, but they were as clear and cutting as fractured glass. "You insult me, Donovan."

They glared at each other for a long, silent minute. To his shame, Donovan looked away first. He heard his father turn and begin to ascend the stairs, one loud step at a time.

Donovan got to his feet and followed his father to the foot of the staircase. "What will happen to Mom?"

His father kept walking. "That is for the courts to decide."

"She'll be convicted of treason and terrorism. They'll send her to the atomizer."

"It is out of my hands."

Something inside Donovan snapped. "You're the Prime Liaison!" His father's bodyguards outside of the house could probably hear him shouting, but he didn't care. "She's still my *mom*. She used to be your wife. Doesn't that mean anything?" He gripped the banister and ran up the steps after his father. "You could keep her from getting the death penalty. You have the power to do that, I know you do. You have the influence to get the courts to make an exception."

His father turned slowly. "Haven't I taught you anything? Power and responsibility go hand in hand. When I go to the Towers, it is as the emissary of humankind for this entire country. It would be wrong of me to abuse that position." He scowled down at Donovan. "Once, only once, have I used my influence to make an exception. I let a criminal escape prosecution, and then I sealed her file. It was a mistake, made in a moment of emotional weakness. Others paid the price. I won't do it again."

"Please, Father." Donovan cringed at the note of pleading creeping into his voice, but he plowed on. "There'll be nothing left of her. It'll be a public spectacle."

His father was terse. "The public event is for us humans, you know that."

Donovan clenched his jaw so hard he could feel it in his eye sockets. You could kill a non-Hardened human in all sorts of ways, but atomization was the only instant, painless way to kill a creature with an impermeable exocel, and thus the only legal form of capital punishment in the Commonwealth. During one heavy period of insurgency many decades ago, rumors began flying that certain executed criminal leaders were not dead after all, because no bodies had been produced by the government. So Congress had petitioned the zhree to allow for public executions. Donovan used to be able to see the excellent logic of it—for those who glorified martyrdom, it was thoroughly unsatisfying to wink out of existence without fanfare. No suffering. No angry mob and weeping relatives carrying your coffin through the streets. Simply . . . gone. As a soldier-in-erze, he agreed heartily with the practice. Right now, it seemed diabolical.

"People will understand if you intervene," Donovan insisted, desperation climbing into his voice now. Did his father have to be so principled and stone-hearted about *everything*? "You can't expect me to watch her being led out and *vaporized*! Even you can't be that cruel."

"Is that what you think my motive is? Cruelty?" His father descended until he stood one step above Donovan. The storm cloud that had been brooding on his face darkened to true anger, the corners of his eyes tightening, as they had last night, when staring at the ex-wife he hadn't seen in a dozen years. "You are a Hardened and sworn soldier-in-erze. An officer of the Global Security and Pacification Forces. I realize that you have a romanticized image of the mother you remember as a small child, but you, of all people, know the importance of upholding the law!" He paused, his shoulders heaving, and Donovan, his stomach in tight knots, fought the instinctive urge to shrink from the weight of his father's authority. The Prime Liaison's voice lowered. "This is precisely why I did *not* tell you the truth earlier. You don't have the mental fortitude that the markings on your hands suggest. Are you no longer in erze? What did that woman tell you in the days you were with her?"

"She said you're a ruthless, self-serving egomaniac," Donovan said. "And she's right."

His father's hand swung up and arced down to strike him hard across the face.

Donovan flinched, waiting for the blow to land. It didn't. His father's hand hung, trembling and suspended, over Donovan's turned face, as if arrested by some unseen force. Dominick Reyes's mouth twisted in pained disbelief and shame. Only then did Donovan realize he'd armored fully—harder than necessary, harder than mere reflex. The impact would have broken and bloodied his father's hand.

His father had never struck him before.

Even so, you didn't raise battle armor to your parents. You just didn't.

For a second, both of them were stunned into immobility. Then, with what felt like wrenching effort, Donovan dropped his exocel completely. He drew every fiber of panotin back into himself and waited, bare-skinned, paralyzed between anger and shame, for his father to administer whatever punishment he was now justified in delivering.

The elder Reyes lowered his hand slowly, wrapping it around the banister, his knuckles white. "This is a trying time for us, Donovan." His voice was a monotone whisper. "Tomorrow the High Speaker will be here. Inspecting. Asking questions. I'm told he's not like his predecessors, not a supporter of the frontier colonies. It's vital that we present a unified front. You will be there to stand honor guard with your erze, and you will not allow your emotions to interfere with anything that happens this week. Is that clear?"

Donovan swallowed a bitter lump. "Yes, sir."

"You must trust me on this, son. It's important." His father climbed the rest of the steps without looking back again.

Donovan watched him go. Then he slunk back to the sofa and sat, staring out the window at the lit spires of the Towers.

20

When Donovan awoke on the sofa in the morning, it was to the sound of Jet buzzing the security system. When he opened the door, Jet took one look at him and said, "You had it out with him, didn't you?"

Donovan left the door open and headed up the stairs without answering. "I need a shower."

It was still dark outside, but his father was already gone, having taken the state skimmercar and his bodyguards with him. Donovan hadn't even heard him leave. Deep sleep had not erased any of Donovan's surreal emotional exhaustion. He felt as hollow as a drum. Partway through his shower, he realized he no longer had a five-minute water limit and stood under the blissfully hot spray for ten more. His mind drifted; he wondered where Anya was now, whether she was okay.

Jet had brought Donovan's dress uniform over from his locker in SecPac Central Command and left it in his room, along with a comm unit and sidearm to replace the ones that had been taken from Donovan when he'd been captured. Donovan shrugged on the starched fabric and stared at himself in the mirror as he fastened each of the small gold buttons. Cleaned up, freshly shaved, and in uniform, he still looked every bit the upstanding soldier-in-erze, the son of the Prime Liaison, a shining example of interspecies cooperation.

He went downstairs. Jet had turned on the morning news. They stood in the kitchen, munching buttered toast and watching Commander Tate hold a press conference. The Commander looked as if she hadn't slept in days; she had bags under her eyes as dark as bruises, but she could barely contain the gloat of triumph in her voice as she made the latest official SecPac statement about the Black Hills offensive. The updated figures were: sixty-three insurgents killed, thirty-nine captured, and twenty-five still suspected to be at large. She also emphasized that a strike team had safely recovered the Prime Liaison's son, killing two of his kidnappers (Reed had bled out in the stealthcopter), and capturing a third, the well-known Sapience propagandist leader known as "Max." "We have dealt a major blow to the enemy," the Commander declared.

"She's going to milk this big-time for Peace Day." Jet slurped noisily at an oversized mug of coffee.

The news shifted to show a series of politicians standing up in Congress to commend the swift, bold actions taken to combat the Sapience threat. Donovan turned off the screen. It was only going to get harder to watch. So far, no one had dug deeply into the identity of "Max." Once it got out that she was the former wife of the Prime Liaison, the resulting media frenzy would take on the veneer of a bad soap opera. And he would be a part of it.

"How are you doing?" Jet asked.

"I'm okay," Donovan said.

"You're lying. But you're faking it pretty well." Jet glanced at Donovan sideways. "Listen, I know your dad probably said you have to go to this thing. But it's just going to be a lot of standing around. If you're not feeling up to it, I'll cover for you. I'll say—"

"No," Donovan said. "You've saved my ass enough lately."

Jet set down his mug and fastened his own dress uniform. After a second, "You'd do the same for me."

Donovan attached the comm unit. He picked up the reissued sidearm and waited for it to calibrate to his exocellular body signature. "Like you said, it's mostly going to be standing around. How hard can that be? Anyway, I kind of want to see it. Historic event, right? How often do dignitaries from Kreet show up for a visit?"

Jet grunted. "Like any of the homeworld zhree care what happens all the way out here. The High Speaker will probably just walk around, waving his legs, while Administrator Seir and the rest of the zun trot out the dog and pony show for him. Then he'll get back on his ship and go home for another fifty years." Jet drained the rest of the coffee. "Step on my foot if I start to fall asleep today."

The calibration indicator on Donovan's weapon went on. He holstered it. "Let's go get this over with, then."

They walked out to the skimmercar. It was still early; the streets were quiet. The skimmercar hit the first major spoke road and took it all the way to the Towers. The sunrise haloed the looming spires in pale light, their faintly metallic sheen winding up and around the many arching causeways and twisting steeples. Thousands of zhree and humans worked inside, tens of thousands in the surrounding area. The Towers were truly glorious, unearthly and beautiful, and the sight of them made Donovan's breath catch. It felt good to be home.

Jet took hold of the skimmercar's manual controls and guided it through the western arch to the main landing field. Several SecPac vehicles were already lined up around the perimeter. Jet parked alongside them.

The circular landing pad was an excited, but orderly, swarm of activity. Zhree and humans of several different erze were rushing to and fro. Raised voices mingled with the frenzied music of shouting zhree and the intrusive babble of translation machines barely able to keep up with the demands of so many conversations. Donovan raised a hand to his eyes as he looked up into the broad morning sky. Not a ship in sight yet. "Come on," Jet said. "Honor guard is supposed to report to the center." They dodged through the crowd toward the easy-to-spot cluster of uniformed SecPac officers.

There were twelve of them, all tugging uncomfortably at their dress uniforms. At Donovan's appearance, there was a renewed round of back-clapping and smiles. "You're here!" Vic exclaimed. The lump on her head had gone down a bit. She bounced on the balls of her feet, hyper with exhaustion. "Nothing keeps you two away."

"Nothing keeps a good stripe down," Thad said, fist-bumping them.

"Nothing," Jet agreed distractedly, gazing at Vic like a painter enthralled by the colors of sunrise.

Others started to chime in, to ask Donovan questions, but Soldier Werth chose that moment to make an appearance. His gait knocked a distinctive triple-beat pattern on the tarmac as he approached, yelling in song and gesturing to Soldiers to take up formation. Light gleamed off his battle-armored body and limbs. He spun into the group of humans and stopped, hard amber eyes taking in all of them at once. They snapped to attention, armor down.

For some reason, Donovan thought of the video he'd seen in the Warren. Had he been alive at the time, Soldier Werth would have given those War Era humans nightmares. He had short, thick fins and larger-than-average eyes; long, powerful limbs and predatory-looking stripes. Despite his fearsome appearance and reputation for being obstinate and quick to judge, Soldier Werth was known to be good to his humans-in-erze. He treated them fairly and with respect. Earth was so far from the rest of the Mur fleet, Donovan's father had explained to him once, that Werth was constantly short on Soldiers and relied on human allies even more than the other zun.

Werth's fins flattened in a gesture akin to a scowl as he surveyed the group of SecPac officers. "Twelve? I requested twice this number from Commander Tate."

Thad stepped forward, hands clasped behind his back politely as he waited for the translation machine to finish repeating the Soldier's message. "Commander Tate sends her apologies, zun. A dozen exos is already more than SecPac can spare right now."

Soldier Werth hummed low—an irritated sigh. "The twelve of you will have to do. The High Speaker will be landing in a few minutes. Take a knee." The twelve of them bent to one knee so Werth stood over them. The Soldier tugged the translation machine close and spoke in a slow musical voice. "The zhree you will be seeing today are not like the ones you are used to. They are strangers to this planet. They may find you odd, ugly, or frightening. Remember, they are to be treated with the same respect as any erze master. You are paragons of your kind. You exemplify the mutually beneficial relationship between our species. Present yourselves well."

"Yes, zun," they chorused.

"Take your positions." As they stood back up, Soldier Werth reached out two of his limbs and clasped Donovan's hand between outstretched pincers, a distinctly human gesture many zhree had adopted. "Donovan. Every exo in our erze is valuable. I am relieved you were recovered unharmed." His alien gaze was inscrutable, but his fins dipped in a solemn nod.

"I am too, zun," Donovan said.

Soldier Werth motioned him back to his fellow officers and took off down the landing field. Werth epitomized the second-generation colonists—he didn't keep humans at a subservient distance the way some of the War Era old-timers still did, but he wasn't as informal with them as, say, Nurse Therrid. Five years ago, he'd scrutinized a room full of young exos and picked out Donovan, Jet, and a number of their classmates for his erze. "I chose your commander as well, when she was a hatchling your age," he'd explained at the reception following their marking ceremony. "I've seen so many exos over the years, I have an instinct for it. I know which ones can carry Soldier markings."

The extensive welcoming party—human and zhree—had just arranged itself into the proper semicircular formation when the High Speaker's ship appeared in the distant sky over the Towers like a sudden celestial miracle. Donovan missed the sight of it first coming into view; when the stir of exclamations made him look up, the vessel and its military escort of zhree fighters were streaking earthward, trailing thick white lines of vapor. People all over the Round and in the surrounding Ring Belt were no doubt stopping, staring, and pointing as the ships descended.

The roar of engines grew from a distant rumble to a wall of noise, drowning out all other sound. The cruiser ship, gleaming in the sunlight, threw an immense shadow across the field as it slowed its free fall and maneuvered to land. The air overhead vibrated madly, lifting the hairs on the back of Donovan's neck.

Slowly, carefully, the oblong vessel lowered itself to the ground. The trio of fighter craft, their spherical bodies rotating inside diamond-shaped wing frames, circled above everyone's heads before streaking up and away, the deafening sound of their departure fading into the sky.

Silence hung over the scene.

The assembled crowd riffled. Zhree fins fidgeted. Light strumming mumbles rose and fell. Seeing their erze masters nervous made the humans nervous too. They exchanged glances, shifting their weight. Donovan found himself tapping his fingers against his thigh. He fought the urge to loosen the tight collar of his dress uniform. He was so close to the ship, the lingering burning smell of its landing thrusters stung his nostrils. It was the most impressive spacecraft he had ever seen. None of the intrasystem vessels and low-orbit transports that usually went in and out of the landing fields compared. Donovan marveled at its size, the elegant curve of its hull, the unfamiliar patterning that he assumed designated it as the carrier of the High Speaker.

Donovan's gaze traveled back across the tarmac. A small procession of zhree was approaching the ship. Administrator Seir, Soldier Werth, Builder Dor, Scientist Laah, Merchant Hess, Nurse Thet, and so on. All the zun—the speakers—of each erze. Behind them walked one human: Prime Liaison Dominick Reyes.

Donovan's father towered over the zhree in front of him. On the shoulders of his dark suit he wore epaulets patterned with the same Administrator markings as his rough, tanned hands—Seir's markings. He walked, as usual, a little stiffly, but he did not seem nervous. He appeared as unconcerned as he had on the day of Donovan's Hardening. He leaned over slightly to hear something that Builder Dor was saying to him, nodding and smiling faintly at some shared observation. The lone human in a group of zhree . . . it was strange to see. It was as if the man was the alien, not the other way around.

A pang of confusing emotion went through Donovan. Fierce pride, or shame, he wasn't sure which.

The bottom of the High Speaker's ship opened and a platform descended. The High Speaker stepped off, onto the field. He was tall, standing chin height on an average human man. His elaborate body pattern was different from any that Donovan had ever seen, but he was clearly the zun of a very important erze. Flanking him were six Soldiers. They drew Donovan's eye at once. They were not *his* Soldiers—they were striped, of course, but the pattern was noticeably different from what Donovan saw on his master's body or the backs of his own hands. Which meant they did not belong to his erze, nor did they answer to Soldier Werth.

Beside him, Jet stiffened. Vic drew a quick breath. They found it disconcerting as well. For anyone growing up in Round Three, the zhree had represented such authority that it was easy to assume that Soldier Werth's erze was the only Soldier erze, that Builder Dor's erze encompassed all Builders, and so on. It was only later, in school, that Donovan learned that wasn't the case. The Mur Erzen Commonwealth encompassed numerous erze of every caste: many different Administrator erze, Scientist erze, Soldier erze, and so on, not only in other Rounds in other countries on Earth but on many planets other than Earth, all the way back to Kreet, the zhree homeworld. It boggled Donovan's mind to think that both the Round and the erze that governed his life, indeed his entire *planet*, were a small part of something so vast—the presence of the High Speaker and his foreign Soldiers were evidence of it.

Administrator Seir was, Donovan's father had told him, the most influential zhree Admininistrator on Earth; he stepped forward to greet the High Speaker, dropping his exocel respectfully so that the hull of his ring-patterned torso lay bare in the stark sunlight for a long beat. "High Speaker, welcome to Earth. Thank the Highest Erze that your journey was safe and comfortable. It is an honor to receive you on your first visit here to our humble and far-away colony."

"Administrator Seir, you've shrunken since the last time you were home. This planet's gravity and low oxygen must not be good for one's health." The High Speaker's voice was unusual. Accented. Donovan leaned in, straining to follow the conversation. There were no translation machines; most of the humans would not be able to understand what was being said.

"One grows accustomed to it, grand zun," said Seir.

Each of the other zhree greeted the High Speaker in turn, dropping their armor in obeisance. At last, Seir indicated Donovan's father. "High Speaker, this is Prime Liaison Dominick Reyes. He is the government representative for the native sentient species over the half of the continent controlled by Round Three. He is a trusted ally."

"On behalf of the government and people of West America, welcome to Earth, grand zun." Dominick Reyes had no exocel to drop, so he tilted forward in a shallow bow. Administrator Seir relayed the greeting to the High Speaker.

The High Speaker's fins made circles of wary curiosity. "What are they called again?"

"Humans, grand zun," Seir replied.

"Ah, yes. They caused a great deal of trouble at first, didn't they?"

"Our relations with the indigenous species have vastly improved since the settlement days, grand zun."

The High Speaker stretched up slightly to look at the Prime Liaison. "I do not recall this one from the history briefing I was given."

"No, grand zun. They do not live as long as we do. We have had three Prime Liaisons since your predecessor last visited." He waved a limb toward the other side of the field. "Let us go into the Towers to speak further. The oxygen is higher inside and will be more comfortable for you."

Seir led the High Speaker forward, and Soldier Werth gave the signal for the honor guard of exos to fall in. Donovan stepped sharply into formation and found himself marching next to one of the foreign Soldiers. He could feel the stranger's multi-directional gaze zeroing in on him. The fins twitched. The Soldier's battle armor was impressively serrated along the rim of the body and down each limb. Donovan looked straight ahead but felt his own exocel layering on panotin.

"These humans have exocels," the High Speaker exclaimed.

Administrator Seir fanned his fins with pride. "Indeed. They are our helpers. We Harden them at a young age and consider them part of our own erze. In a relatively short time, we have gone from conflict with the humans to a cooperative, even symbiotic relationship. It has proved critical to our ability to govern and maintain this outpost at the remote edge of the Commonwealth."

The High Speaker considered this. "They are hideous-looking creatures."

Seir shifted his fins in a way Donovan suspected was like stifling a frown. "Unfortunately, grand zun, that is one reason they were not initially recognized as a Class Two species. Despite their bizarre appearance, humans possess intelligence, emotional range, and social structures similar to our own. For a single-planet civilization, they are an advanced and adaptable race. Most of the erze zun here believe that in the future, significant numbers of humans could live not just on Earth but on other planets as well. Over time, they could become a Class One species."

They entered the antechamber of the main tower. The High Speaker took up the central position of authority, the other zhree zun encircling him in their proper positions, the Soldiers and human honor guard ringing them, and following behind, all the other subordinate zhree and humans-in-erze, who pressed back against the walls. The High Speaker gave an impatient wave of one of his limbs. "Enough about the native fauna," he said. "Let me explain why I am here. The Commonwealth has been through an extended—I would argue, reckless—period of expansion. It is the intention of my administration to correct this. We must evaluate our most far-flung colonial holdings and make the strategic decision whether to continue supporting them."

A ripple of shifting fins ran around the circle. If the zhree in the room had anticipated this, they certainly hadn't expected the High Speaker to bring it up so immediately and directly.

"Earth has always been of military and biological value, grand zun," Administrator Seir replied slowly.

"The planet is remote, difficult to supply, and continues to be a troublesome place to govern," the High Speaker replied. "There is ongoing violent conflict with the natives, even now."

The Administrator thought carefully before responding. "In the initial haste to secure this planet, the first settlers made some mistakes. However, as evidenced by the many humans in this room, the situation is different now and will continue to improve. Only a small percentage of the population is still openly hostile."

"Let me explain, grand zun," said Donovan's father. "Humans often fail to maintain group solidarity over distance and generations. Even after a nation has chosen a course of action, individuals and small groups continue to act unpredictably. They do not reflect the will of the majority. Most humans desire peace and cooperation."

Administrator Seir began to translate the Prime Liaison's words, but the High Speaker interrupted. "Regardless, controlling this planet continues to be a costly endeavor. Given the escalating threat by the Rii Erzen, it is time we consider withdrawing to a more defensible position."

No one replied at first. Not a single zhree in the room moved; they seemed stunned into stillness. Donovan wasn't sure his comprehension of the Mur language was serving him correctly. Maybe the High Speaker's accent had thrown him off and he'd misunderstood. *Escalating threat? Withdrawing to a more defensible position?* What did that mean? The only thing it *could* mean seemed too impossible to believe. Were the zhree . . . were they considering *leaving*?

He wondered if shock was registering on his face because he saw his father catch his eye. The Prime Liaison gave a small, stern, barely perceptible shake of his head. *Don't let them know you understand.* Donovan turned his expression stony, though the magnitude of what the High Speaker was saying made his head spin. *The zhree leaving!* It was exactly what the terrorists wanted, the cause his mother had abandoned him to fight for, the one thing Donovan had always believed to be an absolute impossibility. An Earth without zhree. A Sapience victory. A cooperationist disaster.

Except that, if this "escalating threat" the High Speaker was going on about was real . . . any newfound human independence would be temporary.

Donovan glanced around surreptitiously. The humans-in-erze at the perimeter of the room were shifting nervously, but their faces showed they didn't understand. His fellow exos looked confused, worried. They were hearing the words, but they weren't as fluent as he was and the full implication of the message wasn't registering.

"Grand zun." The rhythm of Administrator Seir's voice was entreating. "In the spirit of the Highest Erze, we must consider all options. However, the Mur Erzen chose to establish Earth as a strategic outpost. We have labored and succeeded in building a viable colony here. Earth contains rich biodiversity including an indigenous intelligent species not found anywhere else. It is a growing exporter of terraforming seed, manufactured algae strains, and luxury wood. Why would we now consider abandoning it?"

"The Rii have become more aggressive. They have attacked two more planets, and the Mur fleet is now engaged in nearly constant skirmishes. Earth is a logical target. From its orbit, they will have access to light-plus transfer points that will allow them to encroach on Commonwealth shipping corridors."

"That is why we colonized Earth to begin with and why it is all the more vital that we continue to hold it."

"We have become too ambitious, spread ourselves too thin. There is a more practical solution. Draw the fleet back to the Hestian system. Blockade the other side of the transfer points from a position of strength. Let the Rii have this remote, ungovernable planet."

Administrator Seir seemed speechless for a moment. When he spoke, his trilling voice seemed muted. "The Rii are raiders, not colonizers. They will not preserve this planet, nor its many exotic native species. Earth is home to many zhree who were hatched here and will not want to give it up to the enemy."

"I suspect just as many will be eager to leave this hinterland and come home," the High Speaker said, fins flattened.

Soldier Werth cut in, fins slicing the air firmly. "With respect, grand zun, I believe Earth is militarily defensible."

"How so?" The High Speaker sounded dubious. "There are not enough Soldiers. The fleet cannot afford to send more out here, and hatch rates on this planet have always been low."

"They are improving," Scientist Laah insisted. "With the construction of new algae farms, we have much better nutrition now. Broods have higher hatch rates."

"The threat from the Rii is imminent. Even if you tripled the rate, we cannot wait for another generation of hatchlings to mature."

"There is another way," said Soldier Werth. "Human allies. The unaltered ones are fragile and short-lived, but the exos are not. Today, Soldiers play an increasingly minimal role in combating hostile humans; instead, human soldiers-in-erze maintain peace on the planet surface, freeing us to defend the system and its transfer points."

"Humans do not take long to reach adulthood," Builder Dor added. "If we were to begin Hardening them in earnest, we could rapidly expand the complementary human force we have—not just of soldiers-in-erze but also Builders, Scientists, Nurses, Administrators, to ensure the colony's stability and self-suffi—"

"Hardened humans!" the High Speaker trilled so loudly his musical voice rang from the walls of the antechamber. "Perhaps being away from the homeworld for so long has sapped your reason. Let me see one of these so-called exos you are so enthusiastic about."

Donovan's lean forward, his look of intense attentiveness, must've drawn the High Speaker's eye because the zhree dignitary stabbed a limb in his direction. "You, human. Come here."

21

Donovan startled at the sudden command, but his feet moved him forward automatically. Swallowing nervously, he stopped in front of the High Speaker and dropped his exocel, then eased it back up to a respectful level. He felt the attention of the entire room converging on him. Donovan glanced at his father. Dominick Reyes's face was an expressionless mask.

The High Speaker raised two limbs. The hard foot plates opened, unsheathing three dexterous pincers each. They reached up and touched Donovan on the head, feeling the texture of his short hair, running down the landscape of his face and stopping curiously at his ears, nose, and chin, then moving down to stroke his shoulders and arms.

Queasy heat burned in Donovan's cheeks. Inside, he trembled from the effort of holding still, of not betraying the desire to smack away the alien hands. He knew what zhree pincers felt like: flexible, like human fingers, but slightly rough and cool, almost reptilian. This touch felt different from an exam by Nurse Therrid, though. He was being treated like a public specimen. The High Speaker tugged on the fabric of his uniform. "Why is it covered with this material?"

"Humans use it for warmth, status signaling, and modesty," Scientist Laah explained.

"Take it off."

Donovan considered playing dumb, pretending he didn't understand Mur. But the High Speaker gestured unambiguously, repeating himself. Donovan had no choice. His fingers slipped on the small, smooth buttons. When he'd shrugged out of his dress uniform shirt, he dropped it to the ground beside him, standing bare chested and praying silently that the High Speaker wouldn't expect his pants to come off too. What would he do? Could he refuse? Could he turn around and leave?

The High Speaker walked a slow circle around him. Donovan clenched his jaw; the zhree fingers were now feeling the musculature of his back and shoulders, probing the long line of exocel nodes, each touch sending a small, unpleasant jolt of sensation up his spine. The High Speaker came back around in front of him. "You can understand me," he said in a low musical hum. "I can see it in those two small eyes of yours."

Donovan wanted to look at his father again, but he felt trapped by the High Speaker's unblinking multi-eyed gaze. "Yes, zun," he said, before realizing the foreigner wouldn't understand any human language. He held up a hand and dipped it in a rough imitation of zhree fins indicating assent. It usually worked with hatchlings.

The High Speaker pointed to Donovan's hand. "You have been given a Soldier's markings."

"Yes, zun."

"Are you bound to your erze, the way these Soldiers are bound to theirs?" He indicated his own retinue of guards.

Where was this going? Why was he being questioned? "I am, zun."

The High Speaker noticed his glance lingering on one of the Soldiers, the one he'd been walking beside on the way in. "He makes you nervous," the High Speaker observed. "Because he is from a foreign erze and displaying his battle armor. A natural reaction for a Soldier." The High Speaker stepped back. "Battle-armor yourself."

Donovan's exocel sprang to life so quickly he realized that he must have been holding it in check all this time. All the stress bottled up inside him, combined with his anger at being interrogated by this stranger, spilled through his system at once. Panotin leapt from his nodes, layering and encasing him in the time it took to blink. It ripped his fingers into blades and crested into serrated ridges up his arms and shoulders. It felt *good*. Like release. Like punching a wall really hard.

The Soldiers surrounding the High Speaker reacted at once, fins flaring in alarm, limbs raising fearsome-looking weapons. Donovan experienced a second of delirious self-satisfaction. He'd scared Soldiers! All his life he'd answered to their authority, but these new ones, they didn't know how things worked here, and to them, he was a large, frightening animal from a strange planet—but striped and armored as they were.

Soldier Werth's voice trilled louder than he'd ever heard it. "Donovan! Armor down!"

He obeyed. His exocel receded slower than it had risen, retreating like melting snow.

"High Speaker, he is not dangerous," Soldier Werth insisted. "Your guards have no need to be alarmed."

The Soldiers lowered their limbs and fins warily. "Not dangerous?" the High Speaker said. He stepped close to Donovan. "You are marked as a Soldier. You are part of an erze. You have an exocel. So are you zhree or human?"

Donovan hesitated; he had a feeling the question was a trap. "I'm human, zun."

The High Speaker's fins riffled in satisfaction. He stepped away from Donovan and addressed the circle of tense zhree zun. "I commend all of you for creating this . . . ingenious relationship with the natives. However, a plan to maintain the colony with exos is dangerously flawed." He gestured at Donovan. "You have endowed a hostile, unpredictable, and primitive species with zhree biotechnology. You've brought them into your erze and treat them almost as equals. But as this one just admitted, they are not zhree. They are humans. What is to prevent them from turning against their benefactors? From becoming a threat to all of us? You had enough difficulty with humans *before* they were Hardened."

There was a silence so profound it made Donovan squirm inside. He felt his father's gaze burning, watchful and silent. The Prime Liaison had said almost nothing this whole time, and the High Speaker had ignored him. He was just a human, after all, not even as interesting as an exo. The circle of zhree fins fidgeted. Opaque eyes opened and closed, exchanging anxious glances. Donovan got the impression Administrator Seir was holding a silent consultation with his fellow zun. Finally, he said, "High Speaker, your concerns are understandable. But they can be dispelled. The exos are an asset, not a threat."

Nurse Thet waved one fin, a subtle interjection. "There are failsafes that ensure this."

"Explain."

"The Hardening process is controlled by Nurses; only zhree determine how many exos there are," the Nurse said.

"Even the number already in existence is foolhardy."

"Humans have a strong sense of social hierarchy and group loyalty, just as we do. In exos, the area of the brain governing those traits is further strengthened; they are as faithful to their erze as we are. Furthermore"—the Nurse paused, glancing uncertainly at the circle of humans—"exos cannot armor to attack zhree."

The High Speaker brought his gaze around, two eyes snapping shut as another two flew open. He pointed at Donovan. "That one battle-armored in front of me."

"Only because you ordered him to," Soldier Werth said, fins moving stiffly. "He could not have harmed you."

The High Speaker moved back toward Donovan. "Is that true?"

Donovan's mind stuttered. *Was it?* He was confused. He'd never had to keep up with such a long, complicated conversation in the Mur language before, and listening to erze masters so at odds with each other was not normal. "I . . . I'm not sure . . ."

The High Speaker stepped closer. "Strike me."

"Zun?"

"You heard correctly. Strike me, if you are able." The zhree dignitary raised a limb and jabbed him in the chest with stiff pincers. Armor against armor, the stabbing limb punched into a spot not far from where one of Kevin's bullets had fractured a rib. Donovan sucked in a gasp of surprise. He heard it echoed from others throughout the room.

"I gave you an order," said the High Speaker. "Do you usually disobey a zun order?" The pincers shot forward again.

Donovan stepped back and shoved them away. *"Stop that."* He'd never spoken in such a disrespectful tone to a zun. But no zhree had ever tried to hurt him before. The High Speaker's gaze was steady and curious; he was prodding a strange creature with a stick, waiting to see what it would do. The foreign Soldiers tensed in anticipation behind him.

Donovan's fists clenched at his sides, armor bristling visibly across his shoulders. He felt the weight, not from the dozens of zhree eyes on him but from his father's stare. His father was watching him, *willing* him to stay in control. This was a test, he knew, but not one he cared to pass. He shook his head, torn between the compulsion to obey and the determination not to be goaded. Even though the foreigner wouldn't be able to understand him, Donovan said, through clenched teeth, "You're not a zun of my erze. I don't answer to you." Seemingly out of nowhere, one of the High Speaker's other limbs arced around and smacked him across the temple. White flashed across his vision.

"*Son of a—*" Jet started forward. All of them—Donovan's fellow soldiers-in-erze—moved with him, but Soldier Werth sang out, "Stay where you are!" with such authority that they froze in midstep. "Grand zun." Soldier Werth took a stride forward, voice vibrating with suppressed anger. "We can show you records to prove our claims. There's no need for you to mistreat a human of my erze to make a point."

The High Speaker gave an incredulous flick of his fins. "Control yourself, Soldier. It's just a human."

Heat rose up Donovan's neck and burned across his rigid face. The sapes accused him of *not* being human, but to the High Speaker he was nothing *but* human. No matter his markings, his armor, his training—he was still nothing of regard. Not worthy of simple respect. Before he could stop himself, he took an angry, involuntary step forward, exocel springing into ridges up his arms—

Before abruptly dropping.

He felt the astonishment around him almost as a physical blow against his suddenly unarmored body. Donovan stumbled back, stunned, not realizing for a second what had occurred. He grasped for his exocel with his will. Nothing happened. A sick sense of panicked déjà vu emptied into his veins. It was just like the night in Dr. Nakada's lab, only far worse, because this time, no one had sprayed anything in his face. In front of the zhree zun, and his fellow exos, and his father, his exocel had fallen all on its own. Donovan let out a choked noise, his body folding.

"What the hell," Jet breathed.

The High Speaker was staring at him with great interest. Nurse Thet spoke up, a little weakly. "It was designed as a safety measure long ago when humans were being Hardened for the first time. A surge in hostile intention toward any zhree reflexively triggers exocel inhibition."

Donovan's face burned. He wanted to flee from the room. It was all he could do to force himself upright and bite out, "How long does this last?" Even as he asked it, he felt faint sensation creeping back into his nodes. With fear and humiliation winning out over aggression, his exocel was crawling to life, numb and tingly.

"You will recover once you've calmed down," said Nurse Thet. "There's no permanent damage."

Donovan couldn't bear to meet the eyes of anyone else in the room. He imagined thrusting a bladed hand into one of the High Speaker's big yellow eyes, and his feeble control wavered. If he ever tried such a thing, his exocel would shut down like a tripped circuit. Shame warred against anger, and he stifled a groan.

Soldier Werth's voice was tight, almost staccato. "Are you convinced, High Speaker?"

"Perhaps." The High Speaker seemed unsure now. "If exos are as loyal and dependable as you say they are, and your fail-safes are reliable, then your plan has merit. But there is only so much you can change a creature's essential nature. Your Hardened humans are an experiment, one you are staking the future of this colony on. I am wary of what the consequences might be."

"Earth is our home, High Speaker," Administrator Seir said. "Those who have not lived here do not appreciate its unique, alien beauty. We have a responsibility to this planet, and to the humans who have put their faith in the promise of being a protected member of the Commonwealth. Earth may be far from the homeworld, but it is still a colony of the Mur Erzen, and it deserves the same regard as Sirye or Hestia. Do not be so hasty in declaring it a lost cause."

"I will consider your plan." The High Speaker began walking. "I would like to see the rest of the Towers now."

The foreign Soldiers fell sharply into step to accompany him. As the exos took their places alongside, Jet picked up Donovan's uniform shirt and handed it to him. Donovan snatched it from his friend's hand and shoved his arms through the sleeves angrily. He didn't look at anyone as he fastened it. He and Jet rejoined the honor guard as it escorted the High Speaker to a waiting vehicle flanked by Builders. One of the accompanying builders-in-erze caught Donovan's eye. Their gazes met, and the man nodded in cordial recognition. It took Donovan a moment to realize it was Danielson, the hefty, rough-skinned man from the construction site who'd waved Kevin's silver SUV through only thirteen days ago.

Thirteen days ago, the world had made sense.

Donovan's father was suddenly behind his shoulder. "We will talk later. Wait for me at home." He did not wait for Donovan to reply but walked past him, following Scientist Laah into the vehicle.

Soldier Werth hung back as the other zhree boarded, gathering his exos around him. "What you heard and saw here today is not to be repeated. Not even to your fellow soldiers-in-erze. That is an order. Do you understand?"

"Yes, zun," came the mumbled replies.

"We cannot afford to have zhree and humans alike roused to a panic." Soldier Werth paused. His voice grew quiet, his fins as flat and scowling as Donovan had ever seen them. "I warned you that some zhree would have different attitudes toward humans. The High Speaker has spent his life on the homeworld, far from hardship and conflict, and cannot appreciate the complexities of the colonies." Donovan saw the exos exchanging nervous glances. Soldier Werth never vented his frustration with other zhree so openly to his human subordinates. "What happened just now doesn't bode well for the rest of the visit, but perhaps the situation can be salvaged. We shall see. You are dismissed from ceremonial duties; return to your assignments.

"Donovan." Only one of Soldier Werth's eyes was looking directly at him. If it was even possible, his erze master looked . . . apologetic. "You are excused from duty for the rest of the day."

Donovan didn't wait for the High Speaker's vehicle to leave before hurrying to escape.

Jet came after him. "Where are you going?"

"You heard Soldier Werth. I'm excused."

"Wait." Jet caught up to Donovan, who kept on walking. "What happened back there—"

"I don't want to talk about it."

Jet reached a hand to his shoulder to stop him; Donovan threw it off and spun to face his partner. "That shroom," he spat, "the High Speaker—the one who makes the big decisions about what happens to Earth—*is a dick*. He made me look like a complete tool in front of all those people. He's never been here before but he's ready to throw our whole planet under the bus. Isn't that *complete crap*?"

"Yes, it is. Very, very much a heap of crap." Jet looked at him with urgent concern. "So where are you going?"

Donovan glared at him. "You're on duty right now, Officer." He started walking again. He knew he was being unfair, snapping at Jet out of his own anger and humiliation, but he didn't stop. From the corner of his eye he saw Jet standing there, looking after him. Donovan rounded the walkway, out of sight.

He followed the curve of the main tower's exterior causeway to the vehicle bay, stewing under a dark cloud the entire way. Most of the skimmercars parked in the bay were unmodified; he'd have a hell of a time handling the zhree-designed controls. He plowed past them to the row of loaner electricycles, intended for use within the Round by any humans on official business for their erze. If you were a squishy, there was a sign-in procedure, but an exo body signature activated any of them without preamble.

He picked one out—they all looked the same—and swung his leg over, settling into the seat. He gripped the handlebars and waited impatiently for the sensors to verify him. The machine hummed to life and Donovan leaned forward, taking it out of the Towers and into the streets of the Round.

He took the first major concentric boulevard exit off the spoke road and flew through traffic, accelerating until the wind stung his eyes, passing archway turnoffs into each of the Round's pie slice–shaped districts. He didn't live far from the Towers, but instead of taking the familiar turn into his neighborhood of well-appointed human dwellings, he kept going. He'd rather drive than sit alone in the empty house. Jet had asked him where he was going, but right now, he didn't know and he didn't care. He felt so . . . *ignorant* and used. For the last two weeks he'd been yanked every which way— by his parents, by Sapience, by SecPac, and now by the High Speaker. He was the son of the Prime Liaison, and exo, a uniformed SecPac officer, and yet he was powerless. Powerless to influence his father, powerless over his own exocel, ultimately powerless, as *all* humans were, over what happened based on the whims of some distant alien authority.

He took the turn off toward SecPac Central Command.

The national command center for the Global Security and Pacification Forces was a sprawling campus of buildings and training fields. On first approach, it wasn't much to look at. Donovan still remembered being twelve and arriving with the other brand-new trainee soldiers-in-erze, all of them standing on the front lawn, rubbing freshly striped hands and thinking, *This is it?* Next to the soaring, curving, fluid lattice metal architecture elsewhere in the Round, SecPac Command was . . . disappointingly old-school human. Commander Tate had welcomed them with a speech that day: "Our duty is not glamorous. It comes without ceremony or thanks. It is dangerous and misunderstood. You have been marked as soldiers, not to wage war but to bring peace. To ensure that the War Era remains in the past, and that Earth moves toward the future."

He didn't take the road up to the main Comm Hub building, where dozens of screens covered the walls in a glowing, shifting ring of grid maps and satellite imagery, and where dispatch controllers, talking into headphones and sipping from mugs of strong coffee, monitored patrol teams across the entire country. Instead, he steered onto a side road. He circled behind the officers' common hall and past the Scroll—an enormous stone sculpture engraved with the Accord of Peace and Governance. He drove past the firing range, where a group of trainees was practicing. There, far from the other buildings, hidden by a row of trees and surrounded by a high fence topped with security cameras, was a nondescript structure everyone called the Pen. The Pen was where valuable or high-profile captured terrorists were kept for questioning—deep in the Round with its layers of zhree security, far from possible jailbreak attempts—until they were turned over to the justice system for trial and sentencing.

Donovan passed his hand under the reader at the security gate and it admitted him. He parked the e-cycle near the front of the concrete block building and approached the heavy steel doors. He buzzed for entry, and a few seconds later, the impenetrable-looking entrance swung open to reveal a small lobby, with another double gate of steel bars at the end of it and an enclosed office to one side, behind a waist-high barricade. As the doors behind Donovan closed, the warden heaved himself up from behind his desk and came out of his small office. "Officer D. Reyes," he exclaimed.

Donovan had only been inside the Pen three times, once on trainee orientation and twice to deliver suspects. He did not, to his embarrassment, remember the warden's name. "I, um . . . I'm surprised you remember me, sir," he said.

"There's only one of you." The warden was a man in gradual but inexorable transition between well-built and overweight. His slicked hair receded well past his brow, and his broad shoulders stretched the yellowed fabric of his uniform tightly across the back of his neck. "When you first came through here as a trainee, I said to myself, the Prime Liaison has got to be a stand-up man if his son is earning his marks just like the rest of us." He held a large, striped hand out to Donovan, who shook it. The warden had a strong grip. He'd probably been in a combat role years ago, back when there hadn't been as many exos and squishies could run ops instead of desk jobs. "What can I do for you?" the warden asked.

"I'm looking for a prisoner who was brought in from Rapid City the night before last. A woman who goes by 'Max.'"

The warden checked the log, then blew out a heavy breath. "You got authorization?"

No, he most definitely did not. What he was doing would probably get him into a lot of trouble. He looked left and right, then leaned toward the warden conspiratorially and lowered his voice. "Actually, this isn't an official visit. My father wants some questions asked, off the record. He knows this suspect, he thinks she might have more information to offer. But he doesn't want anyone to think the Liaison Office is stepping on SecPac's toes, you know what I mean? Political reasons. So he sent me."

The warden nodded in understanding. He was inclined to trust an exo officer. "I take it I ought to keep this visit off the register, then."

"That would be best," Donovan agreed wholeheartedly.

The warden opened a short swinging door in the barricade and ambled around to let Donovan through the secure gates. He opened them one at a time, using a large ring of metal keys, bolting them back shut behind them. Donovan tugged experimentally on the bars. The Pen was surprisingly old-fashioned. It seemed devoid of zhree technology. Just straight walls, square cells, and metal bars. Not so different from civilian prisons, or the stone cell that had held Donovan in the Warren, minus the machine-gun wielding guards.

The warden chuckled as if he'd seen the same skeptical reaction before. "Old human stuff does the job fine around here," he said. "The terrorists are just squishies. That's what you armored kids call us old farts these days, isn't it?"

Donovan said, "Not you, sir. You're a stripe, Hardened or not."

The warden let out a snort, but Donovan saw the pleased set of his mouth as his thick shoulders straightened.

The cells were occupied. Thirty-nine insurgents taken alive from the Warren; no doubt many of them were here. Donovan heard the shuffle of movement as the prisoners drew close to the bars, following the passing sight of his uniform with hateful glares. Donovan walked past Kathy and heard her hiss, "I should have let Javid shoot you."

"You're supposed to be dead," another man's voice growled, so close that Donovan nearly jumped. The prisoner's arms were draped through the bars of his cell, his bearded jaw jutting forward and his neck bulging with a surprise that Donovan felt climbing over his own face. It was Sean Corrigan. Corrigan's hands were swollen, every finger splinted and wrapped in white gauze, so he looked like a cartoon character with comically oversized fists. He held them up to Donovan. "Look what he did to me. You're supposed to be *dead* for this."

The warden rapped his stick against the bars, threatening to smack Corrigan's broken fingers. "Busted fingers are better than what you terrorist trash deserve. Now, get back; you're not to *look* at this officer, much less talk to him."

Donovan dragged his gaze straightforward and walked a little faster, his heart rate rising to match his footfalls. They passed a stretch of empty wall before the warden stopped in front of the final cell. Donovan stepped in front of the bars. His mother sat cross-legged on the bolted-down bed. She was wearing the drab gray clothes of an inmate. She'd been cleaned up and no longer had blood and dirt on her face and hands. Her hair was down; it waved untidily just past her shoulders. Her eyes were closed, her head leaned back against the wall. She wore on her face an expression of weary calm.

"Could I . . ." Donovan cleared his throat and turned to the warden. "Could I have a few minutes?"

"You need anything, just holler, or push that button on the wall. Guards will be here lickety-split." He looked at the middle-aged woman in the cell, then at the young exo, and chuckled at his own words. "Not that *you'd* need any help. If that woman is Max, then she's responsible for a lot of dead people, but you wouldn't know it looking at her now, would you? Heck, she looks like she could be someone's mom." The warden shook his head, then wandered back down the row of cells.

Max opened her eyes. "Donovan." She got up off the bed and came to the bars, reaching her hands through.

Donovan approached, one slow step at a time. In that moment, it seemed to him that she was utterly familiar, and still a complete stranger. He reached out and put his hands in hers. "Are you being treated okay?" he asked.

"Well enough." Her lips twisted into a shape that combined a wry smile and a grimace of grief. "I have nothing to complain about." Not when most of her friends in the Warren were dead. She leaned back a little, taking in the clean-shaven sight of him in his dress uniform. The small muscles around her mouth sagged. Her hands grew heavy in his, like two mounds of sand. "It didn't take long, did it? For him to take you back." Her voice was a bitter whisper. "Did he send you?"

"He doesn't know I'm here." He didn't want to talk about his father. "I just wanted to see if you were okay."

"That means a lot to me."

"I went to the Warren. It's been destroyed, but . . . Saul wasn't among the bodies or those captured." He shouldn't be telling her this; you didn't just give away potentially useful information to prisoners. Donovan squeezed her hands. *Scorch it.* "I thought you'd want to know he might have gotten away."

His mother closed her eyes. Her lashes were wet. "Thank you."

"Mom." Donovan drew a steadying breath. "I know something else that could help you. When SecPac took out the Warren, it didn't get all the files inside—a lot of them were destroyed by the insurgents. Commander Tate knows that Sapience has plans for a major Peace Day operation, but she doesn't have details." He leaned closer to the bars. "But you do, don't you? You're higher up the chain than the other prisoners; you're the closest one to Saul. You know what the plans are."

Max opened her eyes and gazed at him steadily. She didn't say yes, but he saw he was right.

Donovan's voice sped up. "You have something valuable to offer: information that Father and Commander Tate want. You can use it to bargain. You can have the death penalty commuted."

She rubbed the pad of her thumbs over his knuckles. "Do you remember the story I told you about the girl whose mother left her with strangers at the gates to the Round?"

"Yeah. What about it?"

"Over the years, whenever I thought of you, I thought of that little girl. I wondered if God was testing me, punishing me, because I'd been so judgmental and unforgiving of that mother. So He put me in her place, for some terrible purpose. If I could be made as desperate as that woman, if I could do what she had done, abandon my own child, then from that day on, I could do *anything.*"

What was she talking about? Was she thinking about the terrible crimes she'd committed? The ones his father had mentioned, and others he didn't know about and didn't even *want* to know about? "Mom," he said, trying to bring her focus back, "did you hear me? There's a way out of this."

"There's no way out, Donovan," she said gently. "SecPac questioned me all day yesterday. Commander Tate came in the evening and offered me something even better than a way out of the atomizer. She told me I could see you again. If I revealed everything I knew about Sapience's plans, I would get imprisonment instead of death, and you could visit me. Wouldn't I want that?" His mother's smile was unpleasant. "I told her I did. But that I don't bargain with traitors."

Donovan dropped her hands. Commander Tate had dangled him like a carrot for his mom? Slow anger crept up his neck; so he was being used *again*. Then, a second wave of anger: His mother had refused.

"If you cared about me," he hissed, "if you actually regretted leaving, like you keep saying you do, then you'd bargain. You'd try hard to stay alive. You'd negotiate." His fingers curled into fists at his side. "I'm *asking* you to."

She wrapped her hands around the bars. They were so small. "Then let me ask you to do something in return."

He gave a slow nod. "Anything I can. So long as it's legal."

"Leave your erze. Take off that accursed uniform. Run away from the Round and never come back."

He stared at her. "I can't do that."

"You can't? Or you won't?" Her eyes were uncommonly bright. "I think you can. You can break the hold that they—that *he*—has over you."

Donovan slammed a hand to the bars next to her head. "It's still about you and Dad, isn't it? I'm asking you to save yourself, and you're still trying to win the grudge match!" Through gritted teeth, "Whether I can or not, I *won't* break my oaths and walk out on all my friends. Even an unmarked squishy like you can understand that betraying people who trust you is *wrong*."

Max waited a few beats for his words to sink in. "Listen to what you're saying," she said. "We're in complete agreement."

"Urrrghhh . . ." Donovan closed his eyes, leaning his head against the bars. It was hopeless. He could see now it was hopeless.

Her fingers touched his brow. He felt them trembling against his skin. "I'm not a good person, Donovan. I have a lot of bitterness and hatred in my heart. If you knew all the things I've done, you wouldn't be standing here talking to me. Maybe I do deserve the atomizer. But I'm not a traitor. If Saul is alive, he'll fight on, and I won't give up anything that might compromise him."

"Haven't enough people died in the last two days?" His words felt wooden in his mouth. "Most of them were your people. And you want it to go on, for there to be more fighting, more killing."

"We all die, Donovan. It's how we die that matters."

His voice was a whisper; he didn't trust it enough to speak louder. "You said, in Rapid City . . . you said you wanted me back."

"More than anything," she said. "But I can't have you back, I know that now. And the cause is more important, far more important, than what I want. The cause is right; even when I'm wrong, the cause is always right."

"I'm only trying to help you."

"You *have* helped me. You came here today. You gave me the chance to see you again." Her voice cracked. "That's enough for me."

Donovan let his head rest on the bars for another second. Then he took a step backward. Then another. Nothing had changed. He was five years old all over again, aching incurably from an abandonment he didn't understand.

His mother reached for him with her eyes. A long tear rolled down the crease between her nose and cheek. It hung on the top of her lip. "Good-bye, Donovan, my sweet boy, good-bye. You're the only good thing I ever made. I love you."

Donovan refused to reply. *This can't be how it ends.* He might be just one human, as weak as the High Speaker had made him feel, with no control over big galactic problems. But he couldn't be helpless in this too, this one thing. *I'm going to save you*, he promised silently. *I don't know how, and I'm not sure I don't HATE you, but I'm going to save you.*

He took one last look at her face. Then he turned away, practically running back down the row of cells, toward the exit. The Pen had become a claustrophobic, medieval thing all of a sudden. He made himself slow down as he reached the double-barred gates. He waved at the warden in his office, and when the man shambled over to let him out and ask if everything was all right, if he got what he came for, Donovan forced his face into a casual smile. "Yes, sir. Thank you for your help." He burst out of the Pen and into the sunlight.

He slumped against the outside wall for a few seconds, not wanting to move to go anywhere. He wished he could have the last two weeks expunged from his memory. If only he could return to a time when all the pieces of his life—hanging out with erze mates, bantering with Jet, the day-to-day vagaries of patrol duty, even enduring the proud and infuriating role as his father's son—had fit neatly around him as they should. Everything was jumbled now. There were new and mismatched fragments scattered around him in an incoherent mess; he wasn't sure which belonged and which didn't.

Donovan took a few deep breaths and paced back to the electri-cycle. A patrol skimmercar was parked next to it. Jet was slouched against the hull. He did not seem surprised to see Donovan.

Donovan could not say likewise. "What are you doing here?"

"I could ask you the same thing." Jet opened the door of the skimmercar. "Talk in the car."

Donovan got in the car. His partner got in after him and closed the door.

Jet pulled a can of energy drink, dark as tar, from the cup holder. He opened it and took a swallow. "I had to come in for an official reprimand. For breaking that squishy's fingers, you know. Excessive use of force." He rolled his eyes at Donovan's sudden look of worry. "Relax. Five days' suspension without pay. Delayed until whenever I want."

Donovan nodded. "That's not so bad."

"Tate said some stuff she's supposed to say, but she's not even putting it in my permanent record. Soldier Werth said my over-reaction was 'in erze, given the highly unusual circumstances.'" One side of Jet's mouth lifted, but then his expression sobered. "So anyway, since the whole official reprimand took about ten seconds, I detoured to check that you made it home okay." He raised his eyebrows. "Obviously, you didn't."

"What are you, like my nanny?"

"I was hoping I'd find you passed out in front of your dad's booze fridge, but when I didn't, I guessed you'd come here." He set his jaw, serious. Serious wasn't a look that suited Jet particularly well. "This isn't a good idea, D. It's a really bad one."

"What is?" He was having a hard time meeting Jet's eyes.

"Thinking of the woman in there as your mom. The one you

wish you'd had. She's not. She totally walked out when you were a little kid, and she's spent the last twelve years blowing things up and killing people. You know what's going to happen to her. So don't do this to yourself, okay?"

Donovan said, "My dad forced her out because she was going to take me away so I couldn't be Hardened."

"None of that is your fault."

"What if she's right, Jet? What if we exos are bad for humanity? You heard Soldier Werth, he wants to Harden a whole lot more. But you saw what happened today with the High Speaker." Fresh anger warmed his face.

Jet said nothing at first. "The High Speaker is a douche. A homeworlder. The zhree zun don't like him any more than we do; you heard the way Soldier Werth talked about him afterward. What he did to you was a dick move, and it hit you at the worst time."

"This isn't just my issue, Jet. It's all of ours." Donovan leaned back, staring up at the ceiling of the skimmercar. "Don't you think that's one hell of an *oh, by the way* the zhree have been conveniently not mentioning to us? 'Oh, by the way, there's a trip switch in your brain that knocks out your armor if you ever get it into your head to turn it against us.'"

Jet didn't look at him. He chugged the rest of his drink, then pressed the can between his hands until it was a crumpled metal disc. His voice took on an uncharacteristically bitter edge. "It pisses me off too, all right? But what do you expect? We're small potatoes to the shrooms. That's right, *shrooms*—we all think of them that way sometimes. A hundred years ago, I'm betting the homeworlders thought even less of humans than the High

Dickhead does now. The colonists would never have gotten away with giving us exocels unless there was some kind of restriction."

Donovan gripped the armrests of his seat. Panotin thickened his fingers and dug into the fabric. "It's not right. The zhree call us their partners, but they don't trust us enough to give us something important without hobbling it first."

Jet said, "Let's say you *had* attacked the High Speaker. Put a fist in his eye, like we both wanted to. His Soldiers would've freaked and gunned you down on the spot. Kreet would cut Earth out of the Commonwealth like an infected cyst. There'd never be any more exos, period, end of story. Then where would we be, huh? On a backwater ghetto planet filled with squishies fighting each other all over again . . . at least until someone worse like the Rii came and took over."

"Which might happen anyway." Donovan slumped back. "If after everything, the zhree hang us out to dry, then what's the point? We might as well all be sapes for all it matters."

Jet swung around with a sharp look of disbelief. "That's not going to happen. There are smart people like your dad, and Soldier Werth, who know a lot more than we do, whose job it is to solve the political stuff. All we can do is our job—you know, setting an example, proving that we humans can police ourselves, that we have our act together and we're not all extremists. Us exos—we're the ones who can get in on the bigger game, who could be equal to the zhree. That's why the sapes hate us so much."

Jet leaned forward, as if he'd just remembered something important. "My dad told me something interesting from history. You know who first attempted to make exos? It wasn't the zhree. It was the United States military, back in the War Era. They were losing hundreds of humans for every one Soldier and trying to find a way to level the playing field. It was a total failure, of course, but zhree Scientists stumbled across the data after the Accord and did it right. You know what that means?"

"That it's a good thing we weren't born in the War Era."

"That we wanted what they had, almost from the beginning. We knew the rules of the universe had changed."

Donovan's voice came out bitter. "You sound like my dad."

Jet stared at him for a long minute. Finally, he ran his tongue over his lips. He spoke slowly. "There's a syndrome, you know, when a hostage starts identifying with his captors. It's like a way for your brain to cope with the trauma."

"So you do think I'm squishy-brained."

"I don't know what to think. All I know is, something is not right with you. Is it the girl? The one you let escape?"

Donovan felt his mouth twitch against his will.

"She was in one of the photos Thad showed you, wasn't she? You saw her, but you didn't say so."

Donovan said nothing. He cursed his best friend silently. Fooling Commander Tate and even Thad was one thing, but Jet always knew when he was lying. He tried to read his erze mate's expression, but Jet's face had closed like a door. Finally, the silence became unbearable. "What are you going to do, Officer Mathews? Are you going to report me?"

Jet stared straight ahead out the front of the skimmercar. "I've been telling myself that you've been through an epically bad time, but now that you're back, you'll be okay. But coming here to the Pen without telling anyone, and the way you're talking now . . ." He ran a hand through his hair. "The world has big problems, sure.

But we're stripes. We're the good guys. We swore oaths—important, honorable ones. That woman in there"—he pointed toward the Pen—"and that girl, they're sapes, and no matter what happened to you, they're not the answer. You know that, right?" Jet finally turned to him. His voice dropped to an imploring whisper. "Just tell me, D . . . I don't have to worry about you, do I?"

If it ever came down to it, Donovan knew, Jet would do his duty. If he suspected his best friend to be out of erze, he'd turn him in himself, even if it tore him to pieces to do it.

Out of erze. Donovan recoiled from the thought. He couldn't let Jet believe such a thing of him. "The girl," he said at last. "I let her off the hook because she stopped Kevin. She got up and stood in front of him when he was torturing me. I couldn't arrest her when I owed her like that." He nodded toward the Pen. "And my mom . . . I wanted to give her one more chance. I thought she might know about Sapience's plans, information she could give to Commander Tate to save herself from the atomizer. She didn't go for it. I guess I'm not surprised, but . . . I wanted to feel like I did everything I could for her anyway."

Jet absorbed these explanations silently. All of them were true.

Donovan forced a weak smile, then shoved Jet's shoulder. "Hey, you're right—it's been a bad couple of weeks. We all have our doubts sometimes, you know? Don't get so freaked out on me."

His friend turned a pleading look on him. "Don't come back here, okay? Promise me you'll stay away from the whole mess. Let it blow over."

"Right. You know anywhere I could go on vacation for a couple of years?" Donovan said. When Jet kept staring at him expectantly without cracking a smile, he sighed, relenting. "All right, I hear you."

"Take it easy, like Nurse Therrid said. Tate already told me she's taking us off anything having to do with the Warren raid. Regular patrol only. And if you need a break from your old man, you can crash at my place."

Donovan raised an eyebrow. "You're not going to be busy?"

Jet squinted one eye. "It's just a first date. Don't psych me out."

"Where are you going to take her?"

"No idea. Everything in the Round is so overdone, but if we go to the Ring Belt, it has to be classy, you know? You seriously need to help me on this." Jet's comm unit went off and began blinking insistently. He groaned. "I better get going."

Donovan opened the door of the skimmercar and stepped out. Jet leaned after him. "You're going home for real now, right?"

"I'm going to stop by my locker first and change into some civvy clothes because this dress uniform is making me crazy. Then yes, I'm going home to have a shower, take a dump, and eat a frozen burrito for dinner, not necessarily in that order, if it's all right with you, Officer."

"Smartass." Jet flipped him the finger as he closed Donovan's door, but he looked like himself again—smiling. The skimmercar lifted and reversed, then sped down the road and out of sight.

Donovan climbed onto the electricycle and drove it to the officer's common hall. He really was dying to get out of his dress uniform, but he wasn't in the mood to run into other people and talk. Fortunately, the place was deserted. Everyone must still be occupied in the Black Hills, or hosting the High Speaker.

Donovan went in the back entrance and met no one on the way to his locker. He changed out of his dress uniform and hung it up, then pulled on a spare pair of jeans and a hooded sweatshirt. He shut his locker.

He'd promised Jet he'd go home. But now that he was here, there was one thing he wanted to do first, an itch that wouldn't take long to scratch. Before he could convince himself not to, he was walking from the locker room over to the office area, to one of the shared workstations where patrol officers sat to finish up reports, search for information, check messages, or kill time.

It wasn't hard to find Anya's record in the SecPac database again. He ran the same search that Thad must have run earlier, filtering for females between the ages of fourteen and twenty, known to be living in the Ring Belt and flagged as having possible Sapience ties. A few minutes of scrolling through the photos and he found the one he'd seen on Thad's screen—Anya, with black hair, young and petulant. The name on the record was Anne Leah Dodson. He made a face; he couldn't imagine Anya as an Anne Leah. The birthdate put her at sixteen years of age. His eyes flicked to the next field: last-known address.

Donovan's heart tapped a staccato against the inside of his rib cage. He glanced over his shoulder again; he was still very much alone. He turned back around and stared at Anya's file.

What do you think you're doing now? He half expected Jet to materialize angrily behind him. *What was I just talking to you about? She's a sape and you're an exo. Let her go.*

"I can't," Donovan whispered. Before his guilt or common sense could use Jet's voice to get the better of him, he grabbed a notepad and pen and copied out the address on the screen. He closed the file, cleared the search filters, and shut down the workstation. *Sorry, Jet. I just want to know she's okay. That's all.*

— — —

He left his duty gun stowed in his locker and swapped it out for a compact electripulse, easily concealed in an inside waistband holster underneath his civilian clothes. He couldn't very well take an official loaner electricycle from the Towers out into the Ring Belt without it being noticed in both places. He left the e-cycle at a drop point near the perimeter wall and walked the rest of the way down the spoke road to where it ended at Gate 5. There was a short queue of skimmercars waiting to get through the checkpoint, but the pedestrian exit was clear. Leaving the Round wasn't hard; it was getting in that was impossible unless your DNA or exocellular body signature was in the resident database, or you were erze marked and had a valid visitor or worker pass.

Even though Donovan did it almost every day, leaving the Round and entering the Ring Belt really was like going to a different place in a different era. For one thing, there were rarely any zhree to be seen on the streets, and although there were wealthy neighborhoods of erze-marked people to be found outside the Round walls, the majority of humans out here lived in simple wood-and-concrete structures, drove cheap petroleum-burners, and went about their daily lives much as their ancestors might have a hundred and fifty years ago. Having patrolled it extensively, Donovan knew the Ring Belt almost as well as he knew the Round; he walked another ten minutes to a bus stop where he could catch the number 20 to a neighborhood he would normally never consider entering without his uniform and gun prominently on display.

As he waited for the bus, Donovan drew the hood of his sweatshirt over his head. He didn't need it for warmth, but he didn't want his exocel nodes to attract any attention. He pulled on fingerless leather gloves that hid his stripes. On the rumbling bus, he stood apart from the other passengers. They eyed him suspiciously; he wasn't a regular. When the bus arrived at the corner of the second block of Transitional Habitation grids, Donovan waited for the others to leave before stepping off. The afternoon sunlight was stark but exuded little heat. A bitter wind touched Donovan's face, carrying with it the unmistakable stench of urban decay—garbage, urine, and hopelessness.

This is a stupid idea. Donovan fought to keep his armor down and to start walking as if he wasn't already regretting his decision. The TransHabs consisted of six square blocks of identical concrete apartment complexes; originally built by the first postwar government for human war refugees with nowhere else to go, it had somehow endured over the decades, becoming crime-ridden, drug-infested, and full of the poor and the displaced. A prime Sapience rats nest and recruiting ground as far as SecPac was concerned. Donovan was thankful it was cold and there were few people loitering on the street; he avoided a pile of white garbage bags on the sidewalk, stepped around a motionless human form huddled under a pile of wool blankets, and taking a deep breath, walked the concrete steps up to one of the building entrances. A dog tied to a post flung itself toward him, barking loudly—it could smell what he was, Donovan was sure.

Quickly double-checking the address over the door, he went inside and climbed the narrow stairwell, not studying the stains or debris he passed. On the third floor, he hesitated in front of the second door on the right. If no one was home, he would take it as a sign; he'd accept that he'd done all he could and that this was just one final, foolish, indulgent action he was allowing himself before putting Anya out of his life and his thoughts for good. Donovan knocked.

After a long minute, Anya's voice called from inside, "Who is it?"

Donovan's breath caught. It was a second before he could find his own voice. "It's me," he said, trying to speak through the door quietly. "Donovan."

"*Who?*" The door unlocked, then opened halfway. Donovan blinked twice and took a step back, elation collapsing. The woman standing there was not Anya. She had Anya's voice and tiny nose, but she was several years older. She wore a loose pink sweater, frayed at the sleeves. Her prematurely creased face was bored and hostile at the same time. "Who are *you?*"

"I . . ." Donovan collected himself. He tried to act and sound like a normal person and not to slip into the instinctive authority of a SecPac officer. "I'm looking for Anya."

"That what she's still calling herself?" The woman ran a long, hard look over Donovan, her mouth flattening in suspicion. He was clearly not from here. "You one of Kevin's friends?"

Donovan kept his hands tucked into the pockets of his hooded sweatshirt. "I know Kevin, sure," he said, hoping he sounded nonchalant. Behind Anya's sister—for the woman had to be Anya's sister—Donovan glimpsed an untidy green-hued single room no larger than the main bathroom of his father's house. "I just came to check if Anya's all right, if you've heard from her at all."

Anya's sister made a noise of disgust, half snort, half laugh. "How would I know? She doesn't come home. Too busy trying to get herself killed or thrown in jail, thanks to the likes of you." Her voice was harsh, accusing. She began to shut the door in Donovan's face.

"Wait." Donovan shot out a hand to keep the door from closing. "If she does come back here, if you do talk to her, will you give her a message?"

The woman stared at Donovan's hand on the door. He could see her wondering if the gloves hid erze marks, or scars from being stripped, or gang tattoos, or if his hands were simply cold from the autumn chill. He was afraid she'd demand he remove them, but instead she turned to him, arms crossed, her voice slow and frigid. "I don't want to be a part of your world, you hear?"

"It's not that kind of message," he said. "I'm a friend who's worried about her, that's all. Please, if you see or hear from her, tell her—" He hesitated. *Yes, tell her what, genius?* "There's a post outside the front of the building. Tell her to mark an X on the post, and I'll know she's okay. I won't come around here again; just tell her Donovan wants to know she's okay."

He took his hand off the door. Anya's sister glared at him for another second, then shut and bolted it. He heard her moving around the apartment. Donovan stood in the claustrophobic hallway for a long moment, then made his way back down the dim stairwell.

It took a few minutes for him to identify the feeling that made each of his steps seem so heavy. It was the same emotion that dogged him after he questioned people who refused to co-operate, or conducted a search that came up empty—a mix of anger, shame, and defeat. Knowing that he wasn't just unappreciated for his work but *hated*, that perhaps he could have done his job better somehow, that he'd circled the problem but not gotten to the heart of it.

So Anya was still missing, but it had only been a couple of days. Had he really foolishly hoped to find her here? She was probably still lying low in Rapid City. As far as he knew, she hadn't been captured or killed yet. At least it wouldn't be hard, as part of his routine patrols of the TransHabs, to swing by this spot over the coming weeks and see if she'd gotten his message. It wouldn't do any harm; it would mean nothing to anyone but them, this secret, unlikely passing of signals.

He came to a sudden standstill on the sidewalk in front of the building. The dog, a thin, unkempt shepherd mix of some kind, started barking wildly and lunging toward him again, but Donovan stood frozen without noticing it. An idea had come to him in a flash of awful inspiration. He started walking again, his steps coming faster and faster, trying unsuccessfully to stop the plan inexorably forming in his mind. It was such a long shot, and so treasonous, that even rolling it around in his head made him cringe, horrified with himself.

It might work, though. It just might work.

He knew how to save his mom from execution.

24

It was dark by the time Donovan arrived home. The entire hour-long journey back, he'd waged a fierce and silent struggle with himself. He knew what he was contemplating was criminal, and if he went through with it and was discovered, he'd expect to be arrested and summarily relieved of his stripes.

The thought made him feel sick. To be an exo stripped of his markings was unthinkable. There must be something wrong with him; maybe the last week really had damaged his psyche. Exos did not contemplate the sorts of traitorous things he was thinking about. He ought to report himself to Nurse Therrid right away.

Then a different kind of doubt flooded in, and his fists clenched inside his pockets. If he gave up on trying to save his mom's life, if he turned himself in as a mental case just for having disloyal thoughts, wasn't that proving what sapes like his mom were always saying? That exos were made by the zhree to serve and obey; they had no capacity to defy their masters. What had Saul called him? A biotechnological abomination designed to support an alien race.

Donovan ground his teeth. That was *not* true—he, Jet, Thad, Commander Tate, they had free will, they made their own decisions, they pushed back against Soldiers when they had to. Still . . . if he didn't act to save his own mother, was it because Saul was right that he *couldn't*—in the same way that earlier in the day he hadn't been able to raise his armor against a zhree?

He was such a mess of confusion he could barely sit still or eat when he got home. He showered, forced an apple and part of a reheated burrito into his stomach, and tried to calm himself down enough to present the semblance of normalcy. His father would disown him if he knew half of what Donovan was considering; he was determined not to arouse any suspicion.

When he heard the front door opening near midnight, he stood up. His father walked in, took off his hat, and hung up his coat. Damascus and Benjamin nodded at Donovan in greeting before withdrawing soundlessly. Donovan waited for the Prime Liaison to notice him.

"Father." He cleared his throat. "I was disrespectful to you last night. I . . . I'm sorry. I wasn't myself. I shouldn't have said what I did to you." There. Hardest part over.

"Donovan . . ." His father heaved a tired breath. "I realize I'm often demanding of you." He glanced at his son, then massaged the bridge of his nose. "Every decision I've made has been in your best interest, but I know you've been hurt by them as well. Always necessarily, but hurt nevertheless. Yesterday, in my relief at seeing you safely home, I didn't appreciate how deeply you must have felt betrayed. By both your parents."

Donovan had more of a speech prepared, about how he was feeling better and ready to return to duty, or something of the ilk. But he hadn't expected this, the Prime Liaison opening up even a little, displaying anything resembling doubt or regret. It threw him off completely. He felt his poise crumbling. "I feel like I still don't understand anything," he blurted. "I don't understand how you and Mom ended up the way you did. You must have loved each other at some point, right? She said the two of you broke apart over whether to have me Hardened."

His father looked worn down. "That was part of it."

"So I was some kind of . . . pawn in this battle I didn't even know about." His anger rose anew; he couldn't help it. "Just like in the Warren when I had no idea what was really going on. It's the same way the zhree treat Earth—like some kind of chess piece."

He'd ruined the moment, ruined his apology. He expected his father to reprimand him. Instead, the Prime Liaison was silent for a long moment. Finally, he said, "We're *all* part of a bigger struggle, whether we know it or not, and rarely can we clearly see the consequences of our actions. Come here, Donovan." When Donovan drew near, his father put a heavy hand on his shoulder. "I understand how hard it is to let go of the past, to give up on people who disappoint you. To stop thinking about what might have been. But I'm counting on you to do that, to be a soldier for the next few weeks, no matter how difficult a position you're put in. It's important, son. This is a difficult time, for more reasons than I can say."

Donovan tensed. He knew his father was thinking of the humiliating scene with the High Speaker. "What happened this morning . . . I didn't handle it very well."

His father gave his shoulder a slight shake. "You're not to blame for the impossible bind you were put in. No one anticipated how badly the High Speaker's visit would go."

"It was awful. My armor dropping like that, in front of all those people." Donovan's gut clenched in shame. "Why hasn't anyone ever told us that exos can't fight the zhree? Isn't that *wrong*? Even if we *are* in erze, what if we need to stand up for ourselves?"

"Just because you can't use your exocel to attack them doesn't mean you can't stand up for yourself." His father turned away, pacing distractedly, hands clasped behind his back. "We are in great danger, Donovan. You saw how tense the zhree zun were during the High Speaker's visit today. If the Mur Erzen decides that Earth is an unsustainable colony, too remote, too difficult to supply and protect, not worth the trouble of governing . . . what happens then?"

"Would the zhree really leave? And give Sapience exactly what it wants?" The idea of an Earth without zhree, filled with humans left to their own devices . . . He could barely wrap his head around something so inconceivable.

"The consequences would be devastating. Humankind has not governed itself independently for a hundred and thirty years— chaos would ensue. The eighty-five percent of the population that is unmarked would turn on the fifteen percent that is. The violence would be incalculable. But even that is not the worst possible outcome. Not by far. If our strategic position is the reason why the planet is so valuable, and the Rii could exploit it to further their expansion . . ." His father stopped. "I'm doing it again. Speaking to you as a political confidante instead of as a father. All I meant to say is this: Exos are the key. Soldier Werth believes they are the key to combating Sapience. But they are also the key to human security. The best defense we have against the zhree is being invaluable to them. You're not a pawn, Donovan, far from it." He seemed lost in thought for a moment, then shook his head and spoke without looking up. "You should go to sleep. You need your rest."

There must be something else he could say, some way he could get what he wanted without resorting to desperate actions. His father was, above all, a pragmatic man. "Father . . . have you considered that if we spared Mom, Sapience might be willing to offer something in return? She was . . . really close to the cell leader. In a, um, romantic way. Maybe—"

"No, Donovan." The openness, the shade of emotional vulnerability that had been there a moment before, vanished at once. "You've already been dragged far too deeply into this deplorable drama. Despite all my efforts, it's disrupted your life, your career. We've already discussed this. Whatever happens to that woman now, you're not to get involved any further. Do you understand?"

Donovan opened his mouth, then closed it again, his face hot. There was no point in arguing. *Be a good soldier. Pretend everything's fine. Do what you're told.*

"Yes, sir." Donovan's voice came out flat as paper.

His father's voice lost some of its steel. "After the High Speaker's visit, after Peace Day, when things have settled down, we'll talk more. I'll explain more to you than I can now. You must trust me for the time being."

Donovan watched his father's back disappear up the stairs.

— — —

It turned out to be easier to commit treason than Donovan expected. The opportunity came four days later, near the end of an afternoon patrol shift. He and Jet were parked outside a dilapidated single-story home belonging to the Hatler brothers, whom they'd arrested earlier in the day for spray-painting SHROOM LOVERS and MARKED FOR DEATH on the windows of an elementary school in a predominantly erze-marked neighborhood.

"It's not safe here anymore," one of the neighborhood moms had said, rubbing her line-and-dot Engineer's markings nervously as they took her statement. "We don't want the kids to grow up sheltered, but as soon as I'm promoted, we're going to apply for residency in the Round. With both boys Hardened, we have a good chance." Her two sons chased each other in circles, thrilled that school was canceled. The younger one was only five or so, a new-born exo, bald as an egg, nodes curved up the back of his skull like a question mark.

The Hatler brothers were punks. All Donovan and Jet had found in the house were crowbars, two shotguns, empty six-packs of beer, and a bucket of paint in the back of a pickup truck. Nothing SecPac worthy. They'd driven the zip-tied, cursing culprits to the civilian police station and handed them over. Just to be sure they hadn't missed anything, they'd come back to search more thoroughly and interview the neighbors. Jet called their unremarkable report into Command, then punched the line closed. "What a pair of bozos," he said, stretching his arms up to the ceiling of the skimmercar.

"Sape rejects," Donovan agreed. Guys full of hate but too dumb to be real sapes.

Jet pointed to a house down the street they'd visited a few months prior. It felt like years ago. "Hey, isn't that where Ms. What's-Her-Face lives? The lady with the banana bread?"

"Ms. Bissell?"

"Yeah, Ms. Bissell. We should go back for more of her banana bread. Anything we need to question her about?" Following leads, knocking on doors and talking to people in unmarked neighbor-hoods like this one, they never knew what kind of reception they'd get. Sometimes people wanted to kill them. Sometimes they got invited in and served coffee and banana bread.

Donovan slid his partner an incredulous look. "I still can't believe you ate her bread."

"You missed out; it was such good bread."

"She might've been a Sapience sympathizer. She could've laced that bread with rat poison."

"I think I would've been able to tell if it was poisoned."

"No, you wouldn't."

"You were there, so you would've known who'd poisoned me."

"What if *I'd* eaten the bread?"

"But you didn't. I knew you had my six. That's why I ate two pieces." Jet grinned, and although Donovan feigned exasperation, as was their way, a swift, deep guilt stabbed into him.

It was as if everything were back to normal. Jet was in such a good mood, visibly relieved to have his erze mate back on the job and acting like himself. In truth, Donovan hardly felt like himself. He slept badly at night. He worried about Anya, he thought about his mother's upcoming execution, he replayed awful moments in his mind, he was troubled by the things his father had said about what might happen if the zhree abandoned Earth. It took all his energy just to hide his anxieties from Jet; he felt as if he was lying with his whole being.

Jet checked the dashboard clock; he was taking Vic to a fondue place in one of the upscale parts of the Ring Belt that evening and had been counting down the time all day.

"Why don't you take off early?" Donovan suggested. "We're done here."

His partner shrugged. Jet never cut out early, but today he was clearly tempted.

"I'm serious. Go change into something nice, pick up some flowers."

Jet hesitated. "What about you?"

"I don't mind; you covered for me when I went to therapy tank the other day. Gate 3 is like five minutes from here; I'll drop you off, then go calm down the principal at that school and loop back up to Command the long way." When his erze mate still didn't answer, Donovan added, with a calculated combination of jesting and hurt annoyance, "What's wrong? You don't trust me to look after myself anymore?"

Jet had indeed been subtly reluctant to let Donovan out of his sight since they'd been back on duty. Being called out for it now, though, he forced a smile. "I know for sure you're not going to eat any suspicious baked goods." He started the skimmercar and set it into motion. "Well, all right. Thanks for the cover. If you're sure you're okay with it . . ."

After Jet was out of the car and through the gates of the Round, Donovan drove to an address the two of them had searched a month ago: the home of Jim and Mila Guerra, the taciturn couple who were definitely Sapience members but very good at hiding any hard evidence of it. The Guerras lived in a wood-sided duplex in a neighborhood known for being sympathizer-heavy. Donovan parked on the street and sat in the car for a minute, scared stiff by what he was about to do.

Forty-eight hours earlier, Hannah Maxine Russell had been convicted on multiple charges of terrorism, conspiracy, and involvement in an illegal organization. Donovan had watched the proceedings on the evening news. His mother had stood with her manacled hands clasped calmly in front of her as the judge read out the long list of accusations. Her gaze was distant, as if she was only half paying attention. On-screen, she appeared younger and more poised than in person; Donovan wondered if she was consciously playing a part for the cameras.

Only when the judge asked her if she had anything to say for her crimes did she seem to rouse her attention to the bench. "I mourn the lives that have been lost in the fight for freedom. However, in the crusade for the preservation of our species, there are no true innocents. If you are not fighting against the alien, then you are serving it with your apathy. The blood I give is only a small drop in the ocean that must wash our planet clean of its invaders."

She sounded both chillingly sane and perfectly insane. An ordinary-looking middle-aged woman with the conviction of a zealot and a flair for the hyperbolically dramatic. The judge sentenced her to public execution by atomization. Perhaps he too had a sense for the dramatic, because he set the date for October 10—Peace Day itself.

Donovan pulled the slightly crumpled envelope from the inside pocket of his uniform jacket. All day it had been sitting nestled against his chest, feeling as dangerous as a small nuclear device. Inside were three folded pages; they had taken hours of work while his father was out of the house. The first page stated the date, time, and place of Max's scheduled execution thirteen days from today, along with detailed instructions on how to mount a rescue.

It would be near impossible to break her out of Central Command and escape from the Round, so that left the short time during her transport to the execution site as the best window of opportunity. The second page in the envelope was a map on which Donovan had outlined the possible routes to the Steps. The Steps was the largest public square in the Ring Belt. The center of it was arranged like an amphitheater and in the summer it was used for local concerts and festivals. Children gamboled up and down the tiers of brick seating, and planters spilled over with bougainvillea. It was also where most public executions for capital offenses took place. On Peace Day, Donovan guessed the prison truck would take the longer route; the other two would be far more crowded. He'd patrolled those streets enough to be able to mark out the best place to block the road and attempt a rescue.

The final page was a SecPac transport truck blueprint. Every SecPac vehicle went into engine lockdown if the driver activated a remote alarm, but Donovan had marked the hidden reset switch as well as the tracking system the rescuers would have to disable in order to hijack the truck and make an escape. All this and more he'd explained as best he could in the instructions before sealing the envelope and writing *Saul Strong Winter* across the front.

It was the eagle that had clued Donovan in; he remembered that Guerra had an eagle tattoo on his arm—a small but exact copy of the eagle design Donovan had seen in Saul's room in the Warren, that he'd also glimpsed on the back of Reed and Dixon's truck. The eagle was a symbol of freedom, Tate had said. A symbol among Sapience's inner circle, Donovan was sure of it. If Saul was alive and out there, odds were that the Guerras would know how to pass a message on to him through the terrorist network. If it could be done, if Sapience had the information they needed to pull it off, Saul would try to rescue Max from the atomizer.

Donovan had no idea if the message would reach the Sapience commander in time, or at all. He didn't even know if Saul was alive, much less where he was, or if he'd be able to put together a rescue crew so quickly. Even if the letter did find its way into the intended hands, the sapes might decide it was too risky, or conclude that it must be a SecPac trap and decide not to act. Donovan could only hope that Saul would realize it had come from him; no *real* SecPac ruse would be so obvious and detailed, and hand delivered by an officer in a patrol skimmercar.

All in all, it was an awfully thin thread on which to hang even slim odds of success. Donovan stared at the envelope in his hands; before he could second-guess himself, he got out of the car and strode up the short walk to the front of the house. He felt as if he were watching himself and not really in control of what he was doing. It took only a second to bend down and slide the envelope under the door. He tapped the corner with his finger and the envelope disappeared. Just like that. So easily was treachery committed. Had it been this easy for his mother when she'd first started down the path to being an enemy of the state?

Donovan went back to the skimmercar, wondering who was watching him from the neighboring windows. He drove several blocks before parking beside an empty playground because he felt like throwing up. He didn't, but his hands shook so uncontrollably he squeezed them between his knees to try to stop it. Already, he was overwhelmed with regret; he wondered if he could fish the envelope back out from under the door and destroy it before it was found.

"What have I done?" he asked himself out loud. The refrain tumbled around in his skull. *What have I done?* He'd plotted the escape of a dangerous criminal. He'd divulged SecPac information to terrorists. He'd lied to his best friend. He'd betrayed his father's trust. If a high-profile terrorist escaped government custody en route to execution, the Prime Liaison's political standing would be dealt a terrible blow and Sapience would claim a huge victory. It would be immeasurably more awful if anyone discovered that the traitor was Reyes's own son, one of SecPac's supposedly incorruptible soldiers-in-erze.

The ramifications were suddenly monstrously huge; far bigger than Donovan had considered at first, far bigger than the risk of merely ruining his own life. The rescue attempt itself might go horribly wrong. What if his fellow officers were injured or even killed in the ambush? What if innocent people were caught in the cross fire? And if his mother did go free, he would have to live with the knowledge that she might go on to commit further crimes.

Guilt flooded in. Donovan bent forward in his seat, queasy. He ought to be disgraced: stripped of his marks, expelled by his erze, renounced by his father. His certainty of this made him cringe in a kind of satisfyingly cathartic agony. Why had he done it? *Why?*

Because he couldn't shake the image of his mother's tearful face as he'd walked away from her in the Pen. He was the reason she'd been captured. He'd been lost to her, then found, then lost again. They'd only had a few days together, he hadn't even been very nice to her, but she'd been willing to stand up to her own people, to leave Saul and the Warren behind, to risk everything she cared about—everything except the cause itself—for the chance to get him back. It wasn't the same as being there when he was growing up, but it still meant something—it meant a lot. If he couldn't do the same for her, maybe he really was less human after all.

If she went to the atomizer, she would be gone for good. Even when she'd been gone from Donovan's life, the idea of her, the possibility of her, had always been there. It had been more real than she was. In a way, it still was. If he watched her blink out of existence, it would be like seeing a part of himself erased. Negated. If he stood by and let that happen, if he did nothing, nothing at all to even *try* to defy the tragedy of it, he would be only what his father and his erze had made him—an obedient, dutiful soldier. Another powerless human.

Donovan sat with his forehead against the dash until his stomach felt calm enough for him to set the skimmercar into motion. His comm unit flashed; Jet checking up on him from the florist's shop, like a paranoid mother hen. Donovan sent a quick reply, suggesting anything but roses (too cliché) and giving his partner grief for not being able to stay off his comm before a date.

His heart felt heavy; what was done was done, what happened next was out of his hands and lodged firmly in the sphere of fate. He steered the skimmercar toward the Round.

25

Two hours before dawn on the first of October, Donovan was roused from an uneasy sleep by the sound of sirens. Not the pulsing wail of human emergency vehicles but the deafening, vibratory booming of the Towers alarms—a sound he only heard during large-scale zhree military drills. He clambered out of bed, confused. "Father?"

The Prime Liaison was not in his bedroom nor anywhere in the house. Donovan suspected his father had not come home at all last night. He threw on his uniform, checked and holstered his sidearm, and grabbed his comm unit. Outside, the flags over the house whipped violently in the sharp autumn wind. The alarm continued to bellow; it sounded as if a bullfrog the size of a mountain were squatting over the entire Round. Donovan jammed in his earbud, clapped a hand over his other ear, and toggled his transmitter. "Command, what's going on?" The question was barely out of his mouth when a squad of eight Soldiers ran down the street toward the Towers. Donovan jumped back at their passing; running flat-out on all six limbs, Soldiers moved frighteningly fast, their battle armor and hard yellow eyes momentarily catching the light coming from the windows of the human residences along the street.

His comm unit flashed an area-wide SecPac alert: ALL COMBAT-RATED OFFICERS EXCEPTING THOSE ON ACTIVE ASSIGNMENTS REPORT TO CENTRAL. Donovan ran for the garage and took the electricycle. He got onto the nearest concentric boulevard and laid on the acceleration. To his left, bright bursts of light flashed in the dark sky above the Towers. After a second, Donovan realized they were the thruster blasts of zhree fighter craft, rocketing up into orbit from the Towers' launching pads.

What in all erze is going on? Donovan opened his direct line to Jet. "Hey, where are you? Are you seeing this?" No answer. "Jet?"

The alarms suddenly stopped. There were two follow-up blares—one short, one long, signaling the end of the emergency alert—and then the sirens fell silent. What had happened?

Donovan turned into the grounds of SecPac Central Command and slowed; there were vehicles and stripes everywhere, crowding up near the front of the Comm Hub building. He found a spot to park the electricycle and joined the other soldiers-in-erze pushing through the double doors and filling the briefing hall. Donovan looked for Jet; he didn't see him, but he spotted a bleary Leonidas Hsu by the back wall. He started shuffling through the crowd toward Leon, but at that moment, Commander Tate stormed in and demanded their attention.

"Listen up. At approximately zero four hundred hours, orbital defense platforms detected the appearance of three Rii scouting vessels that transferred into our solar system between Mars and Jupiter. The vessels proceeded to slingshot around Mars while gathering information about Earth and its defenses." A murmur swept through the room. Tate adjusted her wire-rim glasses and plowed on, referring to the notes on her screen. "At zero four forty-five, Mur Commonwealth warships fired upon the intruders, destroying one of them. At the same time, the Rounds were alerted to the threat of possible attack, as you all know from the god-awful racket this morning. Additional fighters were launched to support the warships and Soldiers mobilized to defend the Towers and zhree installations in case of surface invasion."

The tension swelled; muttered profanities broke out. "Going to be another War Era," someone near Donovan mumbled grimly. Tate looked up and yanked the glasses off her nose. "Did I say I was done?" she bellowed. The briefing room quieted and the commander continued, "The remaining Rii scouts transferred out of the system shortly after the first one was destroyed. Although all orbital assets remain on high alert, the Rounds are standing down. From what Soldier Werth communicated to me just a few minutes ago, it appears that the Rii were solely on an intelligence-gathering mission and there's no sign of an imminent attack. So don't go bursting your nodes already. *That said*, Soldier Werth has asked me to make a few things clear.

"First, the High Speaker was scheduled to leave Round Three this morning and continue his tour of Earth by visiting Rounds Four, Eight, Nine, and Twelve before returning to Kreet. His departure has been delayed and he remains secure in the Towers until the zhree can be sure the situation is safe for him to continue. That means we're continuing to run extra security in the Round.

"Second, there's going to be a lot of confused people in the Ring Belt today. Most civilians wouldn't be able tell the difference between a Mur Nurse and a Rii Hunter to save their lives. All they know is that there was a lot of noise and ships flying overhead, and they're going to be scared. The Liaison Office is preparing a statement to calm everyone down, but in the meantime, we have jobs to do. Sapience isn't taking a holiday; in fact, they'll be trying to rile up people's fear and hostility. Don't make any statements, to the media or the public, that you don't know for a fact you're authorized to make. Stay alert, be careful out there. Questions?"

Someone in the middle of the room raised a hand. "Commander, if there *is* an invasion, what are we supposed to do? Is SecPac going to support Soldiers in combat if the Rii attack?"

It was a fair question, one everyone in the room wanted to know the answer to. They all bore Soldier's stripes on their hands and were ultimately accountable to Werth, but SecPac's role had always been to manage human threats, not alien ones. Tate glowered. "That is something I am discussing with Soldier Werth and he is discussing with the rest of the zhree zun. When I have an answer, you'll hear it. Anything else?" Silence. "Back to work, stripes."

Leon met Donovan near the door as people dispersed. "Some morning."

"No kidding. Hey, what're you working on these days?"

Leon took out the sketchbook he kept zipped under his jacket and showed Donovan a sketch of a naked fox-woman and a wolf-man embracing. "That's really good," Donovan said. "I like the pencil shading."

Leon shrugged. "I'll probably do it over. Can't get the faces quite right."

"Have you heard from Cass? How's she doing?"

"Okay. Her armor won't ever be the same, though. She might not be combat rated anymore."

"That's awful." They both fell silent for a moment.

Donovan scanned the hall and said, "Hey, have you seen Jet?"

Leon shook his head. "Vic's right over there, though. Hey, Vic, where's your sweetheart?"

Vic's pale skin went pink as they came up. "I haven't seen him."

"He ought to be here," Donovan said, troubled now. He hailed his partner over the comm again and still received no reply. "He's radio silent. There's no way he could have missed those alarms, and we have the day off today, so he's not on assignment."

"I'm sure he's fine, D. Tied up with something. He'll be back soon," Vic said. "How've *you* been? We've all been worried about you."

"I'm fine." Something about Vic's lack of concern over Jet's absence roused Donovan's attention. Vic Kohl was a good soldier but a terrible liar. "What aren't you telling me, Vic? Your face is turning red. Is Jet in some kind of trouble?"

"No, it's nothing like that." Vic's scalp was flushing now.

"Then, what? You know; don't tell me you don't."

"I don't . . . I'm not supposed . . ." Vic stammered. "He's on assignment, is all. That's why he's not here."

"What assignment?" He'd been with Jet less than twelve hours ago; his partner hadn't mentioned anything about an assignment. Jet had secret assignments that he didn't? He turned to Leon. "You know anything about this?"

Leon shook his head. "Bunch of people left here with a prison transport truck when I was getting back from shift around oh-three-thirty, though. Maybe something to do with that?"

Donovan turned back to Vic, insistent now. "They're moving prisoners?"

Vic hesitated, then said in an anxious rush, "It was a last-minute thing. Jet was only told about it yesterday morning, and he was ordered to keep you out of it. They still wanted to do it publicly, but right away, before the sapes could learn about the change."

"About what change? What are they doing that Jet couldn't tell me about?" The answer dropped into his stomach like a stone.

Vic glanced helplessly to Leon for support, then slid Donovan an apologetic look. "The execution. It's happening at dawn. Jet's running security detail for it; that's where he is now."

— — —

Donovan tore free of the hand Vic put on his arm and ran for the electricycle. She yelled after him to please *stop* and think for a minute, what was he—Donovan didn't hear the rest. He leapt onto the vehicle and slammed it into a tight U-turn, tearing down the road out of Central Command and toward the nearest gate in the Round. He was sure Leon and Vic would call in to security; someone would try to stop him. He raced the e-cycle to the side of the road, dodging between skimmercars and running heedlessly over tidy lawns, heart rate skyrocketing. Gate 5 was coming up ahead at the end of the spoke road; guards were hurrying to barricade the exit. Donovan gripped the handlebars, clenched his jaw, and swerved into the entrance lane, flying between the slow-moving vehicles entering the Round. He burst through the checkpoint going the wrong way against traffic, heard the shouts of the guards and the crackle of yelling coming from comm units, and then he was through the wall and out in the Ring Belt.

He turned on the e-cycle's navigation system and swerved across two lanes to hit the freeway entrance that would take him to the Steps. The sky was pale, the streetlights were going out; it would be less than twenty minutes until dawn. Donovan switched on the e-cycle's patrol lights; cars moved out of his way as he shot past them, the wind tearing at his eyes. Fury and confusion lit his brain. The execution wasn't supposed to happen for another ten days! Why was it happening *now*, all of a sudden, with no announcement or warning? How was that even *legal*? Why hadn't he been told? All the information he'd given Saul— wrong, wasted!

Again, he tried to get Jet on his comm. "Jet!" he shouted into the transmitter. "Answer me, dammit!" The words were ripped from his mouth almost as soon as he said them. He almost missed the exit ramp and shot narrowly between two trucks, blood roaring in his ears, exocel bristling at full armor in anticipation of being hurled against asphalt at a hundred miles an hour. He cleared the exit and slowed, but his pulse kept thudding hard and fast. A few more blocks. Just a few more blocks. Ahead of him, he saw a Road Closed sign blocking off the street. He barreled past it, turned the corner, and squealed the electricyle to a stop.

The terraced Steps lay at the intersection of several roads, and from all directions, an impromptu crowd was forming, drawn by the sight in the center of the public plaza: a semitransparent cylindrical chamber on a raised platform, the base and top of it humming with power and lit with red hazard lights. Waiting spectators were murmuring with nervous anticipation. Overhead, Donovan heard the low thrum of a circling T15 stealthcopter.

He leapt off the e-cycle and shoved his way through the outer layers of the crowd, making for the center. At that moment, a figure climbed the three short steps up to the platform, escorted by two guards, and stood facing the assembled throng of people. They fell silent, waiting expectantly for the final words of the notorious Sapience writer.

Donovan stilled. His mom's face glowed with confident serenity. She looked, for the first time, the way he'd once imagined she would look: full of life and uncompromising passion. In a clear, strong voice, she declared, "My life is the least of the things I've given up for the cause. I give it gladly, so that one day we will celebrate freedom instead of peace." The wall of the atomizing chamber cracked open lengthwise down the side. Briskly, deliberately, she stepped inside the execution chamber, as if into an elevator she was eager to take to the top floor.

In the silence, the sound of her shoes hitting the metal surface of the chamber shattered Donovan's immobility. With a strangled noise of disbelief, he fought his way forward, barely hearing the gasps and angry exclamations as his armored shoulders jostled through the press of people. As he rushed for the metal barricade fencing off the platform, he saw Jet breaking free from the line of SecPac officers, moving toward him fast. Pale with shock.

The atomizer sealed Donovan's mother inside. A static hum began to emanate from the machine. Donovan sprinted; he put a hand on the railing and hurdled over it. He launched himself up the short steps of the platform. He could shut the thing down, smash through the translucent hull with armored fists. The nearest officer, Lucius, lunged and grabbed him; Donovan whirled, slammed his elbow back into the man's head without thinking. Armor smacked against armor; the other exo reeled but didn't let go. Donovan drew his gun and aimed for the base of the atomizer. He tabbed the coil charger, his finger curled around the trigger, and then Jet was on him, seizing his hand and the weapon and forcing the barrel of the gun toward the ground. With a sharp twist, he ripped the electripulse from Donovan's grasp. Other arms joined in, grabbing Donovan and forcing him down to his knees. "No, wait, not yet," he choked out. He heard a sound, a soft thud, and looked up; his mother was pressing her hand against the inside of the wall that separated them. She was smiling at him.

Then she was gone.

It happened as these things always did. One second she was there, her eyes so intensely focused on his, the moist imprint of her hand against the surface separating them. The next second, a burst of blinding white light filled the chamber, just for an instant, like a colossal camera flash, burning Donovan's vision in a retinal eclipse. The crowd sucked in a collective gasp. There was no sound or heat; the walls of the chamber glowed but contained the entire reaction. Lightning in a bottle. A faint burning smell filled the air. Donovan blinked, and the cylinder was empty; the last of the particles of ash were sucked downward into the base of the machine until, in moments, they too were gone.

Everything gave way in a wave—first his legs, then his body, then his arms, neck, and head. Donovan slumped forward as if boneless. All the fight went out of him; numbly he let his fellow stripes pin his arms and handcuff him. Jet got up and turned away, his breath hard and ragged. When he turned back around, his eyes held pain, but his voice was all soldier.

"Donovan Reyes, by authority of the Global Security and Pacification Forces, I charge you with interference in a state execution and willful obstruction of justice."

Donovan could hear voices outside of the room. His fellow soldiers were talking about him in the hallway. He couldn't hear all they were saying, but he caught snatches of mumbled conversation: *"squishy-brained"* *". . . think they'll strip him?"* *". . . feel terrible for Jet."* An exo gone spectacularly out of erze was a revolting and fascinating thing.

Jet and Lucius had brought him back to SecPac Central Command and placed him in the small detention room where stripes were held if they were under internal investigation or awaiting disciplinary hearings. Prior to a week ago, Donovan had never imagined he would become familiar with the inside of this room. There was a long padded bench to sit or lie down on and the reproachful seal of the Global Security and Pacification Forces looming over him on the wall, but that was pretty much it. The metal door was locked, but every hour or so, the guard posted outside, a strapping exo whose name Donovan couldn't recall, looked through the narrow spy window to check up on him. You couldn't leave squishy-brained people unattended.

On the skimmercar drive back into the Round, he'd roused himself from misery long enough to ask, "Why was it moved up? Why didn't anyone tell me it was today?"

"Don't talk," Jet had said through a clenched jaw.

"Jet, please."

"Look, I don't know why it was moved. As for why no one told you, obviously it was because there was a chance you'd go insane and do something like *this*." Armor crawled involuntarily over Jet's knuckles as his hands tightened on the steering column. In a defeated mutter, "You're in a scorching hell's pit of trouble and I can't get you out this time. I can't."

"I know," Donovan said miserably.

Jet blew up at him. "What were you *thinking*? You sat in the car with me that day and looked me *straight in the eye* and promised me you had your head on straight. Nope, I didn't have to worry, you were going to stay far away from this whole mess. Then you came back on duty, putting on a show for me, acting all normal, and the whole time you were figuring on trying to bust her out, weren't you? If the execution hadn't been moved, if you hadn't been caught off guard, what would you have even . . ." Jet could barely speak from disbelief. Finally, in a heated whisper, "You really *are* a squishy-brained piece of work."

"My mom just *died*, Jet." Anger penetrated his desire to curl up and fall through the floor of the moving vehicle. "You don't know what it's like to have parents like mine. She was a sape, but I didn't want her to *die*. There's *nothing* left of her now, not an atom, and I'm going to be stripped and my dad is never going to speak to me again, so just *lay off*, all right?"

Jet had been as silent as a frozen lake for the rest of the drive. In the other seat, Lucius had said not a single word and done his awkward best to avoid looking at either of them.

Donovan lay down on the bench in the detention room. He guessed it was midafternoon by now. Lucius had brought him a leftover chicken wrap and a bag of chips from the cafeteria sometime around noon, but Donovan had no appetite. He ate the chips and left the rest of the food untouched. He knew the long wait was on account of Tate having to convene a disciplinary tribunal on short notice. SecPac handled charges against its own quickly and behind closed doors. Since all soldiers-in-erze answered ultimately to Soldier Werth, his erze master would have to be alerted, and it would be the zhree who had the final say in Donovan's fate.

In his solitude, he kept replaying the image of his mother pressing her hand against the inside of the atomizer before everything flared white. The grief he felt was strange—dull, resigned, heavy as lead. Supreme uselessness and apathy. He'd failed in every way possible.

The door of the room finally opened. Donovan looked up and wanted to die. His father stood in the entrance, staring down at him. The Prime Liaison turned and said to the guard, "Keep the door closed and the hall clear. I'd like some time alone with my son, please."

Donovan rose to his feet without meeting his father's gaze.

"Sit down, Donovan," his father said. "Look at me."

Donovan sat back down and reluctantly raised his eyes. His father's face was difficult to look upon—disbelief, shame, and anguish seeping through a cracked mask of stoniness. "You have no idea what you've done, at the worst possible time." The Prime Liaison closed his dark-ringed eyes for a moment, then opened them again. "What do you plan to say to the tribunal?"

"The truth," Donovan admitted. He'd been foolish to think he could change the course of things being decided by people and forces so much bigger and higher than he was. All he'd done was let people down—his mother, his father, his partner, his commander, his erze, even, strange to think of it, Saul and the Sapience rebels who would've attempted to save Max if they'd received the information he'd tried to pass to them in time. "I can't be a stripe anymore."

"You acted in a moment of foolish, impulsive emotion," his father insisted. "You didn't have time to come to grips with the sudden news; you acted without thinking."

"No." There was no point in lying, not anymore. He might as well make it easy for his father to be rid of him. "I did a lot more than that. I came up with a plan for Sapience to rescue Mom. I wrote a letter with all the details of the scheduled execution, the route, the transport vehicles—and I gave it to some suspected Sapience members during one of my patrols, after I tricked Jet into leaving me alone for an hour." It was both excruciating and oddly satisfying to let the words out. Like probing an infected wound. "I'm a traitor, Father. And you know what's worse? I'm not even sorry I did it. I'm sorry I lied to Jet, and I'm sorry that I'm a disgrace to you, but I'm not sorry I tried to save her. Even now that she's gone. Especially now."

Donovan dropped his face, fighting tears. Despite everything, he didn't want his father to see him cry and to be even more ashamed of him. For a long minute, the Prime Liaison was silent. Then he said in a stunned voice, "What you've done goes beyond what can be forgiven. If you admit this at your hearing, you'll be stripped of your markings. You'll be an exo without an erze. An outcast with nothing: no friends, no future."

A sick taste rose in Donovan's throat. There was nothing he could say.

"That's it, then?" His father's voice was rough. "You intend to give up?"

Donovan's face twisted. "What do you expect me to do? I have no choice. I can't be trusted, and I can't do this job, not anymore. SecPac *executed* my mom without even telling me!"

His father stared at him, exhaustion and pity etching lines into his face. "Do you want to know why the execution date was suddenly changed?" The Prime Liaison took two steps forward. "The night before last, your mother made a deal with Commander Tate."

Donovan said slowly, "I don't understand."

"She refused to escape the death penalty by volunteering anything about Sapience's plans or operations. But she did finally offer SecPac something valuable: information on Kevin Warde. She gave Commander Tate several of Warde's aliases and the names of half a dozen of his close associates—two of them were arrested yesterday. Warde is on the run now."

Donovan's mouth opened but no sound came out. His mom had betrayed Kevin? A memory flashed into his mind of the two of them squaring off in the Warren: Kevin's sneering contempt, Max's gritted anger. Donovan shook his head. Had she turned on Kevin, for him? Then, another thought: What about Anya? Was she being hunted along with Kevin?

"In exchange for intelligence on the country's most notorious exo killer, your mother demanded one thing in return," his father continued. "She asked to be executed right away. As soon as possible, with no announcement. Without anyone being told."

"But *why*?" Donovan cried. "Why would she ask for that?"

His father rubbed his eyes. "Isn't it obvious? She didn't want to give her friends a chance to rescue her. They very well might have tried—it was a serious risk even before you did what you did. Most likely they would have failed; she didn't want them risking their lives for her, compromising whatever terrorist plans they'd already made for Peace Day, to save her instead."

Donovan sank his head to his hands. She did it for Saul. To stop him from coming for her. Her life hadn't been valuable to her, not the way it had been to Donovan. The people she loved, and the *cause* she believed in—those had been most important to her all along. She'd foiled him.

He swiped at his eyes, angry and unable to help his tears. His father turned away and paced the small room twice, then to Donovan's surprise, sat down on the bench next to his son. The Prime Liaison looked uncomfortable, perched on the detainee's bench in his dark suit. He laced his fingers together and looked down at his marked hands. When he spoke, his voice was subdued and defeated, devoid of its usual confident authority. "You have something in common with her. Something admirable. You think nothing of risking yourself for others or sacrificing for what you believe in. Even if you must lie and cheat and fight terrible odds, so be it."

"The lying and cheating isn't admirable," Donovan said. "The risk-taking and fighting is just part of being a soldier, part of *these*." He turned over his striped hands.

"It's easy for an exo to be loyal to his erze. It's natural for a man to be loyal to his friends and comrades. What's unusual is seeing something worth saving in people who don't seem to deserve it. Going against all your training and conditioning to preserve a basic human connection to someone you barely know." His voice held neither praise nor reproach, merely resignation, and for a moment Donovan wondered if his father knew about Anya as well.

Had he developed some sort of previously unknown psychic parental ability?

The Prime Liaison's mouth firmed. "You may have inherited a propensity to throw away your own life, but before you do, let me explain to you the wider stakes. This morning, the Rii sent military scouts to evaluate Earth's defenses; it appears increasingly likely that an attack will not be far behind. The High Speaker is grounded on Earth and suddenly paying far closer attention to this planet than anyone from Kreet has since the War Era." His father paused to let out a strained breath. "The most viable plan Administrator Seir and Soldier Werth have presented in favor of maintaining Earth as a self-sufficient, defensible colony involves the partnership of hundreds of thousands of dependable, Hardened human allies. And today, the most-watched news footage in the Round involves an exo soldier-in-erze attacking his own people to try to prevent the execution of a Sapience rebel."

Donovan suddenly felt as if the panotin in his body had congealed, plugging all blood flow to his heart. He hadn't even thought about the fact that he would make the news. Up until now he'd been largely spared from media attention because both SecPac and the Liaison Office had made it unequivocally clear that Dominick Reyes's son was off-limits. Not even the hungriest news organizations wanted to get on the wrong side of both SecPac and the Liaison Office. Now he'd gone and thrust himself into the public light.

"Unfortunately, the High Speaker remembers you well, and when you're stripped and disgraced, it'll only confirm what he already believes—that exos are an unreliable and dangerous colonial crutch, that humans aren't worthy of Hardening. Soldier

Werth's plans will be discredited, and it'll be nearly impossible for the zhree zun to argue against abandoning Earth."

"That can't be right," Donovan said weakly. "What I did doesn't reflect on anyone else—she was *my* mom and what happened is no one's fault but mine. You have to explain—"

Donovan's father stood up. "You know the zhree don't have parental attachments; they wouldn't understand. We're all just humans to the High Speaker—savage and indistinguishable. If one human can defy his erze, why should he believe other humans won't?"

"What do you want from me, Father?" Donovan whispered in anguish. "I feel like you're always looking for something more from me—and I don't even know what it is."

"Hope, son," said the Prime Liaison. "Hope that there's a future." He placed his hand briefly on Donovan's head and left it there for a second before turning and leaving the room.

— — —

The tribunal consisted of Soldier Werth, Commander Tate, Thaddeus Lowell, and, surprisingly, Nurse Therrid. Thad was there because he was cohort captain and could speak to Donovan's character and performance, and Therrid, presumably, had been called in as the medical expert on exos. When Donovan was led into the room, the first thing he saw, besides the presence of the people who would be sentencing him, was the screen on the wall. It was playing the evening news with the sound off, and Donovan cringed to see a blurry video clip of himself kneeling on the atomizer platform, pinned down and handcuffed, minutes after his mother's execution. Tate paused the image and acknowledged Donovan's entrance with the most admonishing of glares. She motioned for the doors to be closed, then picked up her notes.

"This is a closed disciplinary hearing in regard to the conduct of Officer Donovan Reyes, on the morning of October the first, et cetera, et cetera. Present at the hearing—well, you can see for yourself who's present. Remain standing, Officer. Let's be straight." Tate dropped her notes and jabbed in the direction of the screen with her eyeglass frames. "*That* is the most disgraceful one-man circus show I've ever seen. What do you have to say for yourself?"

Donovan found it hard to move his throat to swallow. Thad, who never looked ill at ease, shifted uncomfortably in his seat. Nurse Therrid, standing at one end of the semicircular table, twitched his fins in a sympathetic grimace. At the other end of the table, Soldier Werth made no motion at all—his amber eyes were unblinking, his fins flat with icy disapproval. Donovan forced his attention back to Tate's question. "I have no excuse, ma'am." His voice came out shaky; he cleared it and continued. "I was wrong when I told you I was fit for duty after ... everything that happened. I haven't been feeling right ever since then, and when I found out my mom was being executed right away and no one had told me, I ... just ... lost it."

"You attacked fellow officers and willfully obstructed justice," Tate said. "The prescribed penalty includes losing erze status for life. You're aware of that, Reyes?"

Now that the possibility of it was so close and real, the acceptance he'd felt back in the detention room evaporated and was replaced by instinctive fear. For an exo, the threat of erze expulsion was as bad as the threat of death. Donovan managed to croak, "Yes, ma'am."

"If you were going through emotional difficulties, why didn't you bring them up, as you were explicitly instructed to by Nurse Therrid?"

"I . . . thought I could deal with it."

Tate let out a very slow, harsh breath. "You've caused a piss-stinking mess, Reyes. The public is eating up this story of an exo stripe trying to save his sape mother—they think it's some kind of touching human drama about the tragedy of our times or something like that. I don't even *want* to know how many death threats I've gotten today, or how many pleas on your behalf were called in, not to mention both Kohl and Mathews in my office trying to take the blame and begging for leniency. Bomb threats are more fun than this." The commander leaned forward, dark eyes narrowed and solemn. "You know as well as anyone that SecPac stands for peace and order in this country. A soldier-in-erze that is anything less than entirely competent and trustworthy undermines that in the severest way possible, and has no right to either the uniform or the stripes."

"No, ma'am," Donovan agreed. Jet and Vic had not given up on him—that was the only thing he could focus on from his commander's tirade. Jet hadn't turned away from him.

"Think carefully before you answer, Reyes. Can you continue to wear your markings with integrity?"

"I . . ." His mother's face flashed into his mind, so did his father's words. Tate was waiting for an answer; they all were. "I like to think I can." He glanced at Soldier Werth, still silent and forbidding. "I didn't want my mom to die; I'm human, after all.

But . . . I still believe the oaths I've sworn, about peace, and coexistence, and the greater good. I know it's my job to keep them in mind at all times, and I didn't do that today."

"Do you have anything else to say before the tribunal determines your sentence?"

Now would be the time to confess everything, to unburden himself of his guilt and his doubts, to accept the consequences of his choices. "No, ma'am," Donovan said quietly. "I know I acted out of erze, and I'll accept whatever punishment I'm given."

Commander Tate exchanged glances with the other members of the tribunal, human and zhree, none of whom had said anything the whole time. "Reyes, wait outside in the hall."

He sat outside for twenty minutes before he was called back in. Tate was tapping her glasses on the table, so the discussion must have been intense—but as he entered, she folded and stowed them in her pocket, so apparently a decision had been reached.

"This is an unprecedented situation, to say the least. To your credit, Reyes, your record up until now has been exemplary. Your experience in captivity is also without precedent, and . . ." She hesitated, her expression almost contrite. "We all probably should have taken into account the psychological trauma you suffered and not assumed you'd be able to return to duty so soon. That doesn't, however, excuse your actions." Tate glanced at Soldier Werth for final confirmation before turning back to Donovan. "You're sentenced to seven days in prison, followed by four weeks of medical leave during which you'll be under evaluation and surveillance. At the end of your leave, if Nurse Therrid grants approval, you'll be allowed to return to duty on a probationary basis." Commander Tate sighed. "None of us is happy to see you in here,

Reyes, and I hope this will be the only time it happens. Do you have any questions?"

"No, ma'am." Donovan's heart was drumming in relief. "Thank you."

"Donovan." Soldier Werth spoke for the first time, picking out the notes of Donovan's name with deliberation. "Every year I observe roomfuls of juvenile exos and choose a fraction of them for the Soldier erze. I've selected thousands of humans over the years, generations of the best exos to safeguard the citizenry of this planet. I rarely make mistakes." The Soldier's fins cut through the air and then stilled in a weighty pause. "I hope you are not one of them."

27

There was only one place designed to isolate Hardened prisoners and it was in a medical wing of the Towers. The zhree viewed criminally out-of-erze behavior by a single individual of their own kind as a medical condition, often curable, occasionally not, so the facility was staffed by Nurses and guarded by Soldiers. A few of the cells, or as the Nurses called them, rehabilitation rooms, were separate from the rest and outfitted for human occupation. The rounded walls of Donovan's chamber were made of seamless and indestructible metal weave but one side was open; he could see and speak to people outside, and they could come into his room to keep him company.

Among zhree, the criminally sick were seen as being insufficiently bonded to the erze, so it was the duty of his erze mates to visit him, bring him food and other necessities, and otherwise speed his recovery with their social presence. Donovan had to stay in his room, though; the collar around his neck would shock him into insensible paralysis if he tried to leave.

He ruminated at length on the irony that a few weeks ago, he'd been a prisoner in the Warren, and now he was a prisoner in the Towers. He was more comfortable and better treated this time around, but still, there was absolutely nothing to occupy him—no books, no screens, nothing but his own thoughts, which often turned lonely and dark. He was excited when the prison collar was removed for two hours so Nurse Therrid could escort him one floor up in the Towers to attend his third and final mandated therapy tank session; your life was at a low point, Donovan concluded, when lying motionless in a shallow pool of curative liquid and panotin replenishment gel was the highlight of your day. Every minute he was by himself he longed for someone to visit him to allay his boredom.

When they did come, he was overwhelmed by a rush of affection and gratitude. Lucius brought him a toothbrush, toothpaste, and a hamburger with fries on the first evening, and Donovan nearly wept with remorse for having elbowed the man in the head. Leon sat with him for an hour, showing him new sketches of lewd elves in various states of undress. Tennyson brought him a bottle of armor juice, whispering that he'd spiked it with rum. Even Cass came, her arm in a sling, boasting about how many surgeries she'd had. "We all want you to get better, Donovan," Thad told him.

Prison worked pretty well, he had to admit. Thinking about his mom dampened the effect, but after a few days, Donovan felt so guilty for the burden he was causing his erze mates, so ashamed that they had to see him confined and collared like an animal, and so envious of them being around one another without him, that he wanted to repent every out-of-erze thought he'd ever had and dedicate himself fervently to being a good stripe. He knew it was psychological manipulation of his exo brain, but that didn't mean it didn't work.

It also made him think about Anya, about the visits she used to pay him in the Warren, how much he'd needed them to stay sane. He understood more clearly now that he'd fallen for her for the wrong reasons, that injured and separated from his erze at the time, he'd latched on to her in desperation. Yet even knowing that didn't make him miss her less.

Jet did not come.

"He just needs some time," Vic reassured him. She came alone, miserably guilty for having let slip the news that had landed Donovan in jail and nearly resulted in his expulsion.

"Who's he patrolling with?"

"He's with Leon." Cass was Leon's regular partner and still out of commission.

Donovan tried not to feel jealous. "How are things going out there?"

"Not great. The sapes are hitting back hard. Usually they target people who're marked but not Hardened, because they're easier to kill, but lately exos have been going down too." Vic had a serious demeanor at the best of times; now she looked positively grave. "We get tired working too many hours, trying to cover too much ground. We keep going after we've taken hits and push our armor too far. Round Four lost two guys in a building bomb yesterday, and . . ." She stopped, pressing her lips together as if she was afraid she'd once again let out information she shouldn't. "Let's talk about something else. I don't want to make you feel worse."

Donovan's sentence was scheduled to end the day before Peace Day. He had not seen his father during his imprisonment—only therapeutic visits from members of his own erze were allowed. On the last day, Nurse Therrid examined him one final time and strummed a low sigh. "Physically, you've recovered well," the Nurse said. "There's no lasting damage to your body. It's your brain I'm worried about." Donovan was pretty sure that Therrid had never had one of his exo patients come close to being stripped before; the Nurse seemed at a loss as to how this could have happened. He gave Donovan the daily medication he'd been ordered to take; Donovan didn't remember exactly what Therrid had said it did to his brain chemistry to help him stay in erze, but it did help him sleep better at night. He swallowed the green capsule dutifully.

"While you're on medical leave, be sure to get plenty of sleep, follow my dietary instructions, and check in every second day. Please, stay in the Round and don't get into any more trouble." Therrid removed the prison collar from Donovan's neck and clasped his arm with troubled affection. "What became of that mischievous hatchling who used to pull my fins?"

"Nostalgic for those days when we used to make a fool of you, zun Therrid?" Jet appeared outside the entrance of the room. "We could come up with some prank to mess with you, for old time's sake. You wouldn't see it coming."

"Vercingetorix," Therrid admonished, "don't even *think* about tempting your erze mate into doing anything remotely unusual. You two have caused me enough grief. Do you see this?" He pointed to his armored hull with its swirling markings. "Premature age striations."

"I don't see a thing, zun Therrid," Donovan said.

"Your eyes are too small," said the Nurse.

Jet turned to Donovan. "You ready to get out of here?"

"Yeah." Donovan wanted to give Jet a hug but held back. The smile on his partner's face was cautious, not yet his usual grin.

Jet drove him back to his house. A fall freeze had arrived while Donovan was serving his sentence. It was a brilliantly cold, bright day; light frost dusted the grass and shrubbery. Donovan leaned his head back on the headrest of the skimmercar, luxuriating in the stark sunshine and the sight of the wide streets and the vast white sky. Peace Day decorations were everywhere. Double flags draped in windows—West American stars and stripes next to the Mur Commonwealth icons. Little kids running around with smudgy markings painted onto the backs of their hands, reflecting which-ever erze they most hoped to one day belong to. Doves and wreaths hung from doorways and street posts.

Jet sipped coffee from an oversized travel mug. "So how was lockup?"

"I wouldn't want to do it again."

His erze mate looked at him sideways. "That's good."

"One or two days would be all right as downtime. I wouldn't recommend any longer than that." He stared out the window. "I'm not complaining. It could've been a lot worse."

Jet cleared his throat. "Sorry I didn't visit. I was a crap partner. I know I was supposed to support your recovery and all that." A pause. "Then again, I felt like you were a crap partner first, so there's that. And you made Vic cry, she felt so bad. So I hope you'll understand that I was a bit too angry to come see you and not be a jerk about it."

"At least one of us is smart enough not to do things while squishy-brained with rage," Donovan muttered. "You don't have anything to be sorry for. Neither does Vic—I hope you told her that. It wasn't her fault; I made her tell me and she can't lie to save her life."

"Yeah, I know." Jet smiled a little more.

"How're things out here? How's it going with Leon?"

"He's a good guy. Quiet. Draws a lot. He's not you, though." Jet lifted his coffee mug and winced. He switched the mug to his left hand. "Been a rough few days. I don't know if any of the guys told you, but there was a huge outbreak in Round Four—they've declared a state of emergency. So everyone's really edgy, worried it might happen here too."

Donovan noticed now that Jet held his right arm stiffly; his exocel bulged up around the biceps and shoulder. "You've taken hits," he exclaimed. "No one told me that part."

"Like you needed to know that while you were in *jail*." Jet shook his head. "The sapes have started wearing fake erze markings, so from a distance, you never know for sure who's friendly and who's a sape. A bunch of us got sent to Flagstaff to go door-to-door, searching for the people who've been sabotaging the deep-space antennas. I thought this guy running toward us was marked—until he threw the grenade. All I got was shrapnel, though, no biggie." Jet set his jaw. "You really can't trust anyone who's not Hardened these days."

How very clever of Sapience. Once exos started distrusting even seemingly marked civilians, innocent casualties would go up and SecPac would be blamed. Worst case, the erze system itself could break down, leaving Hardened and non-Hardened people living in fear of one another. "I wasn't going to talk about this stuff," Jet said, glancing at Donovan in worry. "Force of habit, from having you in the car with me. Forget I said anything. You're on leave; put it out of your mind." The skimmercar settled in front of the Prime Liaison's house. "How are things with your old man?" Jet asked, changing the subject.

Donovan looked up at the entrance. "As far as I know, I still live here."

"I'm on duty this afternoon, so I can't stay, but I could come in."

"No, it's fine," Donovan said. "I'm just going to take a nap. Therrid has me on these drugs, but they make me sleepy."

Jet was silent for a minute. "Look, you were right, what you said—I don't know what it's like to have parents like yours, and I didn't go through what you did. I know there are things eating at you, things you haven't told me even now—I can see that." He ran a hand through his short, dark hair and sighed. "I'm not going to push you. I wish I could help, is all."

"You're out there doing your job, Jet. That's a lot more than I can say for myself." He didn't deserve Jet, not remotely. He got out of the skimmercar.

Jet leaned over to ask, "You're going to be at the big Peace Day ceremony thing in Scotts Bluff Center tomorrow, for your dad's speech, right?"

"I'm guessing so. I'll have to wear a suit and tie and everything."

"I'm working security, so jump on the comm and find me if you get bored," Jet said.

"Will do." Donovan waved after the car and walked up the steps to the house. For a moment, he paused in front of the door, wondering if Anya had been to her home yet, to the dirty green apartment in the TransHabs where her sister waited for news of whether she was alive.

He glanced up at the decorative Peace Day bunting draping from the eaves of the state residence. *Peace Day*. What a joke—there was no peace, not for anyone he cared about.

He keyed himself into the house and went in to wait for his father's return.

— — —

Donovan rode to Scotts Bluff Center in the Prime Liaison's official state skimmercar the next morning. It was nothing like SecPac's agile patrol vehicles; it looked like a traditional luxury sedan built by and for humans, all the overstuffed seats fixed in place and facing one direction, black paint so shiny you could see your reflection in it. The insides, though, were zhree technology; the car ran silently on micro-fission engines, banking and moving multi-directionally the same as any zhree vehicle. Just like electripulse pistols, Donovan thought, trying to adjust his tie in the car's mirror. Something once wholly human transformed by alien influence. Just like exos.

His father was on an intense conference call in the backseat, while simultaneously signing a slew of documents one of his staffers was pulling up on-screen for him. After he ended the call, he glanced up at Donovan, then looked back down and continued to sign things while speaking to him. "Unfortunately, you've made yourself into a minor celebrity—far too many people are going to be paying attention to you today."

"I could go home if you want me to," Donovan volunteered. His father had always kept him out of the public limelight at big official state functions, and besides, he wasn't all that keen to spend the day in this uncomfortable monkey suit, listening to speeches and songs.

His father pursed his lips. "I think in this case your absence would cause more of a stir. Better to make an appearance and diffuse speculation. I've asked Damascus and Benjamin to keep the media away from you, but just because you're not in uniform, don't let your guard down."

The streets around Scotts Bluff Center were already crowded with people waiting in line. Ticket hawkers stood on the corners, offering to buy or sell. As the Prime Liaison's motorcade approached, people left their places and poured onto the sidewalks to take pictures, raising small kids onto shoulders so they could see better. Despite the presence of several SecPac patrol cars and dozens of armored officers, the mood was festive. Today's Peace Day celebrations would be the largest, most elaborate ever organized, broadcast live around the country, around the world. In addition to the official speeches, there would be a concert featuring several big-name performers, an elaborate stage and multimedia presentation on the history of the Mur Commonwealth, a zhree symphony (listening to a full complement of six-limbed musicians was an experience not to be missed), and erze knew what else.

The Prime Liaison's vehicle navigated to the VIP entrance. Damascus and Benjamin opened the door for Donovan's father, shielding him as he stepped out. Donovan brought his armor up to the same alert, ready state he maintained while on duty, and followed his father as he was escorted into the stadium. He nodded to the SecPac officers they passed on the way in. He wished he was in uniform too; how was he going to survive a whole month on leave?

"There's a seat reserved for you at the front. I will see you afterward." His father turned and paused, placing a heavy hand on Donovan's shoulder. Last night, there'd been too many staffers coming and going, working late, helping his father prepare his speech—the two of them hadn't talked yet, not really, and Donovan didn't know where he stood in his father's eyes. "I'm glad you're here, son," the Prime Liaison said simply. Then he released Donovan and disappeared into the stadium lounge to greet and be greeted by a lineup of officials and politicians.

Donovan watched his father go, then groaned. The last thing he wanted was to be stuck sitting next to the Secretary of Health, trying to make polite small talk for three hours. He wandered away from the lounge, fishing his comm unit from his suit pocket and slipping in the earbud. At least he could tune in to the SecPac frequencies and monitor what was going on.

The first hour of the program was entertaining, at least. After the opening light show, the band started with a crowd-pleaser, then played two more big songs before closing with a tear-jerking ballad about peace and forgiveness. The stage lights dimmed to a soft glow as a choir of boys and girls walked onstage and stood holding hands with a clutch of zhree hatchlings, all of them singing the refrain in their respective languages, the strains melding together in harmony. Donovan handed tissues to the Secretary of Health. Part of him wished he could relax and join the crush of teenagers dancing and swaying on the floor, part of him wanted to go home and escape all this silliness, and the remainder of him couldn't help running a crowd-threat assessment-check every few minutes.

Everyone was staring at him. That's what it felt like. Sitting there, front and center, he imagined that thousands of eyes were ferreting him out, everyone from the big-shot politicians onstage to the families in the nosebleed sections. They were puzzling over just who, or *what*, he was: son of the Prime Liaison, SecPac officer, Sapience sympathizer, convicted criminal, messed-up teenager.

Donovan's exocel crawled nervously under his suit, making him feel too hot even though people were wearing hats and gloves and he could see his breath in the air.

A ten-minute intermission was announced; Donovan stood up, restless, turning on his comm unit and scanning the stadium entrances for familiar faces among the SecPac guards.

The sudden roar of engines swept over the arena; three zhree fighters ripped long white trails through the sky, tearing over the stadium as they shot up into low orbit. The crowd pointed and cheered, but a second later, Donovan's comm unit came alive: "That was *not* part of the show," Tennyson said. "Something else is going on." Another three fighters followed a few minutes later, temporarily blanketing them all in a rolling wave of sound. Donovan looked onstage; the Prime Liaison did not react outwardly but leaned in to say something to the President. Others around them shifted in more obvious confusion and worry.

"Could it be a Rii attack?" another voice, Antonio's, asked over the SecPac channel.

"There would've been an alarm, right?" Katerina's voice in his earbud. "Could be a training thing? Are we sure it's not part of the show?"

"*Not* our job to worry about that right now," Thad barked. "Eyes on the crowd, stripes!"

An announcement came on over the loudspeaker asking everyone to take their seats as the program was about to resume. Donovan began to obey, reluctantly, then thought better of it and shuffled his way down the row into the aisle. He wasn't accustomed to sitting passively in the middle of a crowd; an hour of that was quite enough. He opened his direct line to Jet. "Hey, where are you?"

"Entrance of Aisle 17," Jet's voice replied a few seconds later. "If you're coming up here, bring some curly fries."

"Please rise for the President of West America," boomed the voice over the loudspeaker. The President took the podium. He was a square-faced man with an engaging, folksy voice and a wide smile. His hands, raised to the crowd in thanks for the polite applause, were unmarked, and Donovan doubted the nominal leader of the country knew more than five words in the Mur language. "My fellow citizens," the President began. "A century ago, this proud nation rose from the ashes of war. Our founders, the signatories of the Accord of Peace and Governance, came from a generation of survivors determined to forge a better future; it is their memory, their optimism, that we honor today." Donovan saw his father standing behind the President, applauding at all the right moments. Perhaps half of the audience was actually paying attention to the speech; the rest were too interested in observing Administrator Seir and the other zhree standing onstage. It was rare to see them outside of the Round.

Donovan began making his way up Aisle 17, standing aside briefly for a man carrying an armful of drinks and a woman in a bulky coat going the opposite direction. Something about the woman seemed familiar—he studied her face for a second but couldn't place it. Curly blond hair, reddish cheeks, and a long neck—he was sure he'd seen her before. She didn't make eye contact with him, merely continued through the stadium with unsmiling purposefulness.

Donovan knew better than to let a suspicion go; he flipped through his memory, frustrated at feeling duller than usual—due to imprisonment, or medication, who knew—until it came to him a minute later. He whirled around, trying to spot her again in the sea of people. "Jet," he said into his transmitter. "I just saw Mrs. Guerra."

"Who?" Jet's voice in his earbud. "That sape couple on Birch Street?"

"She's walking down the aisle right now, in a big brown coat. No sign of the mister."

A short pause as they both ran the same assessment in their heads. The Guerra woman might be here just to watch the show, like everyone else. She might. Or she might not.

"Where are you?" Jet asked.

"Row Victor." Donovan's eyes found the woman, and he began hurrying back down the aisle the way he'd come. "I see her. She's walking across a row now, two-thirds down, ten o'clock."

"Did she see you?"

"Didn't recognize me in my civvies."

Jet said, "I'm coming your way."

The President concluded his speech by reiterating his faith in the country, in humankind, and in the close ties between the species that would improve life for everyone on Earth and elevate the planet as a citizen of the galactic community. "Happy Peace Day, and may God bless our country and all who live on our beautiful planet!" He raised his hands and smiled broadly. Donovan's father stepped forward to shake the President's hand as the massive crowd swayed to its feet in applause.

Thad's urgent voice broke into Donovan's ear over the tumult. "All of you on exterior patrol, we just got an emergency alert about a stolen SecPac transport vehicle—might be in the area. License plate number Sierra Papa Five Five Eight—"

Suddenly, Mrs. Guerra threw off her coat; there was a black object in her hand as she jumped on top of one of the seats and raised her arms over her head. "Death to shrooms and traitors!" she screamed. "FOR MAX! FOR SAPIENCE!"

Donovan had almost reached her; he sprinted the last few yards and lunged across the seats.

Jet was faster; from thirty yards away, he drew and fired, putting two bullets through Mila Guerra's chest. Screaming erupted all around them. Donovan caught the woman as she toppled backward.

He grabbed for the object in her hand as it tumbled from her grip—*Oh God, does she have a*—His heart leapt into his throat; he half expected the world to disappear in an explosion of fire.

The thing was a fake detonator—an electric toothbrush wrapped in black duct tape. Onstage, the President turned, wide-eyed, as another gunshot rang out and Dominick Reyes's head whiplashed back, a spray of red scattering across the podium.

28

Two more shots followed; Donovan would later learn that one narrowly missed the President, who was thrown to the floor by his bodyguard, and the other clipped Administrator Seir across his armored hull as he moved, resulting in a minor injury. At the time, though, all he could see was pandemonium onstage—his father disappearing under an incomprehensible storm of movement and shouting. Donovan was kneeling on the ground with the body of the Guerra woman across his thighs, blood all over his hands and clothes, her open eyes staring up at him in final pain and triumph. He shoved her off his lap, dropped the fake detonator on the concrete, and plunged toward the chaos as if in a dream, plowing upstream against the tide of terrified people stampeding in the other direction toward the stadium exits.

Donovan leapt onto the stage and was suddenly too afraid to go farther; his feet felt as if they'd landed in wet cement and been immobilized. He could see his father's legs, stretched out straight in dark, pressed pants, his polished shoes pointing up. Benjamin had fallen on the Prime Liaison, shielding him with his body, but now the big bodyguard had risen to his knees and was moaning, rocking back and forth in anguish. Damascus, who'd been posted by the stage entrance, rushed into the commotion, shoving and shouting. There were so many people in the way; someone—a doctor?—stood up, shaking his head.

Donovan found his feet again and took a step forward, then another. "Dad?"

Jet caught hold of him, pulling him back in a tight hold from behind. *"Don't."* His partner's voice was like cracked steel, hard and broken near Donovan's ear.

There were SecPac officers all over the place suddenly, swarming the stage, and Soldiers as well, moving with bristling haste, encircling the Administrator and the other zhree and hurrying them away to safety. The stadium was rapidly emptying of screaming people, but the stage lights were still on, giving the entire scene a glaringly stark white quality, as if the whole thing were actually a theater production—fake, impossible, not real. Certainly not real, because even though Donovan knew in a rational corner of his mind, without having to take a single step closer, that his father was dead, it was simply ludicrous to think that Dominick Reyes could be killed instantaneously by a single, stupid bit of propelled metal, as if he were just an ordinary man.

As fragile, in the end, as any squishy.

As if a switch had been flicked on, he heard the SecPac comm channel come alive with frantic chatter. His earbud must have been blaring the entire time, but he'd heard none of it. "No *way* they're in the stadium; the shots must have come from the tower across the street," someone reported. Thad shouted back, "That tower was cleared. We swept it twice. HOW THE *HELL* DID A SNIPER GET THROUGH THE CORDON?" Commander Tate's voice broke through on all channels, crisp with fury. "All units, the suspect is believed to be fleeing in a stolen SecPac transport vehicle, traveling northbound . . ."

Donovan turned away from the stage, registering the rest of the information with the detached single-minded efficiency of a machine instead of a man. He left behind the people crouched over his father's body and broke into a run, bursting out of the stadium onto a street filled with people trying to escape into cars and fighting over space in taxis and buses. Jet was right on his heels. "Where's the car?" Donovan demanded. He spotted their patrol skimmercar among the line of SecPac vehicles parked along the street and pushed his way through the crowd toward it. Jet put a hand on Donovan's arm, looking as if he wanted to say something to stop him, but one glance at his friend's face changed his mind. They got in.

Inside the car, Jet took manual control and said grimly, "Hang on." He lifted the skimmercar up over the sidewalk, punched on the lights and sirens, and plowed backward between parked cars, posts, and other obstacles. A few seconds later, he slammed the skimmercar sideways, shooting through a mostly vacant parking lot, then braked and shot forward into the next street, the skimmercar's gyroscopic engines whining. Donovan called up the navigation system; if the assassin was driving a stolen SecPac vehicle, it should be easy to track. As if anticipating his thoughts, Tate said over the comm, "He's disabled the tracking system; we're going on best guess here, people. Barricades going up now at the following intersections . . ."

Donovan sat back hard, choking down a sob. *Of course.* A hijacked SecPac vehicle to get through the security cordon and escape again. The Guerra woman jumping up in the middle of the crowded stadium to provide distraction for sniper shots at the crucial moment. No way the Guerras could have carried this out without inside information. *Information delivered to them in an envelope under their door.* Donovan gripped the dashboard and his stomach heaved. His mind collapsed upon itself. *I did this.* He'd given Sapience a way to save Max, but it hadn't worked; they'd been foiled by the timing, but they'd used the intelligence to carry out a different Sapience objective.

"We have a visual," Jet said tightly, too focused on driving to notice Donovan's agony. He jerked the steering column and sent the skimmercar careening through a park, narrowly missing a row of poplar trees and scraping the underside of the car against a low park fence as they pulled alongside two other SecPac skimmercars giving chase. Donovan braced himself against the inside of the vehicle, a peculiar burning-cold sensation suffusing him, traveling from node to node from the crown of his head down his spine, as if his exocel was turning to frost. He crawled out of his seat and over to the skimmercar's locked storage compartment, pressing his armored hand to the keypad. It popped open for him; he threw off his suit jacket and took out a spare handgun. It verified his body signature at once; he chambered the first round.

Jet cursed; the skimmercar navigated a sharp turn that sent Donovan sprawling. "He's toast," Jet snarled. The transport truck, a short, stocky vehicle nowhere near as fast and agile as the pursuing skimmercars, was barreling down the road ahead of them like a runaway bull, heading straight for the barricade and another three waiting SecPac vehicles. At the last minute, the truck swerved, sped over a lawn, and crashed straight into the double doors of an office building, sending glass raining down over the front of the vehicle as it lodged itself firmly into the doorframe like a beast stuck in the slats of a fence.

"Holy erze," Jet exclaimed, spinning the skimmercar to a stop in the street behind the wreckage. Donovan was out of the car before it had even stopped moving; he leapt to the ground and crossed the lawn in a straight line, like a man possessed. He brought the gun up but didn't fire; he wanted the killer to see him, to recognize him before Donovan put a bullet between his eyes. No one else in SecPac would get there first; there would be no arrest, no painless martyrdom in the atomizer.

The figure in the driver's seat of the truck groaned and turned his head. Jim Guerra's face was bleeding from glass cuts and quite calm. He met Donovan's murderous gaze—locked eyes with him—then he pulled the door handle and fell out.

"GET DOWN!" screamed Jet, running after him, and all of a sudden the truck and Guerra were gone, and Donovan was thrown backward through the air by the force of the expanding fireball that had taken their place, and everything went first red, then white, then black.

29

He was back in the Towers. He had no recollection of how he'd gotten there, which was strange, because he couldn't have been unconscious the entire time, could he? He vaguely recalled opening his eyes and noticing all the smoke in the air, and how much it stank. Also, Jet's face, smudged with dirt. People bending over him, asking him questions—he didn't remember what had been said or if he'd answered. The rest of the intervening time was a blank.

"Thank the Highest State you have eighth-generation exocels," Nurse Therrid was saying, his voice weak. "Anything less than a sixth and you'd both be dead. Donovan, can you hear me? You have a concussion and some panotin burns, but you'll be all right."

Donovan tried to raise his eyes, but they suddenly filmed with tears and the whole room turned watery. For a second he couldn't remember why he was so upset, then he looked down and saw that he was still in his white dress shirt—although bloodstained, blackened, and mangled, it did not look white anymore. His tie had been removed and the shirt cut open down the front so he could be examined for injuries. He'd dressed himself for the Peace Day celebration that very morning, had ridden to the stadium in his father's car. Now he was . . . an *orphan*. A war orphan.

He pulled his feet up onto the examining table and hugged his knees, dropping his head between his arms. He was sore everywhere. He opened his mouth to say something, but all that came out was a choked, wordless moan. Long racking sobs followed; each one shook his body. Each one hurt.

He didn't even realize Jet was sitting silently next to him until his partner's comm unit went off, beeping insistently. The table shifted as Jet got up. Donovan didn't move; his gasping heaves leveled into shallow, muffled breaths that tugged at his chest and guts.

"I can't leave him like this," Jet said quietly.

"You humans are more resilient than we give you credit for, Vercingetorix," Nurse Therrid strummed softly. "He needs to rest and grieve; you're needed elsewhere. Your erze mate will be safe and cared for, don't worry." He added in a muttering hum, "You would be unendurable without him, so I'm more than motivated to see that he recuperates."

Jet put his hands on Donovan's hunched shoulders and pressed his brow to the top of his partner's bowed head. "I'm sorry, D, I have to go. I'll be back." He held still for another second, quivering with reluctance. "You're not alone, okay? I'll be back." Then he let go of his unresponsive friend and was gone.

— — —

The passage of time took on an indistinct quality. Donovan exhausted himself with grief and regret, he slept, he woke up furious, he stormed and railed alone in the room against everything and everyone in turn before collapsing once more into a wretched stupor. He slept again.

In his dreams, he was being tortured by Kevin, he was kissing Anya, he was trying to reach his mom, he was watching his father fall to the ground, dead. In his dreams, Dr. Nakada said, "I'm here to help you," as he tore out Donovan's exocel nodes with pliers, one at a time, as Donovan screamed and writhed in agony. In his dreams, his father and his mother stood before him and Donovan had a gun in his hand; he had to kill one of them. "I expected so much more from you, son," his father admonished with a frown. His mother hissed, "You're a monster, more shroom than human." The gun wavered back and forth between them as Donovan trembled and wept in indecision, until both his parents vanished in a fiery detonation and again he was hurled through the air . . .

At last, he awoke lucid enough to sit cross-legged on the floor of the room with his back against the wall, and take stock of his situation. He felt as if he'd been through a terrible fever, like what he'd suffered when he was five years old, in the days after his Hardening. He'd been treated like an invalid child too; he'd been changed into clean, thin, hospital clothes, his feet were bare, his hair was damp from being in the therapy tank, though he must have been asleep or sedated because he didn't remember it. He was just starting to think that he was rather hungry, when the door opened and Sanjay walked in right past him with a tray of food.

"How long have I been in here?" he asked.

The nurse-in-erze was so startled he nearly dropped the tray. "What are you doing sitting down there?" he blurted irrelevantly. He set the tray down. "Three days, just about."

Three days; what on earth had happened in three whole days? "Where's my comm unit?" he asked. "Can you bring me a screen?"

"You'll have to ask zun Therrid about all that." Sanjay went to fetch the Nurse, who entered the room a short while later after

Donovan had stoically eaten the bowl of fortifying but decidedly tasteless mush that had been provided for him. The zhree knew what human exos required in terms of nutrition, but flavor and texture were not a consideration. Anyone who needed to stay in the Towers for medical care relied on kind relatives and erze mates to bring in decent meals. Bland food wasn't high on Donovan's current list of hardships.

"Donovan, poor hatchling, how do you feel?" Therrid queried, gently probing the nodes on the back of Donovan's neck. "I'm relieved you're coherent again."

"Where's Jet?" Donovan asked.

"He's on duty. He would've stayed with you, but every available soldier-in-erze has been deployed to quell the violence." The Nurse's voice was grim; his fins moved slowly.

"He hasn't been back at all? What's going on out there?"

Therrid hesitated before answering. "Unmarked humans seized one of the buildings at the algae farm. They attacked it immediately after the Prime Liaison's assassination, when most of SecPac and Werth's Soldiers were diverted. They've taken hostages and are making demands. All part of one coordinated Peace Day offensive, so it would seem. No doubt Vercingetorix and your other erze mates are occupied in the standoff."

The Nurse stepped away from Donovan, fins drooping as he spoke in a musical mutter, almost to himself. "I've heard the old-timers tell stories of the violent settlement days, but that was a long time ago. Why do humans still hate us so much, Donovan? Haven't we governed them fairly, given them all the advantages of exocels, shared technology with them?"

"Only with some of them," Donovan said. "The rest are enemies." He'd already searched the room unsuccessfully for his
clothes and belongings. "Can I have my comm unit?"

"Absolutely not. You're not remotely fit to get involved, physically or mentally."

Donovan could not disagree, but he didn't want to stay in here,
either. "I'm not a prisoner anymore; I already served my sentence.
I can leave if I want to, can't I?"

The Nurse sliced a negative with his fins. "Actually, if you
recall, you are still on mandatory medical leave, by order of your
erze. One of the conditions of your leave is that you report to me,
and considering that you have no other humans to care for you in
your unstable condition right now, I've decided you're to remain
here in the Towers until instructed otherwise."

Being reminded of his orphaned status did nothing to help
rebuild Donovan's fragile sense of composure. "Can I have a screen
at least, so I can see what's going on in the news? Please, zun
Therrid, I'm all alone in here. You know that's not good for me."

Therrid relented and brought him a screen. "If your health continues to improve, in a few days I'll move you near the group
infirmary wing so you can be with other recovering soldiers-in-erze.
You and Cassidy Spencer could give each other a morale boost."

Donovan spent the next twelve hours glued to the news until
his eyeballs felt swollen in their sockets. What he saw made him
feel like he'd been lost in some other dimension and had returned
to find that the world had truly, finally, gone to hell in his absence.

His father's assassination, and the attempted assassinations of
the President and the zhree Administrator, had starkly divided the

country. There'd been a massive outpouring of grief and anger—scenes of people gathering to mourn in public squares; his father being lauded and eulogized; even, to Donovan's uncomfortable shock, people holding prayer vigils for *him*, the tragic son. Others, though, were celebrating; Sapience sympathizers graffitied MAX IS AVENGED and THE DOG IS DEAD on the sides of buildings, held spontaneous freedom rallies, and flocked to join the cause. Riots had broken out in cities across the country, pro and anti-government groups clashing in continuously replayed violent footage of cars and buildings set on fire, people running and shouting, tear gas and bullets being fired.

In Round Three, most of the news attention was riveted on the hostage crisis unfolding in the algae farm along the North Platte River. The huge zhree facility was divided into several sections, each one drawing water from the river to grow numerous crop strains for zhree consumption and export. According to the news crews circling the scene, around twenty armed Sapience members had barricaded themselves inside one of the buildings, trapping two zhree Engineers and six marked human workers inside with them. "As of right now," said the somber reporter in the studio, "it appears as if there is still no progress in the three-day-long standoff between SecPac forces and the Sapience members inside, who continue to publicly demand that all prisoners captured in the Black Hills raid last month be released from imprisonment."

The camera went to the on-site correspondent, who shouted over the blowing wind, "What we do know is that in the wake of the Prime Liaison's assassination, the only two people with the authority to make that decision are the President and Commander Tate, both of whom have reiterated that there will be no negotiating with terrorists. For their part, Sapience has declared that unless the government responds with concessions in the next twenty-four hours and begins releasing prisoners, they will start executing hostages."

The camera cut to a wide-angle shot of the building, a long white hydroponic structure surrounded by untamed prairie grass and riverside stands of cottonwood in the backdrop. Over a dozen SecPac vehicles ringed the property; two stealthcopters circled overhead. Donovan peered at the screen; he could see uniformed stripes, their rifle sights trained on the entrances, and a few zhree Soldiers as well. Even though SecPac had primary jurisdiction over all cases of domestic terrorism, since two of the hostages were zhree, it was no surprise that Soldiers were also involved. Two of them were walking in the corner of the camera's frame; another was talking to a human figure Donovan was sure was Commander Tate.

"We've heard a lot about the eight hostages being held, but what do we know about the Sapience members involved?" the studio news reporter was asking another expert.

"SecPac claims it has identified some of the hostage takers from security footage captured before the cameras were disabled." A video began playing: an interior shot of the algae farm with its long rows of transparent bubbling tanks. Five insurgents ran into the frame, wielding weapons and shouting—the last one to enter the picture aimed and fired at the camera and the screen went dark. The news program replayed the footage but in slow motion this time. The reporter said, "The first man entering the room in this image is the suspected head of the group: Saul Strong Winter, a known Sapience cell leader who escaped the Black Hills raid and is wanted in connection to a multitude of terrorist attacks over the past . . ."

The reporters kept talking, but Donovan had stopped listening. He stared at the small screen, stunned. In the foreground was indeed Saul, in camouflage pants and a bulky panotin vest, his thick arms holding an M16, his face partially obscured due to the angle of the camera but his shaved head and the set of his broad shoulders unmistakable. The video continued playing, artificially jerky. Javid came into the frame, bringing up the rear; he peered up at the camera and aimed his rifle at it. In the second before he pulled the trigger, Donovan recognized the slim figure in front of Javid, and a small strangled noise of despair left him.

Anya was in there. She was one of the hostage takers. One of the sapes capitalizing on his father's murder. In less than twenty-four hours, Donovan figured she would be dead too.

— — —

He turned off the screen and stopped watching the news. There was nothing he could do, nothing he *should* do. He'd tried to change his mother's fate and only made everything worse. If he'd put his head down like a good soldier and accepted that it wasn't his place to make such decisions, maybe his father would still be alive.

He wasn't responsible for Anya. Why, *why*, did he keep letting himself think that he was? She'd made her choices. Just like Max had made her choices. She'd thrown her lot in with Sapience and decided to be a part of this terrorist plot that could only end in tragedy. Didn't she *know* that hostage standoffs always ended badly? Usually with the terrorists being *shot*?

The sapes in there deserved what was coming to them. *Especially* Saul. Jim Guerra had pulled the trigger, but Saul must have planned or approved the Prime Liaison's assassination. Donovan ground his fist into his palm. To *think* that he'd sworn an oath to the man, had actually been relieved to find out he'd survived the raid on the Warren, and had *given him that letter* . . .

Donovan felt himself sliding rapidly back down into the dark hole from which he'd recently emerged; he banged his armored head against the wall and focused on the sharp pain in the center of his forehead to will himself back over the lip. Saul was a formidable man but he'd aimed too high this time; if he was doing this to avenge Max, well, odds were he'd be joining her soon enough. The sooner the better, as far as Donovan was concerned.

As for Anya . . . Donovan put his back to the wall and sank to the floor. He'd tried so hard to convince her to leave while she had the chance. *Stupid, stupid squishy girl. Not my problem. Not anymore.* What they'd had for those few days . . . that one night they'd spent together, the one he kept thinking about with such wishful, torturous regularity . . . it wasn't meant to be. It was a freak trick of his screwed-up emotions, a continuing cruelty that his pulse still sped up madly when he thought of her. Her soft body pressed up against his; her luminous eyes, her small upturned nose, and the faint saltiness of her chilled lips . . . His rib cage contracted with guilt. He'd just lost his parents, how could he even be thinking of Anya?

I just don't want to lose her too.

Idiot. You can't lose something you never had.

Donovan left the room and wandered down the curved hallway. There were several other chambers with patients inside; this section of the honeycombed Towers was where injured or sick exos were treated. The prison where he'd served out his week-long sentence took up the level directly below them, and a shorter, adjoining tower contained the human Hardening facilities and infirmary—the first part of the Towers he'd ever been in. Donovan stood by one of the circular windows, surprised to find himself looking down at a crowd of several dozen small children and their parents waiting to enter the building next door.

Remembering when he and his father had been down there brought Donovan a fresh stab of grief, along with a poignant jolt of sympathy. Those little kids were walking into something they didn't understand yet. A few of them might not survive the procedure, but in a week or so, the rest would be exos, like him. Would they come to see themselves as fortunate or burdened? The lucky ones or the victims? Were they gaining something or losing it?

A hand smacked his ass. "Hey there, good-looking stranger." Cassidy Spencer winked at him when he turned around. She gave him a high five with her left hand—the right arm was still in a sling. "Nurse Therrid said I could find you up here, med-leave buddy."

Seeing his erze mate buoyed Donovan a little. "Hey, Cass, what are you in for?"

She gestured toward her arm. "Checkup and physio. You want to see?" Donovan was about to say that was quite all right, but Cass loosened her sling and pulled it down to show him her bare shoulder and upper arm. There was a lot of scar tissue, but it really wasn't as bad as he'd expected and he told her so.

"The lateral node branch was too damaged, so this is as far as my armor goes now." She armored up but the panotin stopped beyond her shoulder blade, as if it had run out or been halted by an invisible dam, leaving bare, puckered skin exposed down her right arm. "The good news is," she added cheerfully, "because the damage isn't over any vital organs, if I regain all muscle function in my arm, I can still be combat rated."

"That's great news," he said.

"Ugly as a baboon's arse, though." She sighed. "At lease *your* scars don't make you look bad in a swimsuit." She punched him in the shoulder. Donovan winced, not from the punch. Cass's voice softened; she said contritely, "I'm joking around with you because I can't think of anything to say that could possibly make what you've been through any more bearable. I'm sorry about your dad. He was an important person, but he was your dad first."

Donovan blinked and nodded wordlessly. Damn Cassidy—she could make you laugh or make you cry with a few words. "So," he said, clearing his throat and changing the subject, "what've you been doing on leave to keep from dying of boredom? I found out that watching the news is a bad idea."

"Terrible," Cass agreed. "Every crisis you hear about, you know your friends are out there dealing with it, that they're in danger and you're not, and you feel so useless you could kill yourself. I can't watch the news. You know what I've been doing instead, though?"

"What?"

"Chatting with Soldiers." She looked pleased with herself. "You know, trying to improve my Mur language comprehension, so I'll be like you, not even needing the translations. Some of the older zhree are standoffish with humans, but the younger ones don't mind. I think they see a crippled stripe and feel sorry for me."

She rolled her eyes ruefully. "Sometimes they forget I'm there; you wouldn't believe how much they talk around me."

Most humans feared Soldiers—they looked terrifying, and no one had forgotten that they'd crushed humanity during the War Era. Donovan, who understood Mur far better than most, knew that zhree Soldiers were not all that dissimilar from human ones— they dealt with periods of extreme boredom interspersed with periods of extreme violence, and when they weren't seeing action they passed the time complaining, telling stories, making bets, and giving one another grief. "Learn anything interesting?" he asked Cass.

"They gripe an awful lot about homeworlders," she said. "About how the High Speaker doesn't support the colonies. He's still stuck on Earth, you know, inspecting things, asking questions, and it's making them all pissed off and nervous. The Soldiers are all convinced that the Rii are going to attack soon, and the way things are going, Kreet is going to hang Earth out to dry. Some of them have fought the Rii in other places and they think the homeworld isn't taking the threat out here seriously enough."

"There were a bunch of zhree fighters in the sky on Peace Day," Donovan recalled. "Do you know what that was all about?"

"Oh yeah. Rii drones were detected and shot down in Earth airspace. The Soldiers were all talking about it, but I don't think many humans noticed because of the Sapience attacks that were going on." Cass rubbed distractedly at her damaged shoulder, frowning. "It makes me think that it might not even matter whether we win against Sapience or not. We might all be scorched in the end anyway. Someone ought to give that newsflash to the sapes." She shook her head and smirked in self-exasperation. "Man, I'm *really* cheery, aren't I? Let's not worry about it right now. Not much we can do anyway, besides wait to see what happens next."

"Right," Donovan said. *What happens next.* His stomach gave a lurch.

— — —

"I have to go there, zun Therrid," Donovan insisted. "There're only a few hours left before Sapience's deadline, and then they're going to start killing hostages."

"I'm sure your commander and your erze mates will not let that happen," Therrid reassured him, taking hold of Donovan's arm and escorting him gently but very firmly back to his room. He'd found Donovan trying to leave the medical wing. "There is even, I understand, a squad of Soldiers present and ready to take control of the situation."

Donovan pulled his arm free of the Nurse's grasp. "That's the problem." The standoff was a no-win situation. The things Cass had said—they'd suddenly and clearly brought back to mind every-thing his father had told him, right before his disciplinary hearing, about what the bigger stakes were. "SecPac won't wait for the dead-line; they'll storm the algae farm any minute now and kill the terrorists, and if they don't, the Soldiers will." The outcome was obvious to him now. "They *have* to, after everything that's already happened with the High Speaker watching. They can't look weak. They have to prove they're in control of Earth, or the High Speaker will be even more convinced the planet isn't worth hang-ing on to."

"You may be right," Therrid conceded, "but hopefully the High Speaker will think differently if the rescue attempt is successful and the hostages quickly recovered. Soldiers and exos working together to handle the crisis, just as your erze master has been advocating."

Donovan shook his head adamantly. "But that's not how other humans will see it. Some or all of the human hostages will end up dead in the fighting. So it'll look like SecPac slaughtered a whole lot of squishies just to save two shrooms and an algae farm." He paced the room, hands dug into his hair as the whole picture came into focus for him. If SecPac didn't resolve the situation immediately, it would look weak and incompetent to the zhree. If it went in with guns blazing, then exo stripes would be viewed the way Sapience wanted them to be—as villains. Live on international news, the whole world would see armored humans fighting alongside aliens against other humans. Something unnatural, something to be feared and hated, not respected and emulated, as his father had so vehemently wanted. Even if the standoff was resolved to the High Speaker's satisfaction, the outpouring of goodwill following the Prime Liaison's death would vanish, more sympathizers would flock to Sapience, and soon the violence would be even worse than before.

"Can't you make an exception to my leave so I can go there?" Donovan pleaded.

Therrid was patient, but now the movement of his fins grew stiff with displeasure. "Donovan," he said. "You've suffered a great deal. Now you have to stay back and trust your erze. You are one adolescent human. What do you even expect to do if you go there?"

Donovan let out a groan and started pacing again. "I don't know for sure, but I can't just sit here and watch. Things are going to go badly, I know it." Jet would be rushing into a building full of heavily armed terrorists. Anya would be shot dead on the spot. He'd already tried to convince himself that there was nothing he could do about it, that he should leave the fight to others, but as the fateful hours ticked by, he couldn't make the conviction last.

If there was one thing his father and mother had had in common, it was the relentless belief that a person had to act for a greater goal, no matter the personal cost. As much as he wanted Saul to pay for what he'd done, the bloodshed about to happen at the algae farm was something neither of his parents would want. Of that, Donovan was certain. "I have to try and stop it," he said.

He started to move around Therrid to get to the door. The Nurse shifted swiftly to block his way. "You're not to leave the Towers, you infuriating hatchling. That is an *order.*"

Donovan took a step back as if he'd been shoved. Nurse Therrid was not Soldier Werth, he was not Donovan's erze master, but he was still zhree, and a direct command delivered in such an unequivocal tone made Donovan quail under the instinct to obey. Therrid walked to the door, touching a few controls to set it to lock behind him. "You're a brave and well-meaning human, Donovan," he strummed, less harshly, "but this is for your own good."

Donovan trembled, glaring in hurt at the Nurse. The walls and doors of the Towers were practically indestructible; once Therrid confined him in here, he wasn't getting out.

That's it, then? His father's voice came into in his head. *You intend to give up?*

Donovan's fists clenched. His armor wavered, as if it possessed a mind of its own and was not in agreement with him. *I'm sorry, Therrid. This really is going to hurt me more than it'll hurt you.* Before he could think about it a fraction of a second longer, he leapt at Therrid, throwing his body across the Nurse's rounded torso, and punched him in the nearest big yellow eye.

Donovan's armor dropped before the blow landed, completely involuntarily, as terrifying a feeling as if he'd abruptly lost the ability to breathe. If he hadn't known it would happen, hadn't been expecting the physical shock, he would've frozen. Instead, he pushed through it, pushed through the trip wire in his brain that prevented him from attacking zhree. He winced from the unfamiliar sting of bare-skinned knuckles striking a hard, rounded surface, the jarring impact of his mortifyingly vulnerable body hitting Therrid's armored hull.

It was Therrid that let out a high trill of pain. The zhree stumbled back on three legs, two other limbs flailing, the sixth one clapped to his eye. He was more surprised than actually injured, and any zhree, even a Nurse, was stronger than a single unarmored human. If he'd been thinking quickly, Therrid could've easily overpowered Donovan, but he'd obviously never imagined that a human—one of *his* humans, an exo—could turn on him with such suddenness. Donovan didn't waste his two seconds of opportunity; he rolled away from Therrid, jumped through the door, and slammed the lever to slide it closed. "I'm sorry!" he shouted before the entrance sealed, locking Therrid inside. He caught the long, shrill whistle of zhree profanity before it was cut off, and then Donovan was running down the hall.

After a couple seconds, he forced himself to slow to a walk. It wouldn't be too long before Therrid overrode the locking mechanism, or Sanjay or another Nurse wondered where Therrid had gone and found him in Donovan's room. He didn't have much time to get clear of the Towers, but it wouldn't do to arouse suspicion by tearing through the halls as if he were on fire. He took the curving ramp down a level, feeling wildly jittery and a little sick from what he'd done; his armor was still knocked out. *Breathe. Breathe. Calm down*, he willed himself, and as he walked casually out of the building, bare feet stinging from the cold, he felt sensation tingling a little painfully back into his nodes, like a frozen limb regaining circulation. *If Therrid reports me for assaulting him, I'll be stripped for sure*, he mused, but the thought caused only a brief flutter of panic, nothing that compared to his updated standards for true disaster.

Still plenty of likelihood of that—and not much time.

30

It took an hour of tearing down the US-26 on an electricycle to get from the Round to the algae farm. A skimmercar could have made the trip in less time but the e-cycle was the only thing in the garage at his house (his father's state skimmercar was gone) and he couldn't afford to risk being apprehended by spending any more time than necessary within the walls of the Round.

He'd had to go back to the house for clothes and boots, and for a few seconds, he'd paused in the foyer, stricken at the thought that no matter what happened, this would not be his home any longer. His father's belongings were still everywhere—his hat hanging from the coat rack, his papers on the table, even the coffee-ringed mug he'd used on the morning of Peace Day was still on the kitchen counter. It was as if his father were simply at work as usual but would be back; he might walk into the house any minute. The apparent certainty and cruel impossibility of it slowed Donovan as he tried to leave; even in his rush, he found himself paralyzed half in and half out the front door. Only after a moment, when his gaze rose past his own bedroom window to the roof and he saw that someone had lowered the flags of the state residence to half-mast, did the hard truth rear up again: His father was gone and this stately but stiff-mannered house where Donovan had lived most of his life would pass to another Prime Liaison.

Donovan swallowed, then he pulled himself together and ran.

It was already late afternoon on what had been a crisp October day; the sun was on its way down and Donovan raced the shadow of his e-cycle lengthening ahead of him on the pavement. A few skimmercars passed him, but otherwise he was alone on the road, and on any other day he might have enjoyed the long stretch of scenery. This whole area, within a hundred-mile radius of the Round, had been a charred and war-torn wasteland after the War Era; there were large craters and furrowed ridges of earth to either side of the rebuilt highway, but their outlines were obscured by the rolling sea of wild prairie grassland and replanted cornfields that had long since grown over the old battlefields.

Donovan turned on the e-cycle's headlights and leaned forward, putting on even more speed as the sky turned indigo. SecPac would wait until it was dark to attack, when they could take full advantage of night equipment that the terrorists did not have, but they would not wait long.

He saw the cordon miles before he reached it. The first SecPac officer he came across didn't recognize him in the gathering dark, with Donovan out of uniform. "I'm sorry, sir, you're going to have to turn back," said Sebastian, waving him to a halt and pointing back down the highway. The road ahead was blocked by large orange cones. "This is a secure area."

Donovan paused long enough to lift a hand from the handlebars to show the man his stripes. "I need to talk to Commander Tate," he said. "Right away."

Sebastian blinked. "Reyes? I thought you were—"

"Long story, no time to explain," he said, and drove between the cones and up to the main congregation of vehicles and people before the other exo could say anything further.

He'd indeed arrived just ahead of the action; it was an orderly but busy and tense scene he entered. Pulse rifles were being handed out, ammunition loaded, night scopes attached. Everyone with their armor up, talking in terse, short sentences, breath rising in puffs of steam, anticipation and combat readiness in the air. Donovan jumped off his e-cycle and hurried toward the sound of Commander Tate's voice barking out orders.

Thad and Jet were with her, locked in intense conversation. Jet listening, fingers drumming the top of his E201, Thad talking to Tate and pointing at different sections of a screen displaying a blueprint of the building, the Commander with the end of one arm of her eyeglass frames clenched between her teeth as she studied the plan. Donovan ran up to them. "Commander, wait," he blurted. "Don't go in, not yet."

Jet's mouth fell open. It might have been the first time in their lives that Donovan had seen his best friend completely speechless.

Commander Tate recovered from her surprise first. "Reyes." She pulled the wire arm of her glasses from her mouth. Her eyes narrowed in a flat, deadly expression. "What in the name of oath and erze do you think you're doing here?"

"Commander, don't send them in there. We might get a few of the hostages back alive, but it'll be a bloody massacre, you know it will. The whole world is watching. We can't—"

"You are entirely out of line, Reyes. I don't know what is wrong with you, but I don't have the time to find out right now, and frankly, I don't care." Tate started walking away. "Someone get this insubordinate, squishy-brained lunatic out of my sight."

Thad locked an armored hand on Donovan's arm. "Let's go," he said.

"There has to be another way!" Donovan shouted at Tate's back. "I have an idea; there's a chance we can talk them down without any killing—just *please* listen; what have you got to lose?" Ariadne came and took hold of Donovan's other arm, and they began to pull him away; he yelled at Tate, "This is what the shrooms want us to do, but is it what *you* want to do? Is it?"

Tate stopped. She turned around and stalked back to Donovan until she loomed in front of him. In a low, dangerous voice she said, "Watch what you say, Reyes. There are Soldiers stationed around here, and if we don't act tonight to resolve this crisis, they will override SecPac's authority and do it themselves. You have no idea what kind of pressure we're under."

"I do," Donovan protested. "My father told me. If the High Speaker loses confidence in zhree control of Earth and withdraws support, we're scorched as soon as the Rii attack." He kept talking fast, words spilling out of him. "But this isn't like the raid on the Warren and you know it. The gunmen in there know we're coming. There are innocent people inside, and even if we take the building, there's a good chance we'll have to bring the human hostages out in body bags, along with twenty sapes who haven't done anything yet besides make threats."

"Tell me something I don't know," Tate snapped. "You don't think I want a solution that doesn't involve dead bodies on the news? We've gone past that point. The only way this ends peacefully is if those squishy insurgents come out *right now* with their hands in the air and return the hostages with a smile and a 'so sorry for the trouble,' and I don't see that happening, do you?"

Donovan licked his wind-chapped lips; this was it, his last gamble. "Let me go in there. Let me try to talk them down."

Tate's face crinkled in disbelief. "What kind of delusion-causing pharmaceuticals are you on, Reyes? You don't think we've already tried to send in a negotiator? The sapes won't let anyone near the building. They want to see live media coverage of the detainees from the Warren raid being publicly released or they don't talk. What makes you think they won't mow you down with gunfire as soon as you get near the door?"

"Because I'm the son of Max Russell." Donovan closed his eyes for a second. "Saul Strong Winter loved my mom, and I think he's doing this in part because you sent her to the atomizer. There's only one stripe on Earth he'll hesitate to kill, and that's me."

Commander Tate stared at him for a long moment. No one moved, not Thad, or Ariadne, or Jet, who still seemed frozen dumb-struck. Donovan waited, his heart in his throat; Tate was actually considering his wild idea, which was all he could ask for.

She said, finally, "You're not a trained negotiator. If you got in there—and this is a big *if*—what would you say to Strong Winter that might possibly change his position?"

"The truth," Donovan said. "That all of us humans—stripes and sapes—we might all be done for if we don't find a way to walk out of this. That whatever fight we're going to keep having after tonight, let's have it, but this is the worst possible moment for a showdown and if we do this thing, neither side is going to win, no matter what."

Tate said, "You realize there's a damn good chance they will stick a gun in your mouth and blow your brains out before you have a chance to say any of that, don't you?"

Donovan nodded. "I'm counting on the fact that I'm a con-victed criminal who tried to save my terrorist mom to earn me around thirty seconds' worth of brownie points with the sapes."

Tate scowled, then glanced at Thad Lowell. The lieutenant arched his eyebrows. "I hate to say this, but at this point, almost anything's worth a shot."

Donovan pressed on. "If it doesn't work, all you've lost is one man, and you go back to Plan A—storming in and taking everyone out. And then you deal with the fallout." He refused to relinquish his hold on Tate's gaze. "We're supposed to protect civilians, we're supposed to be examples of how exocels and erze markings make us better humans, not worse ones, but instead everyone on Earth, everyone who might one day be a Sapience sympathizer, will believe the worst about us—that we're nothing but trained attack dogs for the shrooms. My father—" Donovan's voice wavered for a moment. "My father would never want that."

Tate's jaw clenched; a vein in her neck bulged. "Let him go," she said to Thad and Ariadne.

Jet suddenly found his voice again. "Commander—"

Tate held up a hand to cut him off, her eyes still on Donovan. "I'm giving you one hour, Reyes. I'll stall the Soldiers for that long. In one hour, whether you're out or not, we go in."

"I understand, ma'am."

"You can't be serious," Jet whispered in mounting horror.

"Get him a uniform and a concealed comm," she said to Thad.

"No," Donovan said. "No uniform or comm. I'm not going in as a stripe. Just as . . . as myself."

"Then we won't be able to monitor you," Tate said. "Things go south, we won't know until it's too late."

"It won't really matter; you'll know in an hour anyway."

"We also won't be able to hear what's being said." She stepped close to him, bending her face down inches from his. "I asked you before if I could count on you to do your duty, and you lied to me. You defied orders *again* to come here. I'm not convinced you're in erze, even now." Her next words were a slow hiss. "Can I still trust you, Reyes?"

"I guess you'll find out."

"I guess I will." Commander Tate stepped back. "One hour."

Jet was shaking his head in furious denial. As soon as Tate and the others turned around to send word through the ranks to hold their places, Jet dragged Donovan aside. His eyes were so wide it was alarming. "*Why are you doing this?*" he demanded. "You're supposed to be in the Round . . . How did you even get out of the Towers?"

"You know how we've been overdue in pulling a fast one on Therrid?" Donovan managed a rueful smile. "Well, I fixed that."

Jet put a hand over his eyes. "I can't let you do this."

"Commander Tate already has."

"You're killing me, D. Just when I think nothing else can possibly go wrong with you . . . you come up with *this* . . . you expect me to watch you . . ." Jet could barely speak. He took a deep breath and pulled himself together. "I'll find her for you, okay? The girl. The one I know you care about, who's in there. Call this off, tell Tate you can't do it after all, and I promise when we get in there I'll do my best to find her and bring her out alive. I swear on my marks. I'll pass the word down; all of us, we'll do it for you. We'll finish this, but we'll bring her out."

Donovan gulped back a hot, confusing knot of emotions. Jet's pledge wasn't just tempting, it was the best chance he had of making sure Anya survived. "You heard everything I said, Jet. It's not just about her. If it was, I'd say yes in a heartbeat. But it's a lot bigger than that. There's a lot more at stake than my life, or hers, or any of ours."

Wordlessly, angrily, Jet unslung his E201 and set it aside. He pulled the night vision goggles off his forehead and unbuckled his sidearm holster. Donovan said, "What are you doing?"

"Going with you."

"No!" Donovan grabbed Jet's arm to stop him. "Jet, *no*. There's a chance, because of my mom, that the sapes will listen to me. That's not the case for you. This whole thing is freaking me out enough without you being in danger too."

"I'd rather eat bullets with you in there than be stuck *helpless* out here."

"You coming with me will doom any minuscule hope of this working."

"We're *erze*," Jet said fiercely. "Not just any erze. We're stripes. We swear the same oaths, we watch each other's backs, we make our stands together. What would you do in my place if I asked *you* to sit on your hands and let me go alone and unarmed into a building full of desperate, machine gun–wielding, exo-hating terrorists with nothing to lose?"

Donovan's throat was tight. "If there was no other way, if I had to do it because it might save dozens of lives . . . I guess I'd pray really hard to whoever's listening. And if you didn't come back out, then I wouldn't feel bad about tearing that place apart and sending as many of those sapes as I could to hell." He couldn't afford to lose any more time; Donovan pulled his stricken erze mate into an embrace, then turned and walked as fast as he could toward the white building without looking behind.

31

Every step of the roughly three hundred meters Donovan had to cross to approach algae farm Building 5 felt like stacking another betting chip on a spinning roulette wheel. Brittle yellow grass crunched under his feet; everything else was silent except for the sound of his own breathing. He kept his arms stretched out and his hands open so it was apparent he was weaponless. They started to ache. Halfway there, two-thirds, three-quarters. Every set of eyes on both sides of the divide must be on him. The building loomed closer: steel lattice frame, off-world fabricated flexible glass paneling that let in the sunlight but was unbreakable and entirely opaque from the outside. Only two entrances, one on the west end, one on the east. It would not be easy for SecPac to storm.

"I'm not armed!" he shouted as he took another step closer, and another. His boots ground on gravel now. "I'm here to talk. Don't shoot, I'm not armed." The entrance ahead of him was closed. Would they simply not acknowledge him? He kept walking; in ten seconds, he'd be able to reach out and touch the door.

It flung open suddenly. The sapes were smart enough to have turned out the lights inside; all Donovan saw was the dim outline of two figures with assault rifles trained on his chest. He stopped, every particle of panotin in his body pouring to the surface, half expecting the gunmen to open fire on him then and there. "Don't shoot," he said again. "I'm here to talk."

"Get in!" shouted one of the sapes, a woman with a black mask over her face. "*Move!*"

Donovan crossed the remaining distance and stepped into the building. The barrels of the rifles never wavered in their focus. As soon as he was in, the door shut behind him and for a few seconds, he could see very little. "*Walk,*" demanded the other sape, a man. A slight waver in his voice betrayed his nervousness. "Keep your hands up."

Donovan took several slow steps forward; his boots clanged on what sounded like a metal walkway. "Keep going." Several more steps. "On your knees, shroom pet." He obeyed, lowering himself to the floor. His eyes adjusted to the dimness; he could see that he was on a wide, central metal causeway that stretched across the interior of the building. On either side of him were rows of massive, open cylindrical tanks, fifteen feet tall, starting one level below ground and reaching to shoulder level on the main floor, the warm liquid inside them bubbling with cultivated food algae.

The two gunmen were positioned behind him; the woman kept one rifle trained on him while the man patted Donovan down for weapons. He ran his hands along Donovan's arms and around his torso. He found only a slim notebook in Donovan's inside jacket pocket; he took it out and tossed it to the floor. He checked Donovan's legs and ankles.

"I'm not armed," Donovan said again. He glanced around, moving only his eyes. A shuffling noise to his left and movement in his peripheral vision. He turned his head very slightly. There, on the concrete basement floor below him, were the hostages. Two zhree Engineers, their limbs lashed awkwardly together with metal wire, were chained to one algae tank; the six humans, wrists bound, sitting on the floor, were tied together and attached to another tank. They looked up at him, their eyes desperate and hopeful.

Donovan placed his hands behind his head; it was dark, but they might notice his stripes and take some comfort knowing he was here to try to help them. "Are you all right?" he asked. If any of them were already dead or injured, negotiating would be impossible.

"You *don't* talk to them," snarled the woman, touching the muzzle of her rifle to the base of Donovan's skull. The cold metal pressed against one of his nodes; his shoulders tensed as he struggled hard not to battle-armor. The woman said to her partner, "Tie him."

I've really had it up to here with being handcuffed, Donovan thought, as the man looped a metal cable restraint over his right wrist, pulled it down, and cinched it together with his left wrist behind his back. "I want to talk to Saul," he said.

A familiar figure approached, emerging from the shadows at the end of the walkway. His boots clanged on metal, then stopped. "Look at this. Our old friend from the Warren."

Donovan's heart sank. "Javid."

Javid's pale eyes stood out like twin moons against his skin and clothes and dark expression. They drilled into Donovan with undisguised loathing. "Do the shrooms always send you ahead, like some kind of trained canary before they descend en masse?"

"No one sent me," Donovan said. "I asked to come. I need to talk to Saul."

"You'll talk to me," Javid said, stepping closer. "You twisted Max's mind, and look what happened to her. Maybe you could twist Saul's somehow, but you can't pull any tricks on *me*. I knew back in the Warren that you were leading them straight to us, and I was *right*. The very next night, they came. I should've killed you when I had the chance, but I didn't follow my instincts, and a lot of good people are dead or captured because of it."

"I didn't lead them to you."

"Don't lie to me!" Javid shouted, spittle flying from his mouth.

Donovan clamped his mouth shut. He couldn't say anything more without revealing the identity of an undercover SecPac operative and putting Brett in grave danger, and the angry man in front of him probably couldn't be convinced anyway. "Okay, Javid, okay," he said. "No lies. Here's the truth: This standoff is going to end tonight one way or another. SecPac is going to storm the building and take it back by force unless you release the hostages."

Javid gave an ugly laugh. "You came here just to *threaten* us? Like the army camped out there wasn't clear enough?" He pointed down at the huddled hostages. "If the zebrahands attack, *they* die. Maybe you're thinking you can rescue them, but you can't. We have explosives rigged to the algae tanks; as soon as we see you coming, we blow the tanks and the entire basement level turns into a giant scummy swimming pool with the hostages on the bottom. Last I checked, armored shrooms and their humans drown at about the same speed."

Oath and erze, this was bad. Donovan peered into the darkness behind Javid. Where the hell was Saul? "Even that's not going to stop them, Javid," he said. "You don't understand. SecPac *has* to attack, even if it costs lives. The High Speaker, the leader of the zhree homeworld, he's here and watching closely and if he..." Donovan trailed off because at that moment, quick footsteps ran up one of the metal stairways from the lower level, taking them two at a time, and the person Donovan most and least wanted to see hurried up and came to an astonished halt beside Javid. Donovan looked at her and their eyes met as if through a wall of razor wire.

A constricting pain wrapped itself like a garrote around Donovan's heart. *Hello, Anya.*

The girl's throat moved in a noiseless gasp. "I'll get Saul." She turned to hurry down the causeway, but Javid shot a hand out and grabbed her arm.

"Saul's covering the other end of the building," Javid said tonelessly.

"We have to go get him," Anya insisted, glancing back at Donovan and pulling against Javid's grasp. "If they sent a negotiator, Saul should be the one to talk to him."

"That boy's no negotiator. He doesn't know anything. They sent him to mess with us, distract us before the main attack, just like last time." Javid's voice had gone flat and detached; it sent pinpricks of cold through Donovan's nodes. "They know what Max meant to Saul, and this is their way of getting to him—it's psychological warfare. We can't let him near Saul."

"You *idiot*." Donovan wanted to throttle Javid. If only he'd gone to the building's other entrance! "SecPac was going to charge in, but I convinced them to let me come here first. I'm trying to save everyone in here from being killed."

Javid's voice dripped murderous sarcasm. "Oh, *of course.*"

Anya tugged again, then stared into Javid's eyes. "He's not like the others," she whispered. "He tried to save Max. I saw it on the news. If he's here, maybe we *can* talk—"

"Don't you get it?" Javid snapped. "You can't negotiate with these people. They aren't even really *human*! All we can do is make a stand. Take as many of them out with us as we can, that's what this whole war is about in the end." The man's eyes were feverishly bright; Donovan felt all hope slipping away. Javid had the look of a wounded animal; he knew he was going to die. "It's Saul's fault we're even *in* here," he went on. "If Kevin were in charge, we would've done this right! We would've blown this whole scorching place to kingdom come and be hundreds of miles away by now."

Javid unslung his carbine off his shoulder and pointed it toward the prisoners below. "We need to raise the stakes. Start sending out bodies so they *know* we're serious."

Donovan felt as if mounting panic would choke him. "You do that and there's no going back, do you understand? You're all dead. It doesn't have to end like that, but there's not much time." How much time had passed already? Twenty, thirty minutes? "*Just. Get. Saul.*" He ground out each word.

As if on cue, there was a crackle of static from the two-way radio unit clipped to the front of Javid's vest. Saul's gruff, slightly distorted voice demanded, "Javid, it's been fifteen minutes already; you going to tell me what's going on at that end?"

They all stared at the radio. Javid reached down and pressed a switch to turn it off.

Anya yanked her arm free and sprinted down the causeway, the echo of her footfalls clanging in the enclosed space. "Dammit, Anya!" Javid shouted. He started to run after her, but she was fast, really fast, as Donovan already knew, and Javid turned back after a few steps, red-faced and cursing. He strode up, madness dancing in his eyes, and raised the muzzle of the carbine to Donovan's face.

Donovan saw Javid's finger curl around the trigger. Time slowed a thousandfold. He was going to throw himself aside; the bullet would hit him but if he was lucky it would graze the side of his skull instead of deforming the center of it. He would roll and swing his legs around and try to catch Javid at the knees. He came by all of these thoughts unconsciously, in one-hundredth of a second—

"Wait!" the woman with the rifle protested. "If you shoot him, the stripes outside will hear it for sure. They'll think we're already killing the hostages."

Javid hesitated, then said, "You're right." He brought the carbine up and swung it down toward the side of Donovan's head like a baseball bat. Donovan lurched forward off his knees. The weapon smacked into his cheek but didn't stop his explosive momentum; he barreled into Javid with his entire weight, shoulder-checking the slighter man in the chest. Both of them tumbled to the metallic walkway with a ringing clatter. Donovan landed on top; helpless to use his arms, he raised his head up and brought the top of his forehead down on Javid's face.

There was an audible crack and Javid screamed, blood fountaining from his broken nose. Donovan tried to raise his body again, but two sets of hands grabbed him and hauled him back violently. Adrenaline surged; his battle armor poured forth into razor-sharp edges. "Don't touch his skin!" the woman shouted. Donovan couldn't stop his backward momentum; he fell, arms pinned painfully underneath his body. Sweeping his legs around in a windmilling arc, he smashed them across the woman's shins, pitching her forward. *So much for negotiation.* He rolled over and clambered up, had almost regained his feet, when the butt of the other sape's rifle connected with his head. Sparks erupted in his vision. Two, three, four more blows to the skull and Donovan felt his body fold and his cheek hit the ground, consciousness scudding away from him.

Javid got up, his face covered with blood, and grabbed Donovan by the back of his jacket. One of the other sapes helped him—Donovan was too far gone to tell which—and together, they dragged him the short distance to the nearest algae tank. They heaved him bodily up the three short metal steps that workers climbed to check on the crops, and before Donovan could utter a final cry, gloved hands forced his head under the surface of the water.

Thick, warm liquid the consistency of spoiled milk closed over him, filling his mouth and nose and ears. He twisted and writhed and struggled in panic and blind fear, but barely conscious as he already was, the oxygen fled his brain in seconds. His legs kicked against the tank, his armor rippled in mad death throes, his lungs shrieked for air it couldn't get.

He felt himself grow feeble. *Jet!*

Desperate remorse over his own foolishness was his last emotion.

And then the weight on his head lifted, and Donovan was yanked up from the tank. His insensible body collapsed and tumbled down the metal steps. Someone was screaming—*Anya*—Anya was screaming, and there was a great deal of other shouting and movement, and Donovan still couldn't see or breathe. Rough hands undid the restraints around his wrists and thumped hard on his chest. Donovan's exocel gave a heroic involuntary spasm, and he felt his lungs contract as if squeezed in a giant fist. His back arched. Gooey water sprayed from his mouth; he sucked in a burning gasp, turned over, and retched uncontrollably, heaving up sour-tasting brine over and over again until his vision throbbed with light and dark patches and he felt as if he'd been turned inside out. When there was nothing left to empty from his guts, he crumpled again, curled on his side, and became gradually aware of Anya's arms over his shoulders, her slight body draped over his shuddering one, her hiccuping breath, and the tears streaking her face.

"You stupid, *stupid* stripe," she sobbed quietly. "Why did you come here? Why didn't you stay with your own people?"

"Couldn't . . . let it all be for nothing . . ." Donovan whispered hoarsely. "My mom, my dad . . . everything."

"Get off of him, Anya." Saul's brusque voice came from directly overhead. "Go help the others watch over Javid, make sure he doesn't try to do anything else asinine." When Anya didn't budge, Saul growled, "I said move, girl. We're in a situation here, and this stripe and I have words to exchange."

Anya hesitated a second longer, then got to her feet and left Donovan lying on the floor, Saul standing over him. Donovan raised his head an inch off the ground. Bright patterns of dots still pulsed behind his eyeballs. He saw, some distance away, Javid sitting on the ground, seething, dripping with algae water, pinching his nose to stop the flow of blood that had dripped down the front of his shirt. The other two sapes, the ones who'd helped him try to drown Donovan, stood beside him looking angry and uncomfortable. All three of them had been relieved of their weapons, and some other sapes, presumably on Saul's orders, were standing in front of them, keeping them well away from where Saul now crouched to speak to Donovan.

Saul said, "You wrote that letter."

Donovan nodded weakly.

"It was all wrong." Saul's glower was hard and accusing, and behind it there was pain. "She was executed the day after I got it. We never had a chance."

"I tried to save her . . ." Donovan wheezed. "But she made a deal with SecPac . . . asked to be executed right away . . . didn't want you to risk yourself and the cause for her."

"*No.*" Saul's face clenched; the planes of his cheeks stood out like stone bluffs. "It was a SecPac trick all along. They wanted her dead as soon as possible." He brought his face directly over Donovan's. "You're *lying* to me."

"Am I?" He lay still, drained. "You knew her a lot better than I did."

Saul forced out a breath through gritted teeth. Then he lurched to his feet with an inarticulate noise of grief and rage. "Dammit. *Damn her.* How could she?" The Sapience commander paced a short circle in front of Donovan, his large hands clutched to his scalp as if he could tear out the hair he didn't have.

He stopped abruptly and looked down at Donovan. "She gave up Warde's contacts, didn't she? That's why they were all nabbed so fast." When Donovan nodded again, Saul let out a sharp bark of humorless laughter. "I warned him not to get on her bad side or he'd regret it. She *never* forgets or forgives." He snorted loudly. "They won't catch him, though. He left the doctor and the girl in a safe house for us to pick up and disappeared like a ghost, but he'll be back. Man's got more lives than the devil himself."

Shakily, Donovan rolled away from the pool of viscous liquid and vomit he'd been lying in and struggled to his knees. "You don't have much time," he said. "SecPac isn't the powerful black guard you sapes think it is. It has to finish this tonight, no matter how bloody the results are, because it can't look weak when it comes to shroom politics right now." He told Saul about the High Speaker's visit, the tension between the homeworld of Kreet and the zhree colonists of Earth, and the threat of the Rii—the scouting ships, the drones.

"The Rii are a myth," Saul growled. "A bogeyman the shrooms and the government use to keep us humans afraid."

"They're not a myth," Donovan said. "If you lived in the Round and could understand Mur, you'd know. Even if you could drive the current zhree off of Earth, others would come. There'd be a new War Era, and we'd start all over again."

Saul bent over and leveled a thick finger at Donovan's face, uncompromising steel in his eyes. "Then we'd *keep fighting*. If we can chase out one set of invaders, then we'll chase out another. There's no limit to human determination. We'll keep fighting for as long as it takes, until our planet belongs to us, or to no one."

Donovan stared past the finger into the man's flushed face. "You want to keep fighting? Then you have to live past tonight. You have to know which battles to walk away from."

The Sapience commander straightened and stared down at Donovan as if he were a two-headed animal. In a lower voice, "You're one of *them*. Why'd you risk your neck coming in here to tell me these things? And why should I believe anything you say?"

Donovan crawled forward, across the walkway, to where the notebook he'd brought with him lay discarded on the floor. He'd taken it from his desk drawer just a few hours ago, slipped it into his inside jacket pocket, next to his heart. Now he picked it up with damp, trembling fingers and rocked back on his knees, holding it up to Saul.

Saul took it. "What is this?"

"Her notebook." Donovan's voice fell. "She used to write poetry in it when I was little. My dad threw out everything in the house that belonged to her, but I saved that one thing. It's . . . it's all that's left of her now." He blinked back the prickling in his eyes. "But it doesn't belong to me. It belongs with you, because . . . because she belonged to the cause. Never to me."

Saul looked up from the curled pages he was flipping through. "This is terrible stuff."

Donovan smiled through pain. "Isn't it?"

Saul snorted a laugh. Tears filled the Sapience commander's eyes and ran down the deep crevices of his weathered face.

Donovan said, "You used the information I gave you to murder my father. You were probably planning it for a long time, but I gave you the final piece. I ought to kill you. I ought to be glad to see SecPac light this place up and take you out. But my mom died wanting you to live, to keep going without her."

He rose slowly to his feet, putting a hand out to steady himself against one of the algae tanks. "I have friends waiting out there, and I don't want to see them hurt. I don't want the shrooms to force our hand and for people to die. I don't . . ." He turned his face aside. "I don't want anything to happen to Anya. Even if I never see her again, even if we have to be enemies, I want her to live. I'd like to know she's safe for another day at least. And maybe one more after that, and one more after that . . . that's all any of us can hope for."

— — —

When Donovan walked out of the building, he made it only partway across the field before Jet, Vic, and Thad rushed to him and brought him back to the safety of the nearest SecPac Humvee. Even Commander Tate looked taken aback by the sight of his bruised face and wet, algae-coated hair and clothes. "You were in there for ninety minutes, Reyes. I'll have you know I've literally been holding back an army on your account."

"Sorry, ma'am. It didn't go as smoothly as I'd hoped."

"Well, you're alive," she noted. "Do you have any other good news?"

Donovan said, "They want five petroleum-burning cars with valid plates and full tanks of gas, which they'll inspect. We're to clear the entire area of any SecPac presence for fifty miles in every direction, leaving behind only one unarmed vehicle with me in it. They release the hostages to me, I wait here until I get a call from their leader confirming all the sapes have split up and gone free, then I drive the hostages out." He gratefully accepted the hot-water thermos that Thad placed in his hands. "Alternatively, if we decide to attack the building, they blow the algae tanks with explosives and the prisoners drown before we can get to them."

There was a grim and resigned silence from the ring of assembled officers.

Jet's eyes appeared sunken into his skull, as if he'd aged several years in a single night. "So we have to let twenty hostage-taking terrorists walk out and go free?"

Commander Tate grimaced. "To save civilian lives and avoid a complete public catastrophe?" She passed a sober look over her troops. "Yes, we do. For now."

— — —

The hostages emerged one at a time, dazed and blinking in the early dawn. Donovan helped them to the van, where a waiting Nurse and a nurse-in-erze—the two additional people SecPac had negotiated with the sapes to allow on site in addition to Donovan—wrapped the freed prisoners in blankets and checked their medical condition. Some of the humans cried; the two Engineers clung to each other with entwined limbs, making that low, barely audible susurrus of a zhree in extreme emotion. The hostages had seen everything that had happened in the building, and even if they hadn't heard all the conversation, they knew they owed Donovan their lives—each of them came to clasp his hand in wordless gratitude, even the two zhree, who Donovan thought might never want to be near humans again if they could help it.

The sapes piled into the cars in groups. Saul gave huddled instructions to each one. They would split up, disappear into the surrounding towns and countryside, rely on the nationwide network of Sapience sympathizers to slip away to wherever they needed to go to regroup and plan their next offensive.

Javid was in the first car to go. His nose had been packed with gauze and the area under his eyes was bruised purple. The long stare he gave Donovan was acidic with hatred, and he was not much kinder to Saul. "This whole thing was a failure and it's because of *you*," he shouted from the backseat of the car, loudly enough for everyone to hear. "If you had half the balls that Kevin has—" Saul slammed the door on him and motioned for the driver to leave. The car rumbled away from the building, kicking up a cloud of dust and gravel.

Anya was to leave in the last car, with Saul and two other sapes. As she passed him, he reached out his fingers, and she reached out hers, and their hands met. She stopped, poised between one step and the next, her gaze luminous behind the faint steam of her breath. She glanced back at the algae farm, then turned aching eyes to Donovan. "This was it, you know. My home. This was where my family's ranch used to be, before . . ."

"I know," he said. "I'm sorry."

Anya dropped her gaze. She whispered, "You really are different. Sometimes, you make me think that maybe . . ." She shook her head and didn't finish. "I'm walking out of here alive because of you, I know that's true."

It hurt to look at her. "That goes both ways."

Anya scuffed the ground with her toe. "If someone had once told me that I'd care so much about what happened to a striped exo, I'd have said they were cracked in the head. But when Javid . . . When I thought . . ." She raised her face abruptly and her hand tightened in his. "You have your armor and your people, but you're not invincible. I hope you never do anything so dumb ever again."

Donovan looked at her very seriously. "That goes both ways too."

Anya's bit her lower lip, uncertain longing in her eyes. "I wish . . ."

"Me too," he said. Then he leaned in and kissed her; Saul was watching, but he didn't care. After everything he'd been through, everything he'd lost, he ought to have this one impossible moment to take away with him, to tuck close to his heart like a well-worn notebook. Anya tilted her face to him and her body softened, and the touch of her lips held a whole world of craving and sadness.

He pulled away first, before he could get lost in her, before he could dwell on how much he wanted more. "You should go." He gave her hand a final squeeze, then let it drop. He made himself smile. "Remember to stay away from stripes." She turned from him, her gaze lingering over her shoulder, and he remembered to add, "By the way . . . go home and see your sister. She's worried about you, you know."

Her eyebrows moved in a question, but Saul and the others were already in the car, and she turned for real this time and jumped into the backseat, pulling the door closed. Donovan watched the car turn onto the road and speed east, growing smaller and smaller. He sat down on the hard ground; out here you could watch someone leaving you for a long time before they were finally gone.

32

The state funeral of Prime Liaison Dominick Reyes was a grand and solemn affair. Due to ongoing security concerns, the procession was confined to the Round, but the zhree allowed it to be filmed and broadcast around the world. People of every erze lined the spoke roads, reaching out marked hands to touch the flag-draped casket as it was carried, not to the sacred top of the tallest Tower, where the zhree atomized their dead, sending their spirits on to await the Highest State of Erze, but to the center of the city park, where he would be buried and memorialized, surrounded by the ongoing life of the Round, by hatchlings and children running between the trunks of the elm and oak trees.

It was an oddly warm, still day, as if the first cold front had been beaten back and winter had paused in its advance to observe the goings-on. Donovan stood with Jet and Vic and the other stripes, avoiding the clusters of dignitaries and political staffers who kept coming up to offer him innumerable condolences. Although the zhree did not usually attend human ceremonies, there were many present to pay their respects to the man who had been their most prominent human ally. They stood in a polite semicircle as the minister read passages from the Bible and spoke of Dominick Reyes as a man devoted to his work, a man of unwavering moral character.

Administrator Seir looked haggard, his fins drooping, his many eyes dull. Next to him stood Soldier Werth, his expression, such as it was, unreadable. At the edge of the crowd, Donovan picked out Therrid's patterned hull, but the Nurse caught his attempt to make eye contact and deliberately closed two of his eyes, avoiding Donovan's gaze. He'd gotten out of the locked room somehow but had said barely a word to Donovan since then, despite the latter's numerous attempts to apologize and explain. It was even more awkward because they had to see each other regularly; Donovan was still, technically, on medical leave—a fact that struck him as painfully funny. He could only hope the Nurse would come around; Therrid might not be talking to him, but at least he hadn't reported him either. Yet.

When the service was over, the politicians and foreign dignitaries began departing for their cars, conversing in hushed, sorrowful voices. The rest of the crowd dispersed in small groups. When most of the others were gone, Soldier Werth walked to where Donovan stood near the casket. Donovan dropped his armor warily—he couldn't tell what his erze master thought of him now. It wasn't often that an exo was reprimanded for disobedience and commended for heroic action in the same week. After a minute of silence, the zhree Soldier said, "He was one of the best humans I ever knew." He touched the casket, then lowered his armor in respect. Donovan was stunned; Soldier Werth dropped armor for no one but the High Speaker.

Werth focused his multi-directional gaze on Donovan. "When you are done here, report to me in the minor assembly chamber in the Towers."

"Yes, zun." Anxiety formed hesitantly in Donovan's stomach. Had Therrid reported him after all?

Soldier Werth left, along with the other zhree. The remaining humans trickled away, except for Jet and Vic, who remained, holding hands tightly. Vic leaned her head on Jet's shoulder and he kissed her brow, then rested his chin on the top of her head, looking out across the green lawn of the park. "You want us to wait for you?" he asked Donovan.

Donovan shook his head. "No, go ahead. I'll catch up with you later."

Jet nodded. He put an arm around Vic, and with a final backward glance, they walked away, leaving Donovan alone with his father's casket and the dense bouquets of flowers left by well-wishers. They stung his eyes with their riot of color, so summer bright against the beige of winter and the starkness of the nearly bare trees. So many of them. His father had been an important man. Maybe not loved but important. His mother too had been important to her followers. One of his parents had died a hero, the other a traitor. The planet could be divided based on who thought which was which. Donovan reached out and touched the draped flag.

"Hope," he whispered. "I'll try to have hope, Father."

— — —

Stepping into the room he'd been summoned to in the Towers, Donovan was at first so taken aback that he forgot decorum. It wasn't just Soldier Werth waiting for him; all the erze zun were gathered. Upon Donovan's entrance, their soft musical conversations faded and dozens of hard amber eyes focused on him.

"Come in, Donovan," said Administrator Seir. "Do you want anything to eat or drink?"

The question was a pleasantry some zhree had grown

accustomed to exchanging with humans by way of greeting. Donovan knew better than to say yes; eating was a private affair for zhree. "No, zun," he said, dropping his armor in belated haste.

Why had he been called here? Awful suspicions rushed to mind. Therrid *must* have reported him. An exo capable of flagrant treachery, of attacking a zhree even with good reason, was abnormal, unacceptable. Had they scrutinized everything he'd done over the last few weeks and decided he was so far out of erze he was to be stripped of his markings after all? Or worse? Donovan's exocel started to crawl with nerves; he forced it back down, standing attentively.

The zhree shifted into a semicircle, surrounding Donovan with armored hulls, limbs, and staring eyes. "You all know Donovan?" Administrator Seir asked the other zhree.

Fins dipped in assent. No doubt they recalled him being singled out before the High Speaker. The more observant ones would have seen him in the human news coverage lately.

"Soldier Werth," said the zun Administrator, "tell us about this human-in-erze of yours."

Werth said, "Donovan is an adolescent nearing full maturity. He was Hardened with an eighth-generation human exocellular system and graduated to active status in the Global Security and Pacification Forces two hundred and twenty-seven days ago. His skills rating is excellent. Both fortunately and unfortunately"— Werth's fins flattened in a frown—"his unusual involvement in recent events has made him well known to a great many humans, both our allies and our enemies. Also, he is the only biological offspring of Prime Liaison Dominick Reyes."

A swell of low humming and fluttering fins. "The *only* one?"

Merchant Hess exclaimed. Donovan refrained from rolling his eyes. The zhree never ceased to be amazed that human fertility was unrelated to social status, and that high-status individuals might have only one or two children, or none at all.

Seir sliced the air with his fins to silence the muttering. "Donovan, we summoned you here for a reason. You know far more about the political situation at hand than most humans. Are you aware that the High Speaker departed the Round yesterday?"

Donovan nodded. The military cordon out to Jupiter had finally been deemed secure enough for the High Speaker to leave safely. Donovan had been glad not to have to stand honor guard this time and had watched from a distance as the massive cruiser ship lifted off and ascended into the sky, escorted by half a dozen fighter craft.

Seir said, "Due to the growing threat of Rii attack, the High Speaker was forced to cut short the rest of his visit. He will return to Kreet, where he will deliberate with the Homeworld Council on whether to continue supporting Earth as a Mur colony."

Donovan was still not sure why he had been brought into this conversation, but he asked, slowly, "And if they decide not to?"

The assembled zhree seemed to shift uncertainly. It made Donovan nervous. After a long pause, Soldier Werth said, "We have already been asked to prepare an evacuation plan."

An evacuation plan? Donovan tried to process the idea. There were billions of people on Earth. You couldn't evacuate billions of people. Billions of *squishies*. When the zhree said evacuation, they meant themselves. In a flat voice that sounded oddly less horrified than he felt, Donovan said, "You mean you would abandon Earth . . . and leave the planet undefended, with all the humans in chaos."

"The Rii would appreciate such a boon," Engineer Phee said darkly. "It'd take no more than a couple of their Seige-class warships to conquer this planet and start looting its resources and infrastructure for their Galaxysweepers."

"They'll strip everything they can for a few hundred years, then move on, as they did with Bithis and Pyrt," said Merchant Hess.

Builder Dor's fins quivered with rage. "Have we given so many lives, so much time and effort, to build this colony, merely to turn around and flee when homeworld armor grows soft?"

"None of this has been determined yet," Administrator Seir trilled loudly. "You can appreciate why, Donovan, I am ordering you not to reveal anything you're hearing now."

"Yes, zun," Donovan mumbled, though he wanted to run from the room. His father ought to be the one in here dealing with such weighty problems. Was that why the Prime Liaison had been so grim and preoccupied in the months before his death? Because he'd foreseen the worst-case scenario unfolding? If the zhree colonists left now, there would be anarchy. And then re-conquest.

Administrator Seir declared, "We must convince Kreet that we have a strong plan to govern and defend the planet. That includes defense against Rii attack, but also ending the human uprisings and political violence, and expanding the erze system and exo programs to sustain the colony in the long run. There is no question that we need human allies to help implement any viable solution. Here in Round Three, we are in immediate need of a new Prime Liaison." He focused back on Donovan. "You are aware, I assume, of how a Prime Liaison is appointed?"

Donovan nodded. "It's written in the Accord. The President nominates five candidates. Congress votes to confirm three of them. Those three are sent to the Towers and the zhree zun choose one of them." He left out how, theoretically, the zhree could reject all the candidates until Congress presented them with someone they found acceptable.

Administrator Seir dipped his fins. "I have asked the human government to begin this process at once and to present us with candidates as soon as possible. Dominick Reyes was our staunchest, most competent human ally; we are unlikely to find a worthy replacement, yet everything depends on it. Donovan, when the time comes, you will help us choose your father's successor. You will act as adviser to the zhree zun until a new Prime Liaison is in place."

He must have heard incorrectly. Also, the translation machine must be malfunctioning. Donovan opened his mouth and closed it again. "I . . . what? Zun, I'm not . . . I'm not even remotely qualified."

"Humans, I have observed, foster close relationships with their biological offspring, regardless of erze assignment. You knew your father better than anyone else. We want you to tell us how he would act, what decisions he would make."

Donovan shook his head vehemently. "There are several administrators-in-erze who worked for my father in the Liaison Office. Any one of them—"

"Your erze rates you highly on intelligence and cooperativeness. You understand our language and culture far better than most humans. You know how things work in the Towers, you are both offspring and apprentice of Dominick Reyes, and most importantly you are an exo, a soldier-in-erze with firsthand knowledge of the Sapience threat. Given the sensitive, dangerous, and urgent situation we find ourselves in, those aspects qualify you above others."

I'm just a teenager! I'm not old enough or experienced enough and I have no idea what my father would do! Donovan opened his mouth to argue, but the decisive sweeping of the Administrator's fins and the authoritative staccato rhythm of his words left no doubt that the decision had already been made. Donovan was being informed, not asked.

"Yes, zun," he said, wondering if he sounded as miserable as he felt.

"This is highly unusual," Nurse Thet said with concern. "We are asking a young exo with a history of questionable judgment to exceed his prescribed role as a soldier-in-erze."

"Perhaps due to some defect in his Hardening process, Donovan appears to be already quite adept at exceeding his prescribed role," Soldier Werth grumbled in a low strum.

"These are unusual times." Administrator Seir took a step toward Donovan. "Do you fully understand all that has been said? Do you understand what you must do?"

What he must do? Donovan's mind stumbled over the question before the enormous, obvious answer hit him: He had to save the human species. A panicked laugh of derision began to bubble from his lips. He strangled it and forced it back down into his chest. This was some kind of terrible poetic justice. Saving humanity was what his mother and father had been striving to do all their lives, in entirely different ways, and look at the price they'd paid for it.

"I understand, zun." There was only one thing his parents had agreed upon: Humans could be *more*. They could rise, against all odds, from conquest and adversity.

He hoped he could prove them right.

EPILOGUE

"Let's wrap it up," Jet said, dropping into the driver's seat. "Vic's coming over at nineteen hundred and my mom's making chili."

Donovan looked up from the notes he was finishing, summarizing their interview with a scientist-in-erze who'd worked with Dr. Nakada in the past and had given them some information that might lead SecPac to the man before he made any more progress on developing an armor-disabling weapon. Donovan sent the report to Central Command, marking it for Commander Tate's special attention, then said, "Can we make a quick detour?"

Jet didn't look happy about it, but he nodded. As he set the skimmercar into motion, he glanced at Donovan. "How're you doing? First week back, not too bad, right? Day shift, short patrol routes . . . They're going easy on you. You're giving me an excuse to slack off."

"I'm just glad Therrid forgave me enough to clear me for duty," Donovan said. "Maybe he was just sick of monitoring me on leave and having to put up with me so often."

"I *still* can't believe you punched a zhree in the eye." Jet shook his head. "Though, hell, I'd believe anything now. If you told me that you'd been sent on a secret spy mission to Kreet itself as part of your new special adviser status, I wouldn't even blink twice."

"You're going to wish you'd stuck with Leon."

"Man, no. Leon's great, but I wanted to break his pencils by the end."

Donovan laughed a little. "You'll get sick of me too staying at your place." A pause, then quietly, "Thanks, by the way."

Jet shrugged. "It's not nearly as nice as you're used to, I know."

"I was glad to move out of there," Donovan said. "Everything in it reminded me of them, you know. Being in that huge house by myself afterward . . . No thanks." He leaned his head against the window, searching for the right intersection.

"You're going to have to tell me where," Jet said.

"Right there." Donovan motioned, and his partner brought the skimmercar to a slow idle along the street curb in the Transitional Habitation grids. A couple of teenagers huddled on a building stoop and sharing a smoke; they eyed the SecPac patrol skimmercar with naked hostility. One of them directed a stream of spittle in their general direction.

"Squishy punks," Jet muttered. "They're lucky we're done for the day."

Donovan paid the exchange no attention. Every other time he'd driven by, the post in front of the building had been bare, containing only the random bit of graffiti or stapled posters featuring lost dogs or sketchy dive bars. Today, there was a white X painted on the weathered wood.

After a minute, Jet looked at him searchingly. "You good?"

"Yeah, I'm good." Donovan felt a real smile climb his face. "Let's go home."

ACKNOWLEDGMENTS

My editor, Jody Corbett, transformed this book. She gave a resounding yes to a story about teenage soldiers, armored aliens, and a dysfunctional family, then pushed me to make it better in so many ways, encouraging me through revisions that shaped this story into something I'm unabashedly proud of. I cannot thank you enough, Jody, for "loving the guts out of this book," as you so memorably put it.

I am grateful to the entire team at Scholastic for getting behind *Exo* with such enthusiasm. Thank you to David Levithan for championing this book from the beginning, Phil Falco for making *Exo* look so jaw-droppingly good, Rebekah Wallin for wrangling every production detail, Jennifer Abbots for tirelessly driving publicity, and Rachel Feld for all things marketing. Thanks as well to Alan Smagler, Elizabeth Whiting, Alexis Lunsford, Annette Hughes, and all the folks in Sales who spread *Exo* far and wide.

There are days when the one thing that makes me believe in my writing career is the fact that my agent, Jim McCarthy, believes in it. Jim, thank you for being unfailingly responsive, witty, knowledgeable, and optimistic, and for finding *Exo* the perfect home.

Thanks to my ever willing and valuable beta reader, Vanessa MacLellan, and special shout-outs to Viable Paradise XVIII, the

Fearless Fifteeners, SCBWI Oregon, Willamette Writers, my faithful monthly writers' lunch buddies, and the wonderful friends I have made in the speculative fiction and YA author communities.

I am, as always, grateful for a family that is proud and supportive of my writing, foremost among them my husband, Nathan. Thank you for being my first and repeat reader, for making me put more romance into this story, and for continually believing that I have more books in me.

This book is dedicated to my parents who, like Donovan's parents, did not always (or often) see eye to eye, but were united in their unconditional love and pride when it came to their children. They both knew I could be a professional writer before I believed I could, and their constant faith in me has enabled me to be courageous in all of my life's decisions.

Finally, my deepest appreciation goes to you, my readers, especially the zeroboxing fans who stuck around to see what the second event would be.

ABOUT THE AUTHOR

Fonda Lee is the author of *Zeroboxer*, which was an Andre Norton Award finalist, a Junior Library Guild selection, and a YALSA Top Ten Quick Pick for Reluctant Young Adult Readers. After spending years as a corporate strategist for Fortune 500 companies, she is now a writer and black belt martial artist living in Portland, Oregon. You can visit her online at www.fondalee.com.